# Soul Juice

## By

## Tony Northover

*"They'll kill you. That is what they do. Either you'll end up an un-dead charred corpse, else they will make you like them - a killer. Either-way the person you are will be gone."*

It is just another day in hell for John Tiber. If school isn't' bad enough he has Danny and his cronies to deal with. Danny will be the death of him one day, he thinks, sooner or later he will go too far. Sooner being the more likely of the two.

But he is wrong about that, there are far worse forms of hell than Danny and the threat of mere death. Something is waiting for him in the Old Manor House. Or rather someone who will change everything for the sixteen year old.

Who takes things further than John can ever imagine. When he initiates him into his world of the Wonder-kind. Where power is almost everything, save for the thirst for the red stuff.

John has a taste for it now, but it looks like it will cost him everything, with his humanity long gone, his sanity is next and maybe even his fast-darkening soul. After all, things look very different if see life out of the bottom of a glass stained red with human blood.

# Other Books by the Author

Sky Death

# Soul Juice

# Wylye Woods

## 21st March 1983: Monday

# Chapter 1

# Living Death

*I taste blood.*

It roils against my tongue, setting taste buds alight, raging with disgust. I had always hated blood, especially the sight of my own. Spit it out, my brain shrieks. Only there is no spittle to get the job done. My tongue moves around like a fish flapping upon a riverbed in a drought, sticking on contact with anything it touches, cementing itself to the roof of my mouth.

I wipe my lip with the edge of my hand. The crimson liquid that is smeared across my index finger runs down along the length of my finger. Dark red droplets falling to explode in little pocks upon the mud-streaked surface of my Clarks shoes.

I feel it in my bones, in my teeth. I fight to halt the sensation of suffocating panic growing in my chest. It blows up, bright and clear, forsaking all else. The world seems to shift a gear. Vision quakes into a blur and the world loses its shape.

"You bloody' cry-baby."

"You…You split my lip!"

"I'll do worse in a minute."

Daydreaming. I am always daydreaming, that is my problem. Everyone says so. Otherwise, I would have heard him coming a mile off. It isn't as if he is the quietest individual in the world. His hand falls like a slab of dead meat on my shoulder. He spins me around just in time to meet his other hand, the one he has clenched into a fist. The shock of the impact brings me hurtling back to reality.

"Morning moron," Danny booms, "You avoiding me or something?"

Stupid, dumb question. Of course I am.

"No," I say. Despite the lie, I try to keep my voice on an even kilter.

My eyelids burn with tiredness. Last night, I lay awake for most of the night, only falling into a dead sleep sometime after four in the morning. My watch said 4.20am the last time I remembered looking at it. I didn't hear the alarm go off. If I hadn't slept through it, this wouldn't be happening to me now. Who am I trying to kid. I Know my luck too well. This was always going to happen. It had to happen. He would have found me. He always did. You can't beat fate, but fate can beat the crap out of you. I should have seen my doom written in my breakfast cereal that morning...

I've been spooning soppy cornflakes around a breakfast bowl. Pretending I don't exist. Trying not to think about going to school. The clock on the wall has other ideas. Fifteen minutes to 9am it tells me. Cutting through my stupor of denial. I should have set off already. No way I could make it in time for the bell: not even if I wanted to.

I put a spoonful of the milk saturated flakes towards my mouth. But just the thought of them all soggy with warm milk makes me change my mind. I let them slop off my spoon, splashing down into the bowl. They are twice the size when sodden. Not the crisp and crunchy flakes covered in sugar with cold milk fresh from the fridge that I enjoy. I have spent too long staring into space. Now they are inedible. It's the same for me with biscuits: you have to dunk them just long enough, just a quick soak. If you leave them too long, they start to bend like rubber. Disgusting! No, things have to be just right, or else what is the point?

The Boomtown Rats are playing on the radio: Bob Geldof's rasping voice merging with the static, making the words difficult to hear. But I know them off by heart. He carries on singing about not liking Mondays before his voice is submerged in the hiss of white noise, whispering corrupted sibilants and vowel sounds.

I heave a sigh.

I get up and turn off the radio. I pick up my duffel coat from the back of the chair. It is a heavy thing, black in colour. After pulling my arms and shoulders into the coat, I thread the horn toggle-fasteners through the corresponding rope loop. Feeling their curved shape – they've always reminded me of the pointed teeth of a sabre-toothed tiger. I force myself to walk in the direction of the front door. I'll have to take a shortcut. I will still be late. That can't be helped. Just not as late.

Called the Ridings, the shortcut is a dirt road running through the heart of Wylye woods. Most people assume the name comes from where people used to 'ride' horses and horse-drawn carriages down the leafy track in bygone days. Half right, the proper name for it is the Raiding, where in more violent times, it was a favourite spot for an ambush, because of the way the track meandered through the woods. All sorts of twists and blind turns to surprise the careless traveller. Or some idiot kid on his way to school.

Walled in on either side by beech trees, narrow silver trunks jut upwards in straight lines. The dark red leaves mix with the green canopy above, like blood clots, arching over, almost to the point of meeting. They partially obscure the sunlight, allowing only the thinnest of yellow beams to shimmer through the leaves. A patchwork of light casts over turbid puddles, full to flooding with cloudy grey-brown rainwater.

"What did you do that for?" The words tremble as I push them out of my mouth.

"Just because," he says.

...I can. I complete the sentence inside my head.

The world is a haze though my waterlogged eyes. I hate anyone seeing me crying. I wipe the wetness from corners of my eyes with the tip of a finger with one hand, while holding the one stained with blood away from me as if it is infected by a creeping necrotising disease. Life is not for everyone. Some of us are dragged through the dirt every day. There is no reason today should be different.

"Oh! What's the matter? Did I hurt you?" Danny coos with zero genuineness.

Danny Raeder is a big guy. Easily the biggest in our year. All too sure of himself and his ability to hit and hurt. Well-built, with broad shoulders and powerful limbs, he moves with big slothful movements. His size and the severity of his face gives people the impression that he is a lot older. He constantly brags about how he has no trouble getting in to see X-rated films, buying cigarettes or any of that adult wannabe stuff. Even though we are about the same age, I am the complete opposite to him. Painfully thin with an explosion of long brown hair growing out my head like a failed science experiment. I look about thirteen years old. When I take the bus to town on a Saturday, more often than not, the bus conductor only charges me half fare. Something that I find insulting but having an extra twenty-five pence to spend more than makes up for the slight.

Danny's eyes are all over me, darting around my face, over my body, sizing me up and choosing where to start on me first. There is no shortage of possibilities. I am on edge – fully primed for the first stab of his acidic scorn. His mouth twists, pulling hard to one side, revealing nicotine-stained teeth. I look away, my face ablaze under his gaze: combusting with shame. I can't look him in the eye; never could. Each time I force myself to meet his gaze, my eyes revolt, just shy away, as if driven off by some invisible force. Cast downward: as if pulled towards the ground by gravity. Looking down at my shoes, at the red splashes of blood.

"Want another?"

"What?"

"Smack in the gob."

What sort of person would say yes to that?

It doesn't matter what I say. If he wants to, he will hit me, and that will be that. It is all so pointless.

"No." I hate it that my voice sounds so whiny.

"Wot? Can't hear you!"

"No!" I say it louder but it still sounds high pitched and weedy.

Pausing to consider, Danny frowns. Weighing up his options. My stomach muscles coil themselves up tight and an unpleasant sensation goes stuttering its way up through my chest.

Weak! I am so bloody weak!

I tense, expecting another punch. Instead, Danny just laughs. The sound is loud, as if to dominate all the other sounds in earshot. He reaches inside his coat pocket. I draw a sharp breath, sucking in icy tentacles of the morning air. Fearing what Danny might do.

Oh no….

Then, I see what he has in his hand. A packet of Silk Cut with only two left. He takes one and pops it into his oversized mouth. I blow out a breath as he rummages in his trouser pocket and draws out a green plastic lighter. He lights the cigarette, breathing in, and pulls smoke into his lungs. The tip glows red momentarily before turning to grey ash. I shiver, flicking a glance at my plastic Casio digital watch:

09.05 AM.

Danny looks at me. He frowns.

"What is it?" he snaps. "Why do you keep looking at that stupid watch of yours?"

"We're going to be late." I glance once more at the watch. We aren't going to be late. We are already late. What we are going to be is very late.

"Think I care?"

"No it's just..."

"You're a right goody-two-shoes, aren't you?"

"Suppose you're staying on next year? Yeah? I don't know why. It's not as if you're any good at anything," he sneers.

"No. No I am not," I murmur. Knowing the truth of it.

"Another month – I am out of that crap-hole, once and for all," he says, taking a step closer.

"I ought to kick your head in," he growls. His hot nicotine tainted breath hits me full in the face. I am so dead.

"Come on then, retard. Ha, ha," he laughs, giving me a sharp push to my shoulder, propelling me in the direction of school.

Danny talks non-stop, delivering a tirade of insults as we walk. They flow carelessly, without pause and seemingly without end. I don't know how to take it, so I take it personally, all of it. My head begins to sag, shoulders hunching over, pushing together my shoulder blades, as if hoping to squeeze and grind myself out of existence, using those two triangular bones. I just want everything to stop. To cease to exist, to feel nothing. Living is not for everyone.

The trees thin out. The woods disappear behind us. Wild hedgerows take their place. Brambles growing out of their mass. Stinging nettles gather in clumps along the grass verge. Behind the hedgerows, brown furrowed fields stretch away to the horizon, forming curved mounds. Up ahead, the green of the sports fields with the rugby goal posts visible and behind that the school itself – St Stevens-Sub-Castle. The track runs all the way up the school boundary to the main gate and beyond. Once it passes the school gates, it carries on past the school and off to God knows where. I have never been up that far.

Approaching the corner of the school playing field, I see the all-too-familiar gap in the hedge. The barbed wire fence that had once spanned the space has its wooden posts uprooted and is then trampled where it lies in the mud and the grass. Flattened by countless student's feet over the years: all taking the same shortcut.

"You first," Danny smirks.

Carefully, I step over the barbed wire fence. I turn to see if Danny is following. Sometimes he skives off school, spending the day in the amusement arcades in the town centre or so I have heard. For the briefest second, there is a desperate hope that springs up inside of my brain, that he will just say: "So long! I don't feel like joining you losers today," and turn tail and leave me alone. But, no, he is here for the duration – to extract as much misery from me as he can.

My eyes turn away from him. Drawn back the way we came. Falling upon the rooftop reaching up over the trees in the distance. On top of the sagging roof, I see four dark red brick chimneys in a stack, With the roof a solitary ait raised up in a lake of green forest. I dab at my top lip with my tongue, as I look at the big old house.

A forgotten memory, like a maggot like trying to gnaw its way into conscious thought, clawing its way in with barbed hooks. Worming its way into existence.

Shut up! I don't want to think about it!

Stillborn, it falls back into darkness. I have the sensation of something curling up and dying deep within my belly. A shiver rides down the length of my spine. Goose flesh climbs my legs and arms.

# Chapter 2

# An Earful

*The school looms up as if out of the earth itself.*

A collection of modern red brick buildings, standing like a huddle of breakfast cereal boxes, some on their sides, others upright. Nearest and newest is the sports hall, resembling a family sized margarine carton that has been placed face down on the breakfast table.

It all looks so harmless from a distance, but the feeling scratching away in the pit of my stomach knows better. The feeling grows more giant with every dreadful step. It feels very much like wending my way into the maw of hell with the devil by my side. That's the warp and woof of it. Truly.

The green appearance is illusory. I slide and sink in the waterlogged earth. Squashing as it sucks at my shoes. Beneath the trimmed grassy blades, the muddy bog threatens my balance at every step.

I follow Danny across the school sports field. Lagging two steps behind him over the rugby pitch. I want to drop further and further behind to be out of his clutches. But I don't have the backbone for it. Besides,

Danny wouldn't allow it. He knows all too well how to jerk my strings: to keep me within punching distance.

He never lets up. All the time, Danny is talking: insults dart from his mouth like blowflies attracted to putrescence. Each and every mental scab opens to greet words that sting and serrate their way in. Laying down their poisonous larva in already festering wounds. To hatch, maggot-like, devouring self-confidence and self-belief, gnawing and burrowing deep into the psyche. To consume everything that is me.

"You think you're tough don't you? You think you're really hard."

"What? No."

"Where did he get that from?" I wonder, genuine confusion buzzing around my brain. I have never said or done anything to give the impression I thought anything of myself – let alone seeing myself as some sort of hard-case.

"Because you're not. You're soft. You're as soft as a fresh turd."

Between his sentences, I heave deep sighs. Dizzying despair claws at the base of my spine, dragging me down towards the mud at my feet. My scampering consciousness, flitting around my skull, is always on the lookout for a way out: a release from these mordant iterations.

"You're just a little turd aren't you? What are you?"

I bite my lip. Tasting the blood as the wound reopens. I feel my cheeks burn. My entire face is hot, as if my skin is about to blister and burst into flame. The simple act of a walking all of sudden becomes difficult. A weight and stiffness infect my stride as if my legs are made of lead or concrete: heavy and inflexible. My eyes cast down to the ground: to my shoes, to the mud and to the grass. *When will this ever end?*

"Say it, you little turd – say it!"

I tighten my lips, pressing them fast together. My heart is pounding, muscles twisting themselves around bones, this way and that. Screaming for my brain to give the order: fight or flight. Fight? I can't imagine punching Danny. If I did, it would wipe his big stupid smile off his face I suppose.

Why don't I just do it? Just throw my fist towards his face and hope for the best? I know why. Yeah, of course I do. I can still feel the bruises on the sides of my rib cage. Every time I move, every time I breathe. Oh yes, I know all right!

Danny slams his fist into my shoulder.

"Say it!"

Then another punch: harder this time, it hits just below my ribs.

"SAY IT!"

"...Because I am a little shit."

"Wot? Can't hear you!"

I say it louder. Danny nods. The muscles to the side of his jaw appear to relax, he smiles and I fall further into a stupor of despair.

I don't want to get there. I dread the thought of arriving in school, knowing what is waiting for me, but I don't want to stay here with Danny either. I look wistfully at the upcoming buildings. They still seem so far away. At least five minutes' walk. Not long normally, but a lot can happen in that time, making it feel like forever.

We approach the tall green link fence that stretches between Newton Block and the sports hall. The only things missing are the guard towers and the barbed wire. But the gate of this prison is open wide. The empty tennis courts wait inside, their nets dropping towards the middle of their length. The two-building tower on either side of me, between the sightless sports hall and the windows of the Newton block staring blindly down at me. No sign of life. Just blank panes of glass with faded yellow blinds. The classrooms have to be full of students by now. But they look empty: desolate. There are about 1300 pupils incarcerated in this school in the daytime, yet it feels as quiet and devoid of life as a graveyard. The silence is a physical thing: heavy, oppressive and bearing down on my lopsided shoulders.

Danny manoeuvres me, over hard tarmac, through the schoolyard, down the short stone steps, towards Cabot block. Its green painted double doors into the English block have seen better days. The paint, blistered and peeling, revealing the woodworm eaten wood underneath. The door bangs closed behind us.

Shadows reach out for me from all sides, the subdued light coming from barely adequate light bulbs under their misty white domes of glass. The lights fail to illuminate anything beyond the empty space directly underneath. Large dark green tiles absorb any light making it as far as the floor. Dank and dark, the space has more semblance to a cellar than a school. The too fragrant smell of floor polish rushes to meet my nose. It coats both my nostrils and tongue with its too sweet flavour.

There are large noticeboards screwed to the walls, overpopulated with A4 paper, that flutters every time the door opens. Exam timetables mostly – just one more thing to dread.

*But what is the point of it all?* Square pegs for square holes. Any other shape just gets hammered in anyway. Only there aren't enough square holes to go around. This is Thatcher's Britain after all. One in ten and all that. Even our careers officer has joked that our school reunion will be held down town in the dole office.

I glance at Danny out of the corner of my eye. *Not long now. I will be rid of you. Just a little further.* I smile the briefest of smiles. Then I freeze, hoping desperately, that he has not seen it. Danny turns to face me side on.

"What are you grinning at, Shit-for-brains? You think this is over. It's only just started," he snarls.

He catches my arm at the elbow, easily pushing it back behind my back, propelling me into the door of the boy's toilets. I fall through the door. He releases my arm. He shoves me again. I stagger upright, turning and retreating a couple of small steps backwards, away from him. He takes a long stride forward and slams the palm of his big meaty hand on my chest. I go back once more. The back of my pelvis is tight against the white washbasin. My shoulders are against the mirror. His hand is still on my chest – pushing into me. I can smell the odour of stale nicotine on his fingers. I hate his touch; I hate it a lot.

"Wait for me at the school gates after school," Danny tells me.

"Wh... why?"

"Then the fun can really begin," Danny says.

"Just do as I say or we both know what will happen." His nicotine breath in my face assaults my nose and mouth. He pulls me forward, using my school tie as a lead.

"Something to help you remember – you little freak," he whispers close to my ear.

He throws a punch at my head, coming hard and fast, catching me unaware. My ear explodes with sharp pain under its impact – it burns like crazy. My hand flies to the fiery flesh, as I fall to my knees. I moan with the pain of it. Danny drives me to the ground with his foot. I fall hard on my left arm. I yelp.

"Stay down till I am gone!" Danny commands. His voice ringing within my screaming ear: abrasive and harsh.

I hear the door slam. Danny's footsteps recede, echoing off the polished bare floor to nothing. I am alone. No one can see. I fall apart. My tears come so hard and fast I cannot stop them. My chest shudders as I lower my head to the floor. It feels cool against my hot cheek and the fiery flesh of my ear.

# Chapter 3

# Stares Back

*I look like roadkill.*

The light in the boy's bog is harsh and unforgiving. Long fluorescent tubes on the ceiling bleach the room with a cold stark mother of pearl brilliance. It is a room with nowhere to hide, a room of radiance and reflection; it makes escape from self-reflection impossible.

I scrutinise the frightening apparition gazing back in the mirror. Ghost white skin, pale to the point of bloodlessness; the only real colour is from where blood has dried, a darker red than the angry swollen skin tissue of the enlarged fleshy lip. My eyes are dull and empty, with no life spark to tell you that someone is living behind those two tiny black holes – that someone is looking back at you. I resemble a breathing corpse.

Dead inside? I wish. But no, my insides hurt too bloody much to be dead. I am very much alive under the appearance of all this deadness, too much in fact. After all, corpses have no trouble sleeping.

No inner or hidden truth here, only pain, with only bone and muscle twisting against each other, trying to wear themselves smooth. It is a wonder I don't catch fire from the friction. There is a twist that runs through my body, finishing up at my squeezed tight shoulders. Even my nose seems to veer off to one side. Danny is right: I am a freak. I don't belong anywhere and I never will. And yet here I am trapped in this space and time with these people who hate me. Stuck with each other until death do us apart.

I wipe the dry blood from my upper lip with a wet folded paper towel. I wet it once more under the running tap. I finish the job cleaning my fat upper lip. Swollen, but it doesn't look half as bad now. I throw the sodden green paper towel towards the bin. It bounces off the metal rim and falls, rolling a short distance on the floor.

I take another towel from the dispenser on the wall. I wet it and then begin wiping my hands, cleaning the brown-red stains from my fingers and thumb. The blood smeared around my mouth has made things look worse than it actually is. It doesn't all come off the first time. I have to scrub hard. I have to get it off. I hate it on my skin. It feels dirty, crawling – unclean.

I press my hips on the white rim of the washbasin, leaning closer to the mirror, examining the damage. The cut is no more than a small red line on my top lip, about the length and width of a paper staple. I dab the small cut with my tongue. I draw in a sharp breath between clenched teeth.

Why? What have I done to deserve this? Why do I have to go through this day after day? Is this what I truly deserve? That old chestnut: *why do bad things happen to good people?* Simple: I'm not good, or good at anything.

I let my head fall forward, to rest on the reflective pane of the mirror. Tapping it gently against the flat surface, looking, close up, into the eyes of a person I barely recognise: a stranger looking back at me.

Is that really me?

I stare into those vapid eyes until my face, body and the room itself blur out of focus and my eyes seem to move towards each other, overlapping. I take in a sharp breath and shake my head, as if to clear it. The room comes back into sharp focus. My eyes return to their usual position.

Why can't they just leave me alone?

My eyes, just for second, flash a side of me that I keep hidden. I want to drive my fist through the mirror, shattering it into a million pieces.

You can just go to hell.

Meet him after school? Why in God's name would I do that? He would catch up with me the day after and get me for it.

*Don't care, don't care anymore.* I shake my head.

I need to stay as far away from Danny as possible. This is not as easy as it sounds. He seems to have a knack of turning up when and where I least expect: as if he has some sort of built-in thug radar.

Jesus H Christ.

I screw up the wet paper towel. I throw it into the bin by the door on my way out. The toilet door swings shut behind me.

# Chapter 4

# Authority Calls

*Temporarily blind, my eyes soften, adjusting to the gloom.*

Dark brown doors, half hidden in shadows, perforate the length of the corridor. Strong and sombre in appearance, although they have seen better days. Generations of students have kicked and marked them with ends of ink pens and other sharp objects. Now, their surfaces are a mass of scratches and scuff marks.

The doors shut off whatever is going on behind them from view. The low murmuring voices indistinct from beyond the thick wood. A sharp raised voice leaps out at me, then dies: returning to the former susurrating hubbub.

It is a strange sensation, being here, outside of everything. When everyone else is where they are meant to be, sat in classrooms, at desks and in lessons, I feel exposed and isolated – uncomfortable in this no man's land.

I start walking towards the stairwell. I screw up my face, running my tongue over the roof of my mouth: I can still taste blood in my mouth.

Bangs and clangs are coming from the direction of the canteen, beyond the double doors at the far end of the corridor. *What are they doing in there?* It sounds as if they are throwing those huge cooking pots they have around the kitchen.

I approach the only open door in the whole corridor. I know who the door belongs to and where it leads. When he said that his door was always open, I didn't expect to ever take him up on the offer. Yet, I seem to have spent more time in that room than anywhere else over the last, painfully long, three years.

The light pools out of the open doorway into the corridor, a sallow oddly shaped beam. The stairs that lead to the first floor, where my first class of the day must surely already in session, are beyond the open doorway. Just out of reach. I bite my lip, regretting it instantly, as the pain shoots up through my teeth and gums into my skull. I swallow the feeling.

Padding, my foot falls, landing soft on the floor. I do not even dare look in as I pass the pool of light. It occurs to me how cartoon-like and ridiculous I must look creeping past his office. If he was to look out and see me, I would most likely freeze before dying of embarrassment.

*I am actually going to get away with this! Just a little way further.*

In my mind, I am already upstairs on the first landing. I push open the door that separates the stairwell from the corridor. It squawks a protest. I can see the stairs with their white steps. I rush towards them. I mount the first stair. My other foot already raised…

Whip-like, a voice cracks:

"JOHN TIBER!"

*Oh no!*

"Yes sir?" I say automatically.

"Would you mind stepping into my office for a moment?"

Tearing my eyes from the stairs. I look towards the open office door, fixing on the silver plaque: "Mr R Stylme" is written in black letters and then underneath, "DEPUTY HEAD."

*What could I do?*

# Chapter 5

# Enabling Rituals

*...Except do what I am told.*

Just like I always do. Conditioned just like Pavlov's dogs to salivate at authority's bark. Whenever a teacher enters a room, we stand until told to sit: part of the multifactorial rituals to instil obedience and conformity. Do this, do that, do the other and do it right now. If not, there will always be consequences. This is the thing with school – you can run but there is nowhere to hide: they always get you in the end.

"Come in, come in!" Mr Stylme's impatient voice sounds like glass smashing on paving stones. He swivels his chair around to face me. Operating under mind control: a zombie summoned by his master, I lumber into Mr Stylme's inner sanctum.

His desk, behind him, is immaculate, ordered to the point of obscenity. Not a thing out of place. The papers are on the desk, all regimented in neat piles, as if arranged using a slide rule. Above the desk, there are two small book shelves screwed to the wall, the books all lined up in perfect uniformity. All are in such pristine condition they could be brand new. They look like they have never even been opened. It is the same story everywhere in this office. Everything is neat, tidy and in its right place. Except me, in my clothes a size too big and my mud-splashed trousers: I am out of place in this ordered room.

Mr Stylme is a small man who sports a Hitler moustache – well almost. It's merely an inch longer on either side than his more infamous role model, but you can see the resemblance. And what are a couple of inches when it comes to a good nickname? It is one that all the pupils use behind his back, and I have even heard some of the teachers saying.

I am all too aware of my hands. They do not seem to belong anywhere anymore. I put them in my pockets. Then I take them out again, only to return them. I shift my weight from one leg to the other.

Mr Stylme slowly runs a hand through his thin grey hair. He examines me with his, penetrating grey eyes. His face is stony hard – unreadable: A face that would scare the most hardened poker player. He is silent for what seems an ice age, then slowly he speaks:

"What time is it, Tiber?"

"Don't know, sir."

"You have a watch; do you not?"

"Yes sir."

"Then you know what time it is."

I shift uncomfortably, my face glowing with hot heat. I look down at my shoes, which are still pocked with blood. I had forgotten to wipe it off. *Idiot!* If I had said that out loud, I am sure Mr Stylme would have readily agreed with the statement.

I start to move downwards to clean the blood from the shoe, but stop myself, suddenly remembering where I am and that Mr Stylme is still expecting an answer to his question.

"Yes sir."

"What time is it then boy?"

"9.20, sir."

"What time does school start?"

"Nine, sir."

"Precisely. Nine o'clock."

"Sir?"

"If you know what time it is, and you know what time school starts, why can't you *be* on school premises on time?"

"I don't know, sir."

*"Don't know sir!"* he says in a high pitched and whiney voice that I was sure sounded nothing like mine.

He shook his head slowly.

"I am sick and tired of your could-not-care-less attitude, Tiber!"

"Yes sir. Sorry sir."

"Let see if detention will do anything to improve things. Report to room C 17b after school, today."

"But sir, tonight I have to...", I start.

Mr Stylme looks up sharply, and I fall silent.

"Make that a week of detentions," he says. A twist of a smile snakes over his thin face.

I want to bite my lip, but stop before I draw blood.

"Well! What are you waiting for? Get to class! Now!"

I make to leave but he is not finished.

"In future, I want you at your desk before nine o'clock every day, before the bell. You hear me, Tiber!?"

"Yes sir."

I hurry towards the doorway. I want to be out of there before he can say another word.

Too late:

"Walk. Don't run, boy!"

# Chapter 6

# Fool Starts

*How much worse can this day get?*

I stop on the first step. More than ready to nosedive into a black cloud of miserable thoughts, When I realise that some good has come out of this after all. I brighten. If I am in detention, then I do not have to worry about bumping into Danny after school. He will be long gone. Mr Stylme does not know this. He has accidentally done me a favour. If he had known, it would have probably sent him into a rage that would end in a cardiac arrest.

*Unless Danny is in detention as well…* No, I can't see that. Can't see a teacher having the nerve. Some kids, the ones that really deserve it, always get away with it. But maybe… *Can't think about that now.*

I take big strides up the stairs, taking two stairs at a time. I just want to get to class – get through this day – in one piece if possible. Halfway up the stairwell, I see the door to my classroom just across from the landing. I rush towards it.

I burst through the door. Miss Sped is leaning over Nicola Leaver's desk, pointing at something in the student's exercise book. They are framed in a wall of light. The windows behind them, the small glass panes framed in a metal matrix, take up pretty much all of the upper half of the opposite wall.

The room is large but doesn't look it, overcrowded as it is, with thirty-five school-desks made of varnished wood with lids that open at the top. Each desk bears its own scars, pictures, marks and names carved into the once smooth surface, arranged in an outer and an inner circle. Miss Sped's desk is a newer and larger office style desk sat at one end of the classroom in front of the blackboard. On the blackboard, there are two sentences. The first is written in white chalk:

Reading Review Essay: 1000–1500 words.

And underneath in green chalk:

To be completed 29th April.

Miss Sped looks up; her mouth falls open as I shamble into the classroom. The door slams behind me. I wince. I try unsuccessfully to smile.

"John!" She says in a tone of mild alarm.

"Sorry I am late Miss Sped," I say, hurrying over to my desk. I fall onto the plastic mounded chair. I lift the top of the desk and start to rummage around inside, looking for my English exercise book. I shuffle through a number of coloured A5 exercise books until I find a green one. I take it to my lap and pull out a worn looking paperback book: 'The Chocolate War' by Robert Cormier, the battered cover says.

I close the desk and put the two books on the top of it. I reach inside my pocket for a pen. I pull it out slowly, knowing full well what must have happened to it. It lies in my hand like a knife that has been used in a stabbing, bleeding ink instead of blood. I check my pocket, which is soaked in ink as well. I pull out a tissue from my other pocket and begin to dab at ink on my hand, wrapping the pen in the tissue before throwing the offending article into the bin.

*Just great! Just fantastic.*

Miss Sped is a tall woman in her twenties. She is wearing a long navy-blue skirt and light green blouse. On the top of that, she is wearing a V-neck dark purple cardigan. She has an open and friendly face; with large brown eyes. She smiles a dead lot – a big genuine smile, not one of those fake pinches of the lips that many people come up with: the ones that make you wish they had not bothered. She comes over to my desk and kneels beside it, leaning towards me.

"John, I don't understand it. Why can't you get here on time?" Her face falls. Her eyebrows pinch together.

"Mr Stylme has asked about you again today," she says.

I look up.

"Yes Miss. I have already seen him."

"And?" She raises an eyebrow.

"A week in detention."

"Oh dear." She shakes her head.

"How is it going with the book?" She asks.

"Ok, I think."

She looks as if she is going to say something. A frown rumples her forehead.

"John, what have you done to yourself?" Miss Sped asks looking at my lip.

"Nothing," I say.

"I fell over," I say.

# Chapter 7

# Playing Ground

*All things come to an end.*

No matter how tedious and long lasting they seem, even chemistry lessons. After Rupert – so-called because he had a thing for wearing yellow checked trousers – dismissed the class, and me and the other students scamper through the chemically scented corridors, like laboratory rats in a maze, all seeking the same thing: an exit.

I am swept along in the current of students, bursting out of the double doors of the science block, pushed along by the throng and spilling out like water shooting out of a waste pipe into the bright midday sun. I shield my eyes from the light with a raised hand as my stomach growls up at me for food. I head towards the canteen in Cabot block. School dinners with their stringy meat, lumpy mashed potato and even lumpier custard are indescribably bad. But when I am hungry enough, I will eat almost anything.

Blinking the sun from my eyes, I scan the schoolyard for danger. Amidst the groups of students gathered in clusters, I see him. Danny springs out of the mass of movement in the playground. He is sitting in the middle of a wooden bench with two of his cronies, Paul and James, on either side of him. I falter and feel the blood draining from my face, looking this way and that, wondering what to do. Fortunately, there is a whole flurry of activity: pupils walking or running between us. I try to blend into the crowd while keeping a wary eye in Danny's direction.

Danny is saying something, turning left then right and gesturing with his hands. His cohorts nod their heads in vigorous agreement at whatever he has just said. Then, all three of them burst into buckets of laughter. Paul slaps his hand down on the wooden surface of the bench by his side.

He hasn't seen me, I know this because if he had, he would not have been able to resist coming over to humiliate me in front of his two friends. This doesn't stop the hot breath of paranoia from breathing down the back of my neck and inflaming my fears. I feel totally exposed and visible – like being in one of those nightmares when you turn up at school only to find that you are naked in front of all your peers.

I take a step forward and then another two backwards. I hover, one foot raised, unsure what to do. My brain is like cheese melting, pouring out of my ears.

I have a problem with making decisions. I can never decide until it is too late. I should be getting the hell out of here: just walking away in the opposite direction. But I am hovering like a turkey that has fallen in love with the glint of the farmer's axe.

Hugging close to the ten-foot tall green link fence that runs down the side of the schoolyard, I slink my way toward the English block. I am on the opposite side of the playground from where Danny and his friends are sitting, If I can stay hidden within the crowd, I should be safe from Danny's roving gaze.

I slide behind a group of fourth-years, their arguing voices emerging out of the general din in the school yard.

"No way! You're mental."

"Yes way!"

"No way are the games on that pile of crap as good as the ZX."

"It's not meant to be a toy."

"And what do you do that's so good?"

"Write programmes."

"Programmes? Yeah, right…dream on."

Abruptly, their voices disappear, as my attention shifts back to the bench. Danny says something, he and nods to James, who returns a thumbs-up. Standing, James looks around and then starts walking through the crowd. I feel my stomach lurch sideways, as he is clearly heading towards me. I look over my shoulder, cursing my bad luck.

But he changes direction, heading towards a small group of third-years – five of them huddled together in the centre of the yard. Their heads are bowed into their circle, as they talk intently with serious expressions on their faces. One, a lanky kid with long brown hair, has his head bowed more awkwardly than the other smaller kids, as if he wants to be the same height as his smaller friends: to fit in. He is holding a plastic carrier bag tightly. He bangs it against his leg as he speaks.

James approaches the oblivious tall kid from behind. The tall kid carries on talking, unaware of the predator creeping up on him. James drops to his haunches, unseen by the circle who are too intent on their conversation. I want to shout out a warning, but don't. Silently, I watch James grab hold of the carrier bag in both hands and stretch the polythene until it rips: books, pens and pencils spew out into a pile on the ground. James grabs a handful of books and starts flinging them into the air. Danny shouts out encouragement. Beside him, Paul is bent double,- laughing.

Everyone turns to look at almost exactly the same time. A howl of laugher surges up into the air, fusing there, the sound reverberating as if one voice. The roar of a gestalt creature that feeds on humiliation. Its rumble is so loud, it is almost a physical thing that vibrates within my rib cage.

The tall kid's face turns bright red as he scrambles across the tarmac., reaching out with his thin long arms for his books. Onlookers jeer as he pushes through the crowd, trying to retrieve one of his books. He is a human daddy long legs, stumbling, fumbling for the book. Then just as it is almost in his hand, an anonymous hand snatches it away from his grasp and throws it back up into the sky. Landing once more, another hand comes to join in the new game, returning it to the air.

With his work done, James swaggers back to the bench. Danny and Paul are laughing as if this is the funniest thing they have ever seen.

I stare stony faced at the whole performance. I look at Danny and his cronies laughing, and then back at the poor kid still rushing around desperately trying to get his books back, only to be thwarted, yet again, by some faceless member of the crowd.

All of a sudden, it's like a light bulb has been turned on inside of my head. Automatically, my gaze flicks in Danny's direction, only to find him staring directly back at me. Our eyes lock. I look away. I feel cold all over.

Danny says something, pointing a finger towards me. The other two, follow the direction of his finger with their gaze. They both smile. Danny pushes up from the bench, and the other two stand. The three of them start to make their way through the crowd towards me. Books are still flying wildly through the air. Pupils are jostling to catch or throw them. Danny doesn't not seem to notice. He walks straight through the horde, shoving aside anyone who has the effrontery to get in his way.

I freeze. I can't move. Valuable seconds tick by. Seconds can be the difference between getting away and getting a good kicking. I glance towards the doorway of Cabot building. Seeing the look on Danny's face breaks the deadlock, spurring my legs into action and I start pegging it towards the building. I crash through the door. My mind is racing. Where now?

# Chapter 8

# On Edge

*Have to get away...but where?*

My head is pounding and my heart is trying to escape through my mouth. Out of control, I scramble down the corridor. I am banging against the wall, half falling, as I twist and thrust my body desperately forwards. My foot slams down heavily on the first step as I hurtle myself up the stairwell.

*Bloody hell. idiot! Wrong way.* I should have run into the chattering sounds of students, coming from the canteen and disappearing in the dinner time chaos. Too late now. I pound up the stairs. Once you are committed to something, there is no going back. I leap up the stairs like a mad thing, flying around corners and using the handrail to propel me: climbing ever higher to my doom. Soon I will run out of stairs. *What then?*

I know the classroom doors on each landing that I pass will be shut – locked up for the lunch hour. My only hope is to run into a teacher patrolling the landings for students to be shooed out into the schoolyard.

Where is a teacher when you really need one? In the staff room with a nice hot cup of tea, I expect.

Echoing up the stairwell, my pursuers footfalls, their voices hollering up at me with howls that sound more animal than human.

"Oi! Oi! Oi!"

"Ooh! Ooh! Ooh!"

My heart is thumping hard, banging against the inside of my rip cage. My lungs are sucking in great gusts of air that rattle around in my bony chest. My legs seem almost supernatural in strength and speed. Adrenaline is pumping hard and fast into my blood stream. But that heartless and pessimistic voice in my head tells me "There is nowhere to go" and I know it speaks the truth when I reach the top of the stairwell.

*I am as good as dead.*

I am standing on the landing at the top of the stairs. A short corridor connects the landing to the rows of classrooms. All of the doors are closed. I try the first one anyway: locked. My heart and brain are racing equally fast. *Damn, damn, damn! No way out.* Except…

Suddenly I remember there is a way out after all. I don't like it: but I have no choice. Desperate choices in desperate times. *Only one way to go; oh hell.* I run down to the end of the corridor where there is a small door at the top of a short ladder, set into the wall with a green sticker on it. On the green oblong sticker are white letters:

FIRE EXIT

Halfway up the ladder, I slam my hands down hard on the metal bar. The door flies open. I half expect an alarm to go off but all I can hear is the wind ripping around the building. As I climb out and on to the roof, the wind plays merry hell with my hair and tugs at my school uniform. I wish I had brought my coat, but it is downstairs in my locker. The roof is flat space, bounded with a small brick wall and capped with small oblong concrete slabs extending over the wall about an inch either side.

I sprint over to the fire escape at the far end of the roof. It is little more than a metal ladder. It loops over the wall and runs down the side of the building. I stand on the wall, one hand on the metal of the fire escape safety rail.

I should be bounding down the side of the building about now. If I hadn't stopped to look down first, I might have been by now. The hard and unforgiving tarmac below is rushing up to meet me. A peculiar feeling rises out of the pit of my stomach as if I am already falling towards it. I can almost feel my face smack into the black surface, crushing my skull, breaking my neck like a small twig. I start to wobble. My ankles and knees are unsteady. I have to get a grip...but it is already too late.

"Hey retard, where d'ya think you're going?" That all-too-familiar voice - behind me.

I whirl around to see Danny walking towards me, flanked by Paul and James, who are trailing slightly behind him. Fanning out, moving in for the kill. I nearly step backwards, remembering in time that there is nowhere to go – except down to the hard ground below.

With three huge steps, Danny is on me, taking big handfuls of my black jumper and red shirt in his big meaty hands. He twists his fists around the material, hoisting me up on to the tips of my toes and forcing me backwards toward the edge of the parapet. A cold wind blows hard at my back.

"No, don't..." I whimper, forcing the words through a spasming jaw.

With my toes barely touching the edge of the paving slap and only fresh air at my heels, my hands fly forward to grab the only thing I can – Danny's jumper. With one hand he bats them away, holding me firm with the other. I yelp with fear as he starts to push me backwards, still further outwards into thin air. Only the tips of my shoes are touching the concrete top of the wall now. I am being leant backwards over the edge. I glance down. All I can see is the tarmac below waiting for my soft body to come crashing down to smash on its hard and unforgiving surface. It doesn't seem real... but at the same time too real. I try to swallow, but my throat is dryer than old bones.

There is something different about Danny. In the throes of terror, I can't put my finger on it. Something in the way he looks at me, his pupils contracted to sharp points. The whites of his eyes are so large it looked as if they might pop out from their sockets. He is grinning at me with his big fleshy lips. The rest of his face is skull-like and utterly white as if completely drained of blood. His face is so close to mine that I can feel his hot stinking breath blasting on my face – stinking of stale cigarettes. I want to retch, but I am too scared to breathe. I try to turn away from his face and those cold and angry eyes. It is at that moment, I realise: *I am going to die.* It is as simple as that.

I feel the tears rolling off my face. Falling downwards toward the tarmac below me. I imagine the tear drops splashing on the ground. *Why doesn't anyone look up and see what is going on?* Would they help if they did? Probably not.

"Danny, you nutter! Someone is going to see us!" Paul says. His face appears by Danny's left shoulder. A deep frown creasing his brow. He flicks a glance over his left and then his right shoulder. As if he is expecting to see someone there.

"Yeah – the little worm's not worth it! Come on!" James says, his voice rising.

At first, Danny does not seem to hear. He just holds me out there between life and death. All he has to do is let go. He looks at me with eyes that do not blink. I try to look away, but this time I can't avoid that savage glare burning into me.

Then it is if a switch flicks in his brain and his eyes refocus. He looks like he is waking up. I hold my breath, unsure if this is a good thing or not. He can just release his grip and I will fall to my death.

"Please...," I say, tears still streaming down my face.

"Fuckin' pussy," Danny laughs.

He pulls me back from the ledge. My feet find the wall, then step down from the parapet. As my feet find the roof, my legs buckle. Danny lets go of my clothes and I fall to the floor.

"Yeah, sure… Later, retard!", he says.

"Don't forget after school; don't make me come find you," he adds.

He turns and starts to walk away.

"Let's go. Either of you two got a ciggy?" He says to Paul and James, his hand already held out.

"Yeah, you can have one of mine." Paul hands Danny a cigarette.

"Boys' toilets?"

"Nah, behind the sports hall," Danny says.

"Of course, mate," Paul says.

I stay where I am, lying on the roof, on my side. I curl up in a ball, hugging my knees to my chest. I hardly feel the sharp stones under my body. I lie there until I have regained enough motor skills to limp off the roof. I am limping, not because I am injured, but because every muscle in my body is shaking.

# Chapter 9

# In Detention

*There is no sound as sad as the home-time bell.*

Especially when you know full well you are not going home. I am still pretty shaken up from lunchtime. Danny has never gone that far before. I have to wonder how much further he would have gone – will go – next time. It is not a good thought. I just want to go home, only I am not ready to go there yet and not just because of Mr Stylme's detention. I am not ready to face my parents and pretend I have had a good day at school: that nothing is wrong.

How bad can it be anyway? It is only for an hour. I just hope to God that Danny is not in detention as well as me. That would be the last straw. I cannot handle seeing his gloating face after everything that has happened today. I walk with an uncertain gait towards the room C 17b. I knock on the door and, without waiting for an answer, I push it open.

I enter a large square room with walls daubed in paint of a varying thickness and colour: ranging from faded yellow to dull white. The room is part of the original building, from back in the days when it had been a girl's school. The windows are small, high up and let hardly any light in. Overhead, there are four strip lights that do very little to help dispel the gloom. They are bright enough, but the room is just too big for them to make a difference. It all has a very unnatural feeling to it.

The desks are lined up in five columns, each in single file and separate from its neighbour on both sides. The students are scattered at different desks in an uneven pattern.

I am instantly ill at ease as soon as Mr Stylme's eyes fix upon me, entering. He watches me in much the same way a large snake would a small furry mammal. A reptilian smile, closer to a sneer, twists across his face. I bite my lip. I must have split it again; I taste the coppery tang once more.

"Well, well, well. I guess we can start now that Mr Tiber has graced us with his presence," he smirks.

I swing around to look at the clock. What is he talking about? I am on time. I frown at the clock: five minutes past four. Crap! Mr Stylme is right: I am five minutes late. I turn back to face him.

Ripples of stunted laughter break throughout the room. Flushed, my face is on fire. Everyone in the room is staring straight at me. My eyes are weighed down by the feeling, finding their way to my shoes. It seems as if that invisible force is holding my gaze down there. Perhaps it is the splashes of blood still on my shoes. I move my tongue around an arid mouth.

"It seems you can be can't be on time for anything," Mr Stylme says, enjoying his role as stand-up comic.

There is more laughter. It is unnecessarily loud. It seems to invade my body – vibrating in my head. I draw in a breath.

"Is it all right with you if we start, then, Mr Tiber?" he says.

I am still looking at my shoes.

"Yes sir," I reply automatically and yet more laugher ripples through the room.

"Take a seat and don't take all night about it!" Mr Stylme snaps.

I look around the room. I check all the faces, and then check them again, just in case. Danny isn't here! I could jump for joy. Only that would land me in even more trouble. I sit at the desk nearest to me, pretty near the back. I slide off my coat and place it on the back of the chair.

"You all know why you are here," Mr Stylme says. He looks at each of us in turn, his face severe, giving the sort of look a judge might give to a room full of mass murderers.

"Yes sir!" we chorus.

"Let's get on with it then, shall we?"

Mr Stylme stands behind the teacher's desk. He turns and goes over to the blackboard. He picks up a piece of white chalk and writes:

"Essay title: Describe the space that occupies the insides of a ping pong ball. No less than 1500 words."

He sounds out each word as he writes it on the board.

*What on earth?*

I am not the only one with this thought. A collective moan goes out from the class.

"But sir...!"

"Silence!" Mr Stylme shouts.

"You know what to do. Now get on with it! Anyone not finished by five o'clock stays until they are finished!" He looks around the room for signs of rebellion. Seeing none, he picks up a pad of A4 paper.

He walks among the desks with the pad, peeling off sheets of lined paper. Four sheets each, he places them down on each desk. He thumps four sheets on my desk, with a more force than is necessary, then before he moves on to the next desk he says:

"I am watching you, Tiber."

I take my pen out from my pocket and hold it an inch above the paper. Part of me is thinking: *What on earth am I going to write? How can I drag this out to 1500 words?* But mostly I am thinking: *what a complete waste of time!* I grind my teeth together.

After about ten minutes, my right hand aches from holding the pen too tightly, and the finger upon which my pen rests when I write is very sore. I look up at the clock face. It is as if time has slowed down to the point of going backwards. If only it had been going at this speed this morning, then I would not have been late in the first place!

Each minute lasts forever. Every word I write feels like pulling a tooth out of a shark's mouth. Each time I wonder if I can manage to get another, or if my nerve will fail.

I have had enough: enough of this crappy day, of school, of Mr Stylme and his stupid essay. A full hour of life completely wasted. I knew it was my fault, really, but that did not make it any better – worse if anything. *Still, no matter how bad any experience, no matter how long it seems to go on, it can't go on forever* I tell myself. *No, but it can feel like it.*


I count the words back to myself, then look up at the clock: twenty-five minutes past five. Could be worse. I get up. I am the only student left in the room. I hand it to Mr Stylme, who looks up. He does an approximation of counting the number of words on the sheet of paper. After a few seconds, he nods. I turn to go. Mr Stylme pulls on an arm of my duffel coat. I have almost made it out, shrugging the coat onto my shoulders. But Mr Stylme can't resist one more parting shot:

"Tomorrow – please try to be on time," he says as I reach the door.

"Yes sir," I say like a good little automaton.

Outside, I take a good deep breath. I breathe in a lung full of fresh air. It is cold on my teeth. I flex my right hand a couple of times. It does not feel any less sore.

*Right! Home. Now. Let's go.* I spur my tired muscles into action.

I walk towards the school gates, passing the sombre school buildings, through the empty car park and passing the bike shed. I cannot decide whether the quietness is soothing or just plain creepy. I look at my watch: half past five.

The sun is sinking. The fiery red orb is disappearing fast, with not much light left on this particular day. It will be too dark to go through Wylye woods. I would be tripping over everything in the dark. No, the safe way home for me.

I go through the school gates and down the short hill and start the slow walk along the winding main road. *At least this day is over and done with.*

# Chapter 10

# Fated To

*I put one foot in front of the other.*

My footsteps make a hollow echoing sound on the empty pavement. Tiredness dogs my every single step. Everything is disconnected – distant from me. I walk slowly along the meandering road. The sun is hovering just above the horizon. Overhead are the dark line of houses and trees. The street lights are only just turning on. Each grey concrete pillar sounds with an unnatural electrical hum.

A Ford Escort whizzes past. I watch the car wind its way around the outskirts of the Heath council estate before mounting the steep hill, where the road hugs the outer boundary of Wylye woods, disappearing out of sight as it goes over the top of the hill.

Coming the other way towards me, a red Mini is motoring down the hill with its headlights barely visible and dispersed by the fading daylight. The car flashes past me. On the other side of the road, a fluorescent kitchen light splutters to life in a window. The shockingly stark glow flares up, illuminating a sparse kitchen in one of the council houses. Inside I can see a young woman with brown hair tied in a tight bun. She moves towards the window to look down at me. There is a look of apprehension on her face. I look away and carry on along the road.

The council houses on the Heath estate are all mirror images of each other. The walls are built out of big rectangular white stone blocks and the roofs are layered with red-ridged tiles. The gardens are the only thing that show individuality: some have neatly cut grass and flowerbeds full of different types and colours of flowers, all uniform and beautifully arranged. Others are overgrown with wild grass and strewn with rusting fridges or washing machines. I pass one with an old Ford Cortina, sat in the garden, with no wheels and its axels mounted on breeze blocks.

An elderly couple putter down the pavement towards me. The man is tall and stooped with short white hair under a brown flat cap. The woman walking next to him is shorter and more rotund in shape. They both scowl at me. The woman is taking a tighter grip on her handbag as they come near. I smile a weak smile until I pass by. A few steps further, I look behind me: the two of them looking back at me, their eyes darkened with mistrust. I never know how to take that sort of thing so I take it personally. The sharp all-too-familiar stab of guilt penetrates between my shoulder blades. *What did I do to provoke this distrust?*

My pace slows and my footsteps drag. My hunched shoulders are the only thing holding me upright. I try to wipe the tiredness from my eyes but I quickly realise: you can't wipe away on the outside what is on the inside. My stomach growls in anger at my neglect of its needs.

*Get home. Get out of the cold. Have your tea. Forget about school and watch a bit of TV. Blake 7 is on later.* But, I just can't forget what has happened today. No matter how hard I try. Had Danny really wanted to kill me? Or was it all just an act? More importantly, will he be having another go any time soon? It doesn't seem possible that he would really go through with it. *He wouldn't, would he?*

*Anyway...nothing I can do about it now*, I tell myself. But, that don't even come close to quieting the turmoil inside my overactive head.

I close my hands around hard and cold disk-shapes inside my coat pocket – coins, my unspent dinner money. I pull the money out of the pocket, counting it out into my other hand. £1.31 in all. I need a sugar rush to cheer me up. I need it now. There is a Newsagent at the top the hill. *Maybe a quarter pound of sherbet lemons or wine gums. How about a Mars bar or three? That would definitely cheer me up.* My pace quickens.

I cross the road.

The parade is a row of five shops. The first is a Fish and chips shop, which is followed by a newsagent, launderette, off-license and an empty shop at the end, which is all boarded up. The hardboard that covers the shop window is plastered in fly posters. These pump out light, blasting it out of their large windows and keeping the creeping darkness at bay. This is with the exception of the last of the row, that looks sullen and sulky in its shadowy darkness.

Outside I can see a few teenagers hanging about in the red and black of St Stephens' uniforms. A couple of them are sat on a low wall sticking out from the end of the row of shops. Away from the glare of the shop lights, I can see the red glow of cigarette ends in the grey half-light. It is a familiar enough sight. The school uniform is no obstacle when it comes to the purchase of cigarettes and a bottle of cider, as long as there are no more than three of you at a time. Everything you need for a good night out: or so I am told. It isn't my sort of thing. I stay in most nights, either watching TV or playing on the ZX Spectrum I was given for Christmas. *Danny is right about one thing – I am a 'goody two shoes'. No perhaps about it. I've never done anything.*

Something in the pit of my stomach shifts uneasily. I pay it no heed, as I am occupied, thinking about how many bars of chocolate I can get for my money.

"Well, well – Look who it isn't?" a painfully familiar voice hisses.

"Come 'ere, moron!" Danny says.

"Oh S…!!!"

My body freezes. Something in my stomach does a cartwheel and my brain yells:

*Run for it!*

And for once I do. I run over the road, pelting over the pavement into the playing field and pegging it towards the tree line on the other side of the field.

Danny may be the strongest of the trio, but Paul is the fastest. It is Paul who rugby tackles me to the ground. And it is Danny who lays into me once I am down on the ground.

"NEVER run away from me, you little maggot!" He shouts. "How many times have I got to tell you? – You retarded or something?"

"Must be!" one of the others says. I can't tell who. I am too busy trying to protect myself from Danny's Doc Martin boots.

"It's going to be worse for you now!" Danny says.

Every cell in my brain is screaming get up and start running once more. But my body is hurting all over and something inside of me tells me that everything is hopeless. Inside I come undone. I lie in the wet grass looking up at the grim, barely visible dark faces peering down at me, made all the more terrible for their facial expressions being obscured from me.

For the thousandth time in my short life, I wish that the earth would just swallow me completely, but life is never that merciful. Instead, uncaring hands reach down towards me, grabbing my arms and pulling me to my feet. Paul and James have an arm each.

"Come on," Danny says.

He leads the way with the other two escorting me towards the woods. I have a horrible feeling that I know exactly where they are taking me.

# Old Manor

# Chapter 1

# Human Sacrifice

*The bloodshot glow of the last of the sun's rays through the trees signifies the coming of the creeping darkness.* The undergrowth snatches at my ankle as they lead me through the trees into Wylye woods. I am marched down the unlit and uneven mud track.

For all I know, they are leading me down to an unmarked grave in a clearing deep within the woods. They could just beat me to death and leave me buried under the dirt and leaves. Nobody would know.

My eyes dart all around, looking for a way out, to escape my captor's clutches. I see only darkness and the threatening dark shapes of the woods; everything takes on a more forbidding air in the dark.

*No exit. No way out. No hope.*

I taste the cold air and feel its sting on my flesh. I hear a creature rummaging in the undergrowth somewhere near. Everything is close and threatening. I cannot see where I am putting my feet. Each step is a step into the unknown.

Tall trees close in on us on either side. I am sandwiched between Paul and James, my limp arms in their iron grip, as they deliberately steer me towards the puddles in the cratered road.

"Here's one!"

"You sure? Can't see a damn thing."

"Yeah."

Splash!

"Told ya!"

"Ha, ha!"

Time and again, cold water floods into my shoes. My shoes squelch as my wet cold socks cling to my feet. My feet begin to feel like solid blocks of ice.

"Come on! Get a move on!" Paul hisses in my ear. That same nicotine charge to his breath. Not as hot and sticky as Danny's though.

Paul was my friend once, a thousand years ago – well four to be precise, but it feels like ancient history. It was at the last school – a lot can happen in the summer holidays. I don't get it. I don't understand what happened. Maybe it had something to do with growing hair in strange places. I don't know. Everything seemed to change – whole personalities. Except me: I stayed the same. The world changed and left me behind.

"Oh no... No, no, no!"

We take a left. I know where we are going. I have suspected it. Now all my worst fears are confirmed. I swallow.

The short overgrown track ends with a giant pair of wrought iron gates pitted between a tall stone wall on either side, stretching in both directions before disappearing into the dark shadows of the trees. It has to be over ten feet: taller than me, taller than Danny even. Through the gate, silhouetted by silver light of the canescent moon, I see it – the Old Manor House.

*Why here! Why did it have to be here!*

I take in a sharp breath of cold air. I had wondered if this would be the place, the place where Danny finished off what he started today on the school roof. *Is this where I am going to die?*

It looks wrong.

It screams out at you, waking, into some dark corner in the older part of the brain. It shouts, not in a way that is deciphered by the conscious-rational mind. It is more something where the only cognizance of it, comes from the deep dark rooms of the unconscious where dark primordial drives run things their own way. It is the part of you that wakes you up in the middle of the night screaming; you don't know why, but you sense some dreadful awfulness waiting for you when you go back to sleep, only to find it standing in the open doorway grinning, machete in hand. Or this is how it feels to my galloping mind.

The Old Manor house waits upon the hill, looking down stone steps, over the wild undergrowth and the sea of bramble bushes, their barbed branches reaching and arching into the air in imitation of the flailing tentacles of an angry sea monster. The steps are almost as steep as those on the side of the pyramid temple of the Aztecs.

*Is this how they felt? Before going up those steps to have their still beating heart cut from their chests? Is this when they realise this is it – everything they could have been is over with. When there was nothing left to do, except to go through the farce of the rituals that would lead to them to their deaths.*

I can feel it looking back at me, boring into my soul, as if somewhere in the depths of its cellars. Its slow beating black heart, amongst the rattling and clanging ancient pipe work and the rats and the spiders, is suddenly beating faster as it anticipates the human sacrifice that has been brought to its door. It waits patiently for my guards to bring me up the stone steps and throw me inside its open mouth, as if it has been awaiting me all this time: to swallow me whole.

"You scared?" Danny asks. I can sense him smirk in the darkness.

"No," I say. I am almost telling the truth: I am not scared – I am terrified. I keep my mouth open, jaws apart. When I close them – when my teeth touch – they start to chatter. This is something I only thought happened in cartoons. Well, now, I know better.

"Well you should be. Very!" Danny says.

"You know what we are going to do to you, don't you?" He growls.

"No," I say.

"When we get you up there..." he says.

"What are you…?"

"Shh! Don't want to spoil the surprise, do we?" he says.

"But don't worry… You will find out soon enough," he says.

Neither Paul nor James seem quite as gung-ho about this venture as Danny. Danny seems to come alive and is glowing with a nervous excitement. I think people like Danny are drawn to places like this: places where no one in their right mind would want to go. Places where the centre of gravity seems to shift and reality slips it noose of ordinariness: where everything is just downright wrong.

They don't say anything – they don't dare – but keep looking at each other and then away. I can see the whites of their eyes dart around, peering at each other almost pathetically. I can practically feel their unease. You could cut it with a knife through the blackness. With Paul, I am not surprised. He has been here before; we both had, a long time ago. The experience must have sat as badly with him as it had with me. If nothing else, the old manor, that old pile of stones, certainly knew how to make an impression, albeit a nasty one.

I catch my breath, exhaling white mist that freezes in the air.

*I am going to die*. I know it in my bones. The only thing I don't know is whether it will be Danny or the house that will get me first. My brain fills to overflowing, with moving pictures of my last moments stuck on repeat.

*I don't want to be here, I don't want to think. I want my brain to shut the hell up.*

*I never get what I want.*

# Chapter 2

# Ancient History

**Monday 30th August, 1976.**

*I jam on the brakes on my chopper bike and stamp both feet down on the ground.* I skid along the dry, caked dirt. A hot dry wind blows through the desiccated trees and the rustling noise sounds almost sinister in its dryness. I look behind me. Paul has stopped a small way behind me. He stands with both feet firmly on the ground and his hands on the cow-handle bars of his bike.

"Come on!" I say.

"Nah," he replies.

"We're just going to have a look," I say. "We're not going in."

Paul shakes his head, then rides up to where I stand with my bike. He gets off and we push our bikes the remaining distance to the tall wrought iron gates. Rust blisters the surface of the gate, where the paint work has long since peeled off. The gates are held together by a thick metal chain wrapped around both gates and secured in place by a large padlock. The chain and the padlock contrast with the old gate, which is bright silver and glints under the midday sun.

I lean my bike against a big oak. Paul props his bike next to mine. The outrageously long cow-handle bars on his bike stick out a mile. Nothing will ever get me to part with my chopper bike, with the gear lever on top of the frame. But I have to admit that cow-handle bars are dead comfy to ride. I am slightly envious, but not much.

I walk over to the ornamental gates and peer through. And there it is in all its scary strangeness. It really was a manor house once: the home of the Sturgess family. They have owned all the land for miles around here but lost it all due to bankruptcy brought on by the various legal battles going on between them. The lands around the manor house have been sold, leaving it to fall into disrepair. The garden has been left to go wild. In the 'water stressed' heat, the wild vegetation has turned a lifeless yellow and brown. The branches of brambles resemble the bones of some monstrous behemoth, the flesh having long since rotted off leaving only the yellow bones.

Silence. No birds, no sounds. Even the wind has stopped, as if holding its breath. The rasping rustling has at least covered up this bare emptiness. Goose flesh covers my skin, stiffening it almost painfully. I feel a chill despite the airless heat burning upon my brown skin.

"…The brother killed the rest of the family with an axe, then blew his own brains out with a shotgun. The blood is still on the walls. They couldn't clean it off. Or so I heard…" Paul said.

"The Sturgesses? That's just an urban myth. My dad said so," I added.

Maybe so, but the dark feeling at this retelling is already here and has already taken root in my imagination.

"That doesn't mean it's not true!" Paul retorts.

I think this is exactly what it means but I don't say anything.

The house is an island of the past that is slowly falling down and sinking into the earth. It is built out of limestone blocks with red bricks sandwiched between the larger blocks, all under a grey slate roof. A good many of the slates are missing. The design of the house has a castle like feel to it – in a faux way. It has two towers at either end and what resembles a gate house at the front, protruding out from the main line of the building.

"Why have they boarded up the windows?" I ask, disappointed

"Had to... The council. Health and safety, or so my dad says."

"Yeah?"

The house scares the pants off me, but at the same time I am curious about the place. It contains a morbid fascination for me. I wouldn't mind peeking through one of the windows if they were not boarded up and maybe even…

"My dad says they're itching to tear the place down… But some dodgy solicitor in London keeps blocking it. This solicitor won't even say who owns the house."

"An overseas client. That's all he will say," Paul adds. But I'm not even listening. The house seems to be reaching out to me:

*Come on in! You know you want to…*

Drawing me in, a sirens voice is almost singing…

I start. I feel something on my shoulder. I swing my head around to see Paul. He is shaking my shoulder. I pull away.

"What?" I say – irritated.

"You're not listening to me," he replies.

"What? Yes…no – what were you saying?"

"I don't like it here! Let's go!" Paul says. "It gives me the creeps."

"You're not scared are you?" I say, smiling.

"Of course not. I just want to go," says Paul. But his creased face tells a different story.

I look back at the house longingly. Just for a second. Then I look back at Paul's creased face. Then, the spell is broken.

"Ok…ok" I say. "Let's go."

I turn and we walk back to our bikes. I put my foot on my bike's peddle to push off. I cannot help but turn back to the house, for one last look. Everything is still – but I am sure I hear a voice inside my head plead:

*"Come back…don't go."*

*"You'll be back."*

I shake my head and turn away. Paul has already set off and is looking over his shoulder at me. I push off and start to peddle after him.

I have pushed the memory into a box marked 'do not open', dropping it in the abyss of my unconscious and forgetting all about it. However, a shiver of fear runs down my spine every time I think of the Old Manor House – just for a moment, before I push the thought out of my mind. But now that box is broken wide open and I cannot control my shakes or the dark thoughts that run through my mind. *I thought I saw the slightest flash of recognition in Paul's eyes. I could have been mistaken. But I was sure I saw it. As if he too was remembering that day. Then the hardness returned to his face. He would not be saving me a second time.*

# Chapter 3

# Canescent Moon

*Tonight, even the moon is insane.*

Bleeding moonlight: under its canescent beams, everything looks unreal. Beyond the gate, the landscape with its dark mass of vegetation is tipped white at its edge by the moon's light. It looks like another world – both alien and monstrous.

Danny, his face in darkness, his blonde mop of hair silver in the light, looks up at the top of the gate. Then he looks at James.

"You first," Danny says.

"Ok," James says. No one says no to Danny.

James grips the bars of the gate and with the agility of a monkey, he scales up the metal frame and flips over to the other side, dropping to the ground.

"Ok?"

"Ok."

*They are really going to do this. Hope has really left town, leaving misery in charge.*

"Your turn now, retard," Danny says, turning to me.

"I can't…"

"Get up there!" he hisses.

My arms shake as I put my hands onto the bars of the gate. The metal is cold to the touch. Rust crumbles underneath my fingers as I grip the top of the gate. I try to lift my own body weight with my scrawny arms, with one foot on the gate, trying to help myself up. The gate quakes on its hinges – wobbling. I feel my face burn as I drop back to the ground: exactly what I had expected. At school, I was not known for my athletic prowess, rather for the lack of it.

"Pathetic!" Paul shouts.

Danny sighs: "Come on he's just too bloody feeble. We'll be here all night!"

"Grab the other leg!"

Taking one leg each, they launch me upwards, pushing me, none too carefully, towards the top of the gate. I grab hold of the upper ridge, gripping the rust covered surface for dear life. I heave my body upwards. Throwing a leg over, I sit precariously on the top – one leg either side. The gate rocks and shifts under my weight. All I can think about is falling off this unstable perch. I quickly pull my other leg over, but then lose my balance and footing.

I fall. The rush of fear comes at the same time as the ground rushes up to meet me.

I land awkwardly on one foot. My ankle twists over. A sudden spasm of pain shoots through me.

"Ha, ha, ha!"

I want to cry out but I don't. It is not as if I would get much sympathy from this crowd. I run a hand down my trouser leg. There is a rip at the bottom of my trousers. I must have caught it on the gate when I climbed over. I didn't feel anything at the time, but here it is. I run the hand across the painful surface of the back of my leg. I run my fingers over the skin towards the centre of the pain. There is wetness there – cold and sticky on my fingertips. I swallow and look down, under the silver of moonlight, and the dark coloured liquid on the tips of my fingers looks like black oil.

Biting my lip, trying not to react to the pain, I look around.

Plant-life has conquered the driveway. Wild grass and weeds are pushing up through the small stones. Ahead of me, there is a narrow pathway through the overgrown vegetation. The undergrowth on both sides is all set to consume the diminishing pathway: to bury it beneath its dark mass. The pathway runs through the middle of the valley of thorny tentacles to the steps leading up to the house.

Ancient oaks of great girth are strewn around the wild landscape, split with age, surrounded by the swarming of bramble bushes. In front of me, at the end of the driveway, are the stone steps that would take us up to the house. Brambles lash across the steps on both sides, like steps to a lost temple hidden by a jungle.

The gate clangs and rattles behind me. I turn to see Danny scale the gate in big brutal movements and wonder if he will damage it. He jumps down, thudding into the soft ground.

Paul clambers up and over the gate. I watch his movements – fast and without hesitation, he flies over the apex of the gate, after dropping to the ground, springing up almost immediately.

"See, that is how you do it!" Danny brags.

"Easy!" Paul agrees.

"If you are not a freaking spineless weasel. that is!" James says.

After a while, I stop following who is saying what. It all sounds the same. As if they have become one person. They will be completing each other's sentences next. Three little psychopaths melted into one.

"Come on!" Danny says, reasserting his leadership credentials once more.

He starts down the overgrown path towards the steps.

"Get going, moron!" Paul says, giving me a shove. I do as I am told.

Danny leads, striding up the path, through the undergrowth, pushing the branches of brambles to one side as he negotiates the wilderness. I follow with Paul and James behind me: a rear guard, in case I try to make a run for it. I push through the wild grass and the vicious branches of brambles that grab at my coat with their thorny lengths. If things were not bad enough already, Danny thinks it jolly good fun to hold back a branch of one of the brambles from time to time, until I come near, when he releases it, making it spring at me like a whip. I jump back, but to no avail and it whips across my face and my duffel coat: digging its hooks into the thick material.

"Oh Whoops!" Danny says.

And I am silent.

"Oh, and again! I am just so clumsy today!"

"It just slipped out of my hand!"

I am silent.

"Accidentally!"

"Accidentally on purpose! Ha-ha."

I say nothing.

It takes me several seconds to unhook myself, by which time Paul and James catch me up and give me a shove.

"Come on. Hurry up," one of them says and whoever is directly behind me gives me a push. I don't know how they are managing it. The path is narrow: too narrow for one person, let alone two. But, somehow, they manage to swap places. Maybe they don't. Maybe it is the same person all the time. I don't know. I am beyond terrified. I am out of my mind with fear. Anything is possible, heading up these fateful steps.

The grotesque silhouettes of misshapen trees surround us, their giant shapes reaching, more and more of them, clawing like giant black swollen fingers. Their trunks, thick and deformed bodies, leaning at odd angles, with swollen joints in the shape of tumorous human heads. The dead limbs seem to me as if they are trying to reach down towards me. I bite my lip.

At the summit, the remains of a water feature loom out in front of the house, now little more than a wide stone dish, with a huge crack on the far side. Four cherubs, made plain by the light of the moon, dance around the central head of the fountain, their faces worn away, and one of them having lost its head completely. The rough surface of the stone, where the head had once been, looks as if it has been snapped clean off.

In its day, there would once have been a powerful spray of water spurting into the air and filling the dish of the water feature, where there is now only the brown mush of dead leaves and rainwater leaking from the crack in the side in a thick brown trickle. The moon reflects out of the blackness of the dark water, wavering, its outline vague —a long round shape flickering in the stagnant water.

Everything here is in a state of decay. This whole place, everything here, is sickly, as if it is waiting to die.

Danny walks around the stone basin and towards the porch and the main door. He mounts the first of the four wide stone steps. I meekly follow him towards the wooden doors: doors that make even Danny look small when he stands in front of them.

Everything seems to halt – all the vegetation and even the grasping talons of the brambles have died away the on way to the steps, as if they were too scared to grow too close to the house: shrinking away. I cannot blame them. It is how I am feeling inside. My stomach is lurching at every opportunity it gets and a sinking feeling is descending upon me as if I am on top of a perilous, high up ledge and the vertigo has just started to kick in. I try to suck in air, but there does not seem to be any. I steady myself on one of the stone pillars. My legs feel weak. I wouldn't have thought it possible, but my anxiety levels are rising, going up and up, without pause or any indication that the feeling will ever abate.

Danny lifts one of the sizeable wrought iron rings that serve as door handles. He pulls. The door groans, but does not budge. There is a loud bang as Danny drops the ring. If the house did not know we were here. It does now.

# Chapter 4

# Dark Threshold

*Danny gives the door a savage kick.*

But it does not move. It makes a reassuring thud when his booted foot hits the wood. At last he has met his match. Danny has found something that does not automatically bend to his will. *Hope you break your flipping toe!*

"Bloody door!" He rages, giving it another kick.

I edge into the darkness, behind one of the stone pillars, out of direct sight, before he turns on me, making me a punch bag for his anger. I keep my face blank. Not that he can see it. The inside of the porch is dark. It is impossible to see anyone's face, let alone their expression, but my ear burns hot as a warning. I am not about to take any chances. Whatever Danny has planned will be bad enough. I don't want to add to it by pissing him off.

"Shh! Someone might hear," Paul says, scratching at his cheek, looking around.

"Dickhead! Who's going hear?" Danny shouts.

Paul takes a step backwards.

"No one comes out here!" Danny raises his hands in mock desperation.

He puts his hands around his mouth and yells:

"HELLO, ANYONE!"

"See!" he says, smiling.

This reminds me just how precarious my situation will be if things turn nasty for me, which they surely will. Danny is right: no one ever comes out here. It feels like being on the edge of the world, about to drop off. I shift uneasily in the dark. I look back the way we have come. Everything up to the tip of the gate is visible under the streaks of moons light; beyond that, all is submerged within the darkness, indeterminable in that one shade of black.

I have to keep hoping against hope that I will survive this night – a few more bruises, even a couple of cuts, but alive. I will get home and tomorrow things will start over again... My rotten existence will just carry on, without point or reason, but it is life, the only one I know and will cling to desperately. Even if I am slowly dying inside and gradually turning to mud, lifeless and malleable, it is all I have.

But it isn't just Danny anymore. Something else is hanging over me like a thick miasma and it feels like death. It had felt bad enough from behind the gate, but now that I am close to it – the house – it feels a million times worse...

Waves of nausea run through me. All of sudden, I am not getting enough blood to my brain – the world flies into the air and all the time an unpleasant sensation is ripping through my midriff.

"No..." I say. It is barely a whisper.

I slip to my knees, crouching, with one hand on the cracked stone floor. It is so cold, numbing the skin on my palm and fingers. Even so, all I want is to lie down on that cold surface, until all of this has passed. The others have moved around to the side of the house and are checking windows by the sounds of it. I am left – forgotten for the moment. No doubt they will remember their toy soon enough. The further in the future that is, the better. So I suffer in silence, in that dark corner of the doorway.

I can see them trying to prise the wood from one of the boarded-up windows. I think about running for it. But all three of them are faster than me. Anyway, how would I get out? Over the high walls or the iron gate? Ask for my tormentors for help again to get out? Ha! I can see that happening – *not*. Besides, my leg is still throbbing with pain and when I try to stand, I feel anything but steady. So, I stay where I am, listening to the voices of the others, dreading the moment when their attention will return to me.

"This place is shut up tight! We're wasting our time," James' voice drifts out of the darkness.

"Yeah we need a crow bar or something," Paul says, rubbing his knuckles.

"Or a screwdriver at least," James says.

"Let's get out of here," Paul says hopefully.

"Nah, let's try round the back," Danny says, his voice louder than the others.

"Grab 'im," Danny says, pointing in my direction.

Still feeling sick, I stand, sliding up the wall, when Paul and James approach me. They grab my unresisting arms and steer me out of the porch. I am marched down the side of the house. Out of the light of the moon, it is almost pitch black, with the only light coming from the end of the pathway, which fails to penetrate down the side of the house. We pass under a stone arch, looming up out of the darkness, a darker shade of black than everything else. With each step, I have no idea where I am putting my feet. Every footstep is falling upon the unknown and an uneven pathway. If there is a deep hole or an open drain cover, I will not know until it is too late: until I am at the bottom with a broken leg. I am urged on by the occasional forceful push. We just keep heading toward the light up ahead.

We emerge from the darkness into an ocean of silver moonlight that rolls over the wild grass that runs downhill towards a meadow. I can see the river Wylye snaking through the valley below, its water surface appearing as a continuous black surface whittling away into the distance. On both sides of the riverbank, trees cluster, as the river meanders towards the city: all lit up in white and orange lights. Somewhere in that mass of lights, is a street and down that street is a house: my home.

*I should be there now, in the warm, sat in front of the TV, watching my favourite programmes, with my tea on my lap: safe. Instead, I am out here, cold, frightened and the night is not over. Why did this have to happen? Damn Danny. And Paul and James. Damn them all to hell.*

Danny checks the windows on the ground floor of the house, without success. They are boarded up as tight as the ones at the front.

*Good. I have no wish to go inside. The idea…Well, let's just say I don't want to go in the house and leave it at that.*

"Hey! Wait a minute…," he says.

*"Oh no!"*

Danny stands at the side of a small wall. Nearer to the wall, I see the flight of steps leading down, running below ground, tight against the wall of the house. Danny bounds down the steps into the darkness below, disappearing from view. My keepers stand on either side, watching me, their complexions pale white in the moonlight. I hear Danny pulling at the door. I hear him curse.

He tries again.

And the worst possible thing happens. I hear the screech of wood as the ill-fitting door scrapes across the stone surface. He must have forced the door open. He bounds back up the steps with a big grin on his pale moonlit face.

"Yes! We are in!" He says, as his face appears above the small wall.

"Bring 'im down. We are in business!" He says.

I look up at the moon with the finality of prisoner who is just about to be led to the gallows. It is completely radiant in its fullness. Typical. The moon overhead will go on shining, tonight, tomorrow night and the next: as it has for millions of years. I resent the moon for that but, at the same time, it comforts me. I walk down the worn stone steps to meet my fate. Someone's hand helps me on my way with a half-hearted shove.

At the bottom of the stairs, I pause. I can't see Danny's face in the darkness, just his big silhouette. He is standing close, too close to me, his breath, hot and unpleasant on my face. It brings back the image of the school roof top: my legs dangling in mid-air and a cold chilling look on his face. And something in the gloom behind him seems, to be grinning out at me as if enjoying some secret access to the images in my head.

Danny grabs my arm and twists it. I yelp and he thrusts me towards the dark emptiness of the doorway. Fear spikes and flies upwards.

"No, no, no," I plead as I look into the abyss, my eyes straining to see into the total blackness beyond. I can see neither shape nor form: nothing, just a black wall.

"Bring us back a souvenir!" Danny sneers.

I feel my arm release from his grip, while another hand slams into the middle of my back, propelling me forwards into the wall of darkness. The Icy breath of the house rushes to greets me. My sightless eyes widen. I stagger over the threshold into the black.

# Chapter 5

# Dying Light

*I stumble into the cold blanket of darkness.*

Falling and landing face down. My reactions are too slow to stop my head from banging down on the stone floor. I don't feel it. I am too terrified to feel pain. My head is a junk-shop of disconnected thoughts. I breathe in the cold musty air. It smells like a tomb: mine.

Dust is thick on floor, with my fingers deep in layers of it and the air choking with it. I can feel it at the back of my throat, irritating the soft skin there. I cough out a lungful, staring, wild, into the darkness.

I am spinning towards the door. A narrow shard of moonlight shines down from above the doorway. I can just make out a dark shape standing there, filling the door frame with his large bulk. Demonic looking, the only thing missing from the shape is a machete in one hand and a severed head in the other.

"What are you doing?" My voice quivers in the dark, the sound seeming not to come from my mouth but elsewhere in the room.

I cough.

"So long shit-stain," Danny says.

"Yeah nice knowing you!" James pipes, the round umbra of his head appearing at Danny's shoulder, making it look as if he has two heads.

"Enjoy!" Paul says, from somewhere behind Danny.

"See you around... not!" Danny says. He starts to close the door.

"No!" I yelp.

I am on my feet, with no idea how I got there. Without thinking, I run for the door, only to meet with Danny's fist coming in the other direction. It hits me square in the face, its force throwing me backwards. Eyes watering, I fall upon the corner of something hard.

"I told you…" Danny says.

Thud. I go down like a sack of spuds.

Huh, what?

Why does my head hurt? It pumps pain through my head and down my neck. I open my eyes. There is only darkness.

*Where am I?*

*What happened?*

I have a moment of anxiety as my brain tries to track down the elusive memories that led to this point. I feel the hard stone beneath me; it is cold against my cheek. Then I realise where I am and start to really panic.

*Bloody hell! I am still inside that old relic of a house.* I look around and crouch like a wild animal: listening.

I remember Danny's punch, then nothing, then being awake once more. It is as if consciousness has been sliced in two and then taped back together again, with only the rough incomplete edges to show the break between the two.

I put my hand to my aching head. My forehead is wet. I sniff it and then I taste it, knowing full well what it is before my taste buds tell me:

blood. I must have hit something before I fell. I check my nose which also hurts. Nothing is broken.

All at once, I have the distinct feeling of being watched – that someone is in the dark, silently laughing at my distress.

My eyes strain to see something, anything. But the darkness is total. The dark is a place of infinite possibilities for concealment, from the lunatic with an extra sharp butcher's knife to the hideous blood sucking ghoul that has just stepped out of the imagination into the world of flesh and blood. My brain starts to melt in a blind panic. I swallow, then bite down on one of my knuckles until it hurts. My skin is ablaze with goose flesh all over.

"Danny?" I ask the blackness.

He could be right in front of me and I would not know. For a second, I think he might be in here with me. I freeze.

Silence.

He and his pals must have been long gone, leaving me alone in this haunted place, trapped in the dark. I can't even see my own hand if I wave it in front of my face.

At least that is something: they have gone. I relax slightly.

What is the matter with me? I am so jittery that if someone tapped me on the shoulder at this moment, I would drop dead from a heart attack.

I tentatively put out a hand into the darkness.

*No, no don't!*

There is no one or nothing there. But in my head… No, I have just worked myself up. I have blown the whole thing out of all proportion. *Nothing new about that!*

I reach out, my hand in front of me seeking, but not wanting to find. I'm not to be disappointed. I find…well nothing. I claw the empty air.

I let out a huge sigh.

I crawl along the floor in the direction I think the door I came in is located.

*Oh!*

It is only a big empty old house. That is all. I just need to get out. To go home. Reaching out with one hand, I find the wooden door. I kneel up. With my hands outstretched, I feel its edges on either side where it meets the stone of the wall. I pull myself upwards, seeking the door handle. Finding it, I try to pull it downwards as I push at the surface of the door. It does not move. I put my bony shoulder against the door and push. And I get a stab of pain in my shoulder for my trouble, but the door does not budge.

I bang my fists against the door, hard at first but then the blows become weaker as feelings of hopelessness start to bite. I freeze. I am making enough noise to wake the dead.

*How am I going to get out of here?*

*I am not thinking!*

This can't be the only way out. If not a door, a window. It can't all be boarded up. It doesn't even have to be that big: because of my narrow frame, I could squeeze out of the smallest of openings. Failing that, I could find something heavy that I could bash out the window with.

I start to edge away from the door, along the wall, my hands seeking guidance from the rough surface that crumbles under my touch: damp flakes of paint and plaster coming away in my hands. I make good progress until I touch upon something solid blocking my path. I stop.

*A table?*

I reach out towards the object, leaning forward, my hand passing through something soft and wispy, it wraps around my hand and I feel something soft brush across my face, tickling it.

"Urgh! Cobwebs!" I say, withdrawing my hand quickly. Rubbing my hands against my trouser leg to get the filmy stuff off.

"Spiders. Yuk!" I imagine them crawling all over the table the floor, crawling up my arm, swarming...

I become aware of a sense of panic that sits deep inside my gut. I feel like a trapped rat that will do anything to escape its confinement.

I try to calm myself. I touch the edge of the table, my fingers running through layers of soft gritty stuff. I follow the table, my fingers trailing the edges, away from the wall, into the room, into the unknown. Following the curves and protrusions of its rough surface, I worry about getting a splinter from the warped wood. But better that, than losing contact with the surface of the table. It's my only guide back to the door. I need to know I can find my way back to the door. I don't know why. But it seems important. I need something to hold onto after all.

I reach the end of the table. I step forward. Stretching out, blindly, grasping, I find the edge of another piece of furniture: another table or workbench. I take another couple of steps and then, already off balance, I stub by toe on something. I trip and fall. My hands flail in the darkness. I grab onto something as I fall heavily into the side of the table. It all comes tumbling down on top of me: boxes, crates, magazines, pieces of furniture and whatever else has been stacked on the table. It creates an almighty noise, as objects big and small clash down and clatter across the floor.

"Aaagh!"

I lie under the pile, stunned. The sounds of smaller metal objects are clattering across the floor, ringing in my ears. I splutter and wheeze. My nostrils fill up with so much dust I can taste it. I rub itching eyes. Getting my breathing back under control, I start to disentangle myself, pushing a wooden chair off. I turn over, putting a hand down to steady me. My hand finds a single shoe.

*I am ok,* I try to reassure myself. *No real damage – maybe a couple more scratches and bruises but no broken bones.* It doesn't work. If something happens to me here, if I break my leg or worse, that would be it for me. The only people who know I am in here are Danny and his two cronies and I can't see them lifting a finger to help when I don't turn up at school.

"Good riddance to bad rubbish," I expect they would say.

My parents would go to the police and I would be registered as a missing person. But would anyone really miss me? Would anyone think of looking for me in this old house? Probably not. Maybe after I have been lying rotting on the floor for a few years, someone – kids on a dare or a tramp or something – might find me... *God, morbid much…*or just scared out of my mind. One thing is clear though: I am on my own. No help will be coming. I am the only one who can get me out of this mess. So I need to stop faffing around and get on with it.

The shoe is still in my hand. I frown. At first, in the dark, I wonder if it is mine. I wiggle my toes on both feet to make sure. It must have fallen off the table with all the other stuff. Maybe there is another one lying around to make the pair. I grip it harder. I pull at it. I want something to throw across the room in frustration, in anger – both? Who knows. Only I couldn't. The damn thing would not move. It seems glued to the floor, as if it is attached to something. My breath catches at the back of my throat. Worse, the shoe doesn't feel empty. It feels as if there is a foot already inside. I tear my hand away in shock.

"Bloody hell!"

It can't be. I am just freaked out about being locked in the dark. I explore with my other hand. I find the shoe. Going upwards, I find an ankle and the start of a leg. I feel the hairs on the skin, the warm softness of flesh. Losing my nerve, I whip my hand away.

"S…Sorry!"

Silence.

"Er, um, do you know a way out?" I say nervously.

Silence.

A tramp asleep in here? My mind flails. I shake his trouser leg.

"Excuse me, but do you know the way out of here?" I say, louder this time.

Silence.

Then it struck me, a terrible thought, one I did not want to be true. The skin had felt warm but lifeless. And... *No don't say it. Saying it will make it true.*

No. I won't believe it. If he is dead, he will be cold. I know that for sure. *And how would you know? How many dead bodies have you touched? A big fat zero*, I chide myself.

I don't want to, but I have to know. I reach out once more, dreading the touch, fearful of what I will find. Some drunken vagrant cussing and beating me away is a positive outcome here. My stomach curls in a tight ball as I stretch out my hand once more.

I find his chest this time. The shirt he is wearing has buttons down the front ripped open. His chest is hairless and bare. I go higher. I find the face and touch the cheek, which is warm and soft. Its lifelessness and the way the head moves on the neck without restriction confirms my worst fears. My hand seems to leap back of its own accord. I have never seen a dead person before. And I have no doubt in my mind that what I have just touched is a dead man. Before I have time to think about it too much, I put my hand on what I think is a pile of sacking under the body.

It isn't. My hand lands on a shoulder. The texture of the material covering the shoulder is velvety and smooth, like the sleeve of a dress. I move my hand upwards to find a neck and it is as lifeless as the man's. I have the impression there are more bodies here. But two is more than enough. *Why is there no smell? I wonder. Aren't dead bodies supposed to smell?*

The gloom surrounding me seems to descend upon me, pouring in my blind eyes and infecting my brain with its malevolence. A scream comes up inside of my throat but stays there: trapped. I stare around uselessly in the darkness, my eyes bulging, trying desperately to see – trying to see the killer coming towards me out of the dark.

All imagined fears have been made real in an instant. My mind juggernauts to one single neon-lit conclusion, the only one possible. There is a killer. Who killed these people. He may come back or, worse, he could still be in the house.

*Shut up! Shut up! Think!*

All the possibilities melt into one, certain and wholly unpleasant thought. My heart has just tripled its beats per minute, pounding loud in my head, behind my eyes. Then, right on cue:

"You have seen a little too much," a voice says. It is low, and without real expression or emotion. It has a smooth, silky quality to it that reminds me of the dead woman's dress.

I try to speak, but everything has stopped working. My mouth, legs and arms are all frozen in place: immovable. Nothing works, except my heart, which beats even louder, while the insides of my chest and gut liquefy into pure terror.

Nothing I can say will cut much ice with the giant that descends upon me. I could scream, but no one would hear. I could plead for mercy, but the pile of bodies on the floor suggests he is not a merciful man.

I don't even hear him approach. *How long has he been in this room with me?* Even before Danny locked me in? It does not seem to matter, not really, not in the grand scheme of things. These are like the stray thoughts of another person, not remotely connected to me. Impossibly large hands grab my upper arms, lift and practically carry me across the room. My mind turns to mush, a terrified incoherent lump that refuses to think or do anything other than to whine, repeatedly:

*No, no, no. Please no!*

As if this will magically stop what is happening to me. As if anything could possibly save me. If an axe murderer comes into your bedroom, you hide under the covers. As if that would save you. How are those few layers of sheet and blanket going to stop the blade of an axe falling at speed towards your vulnerable and soft body? The mind just clings to the smallest hope, however farfetched and unlikely.

He drags me through a door hidden on the other side of the room and down corridors that take us deeper into the house. Then he picks me up in his arms as if I am nothing. No heavier than a feather pillow, I don't resist. I do not do anything.

*I am going to die.* The thought has no bitterness to it. It seems in a way as if it is someone is doing the thinking for me. It is just a pure and simple statement of truth, of what must happen next, at the journeys end. Hot tears form and stream down my face. But they don't mean anything.

He carries me down two flights of stairs. *He is taking me down towards the cellar.* I am being taken to the heart of the house, cradled in the arms of a mass murderer.

# Chapter 6

# Death's Door

*"I can just snap his neck if you like?" the man holding me growls. "Just say the word."*

We are somewhere in the labyrinthine depths of the Old Manor House: in its very stomach. I know that much, but not much else; the darkness is total.

I am trembling, inside and out. I can't stop shaking. The only stillness my body has is where my captor is holding it in a vice-like grip.

"That would be simple, but such a waste!" another voice says. It is a woman's voice, well spoken, musical even.

I peer into the darkness, my head turning, uselessly, this way and that.

"I think we should eat him while he is still fresh," she says.

Eat me? The words hang in the air. The meaning is unambiguous, but my mind can't digest the words. I can't think what they mean. I can't think at all.

My feet do not touch the ground. They hang down and the floor lies below them somewhere. The giant holds me up in the air without obvious effort.

"Drain him of the very last drop of blood," she says.

*My blood? they want to drink my blood?!* My thoughts are murmuring and inarticulate compared to the whip lash of each of her words – sharp and dangerous as a stiletto blade.

She goes on:

"Awake and aware, till the very last moment!"

*Schsssss.* There is the sound of a match being struck, the smell of sulphur and a light flaring in front of me. The spark explodes into flame, hurting my eyes after the total blackness. The match hangs in the air, burning upwards from the end toward the tips of the fingers that hold it. It is stationary for a few seconds, then the burning flame moves in the darkness. The wick of a candle is lit. An orange flickering light glows outwards and shadows climb the walls. Outside the small sphere of light, not going much further than the coffee table itself, I can only make out dark shapes.

"I do love it – when they know they are going to die," the woman says.

I strain to see her face. All I can make out is a tall elegant silhouette, whose movement is only thing that separates her from the darkness.

"You can see it in their eyes, all hope dimming. Ah, lovely!" she says with a sigh. The pleasure at her recollection is unmistakable, even to my terrified mind.

*Two of them?* The woman who is talking and the giant who held me. But I can sense another presence – a third. There is someone else there, I am sure of it. There is something familiar about it. I can feel their eyes on me: watching me from the dark. It is enough to push me over the edge. I want to scream. Instead I bite down on my lip.

"Oh what to do? Clearly we can't let him leave. No, that would not do at all," a man's voice says. It is very different from the other two, in its way, more menacing: slower, more thoughtful. And it is an even colder sound, colder than the other two put together.

The giant drops me onto my feet, but still keeps hold of my shoulders with his big hands. I struggle to stay standing. My mind is numb. Who are these people? *Murderers*, a voice inside my head, whispers darkly.

"And what do you think? What should we do with you?" he asks, his disembodied voice floating out of the darkness. His voice is deeper than even the giant's voice. It is a voice accustomed to not only being listened to, but being obeyed. It has that resonance to it: louder than absolutely necessary. I tremble with each word he utters.

"He asked you a question, maggot," the giant says, gently squeezing my shoulder, crushing at the flesh painfully.

I hear the mysterious man stand. There is a thud; as if something has fallen off his lap as he rises. The top half of a man with short blonde hair, rolls into the sphere of the candle light. One arm flops out to one side; his neck is twisted to an improbable angle and his sightless eyes seem to look into mine as he lies lifeless on the floor. I try to swallow; but the area at the back of my throat is as dry as fossilised bone.

Every muscle in my body trembles as I attempt to get the words out of my dry non-functioning mouth.

"I...I... just want to go...home," I manage to squeeze out. I don't know how. My legs and arms are shaking uncontrollably. I try to breathe.

"You just want to go home! To see your little Mummy and Daddy! How sweet!" he says, his voice a parody of my own. Then his voice hardens:

"But how can we let you go when you have seen all this? Tell me that?"

"I, I, won't say anything. I won't tell anyone!" My voice is rising to soprano.

"Well that is very commendable I am sure," he says, "but you humans lie through your teeth. You can't help it I suppose. It is your nature…"

"It's true," the woman says, "They will say anything to save their rotting skins. And the moment your back is turned…"

"So we can't possibly let you go," the voice behind me thunders. I feel it vibrate at through the back of my ribcage as much as I hear it.

"What to do. What to do!" the voice says.

I know he is only playing with me. I can hear it in his voice.

*This is it. The end of me. To think I had been so afraid of Danny and his cronies all these years. This is real: these people are real killers.*

"We are wasting time!" the woman says. She walks into the light.

She is tall and thin: easily six foot tall. She wears a black trouser suit with a puffed up white blouse with the white cuffs of the blouse extending from the jacket. She has a sharp nose and an equally sharp chin. Her hair is a dull black, tied back in a tight ponytail behind her head. She looks out of place and as if she would be more at home in a top floor office, surrounded by aids and assistants, not in the basement of some dilapidated house.

"Kill him," she says.

Those two little words pop out of her mouth as easily as she might say: "Could you photocopy this report by five o'clock?"

"No I think not. I have other plans for Mr John Tiber here," the man in the centre of the room says.

*They know my name! They know me. How?*

"You don't mean…No…You won't… You can't!" Now the woman sounds shocked and clearly more than a little panicked. I haven't known her more than five minutes but, even so, it seems shockingly out of character for her. I have had the impression that cold and calm is her usual modus operandi.

"It's my decision… and I think you will find that I can," the man says.

"But that… He is no more than a little runt…What possible use can he be to us?" the man behind me rumbles.

"You can't…It's an insult…a sacrilege!" the woman shrieks.

"I can," the man reaffirms.

"They'll kill him anyway," the woman says.

"Well, he will have to take his chances."

Then, finally, the man walks into the light at the centre of the room. I am expecting another giant, but he is only about five foot five, if that. He wears an old-fashioned black three-piece suit. The jacket is open at the front, where a gold chain loops from a low pocket. His face is layered and lined and his hair is short – a black-brown colour. His eyes are deep set: the skin inside those deep sockets seems to fold in concentric circles like whirlpools that pull towards his sharp dark brown eyes.

"Do you want to die? Now? In this cellar?" he asks. I feel his wet finger running down my forehead, massaging the wound, going in and out of the cut. He puts the finger to his mouth and sucks at it. His eyes fix on mine the whole time. I try to look away, but find I cannot.

"Nnno!" I stammer, my teeth chattering.

"Right then. That is decided, then!" he says cheerfully, shooting the woman a look.

A twinge of hope springs forth. I might get out of here alive. *Oh please God!*

I don't even see him move. One moment he is stood looking at me. The next, he is at my throat. I feel two sharp needles puncture my neck. I don't even scream. I feel, as much as I hear, my heart pound loudly in my ears. Then the small pool of light in front of me starts to swim and fly up towards the ceiling. And I drift into darkness. But just before the darkness swallows me up, I think *This man is not a man at all*. He is a snake: a man-snake with two razor sharp teeth sinking into my neck, sucking the life out of me. It doesn't seem real. And then I just disappear into the darkness, as if the candle has been snuffed out.

# Chapter 7

# Waking Up

*I feel the warmth of the sunlight on my eyelids.* I smile at that warmth, stretching out. Then the dream, a nightmare really, comes back to me. My smile fades, a grimace taking its place. As I remember:

*I was trapped in cellar full of snakes, they all had human faces. There were thousands of them, they swarmed and slivered all over me biting, taking out huge red and bloody chunks as I fought against them. Then one rose up in front of my face. There was something wrong with the snake's eyes: it had these circular folds of flesh all around its eyes. It lunged for me with huge long white fangs.*

*Then, I was climbing up the walls of the cellar. The wall was coal black in colour, in fact everything was dark and dungeon like. The snakes were still biting at my ankles and legs as I tried to kick them off. The wall seemed to go up forever, in the way that they do in dreams. Finally, I reached the top. I put a hand over the parapet on the top of the building. I was standing on the roof. I looked down; my legs had gone, replaced with the scaly light green skin of a snake. The scales crawled upward over my stomach, my chest and towards my head. I screamed. Then I broke the surface, being pulled upwards towards the warmth of the sun.*

I open my eyes to find that I am in the most familiar place in the world. But something about it seems strange and unfamiliar. I blink, unsure of what is real. I am relieved that I can move both my legs separately, that they are still – well, legs.

I am in my bedroom in my bed. I am lying on the top bunk of the bunk bed. Sunlight blasts through the light blue coloured curtains. I rest my head back on the pillow. I sigh.

Lifting my head and look around the sunny room. Why is it so bright?

Everything is razor-sharp: lucid. A surge of sensations is cascading over me. The colours, the smells and sounds, all at once, are overwhelming: too many things to experience at the same time.

The blue-green-brown carpet ripples with too much colour, a pattern standing out from the rest, then fading as different colours come to the fore and another pattern is forced into existence. The sunlight pours through the spaces in the curtains, setting alight anything the streaming beams of light touch with fantastic colour. I hear a whispering noise that susurrates from somewhere in the house. I recognise the sounds as they begin to separate out as the voices of my mum, dad and little brother. I can almost hear them; I know that if I listen a little harder, then I will be able to hear what they are saying...

Memories of the previous evening flood my brain. I soon throw these memories back down the stairs into my unconsciousness, dismissed out of hand as not even a possibility. My brain just refuses to believe it. It is all too outrageous to be real. *It could not possibly have happened*, I tell myself firmly.

My pyjamas cling to my body, sodden with sweat, I feel the cold wetness against me as I move.

Have I dreamt it – being in the cellar with those evil people? I must have! What else could it be? There is no other explanation. There is no way that it could have actually happened could it? It is just not possible. The Old Manor House has always held a primal terror for me. So, it is only natural that I would dream about it: or so I try to convince myself.

Oddly enough, sat up in the top bunk, what bothers me the most is the fact that I am wearing pyjamas. Nothing strange in that; I always wear pyjamas. I am wearing my favourite ones: white cotton with a picture of a samurai brandishing a sword on the back. What is strange is that I have no memory of going to bed or, more disturbingly, getting reading for bed. I don't even remember coming home last night. I just hope that it was not my parents that had undressed me and put me to bed. Now that would be embarrassing... How did I get home? I have a nasty feeling rising in my stomach, telling me I am not going to like the answer to that particular question.

Suddenly my consciousness snaps towards one sound and one sound only. It starts as a loud rhythmic drumming noise – then intensifies. The sound captivates me. I am transfixed: totally focused upon it. My head starts to pound with my quickening heartbeat. I feel blood rush to my head and limp in a great whoosh: I think my head is going to explode.

It sounds like the steady beating of a drum. It is getting stronger and louder. I try to ignore the sound. But something about it draws me back to it each time. I have no idea what. It is something about it, something beautiful… about the sound.

The drum beat is getting incredibly loud; too loud. I put my hands to my ears. It does not help. Then the door opens. It bangs on the side of the bed. I wince at the noise.

"Andy! Not so loud!" I moan as my younger brother comes into the room.

I throw back the sheet and blankets. Then, I start to climb down the short wooden ladder on the side of the bed. I feel the bristly texture of the carpet under my feet. The nylon fibres make me feel like I'm standing on steel wool.

"What happened to you last night?" says my brother. "Mum and Dad are going up the wall."

*Duh-dum, duh-dum, duh-dum, duh-dum.*

The drumbeats were loud now. His face: there is something wrong with his face. It is moving, pulsating, to the beat of this loud drum. It looks as if he has worms under his skin, wriggling around.

*What the hell?*

"Don't remember" I say.

"Have you been drinking?" he asks

"No."

"Drugs?"

"No."

"Glue?"

"No!"

"How can you be sure if you don't remember?"

"Smart Alec!" I say. I look around for something to throw at him. There are plenty of candidates but nothing I want to risk damaging.

I push past him. The beating noise is almost deafening. I catch sight of his very white and long neck as I pass. I see long snake-like lines beneath his skin, twitching to a regular rhythm. I tear my eyes away. Who looks at their brother's neck in that way? Most people who have seen enough horror films know the answer to that. The word 'vampire' is very much part of our cultural lexicon. But that would be ridiculous, right? Right?

I head straight for the bathroom. The deafening beat starts to recede, giving way to the sounds of others further away, beneath my feet and beyond the wall – almost a chorus, an orchestra, a steel drum band.

*Duh-dum, duh-dum, duh-dum, duh-dum.*

The strongest urge swells up within me to smash through the wall or rip through the floorboards: to get to the source of that sound. I lick my lips. My mouth is flooded with too much spittle. So much that I have to swallow twice to prevent it pouring over my lips. A chill runs down my spine. I know what the sound is. I see it now in stark clarity. There can be no other explanation.

*Stop! This is crazy.*

But that is the thing. Once my overactive brain starts thinking, there is no stopping it. I walk faster, along the landing towards the bathroom, as if sanity will somehow return once I am behind the bathroom door.

# Chapter 8

# ...Never Lies

*Hands shaking, I lock the bathroom door.*

I slam the tiny copper coloured bolt across the door: a bolt that a charging guinea pig could snap if it launched itself at the door. I fall heavily against it, sliding slowly down it to my knees.

*What the hell...what is happening to me?* The room won't stay still. Everything seems to shift: coming undone. A thought strikes me, like one of Mr Stylme's slaps across the head in maths. *Am I losing my mind? Is that it?* I put my hands to my eyes and rub vigorously. Am I going to break down and start crying buckets of tears? I wonder but nothing comes. My eyes remain dry.

*This is really happening?* It is a crazy idea. One that can't be true. But it is a case of either that or accepting I am completely stark raving barking insane. And I don't feel insane.  am tense to the point of breaking. Insanity is something that has figured large in my future, sure. But not now, not yet. What else would explain what am experiencing? I can still hear them. Their hearts beating – it is difficult to think with that sound. It echoes in my teeth and bones. Calling to me.

*I have to know – whatever the cost, whatever the truth – I have to know.*

At the same time, I really don't want to. I want to go back to my bed, hide under the blankets, until all this craziness just goes away. I want that more than anything: for it all to just go away!

Half out of my mind with fear at what I might see, I stand. I walk over to the bathroom medicine cabinet, above the washbasin, and look into its mirrored doors.

And I see…

…My face looking back at me. The inner sides of the mirror doors, where the two join, cut my face down the middle and shunt the two sides together with half an inch or so of the middle of my face missing. But it is me. Sighing deeply and let my muscles relax.

I have been though a lot recently, no matter how much has just been a dream. Danny. There is always terrible Danny. Did he try to throw me off the top of the school roof or have I dreamt that too? Is it Tuesday? It has to be Tuesday today. Another school day and no doubt he would be waiting for me… I could pretend to be sick I suppose, which would not be much of a pretend this morning. I could get Mum to write a sick note: *Dear miss sped, John will not be in today because of a sudden bout of raving lunacy – he thinks he is a bat. The doctor says we should keep him locked and restrained for the rest of the week…*

I sigh, looking more carefully at my face. The person I see in the mirror is me. At the same time, it isn't. It doesn't look like the corpse that I glimpsed yesterday in the mirror of the school toilets. The usual black rings around my eyes have gone. My face has colour: it has a healthy rosiness to it. More, it is smooth and unblemished, with no signs of cuts of bruising. My eyes look bright and alive. My lips are a coral pink and the cold sore that has been disfiguring the corner of my lips has gone. It is as if an alternative version of me has stepped in and taken my place. I look as if I am alive for the first time. For that reason alone, the person staring back at me is a stranger: a stranger who seems to be leering – no, laughing – at me.

I have to wonder how my brother recognised me. It seems to me an extreme transformation. I guess people only see what they want. The tags they want to remember...

And my leg! Which I hadn't given a single thought to since waking; there is no pain at all. I try to remember which one it was I hurt coming off that iron gate: left or right. I kneel to check the calves of both legs, but it is the same story as my face. If there had been a wound, it is now completely gone.

*What has happened to me?*

I can remember being in the cellar. That man, he attacked me. Then… I was here?

*How did I get home?*

I open my mouth and examining my canine teeth on the top row. Do they look bigger than before? *I don't know… How had they looked like before?* I think they look bigger now, and when I feel them with my finger, they seem bigger. It could be just my mind playing tricks on me. Trying to scare me. Fear makes everything seem out of proportion. It occurs to me that I don't even know what vampire's teeth look like anyway. I have seen Christopher Lee's on television, but he is not a vampire; he is an actor. The teeth he wore for the film were probably plastic.

*Oh! This is nonsense!*

A sense of relief floods my brain; my body sags and relaxes as I think how stupid I am being. I am no more a vampire than Mr Lee is. Vampires do not exist. Well, not outside the deepest, darkest parts of my unhinged mind, they don't.

"Ha!"

I bite down, then it happens.

I step backwards, not believing, for one single second, what my eyes are telling me. I nearly fall over the purple bath mat that someone has left on the floor. I look but I can't process it.

"My God! This can't be real. It just can't," I whisper.

Two long teeth curve down from my upper gum, above the regular human teeth. They resemble snake's fangs: ivory white, elongated and a slight curve down their length. I freeze, just staring at these abnormal dentures. They don't look like the vampire teeth I have seen in films, but brutal, cruel looking things and worse for the fact they look real. There is no point in denial anymore. The simple fact is there is something not right with me. I tentatively reach out towards the tip of one of the fangs that has sprouted from my mouth with my index finger. The tip is as sharp as it appears. Drawing blood at the touch. The sight of the crimson liquid stirs something in me. It isn't nausea or revulsion, but a feeling I cannot even put a name to. I put my index finger in my mouth and suck, and something lights up within my brain.

For a terrible few moments, I am frightened that the teeth will stay as they are and that I will have to go around with an enormous fake moustache. I can't see anyone swallowing that in the 1980s, least of all my family. Also, to date, I have been unable to grow more than a few lines of bum fluff on my upper lip.

To my immense relief, after messing around with different facial and jaw muscles, I find the ones I need. I flex the mysterious pair of muscles and the teeth retract back into the gums. I pull up my upper lip with my fingers to get a good look at the where these fangs have come from. I can just about see where they have come out. There are two small bumps with holes in the flesh there. I can see two white spots: the tips of the fangs themselves. I flex them once more and the teeth spring outwards and lock into place. I think I hear a small click. I try it a couple more times: out then in, out then in.

This isn't a game. This is deadly serious. Everything I remember is true, meeting those people, those things in the basement. They have done something to me, impossible as it sounds. They have turned me into... I can't say the word anymore. Not now its implications are so dire. Am I really now one of the un-dead?

*You don't know that!* Says a voice, the quiet and reasonable one inside of my head.

*But I have bloody great big teeth!* a more disdainful voice says. This voice is the one that is used to getting its own way.

*What do you think they are for? Cleaning out the dirt under your fingernails? Sunshine, you are a goddamn blood sucker! And you know what you have to do, don't you?*

*No... Please.*

*It's not fair –*

I hear someone banging at the door of the bathroom.

"John? Are you there, son? Are you ok?" my Dad's voice asks.

I swallow hard. My mouth is so full of saliva that it is practically dribbling it from the corners of my lips. I wipe a hand over my mouth.

"Yeah Dad, I am fine. Just washing my..." (*My what?*) "Er-um...face. I'll be out in a sec," I say.

"Ok son. Your Mother and I would like a word before you go to school. Ok?"

Huh? School that is one nightmare I won't be having to face anymore, not ever again. Then I think of Miss Sped. A wave of sadness hits my brain.

"Ok Dad. I'll be down in a second."

*And I hope I have the restraint not to rip yours and Mums throats open.* My new fangs have other ideas at this thought, at my horror at the idea, and slide smoothly out into view, as if someone has told them it is dinnertime. I want to lick my lips. I don't because that would really not be appropriate.

# Chapter 9

# Concerning Food

*"We were worried."*

In the sitting room, I sink into a chair that looks far more comfortable than it actually is. For the sake of appearances, I am wearing my school uniform. My parents are sitting side by side on the sofa opposite.

The sofa and the chair are part of a matching set: cream coloured with red lacy cushions positioned in the corners. The cushion on my chair sits uncomfortably at my lower back. I shift in the chair – trying to get more comfortable. Every adjustment I make fails to improve matters.

My parents sit together with identical expressions fixed on their faces, wearing furrowed brows on their screwed up 'worry faces'. I pretty much know what is coming. I grind and scratch at the arm of the chair. How much of this can I stand before I snap?

"When you turn up at the door step after midnight..."

"...Slumped on the doorstep."

"We were going to call the police!"

"We were worried!"

Mum and Dad are a double act. Each completing the others part. Have they always been this way? I don't know. I can't focus. I am transfixed by their twitching distorted faces, muscles pulling them out of shape under the cling-film of skin stretched over to both smoothing out and constraining them. They remind me of manikins - fashion dummies or they would, if manikins had throbbing veins and arteries, thrumming to the deafening beat of two hearts, almost in tune and almost beating as one. As one sounds, the other answers. They speak in the very same manner.

"Are you on drugs?"

"No."

"Have you been drinking?"

I can only think of one thing and one thing only. Its colour begins with R and ends with my parents dead. All I can conceive of is blood, their blood, pulsing through a million tiny tubes. My tongue finds my top lip and runs along it length. I realise that I am doing it. Abruptly, I stop.

*This is my mum and dad, for Christ sake!*

*Blood.* Don't ask me how I know. I just do. It will solve all my problems and ease the savage gnawing at my gut. More than that, it would satisfy me completely. I have always hated the sight of blood. It used to make me feel ill just to think of it. But now I desire it above all things. Everything else is expendable, even the lives of my parents. *I am going to kill. I am going to feed. It will feel wonderful.*

"If you have, well, you can tell us. We won't be angry..."

The same questions my brother asked. Normally these would irritate me. What bothers me now is the way their skin moves. Beneath their skin, I can see blood vessels twitch, pulsing to every single beat of their heart and pushing the beautifully warm and tasty crimson goodness around their bodies: bodies just waiting to be pieced and drunk from; asking for it. My mouth is full of so much spittle; I have to swallow repeatedly, trying to drain the liquid from my swamp of a mouth, to prevent drowning in the stuff.

Each contraction of each blood vessel and each beat of the heart is calling to me, inviting me. It is unbearable. I know that if only I could bite into one of those teasing blood vessels... I know that things will be ok. It will quell this intolerable thirst.

Only it won't be ok. Nothing is ok, nor will it ever be ok ever again. I can see it in my mind's eye, drinking from their throats, unable to stop until they are both dead. Even then, would it be enough? After I have drunk them dry, will I go looking for new, fresh victims to feed from? I think I know the answer.

I shake my head. I look down at my shoes and then at the pattern on the carpet: red-green-blue shapes. They seem to change as I focus on and let my eyes cling to the flowery shapes that rope up and down the floor. I follow the knotty pattern to the wall and then up, following the wallpaper. It has a similar rope-like pattern. My eyes drink in the winding brown interweave.

*Just look at the pattern. Don't look at them,* I tell myself, as I gently gnaw at my upper lip with my incisors.

"I am sorry," I say. My voice sounds remote and lifeless.

"Where were you anyway?" Mum says.

"I don't know. I don't remember."

"Do you need a doctor?" she asks.

"No. I don't think so."

"So you will be going to school today?"

I look back down to the front of my school uniform: red shirt and black jumper and trousers. Of course: my Clarks shoes. The blood stain is still there. *Don't look!*

"Suppose," I say. My eyes snap back to the wallpaper.

*Just look at the wallpaper. Follow the loops and curves.*

The shapes join to form what looks like a man clapping his hands and feet at the same time... I can see the perforations in the wallpaper itself, the lumps of the uneven wall below and the unevenness of the lines at the bottom where the wallpaper meets the skirting board... But I can't block out the sound. It's too loud:

*Duh-dum, duh-dum, duh-dum, duh-dum.*

I grind my teeth. I put a knuckle to my mouth and bite into it.

*Block it out! You can't, you just can't do this...They are innocent for God's sake! They don't deserve a brutal bloody death in their own sitting room.*

Just a little...

No, I won't. I won't.

Then, to make things worse, I can hear another three heartbeats drumming through the wall to my left: the next-door neighbours. I am so very thirsty. I feel light headed. I think I could just... Just what – just kill them? The very idea is monstrous. It is inhuman. It's...*what, vampire-like?*

The patterns on the wall turn from dark brown to dark red, pouring like blood down the wall. My parents just sit with their fixed concerned parents look. Nothing in their expression says *blood all over the carpet*. They seem not to notice because it is not there. It slowly disappears as if absorbed into the walls and skirting board. I really am crazy.

Not real! Not real! I repeat silently to myself.

"We'll talk about this later – this evening," my Dad says rising from the sofa.

"I want you home on time," he says.

"Ok," I lie, though I suppose I will be at home if I go through with what I have in mind. I get up and hurry from the room. I don't look back, even though I know this will be the last time I will see them, ever again.

*Have to stay in control.*

I am still the same person; I just have something else inside of me now, something that wants to kill my family and, well, everyone with a pulse. I can feel my heart beating in my chest. It feels like a huge decaying thing at the centre of my rib cage, pumping poison into my blood stream. As black as tar, and slowly, little by little it will seep through my arteries until it possesses me entirely.

# Chapter 10

# ...Is Painless

So *just do it.*

I have never wanted to hurt anyone, but now I have no choice. I know what I have to do.

When I saw my reflection in the bathroom mirror, I thought I was off the hook. I was the same as I ever was. But the teeth... How on earth could teeth like that just grow over night? Worse, I can feel something that isn't me – something destructive and hungry coursing through my veins, existing in every pore. It is growing by the minute – consuming me. I know – just know – that sooner rather than later I will feed. And then what? What will I be then? Will I even be able to stop myself from killing? I don't think so.

I have endured everything, from the attentions of Danny and his friends to the sheer grinding boredom of existence, without once thinking of doing myself in. Throughout all I have endured, the one idea that keeps me sane is that *this may feel bad, but bad as it feels, it cannot and will not last forever*. I repeat this mantra, over and over.

But this won't go away. This is for keeps. I am damned forever. Unless I do something about it. I have to end it: kill myself.

Anyway...

I will have to kill others to buy my immortality. *How many and how often?* Well, this does not even bear thinking about; in my book, one is too many.

*Even if it is Danny?*

"Yes, even him," I sigh.

I just can't bring myself to do it. I just can't; I cannot be that destructive, that selfish. I do not want to hurt anyone. I've never wanted to hurt anyone, and that is the thing. I see it for the first time. This is why I never struck back at Danny or any of the others. This was what I was hiding from: not just the fact that I was scared – and it wasn't even that I was weaker than most. It is that it is not in me to fight back. I just never want to hurt or be cruel to anyone, no matter how cruel or deserving they might be.

*You could be insane of course.* "If only I was." *Well you are talking to yourself. First signs and all that.*

That would be better: get pumped with loads of drugs in the mental hospital of my choice. At least I will not be able to hurt anyone in one of those white cardigans with the arms that does up at the back. And I would get my very own padded cell. But I don't think I am mad, or at least I did not feel that I am. I suppose no one ever thinks they are mad. That's what makes them mad I suppose: thinking your Napoleon and seeing nothing wrong in that. But being a vampire? Isn't that what a crazy person would think? The very idea is ridiculous... well, insane. How can you be something that cannot possibly exist? The idea is laughable. *Ha! Ha!*

Yet I know it is true, deep down.

So I have no choice do I? I have to end things before I do something I cannot live with – before I kill someone.

At last, the house is empty. It has that empty feel to it; that eerie echoing quality hangs in the air. The loneliness to it has an almost physical texture: almost like if I could reach out and touch it as it surrounds me with its suffocating miasma. I couldn't be more alone... knowing what comes next.

My hearing has become a creeping thing, reaching out, slinking its way into places it has no business being. I am hearing the last thing in the world that I want to hear: the beating of a human heart. It has a muffled quality to it. It could be because of the extra thickness between the walls or the wall insulation. *Who knows; who cares.*

It is the sound of one large adult heart beating steadily and two smaller ones, the sound softer and the speed quicker. The shrieks and the pattering of feet set my teeth on edge. I imagine they are running around, chasing each other, while the mother watches some god-awful programme on the TV. I hear its blare in the background: dull, because it is of no interest to my acute hearing.

I am left to my own devices, left to myself to do what has to be done. Sunlight has not worked for me. Vampires are supposed to burst into flames. Isn't that it? I shudder, imagining what it must be like to glow red and burst into flames, dissolving into ash. I always did have too good an imagination. It is certainly not a nice way to die. But is there one?

The idea of taking your own life seems depressingly worse than any other death. There is a sadness – no, sadness is too soft a word, but I can't think of a better one. It is a sense of reaching a brick wall, of being confronted with something that cannot be overcome or gotten over: a trap sprung. As horrible as the idea of burning is, it would mean that I would not have to do this, now. Sure, it would be painful, excruciatingly so, but this seems so much worse. I am sure of that.

This, I have to do myself. It scares the hell out of me. *Hell...* That is a point. Is that where vampires go after they die? They are, after all, creatures of evil. If there is a god, he isn't going to be best pleased to see me. I would definitely be going to the other place. Not so much for what I have done, but for what I haven't. I have never done anything with my life and now it is over. The parable of talents doesn't exactly show me in a good light. If I have any talents, they are buried so deep, it would take a JCB to find them.

I don't know what I believe. I have thought about it a lot but never reached any sort of a conclusion. My parents don't believe in a god or an afterlife: that, in my book, would be a result. The alternative to being burned forever in the bowls of hell mortifies me. The thought makes me want to chicken out of the whole thing. I would too if it wasn't for the fact I keep thinking of a blood fix. I am surrounded by people in their houses going about their mundane and ordinary lives. The last thing they would suspect is for a vampire to come calling. It would be too easy. But I can't do it. It is against everything I believe in. I just can't. I have to go through with this. *No choice.*

I go out into the back garden. The garage door is a rickety wooden thing that won't quite close. I unhook the metal chain and go inside to make a start. After about an hour of work and a couple of failed attempts, I have what I am after – a wooden stake. I have sawn off the end of a broom handle and then chiselled the end to a point with one of my Dad's wood chisels. Now it is done. It looks a bit rough but I am sure it will do the job. I would not get a high mark for presenting this in woodwork class, but that does not really matter. Nothing matters, except to stop me from killing anyone. This matters to me. But, as for everything else, well... It is all too late. It is all over and done with.

*Am I really going to do this?*

I sit in the garden on the grass for a while. The wetness of the grass seeps through my trousers to my skin. I don't care. I have weightier things on my mind than a bit of morning dew. With my legs crossed, I sit looking up at the house: a red brick semi-detached with French windows on the ground floor. I lift my gaze upwards. It is an almost clear blue sky. There are only a couple of clouds, rushing over the house, being pushed along by a fast, strong wind.

I can't believe I am really going to do this. It doesn't seem real. None of it does. I am a vampire and that is as unreal as it gets. I keep thinking that something might save me at the last moment, so I will not have to go through with it. I am hoping someone will stop me. This is all very well in the movies, but in real life, they never do. I just have to accept it. Get it over with.

I stand up. I pick up the home-made stake and wooden mallet I had taken from the garage and start to walk towards the house slowly, like a prisoner on death row walking to his own execution. *At least they don't have to flick the switch themselves.*

"How the hell am I going to do this?" I mutter.

I really do not know. I don't mean technically. That is simple enough, I mean how am I going to have the heart to go through with it? I just keep hoping that I will wake from this nightmare at any moment. I know I won't. I am going to die. Even as I think the words, I do not quite believe them.

"Oh well. Better get on with it." I almost laugh at my own words.

I go upstairs and into the bedroom. I peel off my black jumper and then climb up onto my bed. I just lie there for a while and then, realising I have left the mallet and stake at the foot of the bunk ladder, I go back down and retrieve them, returning to my face up meditation upon my dark blue and red striped duvet. The mallet is in one hand; the stake is in the other.

*I don't want to do this. I don't want to die.*

I feel a pricking sensation at the corners of my eyes: tears are on their way.

It isn't fair. It really isn't. My life has hardly begun and now it is over. I think of my parents. I think of them finding me here dead. Or will I just crumble away to dust? That would be better for them.  For me, it seems so much sadder: vacuumed away by my mother when she is doing the cleaning. If that happens, I guess they would just think that I had gone to school and never returned home. They would never know what really happened to me. Just as well. It might be just as well they don't know...

*This isn't fair. Well, nothing is – you self-pitying bastard.*

With the energy that flash of anger brings, I pick up the stake and the mallet. I position the stake over my rib cage, low on the left-hand side. I feel for where the heartbeat seems strongest. Finding it is no problem at all. I position the sharpened point between two of my ribs, then, raise the mallet and strike the stake home with a force I did not think I was capable of. It punches through the skin, deep, going inside me. I feel warm liquid pool around the hand that holds the stake. I scream, then hit it again, and once more. The pain is... indescribable. I beg for the pain to stop. Pain throbs, coursing through my entire body, as I wait for death to come. I wish it would get a move on. What is it waiting for? A written invitation?!

# Chapter 11

# Preternatural Problems

*But it doesn't come.*

My new preternatural body doesn't go much on the idea of death and it does not much like being stabbed with the pointy end of a wooded boom handle, and so it does the only thing it can: it spits it out with considerable force, so much that it wedges itself into the ceiling above me. It is all quite a shock.

I have been on the bed writhing with pain, hoping that death will come quickly, because I cannot take much more of this. I think I will pass out. Then, all of a sudden...

*Whoosh!*

The wooden stake shoots out of my chest at the speed of a bullet and thuds into the ceiling with the sound of an arrow thudding into a tree. The wounded house shakes and groans all at once. Fragments of plaster tinkle down the wall, behind the wallpaper.

I stare wide eyed at the ceiling. Cracks in its white surface radiate out from the point of impact. My eyes fly to the point of entry and exit: my chest and my school shirt. It is red anyway, but now has an inch-wide hole. I should have taken it off first. I shake my head. Best laid plans and all that.

"Mother is not going to like that," I say, considering the ceiling and the stake. I turn my attention to my shirt.

I put an index finger through the hole in the shirt – touching the skin. I can't feel a whole or a scar. I unbutton the front of the shirt. I sit up. I look down at my chest – nothing but a few streaks of blood, fast drying and staining my chest. I feel for the hole where it should have been. The skin is smooth and unmarked. Maybe I can feel a slight mark there: the skin is slightly raised. But that is all.

My plan has failed. Maybe I used the wrong type of wood. It's possible. Just like the mirror and the sunlight thing. Oh, and the little ol' fact that they are not even supposed to exist in the first place. It is likely that everything I knew about vampires was just a load of old tosh. Except for the blood thing of course. That is real enough. After all, it's the very definition of being a vampire, the blood drinking business.

This leaves me with a problem – I have no idea what is true. Is everything I thought I knew just a tissue of lies? Something you tell your kids when they are young: that world is this rational place, free of monsters, when all the time… Do my parents know about the vampires living in this city? I am pretty sure they don't. But I am just questioning everything. When you find out your core beliefs are wrong, this is the sort of thing you do. Where am I going to find out the truth about what had happened to me? The library? I don't think so. They aren't likely to stock a self-help book on the subject: "Feel the fangs and bite your friend's neck anyway.". I think not.

*What the hell am I going to do?*

I can't stay here, not in this house, not with my family. I was lucky this morning. It frightens me how close I came to murdering my family. It is only a matter of time before my control breaks down. Then what? I kill. Simple as that.

*Where can I go?*

Only one place comes to mind: a place I never want to see ever again. But I am all out of options.

Will I even get any answers? They did this to me; don't they at least owe me that much? Answer a few questions? Like why do this to me? That would be a start because I can't think of a single reason. Why didn't they just kill me, feed on me and leave me on the pile with those other poor bastards? What is special about me? Nothing. Was it a joke? Had that man just done it to spite that well-dressed woman? Those vampires were three shadows in that room. Were there more? I can't see them being pleased to see me. What else can I do? Where else can I go?

*Anyway, what is worst they could do? Kill me? Tried that; it didn't work.*

# Chapter 13

# Nobody Home

*All things hum with life.*

Everything is vivid and so alive. The street is unrecognisable as the one I have lived on for the last 13 years. I swear that I am seeing colours I have never seen before – that I don't think there is even a name for. Every living thing has a slight glow to it: a halo of colours.

It is all too much. I stagger down the pavement like an old man. I must be the most decrepit vampire in the history of forever! All five of my senses are overloaded with sensation. The external world pours inside of me in a deluge. My brain struggles to process it all. Much too much to bear.

It batters my poor brain like a migraine headache. The noise of passing trucks and cars is unbearably loud. I am forced to clamp both hands over my ears as a lorry speeds past me. It is like a physical wall of sound that penetrates my chest, vibrating it as if it were a brass tuba.

I am having such a hard time trying to cope with everything. I forget about feeding; putting one foot in front of the other is all I can manage.

But things are improving all the time, I am getting used to the sensory onslaught.

It's that time in the morning when there are not many people about. Not on foot anyway. Between the rush to work and the lunch hour, there are plenty of cars and trucks. But I only meet three pedestrians. I pass on the other side of the road – to avoid temptation. Two out of the three give me a filthy look.

*Humans. I never understood them. Now, I am not one of them, I guess I never will…*

The sun burns hard on the side of my face and the wind blows cold on my exposed skin. I have my duffel coat done right up. I have always felt the cold, but this is a whole new kind of deal. It is like being burnt and frozen at the same time.


I walk once more down the dirt track in Wylye woods. The lines of beach trees provide some shelter. The wind breezes around the trees, rustling through the leaves. There is a strong smell of wood all around, with decay: layers of rotten leaves and dead animals, hidden out there somewhere, slowly rotting into the soil.

On both sides, among the rich deep greens of the undergrowth and the blood red leaves of beech trees, a pale green radiance seems to come from every tree and every plant: I hear small animals scurry through the undergrowth, their little hearts beating fast. I can smell them. It is the smell of fear, as they scamper with their little legs through the un-dergrowth, trying to keep out of sight of predators. They have nothing to worry about from me, their fast little beating hearts do little to excite me, not the way the bigger and louder human ones do.

It is good to be alone. I almost relax. I walk down the dirt track once more. Not a single human heartbeat is to be heard. The hunger doesn't wane; it still burns bright deep inside of me, purring its desire.

I approach the gate and the wall that marks the boundary of the Old Manor House. The trauma of the night before is resurfacing in flashes of badly edited memory: taunting me. Ignoring the gate, I walk up towards the wall. The large blocks of stones are piled on top of each other, cemented in place, with green moss pouring down the blocks, filling the lines that separate each one. I study the wall, its height and the flattish surface that runs along its top, unconsciously calculating. I know I can do it. I feel it in every cell. I run towards the wall and leap upwards, landing upon the balls of my feet on top of the wall, all cat-like. I perch there on my haunches, looking around, scanning the house first and then the turmoil of the foliage that lies between.

At the slightest movement in my peripheral vision, my eyes snap in that direction, sucking in vision and scanning for more movement. But there is nothing, just the wind scouring the wild landscape. I glance once over my shoulder. Then, I drop down the other side of the wall in to the long grass. I land perfectly. My legs feel powerful, ready to leap. All traces of my earlier discombobulation have gone. A feeling of strength is surging through my body. I have never felt so powerful. It is dizzying knowing I can do anything I want: like jump ten-foot high walls.

I don't know what I am expecting to see. It just looks like a big empty shambles of a house, devoid of whatever threat it once held for me. It is just a house – nothing more. It is the people inside it who are dangerous. I have no wish to meet them again. I really don't.

*This is a crazy idea. True, but I have to do something.*

Do they live here? Is this why I had been frightened of this place for so long, not because of the house, but because of them? No I can't see that. Not from the way that horrible woman was dressed. She wouldn't be dossing down in the cellar with all the dirt, cobwebs and rats. Why were they here last night then? And what I am going to do when I find the man who had done this to me? Wouldn't I be thanking him? No, definitely not. What then? Revenge... Is that what this little trip is all about? No, I don't think so. That sort of thing is all well and good in the movies but in real life, no. I am strong, but he had to be stronger than me. It stood to reason. And there were three of them. I am definitely outnumbered. And one of them is a giant. It is answers I want – Yes, answers would definitely be a good start.

*Then what?*

I spring to my feet and start to stride through the undergrowth and climb the stone steps, retracing my steps of the night before, around the back of the house.

*What the hell?*

I am looking down the stone steps at the door that Danny and his mates had forced me through the night before: the entrance that had been the taken me to my present precarious situation is boarded up tight. Thick wooden planks of wood are nailed across the doorway.

A feeling of unreality eats at my mind as my brain does a couple of half cartwheels. Even after everything that has happened recently, it is as if I can no longer tell what is real. Have I even been inside the house?

Of course I have! Anger flares inside me. I was in the house and they – the vampires or whatever the hell they were – did this to me. I need answers and I will get them even if it kills me. I bound down the steps towards the door.

I don't need keen eyesight to see that it is a recent job. My first thought is Danny. But why would he do that? What is in it for him? The only ones with any kind of motive for this would be the people – no not people, the vampires – I met in the basement. Why? Are they still here? I find that I hope they are. I am depending upon it. If not, I don't know what I am going to do. My stomach drops.

I rip the planks away in a heartbeat. I pull at the door handle. The brass knob comes away in my hand. I throw it to one side. I kick the door open. The sound of the wood splitting and hinges snapping is a very satisfying noise. The door falls inwards, making a loud bang as it hits the stone floor. The door is a solid thing. No wonder I could not shift it last night. I step over the small uneven rectangle of sunlight and walk over the threshold.

Beyond that patch of light, where there should have been darkness, I can see clearly: black and white with a hint of colour here and there, as if I have stepped inside one of those huge old televisions. I feel like I am walking around the set of some spooky old programme from the 1950s.

In many ways, it seems more natural: this achromic world with its tint of gold-yellow colour dappled at random. If nothing else, it is easier on the eye than full-on bright daylight outside. It is almost relaxing, look-ing around. Yes, I like it. What I don't like is what I see.

The room seems smaller than it had felt the night before, sightless in the dark. It also seems emptier. The tables that had been piled high with boxes and broken furniture, covered in cobwebs, have gone. The pile of human bodies has disappeared too. I kneel, running a finger over the cold naked floor. There is no dust; it has been swept clean.

The only things remaining are the scuff marks upon the stone floor. I can smell the faintest traces of stale blood. When I examine the floor, I can see dark patches of dried blood on it, leading along it. I suddenly become aware of a flood of drool within my mouth, and the painful pangs deep inside of my gut.

Someone has been cleaning house. It is a bitter thought.

With panic rising in my chest, I try the door on the inside wall. This has to be the door to the rest of the house, the one the giant dragged me through. It is the only other door in the room, so this is not really a great piece of deduction on my part, just me concluding the obvious. Talking of the obvious, if the giant could see as well as I can in the dark, it is no longer a mystery as to how he managed to creep upon me. He could see when I could not: a bit of an advantage. I smile, as it becomes clear to me, but the smile fades – I *am one of them now*. I remember their words and the cruelty behind them. They were not people I would choose to spend five minutes with, yet here I am looking for them, hoping they are still here.

When I get to the cellar door, I don't know what to feel or whether I am pleased or disappointed; my emotions are completely played out. I open the door. It is a big place, made up of a number of other doors. I can't remember exactly where the giant took me.

There are three possibilities: three rooms that could have been the one. There are many more. I looked in each one, but they are either too small or packed full of junk and old iron work.

There is no sign of anyone – no sign that anyone has been down here. There are no vampires and no dead bodies. Nothing. Even the candlestick has gone. It is as if I had imagined the whole thing. There is no dust on the floor in these rooms either. Vampires who spring clean... Well, what are the odds?

I slump into one of the corners of the room, my chest and head leaning forward towards my lap. I sniff, smelling the heavy aroma. This is the place alright: the smell of blood and of something else. I sink back against the wall. I put my fingertips together over my nose. I stare at the wall.

So this is where it all takes place. Where I was changed from something living to something dead. True, I have plenty of add-on extras. But, a dead thing is a dead thing. The future, I can't even see it. I cannot imagine it.

*So what now?*

I don't know how long I have been sat here, just staring at the wall.

So where are they? Why have they left? They wouldn't be scared of me. Did they think I would call the cops or something? They didn't appear to me to be people who were scared of anything. No, they wouldn't be scared of the human constabulary.

"What do I do now?" I repeat aloud this time.

There is of course no answer. There is only the sound of the house shifting and groaning. Everything feels utterly hopeless, as if the entire weight of the house is pushing down on me, crushing the life out of me.

If only…

# Chapter 14

# Letting Loose

*Outside, the sun is a raging globe of searing heat.*

Its fierceness pours down on the top of my head. I feel it especially keenly after the damp coolness and the soft, muted monochrome of the house, as if the sun is inside my head burning its way out. When I first step out of the backdoor and walk to the top of the steps, I really do think I will explode into a million tiny pieces of ash. I screw my eyes shut. Nothing happens. I blink. My eyes adjust to the brightness. The sun still feels hot on my skin, but I haven't spontaneously combusted.

*What the hell do I do now?* I can't go home. The hunger is getting worse. It rips through me, gnawing at my stomach and clawing at my mind, with its outrageous demands. My entire body aches with it, my nerve endings burning as if on fire. I know what it wants. It is only a matter of time now.

*No, I can't go home. Not ever again.*

I walk towards the steps, past the fountain, its grey stone half covered in green and yellow lichen. The brown slop inside looks even more disgusting than it had at night.

Even in the daylight, this place seems a cancerous aberration of nature. Wild grass and bramble bushes choke up the grounds. The grass is tall and everywhere. Its colour: pale, sickly yellow. The brambles: a leafless brown. In amongst the ailing vegetation are several ancient oak trees, their girth enormous, black and rotting, surrounded by their fallen limbs: the twisted arms of giants, decaying into the ground.

Apparently if you dance naked anti-clockwise around an oak, you summon the devil. No need for that. He has already been here. I met him in the basement last night.

I can hear no signs of life – no bird song, nor animals scampering though these toxic grounds, not like the woods. Out here, there is nothing. Only silence. A shiver runs down the length of my spine.

*Shouldn't I be at one with this – evil?*

I don't feel that at all. I have to get away from this place. I have no idea where I am going; I only know I don't want to be in this dead place: it reminds me too much of my own living death.

I make my way down the stone steps towards the wall, jump up onto it, then flop down the other side. I start walking down the dirt track. The smell of rotting vegetation gives way to the over-powering stink of stale cigarettes mixed with the smell of stale body odour. The smell upsets the soft sensitive areas inside my nostrils. It is foul. It is familiar.

"Oi, moron!"

Oh great, just what I need right now. I might have known that however bad your day gets, it can always get worse. I should have heard his heartbeat, of course. There is no way I should have missed that. It thunders in his big chest as his heart tries desperately to pump blood through his big body. But I am too preoccupied with my own problems.

I freeze. Eyes wide and my mouth open. It is as if my mind has been wiped clean of everything that has happened and fallen back into the well-worn groove of habit. I lower my gaze, take a step backwards and clench all the muscles around my shoulders and neck. A pang of fear forms in my stomach, then works its way up into my chest and throat, until I choke upon the feeling.

"Well, well," Danny says, "If it isn't the biggest dickhead in dork town."

I look down at the grey-brown mud smeared on my shoes and don't look back up. After all I've been through, I still cannot look at him.

His voice booms out too loudly. It hurts my ears. I want to turn and run. But I don't.

He walks towards me.

"So you got out then? Shame. I thought the rats might get you. How did you do it? Get out of the house? Thought we locked it up tight," he says, taking a long drag on his cigarette.

I am silent, listening to something else.

"Not speaking? Eh, eh?"

*Duh-dum, duh-dum, duh-dum, duh-dum.*

The sound of blood gushing from one chamber to the other, then forces through to the next, before being pushed out around the body, pumping day and night, never tiring. It is such a beautiful sound.

Danny takes a final drag on his cigarette. He looks at the fag-end for a moment, perhaps wondering how it had burnt towards the butt so quickly, and then he throws it down, screwing it into the ground with his foot.

Suddenly the dark creature inside me looks up. My eyes snap around and lock onto Danny's face. They feel like they are on fire and bulging out their sockets. For the first time I look at him, I mean really look at him. The expression on his face is one of incomprehension. The pupils of his eyes dart around in agitation as his eyes move up and down my face. His mouth is no longer a sneer, but a gash of uncertainty.

My skin hums with life, my spine curving forward, my head cocking to one side, my eyes sucking in all the visual stimuli it can. Danny's skin is a white-yellow colour. It stretches over twitching muscle, thinly covering the mass of blood vessels spread under its surface, a vast network of gossamer-like strands that leap and pulse. I can feel each contraction like they are a part of my body, as if our hearts are joined, beating as one. My eyes glue themselves to his skin, scanning its surface, noticing its unevenness, the crease marks and the forests of acne that cluster around his jaw like a range of bright red volcanoes ready to erupt. Inside the V of his open shirt, there are blue and yellow blotches of skin. The discoloured skin leads down, out of sight, covered by the red of his shirt. I know what this means, but I cannot think clearly, due to the sound of the blood pumping and gushing through 60,000 miles of organic piping. I can hear it, see it and feel it. The red torrent beneath his skin is rushing, surging, trying to escape the endless track and asking to be liberated. And I want... I want it so badly.

*I can't. I won't!* I repeat this in my head as a mantra. I am losing the fight and I know it.

It is murder. Plain and simple.

*It just means that someone else won't suffer the way you did*, a voice from deep down in my unconscious counters.

*It's only a matter of time before he really hurts someone,* the voice hisses. *If it has to be someone, why not him?*

*But he is too strong!*

*Not anymore…*

"Get out of here! Get lost!" I roar at Danny.

He stares at me with uncertainty in his eyes, looking at me as if a I was a dog that had suddenly started shouting at him.

"Who do you think you are?" he yells at me, almost spitting the words. "You don't tell me anything. I'm the one who does the telling."

I bite my lip, turn and start to walk away.

*Keep walking. Don't look back.*

A hand lands on my shoulder and I close my eyes. My stomach sinks like a lead weight falling through tissue paper.

"Don't walk away from me!"

I spin around.

"Don't!"

"Or what?" he says. "What are you going to do, shit-stain?" His face is a deadly white, his expression twisted. He raises his fist.

There is dark thunder inside of my skull. If it wasn't for him and his incessant need to make himself feel big by hurting others, by hurting me, I wouldn't be in this mess. I would never have gone to that bloody house… I wouldn't want to murder my family. I would have a home, a life – such as it was. Right here and now, I hate Danny with intensity and malice I haven't known before. I want him dead.

"I'll teach you to play dumb with me!" Danny snarls.

Everything changes, in that second, as Danny lets loose a well-aimed fist at my face. It is a powerful punch, but it seems to me as if it is travelling in slow motion. I could step out of the way, but I don't.

My body appears to react all by itself. I am just the backseat passenger. I watch my hand smoothly raise into the pathway of the approaching fist. It flops into my hand. I barely feel any force behind it. I gently squeeze. I feel the bones in Danny's fingers splinter and shatter, as a series of loud cracks echoes through the woods. Danny's fist morphs into something that no longer resembles a human hand: a claw-like mass of blood and bone, the bone protruding through the skin. Danny gawps at his hand, his brain registering the pain. Then, he is screaming – in long ear-splitting shrieks of pain punctured by heavy breaths.

"You, you…"

I can feel the warm liquid flowing over my fingers, running down my hand. The smell is rich and overpowering. I let go of his hand. I put my fingers to my lips and lick at the blood. My taste buds explode with exquisite taste. Danny falls against the tree clutching his arm, his eyes wide.

If that is bad, what comes next is worse, as my hand reaches towards Danny's throat, my snake's fangs already sprung out extended to full length, in expectation of blood.

"What are you…" Danny screams.

He struggles and fights back, "There is no way you are going to get the better of me you little faggot!" His neck and shoulders are a rigid wall of knotted, straining muscle, trying to twist away from me. It would kill him to know how little effort I am putting into it. I am surprised by how comfortable I feel close up and personal with someone I hate. But his blood is all I can think of. All I want. His body, its smell and its heat are not even a consideration.

Sinking into warm flesh, my teeth pierce the walls of muscle like two hypodermic needles. They brook no resistance, going in nice and easy and there is a popping sensation when they penetrate the artery. There is a stab of sensation in my stomach, which is part fear and part excitement as the pressurised blood spurts upwards into my open and eager mouth. The blood flows in, over my tongue, and then I drink in deep and frenzied gulps.

"Please," Danny whispers. I feel the word vibrating through his neck. But I am no longer listening. Blood, its taste and its thrill, is everything now. It is like watching someone else, the real monster, through my eyes. I am feeling all the sensations and the pleasure, while at the same time hating them and being totally revolted by the act.

Something deep inside me starts to suck. The hot liquid pumps into my mouth, aided and abetted by Danny's treacherous beating heart. As it passes over my tongue, every taste bud becomes alive – set on fire by the most delicious taste imaginable. The rich dark taste causes my brain to explode with excitement and pleasure. My tongue is tingling as the rich dark liquid speeds over its surface and something dark and other screams in the depths of my soul for more of this delicious nectar. I am drinking fast and deep now. The dark rich flavour engulfs me and swallows me whole. I am savouring every second, lost in the moment, enjoying the exquisite sensations, as I try in vain to sate an impossible thirst.

# Chapter 15

# Broken Ruins

*A low moan escapes Danny's lips.*

His body shudders, then falls limp. I sense the change without looking at his body. Death: I am so at ease with it. I let his body flop to the ground. His head falls against the side of the trunk of an oak tree. His head makes a sickening thump as it hits it.

Numb, I look down at him. Seeking in his face any sign of life. I can't hear his heart anymore. There is nothing. Just his blanched, twisted face and unseeing eyes. I am forced to face the truth of the matter. Danny is no longer here. Just the empty flesh of his body. I feel more alone that I have ever felt in all 16 years of life.

All I can hear is the wind blowing through the leaves of the trees, as if hundreds of voices are speaking in soughing whispers, barely audible, but with the meaning clear as day. Because they are the same words that fall and clamour down inside my head:

"Murderer... Murderer...Murderer..."

Overwhelmed by the word and the horror of what the word means, I would take it back if I could. But I can't. I try to pull in large mouthfuls of air, it feels like breathing vacuum. Panic rises in my chest and just keeps going: up and up.

I have to get away...

I turn and run through the woods: jumping fallen trees and leaping over bushes. Branches whip at my face and body. I hardly notice. I just run and run, burning hot tears streaming down my cheeks:

"What have I done?"

Stupid question. I know what I have done. My insides are still quivering, mostly from a blanket feeling of revulsion, but also from horror at a warm and pleasurable feeling shooting up from my gut. I want more; I want to do it again and again. It is only a matter of time before I find another victim. I am damned. I run faster, the trees and ground becoming nothing more than a blur.

I stop dead and fall forward against a mighty oak tree, my fingers clawing at the thick rough bark. I bang my head, none too lightly, against its surface. Tears pour freely down my face like little hot rivers. Shivers rack my body, beyond all endurance.

I gaze up the trunk of the tree, towards its boughs and branches and the partially obscured blue sky above. The tree seems to be glowing a gentle quiescent green, which surrounds me as I cling to it. I breathe it in. It calms me. It seems stronger now, with the glow thicker than the air, almost physical. I am still aware of all I have done but breathing in this life glow distances everything so that it appears far away. I turn and collapse to the ground, leaning against the oak. I sit there looking around. The glow is everywhere: all different colours, both intense and soothing; both intoxicating and calming; like a lullaby from childhood.

From the tragic broken ruins of my life, all I can see is beauty: the beauty that pierces your heart and leaves you with no choice but to stare, open-mouthed like an idiot. It is as if I am seeing this ancient forest for the first time. Its spectrum of greens, from the very darkest to palest, mix in with the blood-coloured leaves of the beech trees. And then there are the whites and blues of the wild flowers peppered across the forest floor: All glowing bright like ghost light, there is a halo around every living thing. All I can do is drink it all in and let it consume my consciousness. I can just lie here breathing in and out the colours and the strong rich fragrances of the forest.

# Tumbling Down

# Chapter 1

# Broken Bridges

*Under the iron bridge, I cower.*

Traffic rumbles overhead, the bridge shaking with the endless on-slaught of motor vehicles on their way to wherever. Away from here if they have any sense. The bridge used to span two railway tracks. They are long gone. Maybe before I was born. I don't know. I can't remember there being railway lines here. The rough pattern of where they were has stretched away, disappearing around a bend. It is slowly being devoured by the clawing undergrowth crawling down the grass banks of green onto the long strip of wasteland. It is not used for anything now – except fly tipping. Between the bushes, brambles and the tufts of wild grass, junk and rubbish pit the landscape. There is every bit of junk you can imagine here: empty tins of paint, old fridges, the shells of washing machines and even the rusting remains of a wheelbarrow, its rubber tyre frayed away to almost nothing.

I don't feel right.

Under the thunder of the traffic over my head, I vomit: a mass of black sticky liquid streams out of my mouth and nose. It reminds me of the nosebleeds I had as a kid. It feels like there is gallon of the stuff coming out of me in a never-ending flow. When it does eventually stop, I fall on my knees gasping. The inside of my mouth tastes foul. I spit, then wipe my lips with the back of my hand.

Jesus wept.

My thoughts run in circles, replaying images in clear Betamax definition, going around and around. Each lasts too long, then rewinds and replays. I bring up my hands to cover my eyes and block out the painful sight. I see Danny's white-grey face as clear as it is still, directly in front of me: his eyes open unblinking empty orbs – staring, always staring. All the time, I am waiting for the police to find me. How will I ever face my parents? It's an absurd thought. But it's one that cuts me deep.

*I wish I was dead. But death doesn't want me.*

Even in this refuge for the unwanted, this dumping ground for the cast offs, I am out of place. I go deeper into the shelter of the bridge. Built on an angle, it is like two separate bridges have been welded together. I am desperate for blackness. I want it to swallow me whole. But my monochrome eyesight thwarts me at every turn. The brick legs sit under and support the iron structure above, with the texture of the iron and brick. The broken bricks, empty booze bottles and puddles of rainwater are strewn over the chalk ground. The sound of rainwater pouring down the walls echoes within the enclosed space, a grating sound, audible even against the roar from the road above. My duffel coat is wet through – my clothes are sodden but I don't care. The cold damp registers, then fades to grey background.

Is there anything left of me? Is there anywhere I can go? I can't think. I walk towards the centre where both ends of the bridge join. I sit down and pull my elbows and knees to my chest. I roll onto my side and curl up in the darkness. It is what I crave with all my heart. To wrap myself in darkness and fall into its depths, never to return. Closing my eyes is the nearest I can get to it. It doesn't work. I see red, dull and pulsing, to the thump of my heart, which seems to be banging against the inside of my skull. The neurons inside my head are sparking and flaring. My senses are reaching out, wanting to join with the movement above my head: to rip into those metal tin cans and tear into the fleshy contents within; to devour every living human on the planet; to drink the world dry. And I used to be such a good boy. "Wouldn't say boo to a goose," my nan always used to say.

The sun goes down and comes up again. I stay where I am, curled in a ball, desperately wanting the world to go away or just end. I wonder if I would survive if the Russians fired off a pre-emptive nuclear attack. Probably, most likely I would be the only one left: left to walk the ruins of this city, with the dead and the dying all around me, radiation poisoning painfully destroying their bodies. Killing my family, Miss Sped, everyone I knew. Me, doomed to walk the earth forever, alone.

Maybe that is all I deserve. I used to imagine the end: the three-minute warning and then seeing the mushroom cloud rise up over the city, then darkness as the light of the blast burns out my retinas and then consumes me. Or dying blind in a gutter, slowly, my body cancerous and decaying. It had scared the life out of me. It did not help that the walls in most of the classrooms at school were covered in Protect and Survive posters, between posters of animals with little words of so-called wisdom – sickly sweet and insanely positive.

*Morbid much? You fucking kidding me?* ***I am death walking****.*

The F-word? I have never used it before – well maybe once or twice. It always sounded so artificial and lacking in vigour coming out of my mouth. Strange how now it carries so much venom and fullness of sound.

My head is so alive with desire and sensation. I am totally awake and alert. I bury my eyes in my arms, the ground pressing into me, unyielding, cold and hard. I rub my face against the chalk, in small repetitive circles. My eyes burn through closed lids like they are orbs of burning coal. The surge of each insatiable beat of my heart is coursing fast and furious, like a sugar craving, only much stronger and a thousand times worse. Something deep inside me screams to be let out.

*Sleep. I just want to sleep.* But I'm too on edge, too alert and too awake: I feel too alive. I am desperate for sleep to rend me from this world, into dreams of some other form of existence. Just to be free of these manacles of reality for a short time. But it doesn't come. It feels like it never will again.

# Chapter 2

# Night Falling

*The wind pulls at the bottoms of my trousers like a pair of over excited terriers.*

It tears at my clothes and hair. Pulling it out long and blowing it over my face. My duffel coat is undone at the front, flowing out like a black cape. I stand there. Just looking. Standing on the roof, on the edge of a block of flats on the parapet. I love the night time. I never used to. Things change. There is so much to see, and so much to experience.

I see everything. The grey monochrome of the buildings, laced with a patchwork of lights. The yellow-orange of the street lights curve and arc over the city sprawl. Office blocks are patterned by windows lighting up the stark white lights. I can see them turning off and on all over the city. The traffic moves like a stream of blood cells along vessels of concrete and tarmac, feeding the machine of light. The air is fresher and cleaner this high up. I breathe in deeply, as if it is my very first breath, as if I am alive for the very first time.

Everything seems new and fresh and totally alien. Down there is a world I am no longer a part of, that I no longer understand. I am just an outsider looking in. The ordinary world, the one that I had shared and taken for granted for sixteen years now looks like nothing more than a freak show, with its regularity and pointlessness. It all comes down to irrational emotion: a feeling of belonging. Once that is gone, it is gone and all that I had carpeted over has now come to the fore. I miss it: the world I have left behind, at the same time, I don't. The latter is becoming stronger with every day that passes. With it, my humanity and compassion has started to slowly dim to a shade of grey.

I breathe in the feeling of complete and utter freedom. Why not? I have paid such a high price for it. That's the thing: for everything there's a price. Nothing for free.

It is as if the darkness has hidden what I have done. I live as two separate people: one in the daytime and one at night. At night, I am almost content, almost happy. In the daytime, I am haunted by thoughts of Danny. I see his lifeless eyes staring at me. He deserved many things. But he didn't deserve to die and not like that. Nobody does. We both had our lives cut short at a young age, but I have lived on to experience all the fury and the pain. I will go on to feel all the things that Danny never will thanks to me. Life is for the living and the living dead.

In daytime, I think of what I have become – a murderer, and that is the charitable interpretation of what I am: a murderer who is most likely wanted by the police. I keep wondering if they have turned up at my parent's house by now. In my mind, I see my parents' mortified faces: my dad partly horrified, partly disbelieving, and my mum in tears on the doorstep... And what would they even say?

"Yes, officer, he has been behaving very strangely recently..."

Or:

"No John would **never** do anything like that. You must have it wrong."

I drive myself halfway to crazy with these thoughts until I can't take anymore. I tell myself my life is over. I am a vampire, a monster and a murderer, and that is that.

Anyway... It is not as if I can change anything.

It is very beautiful. The stars are out. The moon is shining bright over this sea of lights. I can almost forget who I am for a time. Until I get hungry again. I have tried. I really have tried not to feed... But the need is too deep, too powerful... I hate myself. I sink into a depression soon after the high of ingesting human blood. I am getting the feeling once more, that familiar gnawing in the pit of my stomach: the insane craving...

I flex my feet, going up on my toes, and stand on the very edge of the parapet. I take a step forward... Then I am falling. I look on with interest as the ground comes rushing up to meet me.

The block of flats is 25 stories high. The council has put a limit on the number of stories they can build: 25 is the limit. I think Auntie Janet used to live in this block of flats or one of the others nearby. There are about ten blocks of flats in all, with small council houses jammed between the red brick towers. I can't remember which is her flat. They all look identical. Anyway, it seems a long time ago. It isn't. It is just that my previous life seems to me like something that happened to someone else. Or a dream. Anyway, it doesn't matter anymore. none of it does.

My clothes flap violently around me as I fall – headfirst. Smiling, I spin out of control – falling and spinning. Then, starting with my stomach muscles, I twist my body around. All of this is automatic. I don't even have to think to do it. It just happens – like a natural reflex: like a cat.

I hit the ground – landing feet first. It is a perfect landing. But there is nothing special about that. They always are. My legs easily fold down into a squat. Then I leap up. I sprint across the grass verge, over the pavement and over the road; distances just seem to melt when I run.

There is no doubt that my body has changed beyond all recognition. I can do things I would not have thought possible. The only thing that I can't do is fly. I have wondered, you know, about the whole vampire bat thing. Well, it just didn't really work out. But I think we can skirt over that painful and embarrassing little episode…

Anyway...

I sprint towards the next block of flats. I jump through the air. I land, silently, on the top of concrete porch over the entrance. I hurry to the wall and start to climb. My fingers push into the cement between the bricks. I easily lift my body up the wall, with my feet adding extra purchase as I scale the tower block. I am certain I must look like Spiderman, only with a duffel coat and Clarks shoes.

Soon, it takes mere seconds; I am standing on the grey roof at the top of the building. I walk over to the other side of the roof. I peer down at the lights in the houses below. In one of the houses, the downstairs light flicks off and the upstairs bathroom light comes on soon after. There is enough time for a human to scale the stairs, but to me it seems to take an eternity. Several of the houses are already in darkness. In two or more of them, the lights are still on downstairs. One has left the curtain drawn open for the whole world to see inside their living room. My Gran would not have approved. I can see a couple sitting on a sofa. They are young, though older than me – in their twenties perhaps. The man's arm hangs lazily over the shoulders of the woman. The only light is the flicker of the TV that blares out. All these people have homes, families and friends. They belong somewhere. I try not to hate them for it.

I cross the rooftop. I stand on the parapet once more, crouching down on the edge with my thighs tight to my chest. I look up at the sky. It is like the stars are raining out of it. Their brightness is dazzling – pure white light against a background of black. Above me is the moon; looking down, bold and bright, unchanging. A smile crosses my tight lips.

# Chapter 3

# Domestic Dispute

*I am climbing the wall of the block of flats.*

I notice that a window has been left open. Light is glaring out from behind the thick yellow curtains. I slide over. I peek between the curtains. I can't see anyone. The television is on, playing to an empty room. It is big and old. It sits on top of a brown wooden TV stool in the corner.

I can hear them moving around: two of them. One has a heavy step, the other lighter. I can hear them despite the noise from the TV. This surprises me. My hearing is not only much improved but could also discriminate and hone in and attune itself to different sounds. Vampirism: the gift that keeps on giving.

I slide silently into the room. I can hear two heartbeats pounding away in a nearby space. Two people, a man and woman, are talking in low voices:

"And you know, she was like all upset and I just say, 'You know, it's your own fault'," the female voice says.

Why had I come in here? Did I want to eat them? Drink their blood? Well, of course I did. I bit my lip. I was sure that Christopher Lee never bit his lip.

I looked around the room. It was shocking: everything was either dark brown or bright yellow in colour. The sofa was coffee stain brown and in front of it there was a lighter brown coffee table. The walls were yellow. In the corner, there was a glass cabinet filled with plastic dolls dressed in the stereotypical national dress of various countries.

I wonder what will happen if they come in now and discover me here. Will they try to call the police? I notice a cream coloured telephone with a plastic dial on the front in the corner of the room on top of a pile of magazines. It will take too long to run the dial around the face three times. I will have killed them by that time. Or will they try to attack me, or run or shout at me? And what will I do? Overpower them? Kill them? This is a bad idea, coming here. I know, but still I do not leave. I just rock on my Clarks shoes, feeling the texture of the nylon carpet under my feet. And yes, the carpet is yellow too.

Saliva overflows from my mouth. Wetting my dry lips, it feels cold as it trails down the side of my mouth. My fangs are out ready. I am listening, their heartbeats inviting me to feast. It will feel so good. I know.

I can feel my self-control slipping...

I do only one thing. I walk over to the TV and flick the channel from ITV to BBC 2. Just for something to do really. Then I leave as silently as I have come in. I jump onto the window and dart out, falling downward. I land on the grass below when the voice starts yelling:

"Well I never changed the channel!" a woman's voice shouts.

"You must have! There's no one else here. And I didn't bloody well do it!" The man yells back.

"I don't know why you have to watch that trash anyway. There is never anything good on that station," she says.

"I like it, alright? God Knows I don't get much enjoyment..." he says.

And so it went on.

"Ooops, oh dear," I think. "It is always the little things."

I quickly get to my feet and pelt away into the darkness. Keen to get away.

# Chapter 4

# Inside Out

*The house is in darkness.*

It has been for a few days now. I put fingers around the edge of the metal of the window frame and mangle the catch and handle as I pull them out towards me. There is some noise but not much: quieter than smashing the window. That would be a dead giveaway. The blaring TV next door helps too.

I slide into the darkness of the room. I slink about the place until I find what I am after. I slide a fifty pence piece into the slot and turn the butterfly shaped dial. There is a clink as it drops into the box beneath: metal on metal. The sitting room light comes on instantly. I rush to find the switch and turn it off. It's not as though I need it. It will only attract attention. The last thing I want is a police patrol car pulling up outside. Still, maybe I am being paranoid.

I find it in the kitchen. I turn it on and return to the sitting room. I settle on one of the chairs, curling into a more complete ball than I ever could when I was human. I wait in this strange house, where the walls beat to the sound of bad TV and the thumping of many human hearts singing their sweet siren songs in the neighbouring house.

The bathroom is small, barely big enough to contain the bath, washbasin and toilet that are all wedged in so tightly together that they almost touch one another.

I avoid my reflection in the bathroom mirror above the washbasin. I don't want to see my snarling bitter face looking back at me. All these years of living in fear of others and it turns out the one person I should fear the most is myself. I am sure there is some deep ironic philosophical point there. But I have no use for it. I take the bathmat from the side of the bath and place it on the floor. It is one of those with twisted tassels on the 'up' side. The toilet lip cover is made of the same stuff.

I put the plug into the hole of the bath and turn on the hot water. Water steams into the tub. After it fills with two inches of hot, I turn on the cold tap.

I take off my duffel coat, fold it and place it on the top of the loo lid with its tasselled cover. The rest of my clothes follow. I peel off my red shirt with the bloody hole in it at last. I lower myself into the bath, enjoying its warmth. The rising steam around me tickles my nose. I let the feeling of warm water against my skin take me as I lie back in the water, relaxing for the first time in ages in a bath in a stranger's house.

I was never bothered about bath time before. In fact, I hated it. I hated getting in and hated getting out. The time between the two... Well, that was alright I suppose… Everything now is heightened. The sensations stretch to the sky as I lie in a state of sensual bliss for some considerable time.

It seems like only minutes have passed but it must be closer to half an hour. The water has gone cold. With my big toe, I nudge the hot water tap on, hoping for a return of the warmth. But only cold water pours out. I grimace, promptly withdrawing my foot. *The hot water tank must be empty*. I sigh, pulling myself out of the bath. I reach for the bath towel on the rail and start to dry myself. The rough texture of the polyester mix in the towel is like fine sandpaper against my skin. There is no window in the bathroom. So I risk turning on the light. It flares bright and white. I see the image I have been avoiding in the mirror looking at me with alarm. And a good job too. Even though I have just washed, my lips and teeth are still stained red with blood. Danny's blood. I take the toothbrush from the glass on the sink and the toothpaste and set about cleaning my teeth. I finish up and dress. Taking my duffel coat over one arm, the towel in the other hand and furiously rubbing at my head, I leave the bathroom.

Downstairs, my hair still wet, I rifle through the drawers of the sideboard: coasters, table decorations, tablecloths, a hair brush and nail clippers. Nothing of any use or relevance to me. Not anymore. I close the drawer. I go over to what is meant to look like a bookcase. But the books are all plastic. I push the mounded plastic front. It rotates, revealing it to be a booze cabinet. I pass over the cheap sherry bottle and find a bottle of Teachers: half empty. *Maybe it will help me sleep?* I unscrew the top and put it to my lips and pour the liquid into my mouth. The fiery liquid burns its way down my throat. The thing deep down there in my throat somewhere goes berserk, spasming and writhing with effrontery at the unwelcome rough tasting liquid. I look at the bottle. *How does anyone drink this stuff?*

"Well son, it's an acquired taste," in memory, I hear my Dad say.

He had been talking about beer – well, pale ale to be exact – but I knew he liked whiskey too. He had given me a sip after I had constantly begged to be able to taste this adult drink. Now the memory slices straight through me, making me feel more alone than miserable. I would not have thought that possible, but no matter how bad things get, there is always somewhere lower to fall.

I curl up on the sofa, pull my duffel coat over my shoulders and try to sleep. But the outside world won't let me. My head rings out with thunder as fork lighting electrifies my brain. The sounds of drunk voices and the empty echoing footsteps beyond the window and thudding of heartbeats play havoc with my nerves. The constant fear that the owners will return at any moment – an exciting and dreadful thought – serves to keep me on edge and maintain my body in a state of agitated discomfort. Sleep just isn't coming. I haven't slept for weeks now. I don't feel any worse for it. Except my resolve to never feed again is weakening. It's just a matter of time.

I give up. I put on my coat and slide out of the window I came in. Rain streams down my face as the wind pummels my body as I face the storm. I am climbing the nearest and tallest building I can find. I reach my hands back to find my coat pockets. Pushing into them, I pull the coat the coat flaps out, stretching them into triangular wings as I dive off the building. It's the same way I used to pretend being an airplane with my friend in junior school, bombing around the playground, hands in pockets. I do look bat-like after all. The rain and my tears become one as I fall. I don't belong inside houses, snug and warm: it is out here where I belong, in the wild stormy weather, outside of everything.

# Chapter 5

# High-street Treats

*It is going to happen.*

I can't feign surprise, not anymore. It is deliberate. It is the reason I am here. To kill. After all, that is what killers do, right?

I give up. I can't fight it anymore. Hunger gnaws at my stomach. I am insane with it. I head towards the town centre, where there are people: lots of people.

In their darkness, not mine. I can see just fine thank you very much. I can't see the dark, but I can feel it all about me, curdling around me as if it were a part of my being, my nature. I use it to take shelter from the street lights, in dark alleyways and the shadows. I slip down the alleyway between two shops. I climb the wall. The old brickwork crumbles at my fingertips.

Most of the shops on the high street are old Edwardian buildings, three stories high and converted into shops, with flat roofs. I jump from roof to roof.

There are plenty of dark spots to hide, but I really don't need to. People never look up. I stop on a rooftop, peering down into the main high street. It is busy: excited, raucous and piercing voices coming from below. As the crowd swarm along the pavements of the main road, they spilt spill out of pubs and restaurants, feeding in and out of the smaller streets that intersect the high street. Pulsing with life, there are hundreds of heartbeats, and the grating rasping of breath: short and fast, long and deep, and everything in-between. Has life always been this noisy?

The top tiers of the buildings opposite are grey and austere. Down at street level they are bright and full of life. The shop windows are lit up with small spotlights shining down on the goods they have on display. The soft warm glow matches the mood of the crowd.

On the other side of the road, there is a fish and chip shop with a queue that trails out into the street. At the head of the queue, a man in a leather jacket is arguing with the rotund woman behind the counter. She looks to be giving as good as she gets. My vision snaps onto the man with the leather jacket, then out again, looking up and down the street and fixing to look at this person or that. All it takes is a decision, to choose one, and they are as good as dead. I am like an owl looking down at a barn full of field mice scampering around the floor: waiting to swoop and devour my prey.

*What am I even doing here?*

*I don't want to...*

*Want has nothing to do with it.*

That is when I see him. He is walking out of an amusement arcade a little way down the street from the chip shop. James, he is down there with Paul and another kid. I don't know the third boy. I don't think he even went to St Stevens. He has a skinhead haircut and is dressed all in blue denim. They are laughing. The laugher cuts through me, grating upon my nerves. They walk in a pack down the high street. I follow them on the rooftops.

They cross the bridge over the river, then take a left, turning down an alleyway that runs alongside the river. A long and low brick wall runs the length of the river. To the other side of the path, there are a couple of small shops, closed, in darkness and backed on to a ramshackle mix of housing. The roofs, walls and windows point in all directions in an Escher-like formation. It is difficult to work out which door, window or roof belongs to which house. A few of the houses have the lights on: dimly lighting up the dowdy curtains. For the most part, the houses are in darkness, solemn in their stillness.

*Am I really doing this?*

It is as if I am sleepwalking. Something is leading me by the nose. My mind just closes its eyes, refusing to acknowledge the truth in hand.

I drop silently to the footpath. James is just a little way ahead of me. Keeping to the shadow is not a problem for me. The street lights on this stretch of pathway are few-and-far-between. Good.

My blood is on fire, burning as it works its way around to my brain – lighting it up with foul images of blood and slaughter. A discordant feeling in my stomach resonates on up through my chest to my brain. The thirst sings loudest in my heart, driving me forward, responding to the urge. I want to sink my teeth into one of those pale white necks. I want to get drunk on blood right here and right now. Instead, I bite into my lower lip.

"What's that?" James says, turning.

The other two carry on walking.

"Nothin'. Come on!" Paul calls over his shoulder.

"Probably..." James mumbles, turning back.

I rush forward.

"What the bloody hell are you..." James begins.

I put a hand over his mouth, silencing him. At the same time, I put the other arm around his neck. I drag him, struggling, towards the shadows.

"Come on James... Stop messing about!" a voice says.

I barely hear it. I can feel the almost tropical heat of his body. I hate it. I hate the closeness and the heat, but I can feel the hot liquid beneath his skin, pumping fast. I want that so badly I could weep.

"Mmmph!"

He tries to fight me, trying to pull my arm away from his throat. My grip is cast iron – irremovable. I drag him through a brick archway into a backyard. I pull him deeper into the shadows. He starts to kick and fight against me, attempting to break my grip once more. Fat chance.

My main focus is on my prey, but my peripheral vision takes in the surrounding area, scanning for movement. The yard itself is narrow and short. A washing line runs from the house to the wall at the end of the yard, where it is attached to a metal loop in the brickwork. There is a concrete path and a bit of grass on either side scattered between the mud patches. The house is as narrow as the yard. Two windows, identical, one on top of the other, stare blankly out at me. The curtains are open wide, but there are no lights on inside. The gutter on the side of the house is broken. There is a stain where the water has run, for no small amount of time, down the brickwork. It is a sordid place, just right for a sordid act.

James thrusts an elbow into my stomach a couple of times. This is a favourite move for James. I have seen him do it to others. They would fall quickly to the ground under the onslaught of this bony weapon. Then he and the others would finish the job with boots or fists. He has done it to me before. This time, I feel next to nothing as his elbow slams into me. He hits me with it again and then once more. But the next time it goes wide. I pull his head back. My teeth lengthen automatically. I don't even notice. It is pretty much an act of faith. I have just assumed that they will be out and ready for action.

With deliberate slowness, I lower my head toward his neck. His heart is beating loud and fast. His body is shaking. The skin itself is running tremors as I sink into the flesh of his neck. They go in easily like hot steel through butter. I feel the tips of the teeth tap against the artery. My fangs pass through them easily enough. I feel a small pop, like bursting bubbles in a sheet of blister packing.

My mouth is running with saliva, as if it were on tap, flooding out of my mouth, down my chin. The thought of the exquisite red liqueur over-powers all other thoughts. Is this how a drug addict feels? When they push the plunger, when the needle empties it payload into the blood stream, before the drug goes speeding towards the brain to explode into electrical impulses of pure pleasure

When you pierce an artery, the blood does not so much pour as spurt: a geezer of blood that could easy arch over six feet high. Not a problem. Not only are my jaw muscles a lot stronger, but there are new muscles at the back of my throat which seem to operate as a pump, not unlike a heart. They expand and draw blood into my mouth and when they contract, they push the blood down my throat. At first, this was a very strange and unsettling feeling. But it's one I've got used to.

# Chapter 6

# All Things

*It is only a matter of time.*

I know where Paul lives. I don't go straight there. I have mixed feelings about the whole thing. Despite the gnawing hunger pains in my gut. Despite the fact I haven't fed for days. Despite every molecule in my body screaming at me: feed me. All my thoughts are coloured red. Red is for the anger I feel all the time. Red is for fire – the way my skin and insides burn like red-hot steel pincers on naked flesh. Red is for blood, to take the pain away...

Paul was my friend once. James never liked me. I didn't have anything against him, only that he had gone out of his way to make my life a misery. I don't think he deserved to die for that. I killed him three days ago. Now all that is left of him is the blood stains on my finger nails. I wonder if they have found his body yet? Or if it is still propped up against the wall in that grotty yard? Everything I have done is wrong – evil even. But the die is set. I could pretend, but I can't hide from the anger and hunger that is in me now. I would kill again. That is the simple truth of the matter.

For a couple of hours, I entertain myself by jumping from tower block to tower block, enjoying the feeling of freedom, it gives. And I pretend I am not going to go through with it. The hunger will just magically disappear and I will... Will what? I don't know.

Enjoying the sensation of seeing, if not everything in my horizon of vision, then near as damn is to swearing to it. When I am falling towards the ground, I almost forget the pain, the hunger pangs and the guilt. I feel alive in a good way: just for those few seconds with the rush of air and the ground coming up fast. There is a state of numbness, of nothing mattering. It must be what dying is like – falling. Falling into what? I will never know. I won't ever die. That is what the myth says. Eternal life for those who feed on the blood of others. I don't know if it is true.

The person I am inside is dying. After Danny, the killing part has been getting easier. Soon I will feel nothing. Then I won't be me anymore but the creature I am becoming. Part of me welcomes it and the other part is terrified: terrified of what I will do, how far I will go. Already I have stopped seeing humans as human beings anymore: just blood bags and meat all wrapped up in polythene, waiting to ripped open, penetrated and consumed, the blood being released into my drooling mouth. I don't see them as human anymore, but it was me not them who has changed. It is me who is no longer human.

At 2am or thereabouts, I turn up outside Paul's house. It is one of those small two-bedroom terraced houses. I went inside it, years ago, when we were still friends. I wonder if his bedroom ceiling is still covered in model aeroplanes, suspended at angles with cotton thread, held in place by drawing pins. Probably not.

All the lights are off. I go around the back of the house, taking the alleyway that loops around the whole row of council houses. There is a high wooden fence at the back. I scoff at it, then leap over, landing in a small garden. it is all grass, except for the pathway that goes up the centre to the back door. I try the handle. Locked. What else was I expecting? Suddenly I am gripped by a thought: can I enter the house? Aren't we vampires supposed to not be able to cross the threshold without an invitation? Then I remember that this didn't apply to any of the other houses I have broken into. *Yet another lie.*

I wonder about putting a fist through a window. But that would wake up everyone in the house. I only want Paul. At least I think that is all I want. I back up a couple of steps and peer up at the house, looking for an open window I can climb in. I spot one. I move forward. I feel a hand rest my shoulder. I have heard nothing. Nobody can creep up on me. Not anymore. I whirl around. My fangs spring out: ready to kill the person who has startled me.

"Easy," the man says.

"I think you have had more than enough fun. Now it is time to face up to your responsibilities," he says. I instantly recognise the voice and the eyes as they bore into me from those dark hollow sockets. How could I not? They belong to the creature who did this to me, the one who had turned me from a shy messed up kid into a murderous monster. So, naturally, I want to kill him more than anything in the world.

# Chapter 7

# Ropes End

*Hatred has a sound.*

A low hiss emanates from deep down in my throat and wrenches its way out of my mouth, cutting the air. It is an eerie sound, one that seems extra-terrestrial to me and I would not have guessed I was capable of making, but here it is, hanging in the air.

I am very aware of my extended teeth and the man's thick short neck. I want to rip his throat out.

"Now, now – There is no need for that!" he says gently. His eyes glance into mine. Then he looks down at his nails, as if unconcerned.

"Henry Hrot at your service. That is H.R.O.T. But Mr Hrot to you," he says.

This infuriates me. Before I can act, a monster of a man emerges from the shadows. He was also in the house that night. He was the one who first grabbed me. He looks even bigger than I remember him, although this could be the big fur coat and hat he is wearing.

"You want me to slap him about a little bit?" the monster says. He rolls the R at the beginning of Hrot's and leaves the h silent. So it sounds more like *Mr Rrrrot*.

"No that is ok, Gunnar. We are just talking."

Then to me:

"Really, there is nothing you can do to me. I transformed... released you from human form. So you can't lift a finger without my say so."

This makes me even angrier. It is his calmness, his haughtiness and his superior attitude. It makes me see red. But what is most irritating of all is that he is right. I just can't move from the spot. I can't take a single step forward, let alone take a bite out of his neck.

"I'll let it pass this time. Because you don't know any better. But raise a hand against one of your betters again and I will put you down like a dog." His tone is even and his voice soft but there is definite menace in his voice that gives an extra level of meaning to his threat.

"Anyway, enough of all that. Let us get out of here. These hovels, they depress the life out of me."

He turns to the giant:

"Gunnar, you tie business up here. Then proceed back to the Chateau. I can take things from here."

"If you are sure Mr Hrot?" says Gunnar. At the same time, he eyes me with suspicion.

"Yes, yes. I am a big boy. I can handle things from here," Mr Hrot says.

As the large shape of Gunnar disappears into the shadows, Mr Hrot turns back to me:

"Come on. We have to make tracks. We have a long journey ahead of us. My car..." he says, gesturing vaguely with his hand.

I follow him out of the garden gate, then back down the alleyway. From there, we walk down the street side by side.

The long black BMW looks out of place among the Ford Cortinas and Escorts parked up and down the street. I move into the road. I have planned to go around the other side of the car to the passenger door. But Mr Hrot shakes his head, waving me around to the back of the car. He unlocks the boot. There is a heartbeat coming from within the car: firm but steady in its rhythm. He opens the boot. It glides up smoothly and a small light comes on. I peer inside.

"Is this what you were looking for?" he says.

Inside, curled in a foetal position is Paul Flustrian. He is breathing, his eyes are closed and his wrists and ankles are tied.

"What...? Why is he here?"

"It is a sweetener. You will come with me anyway. When we get to where we are going, you can have him. He will be all yours to do with whatever you want."

"I am not hungry," I lie.

"Well we have a long drive ahead of us. If you get peckish then just let me know and we will stop off for an all-you-can-eat buffet."

"Well, we must be getting going. Get in," he says.

"Where are we going?" I ask, as I open the passenger door. If Mr Hrot hears me, he makes no sign of it. I get in anyway. I sink into the leather seat as he turns the key in the ignition and then smoothly drives off, headlights blazing.

# The Wonder-kind

# Chapter 1

# The V-word

*The car accelerates into the gloom.*

The dashboard glows with green light inside the car. But I can see perfectly. The car slides smoothly down country lanes, gunning through the night – or, rather, morning if the digital numbers on the built-in clock are to be believed.

The city lights fade into the distance, leaving behind everything I know. It has a terrible feeling of permanence. There is security and familiarity in the place. Now, it is disappearing behind me. It is the end of everything familiar – like falling off the edge of the world. I have lived here for sixteen years. I am acquainted with every pothole and every sign post on every street. Now, all of it is receding in the rear-view mirror. I will never walk these grey streets again.

And where am I going? All roads lead somewhere. There are some you really don't want to go down. The Ridings is a prime example of that: being driven by the vampire who killed me, who destroyed my life. Well, as portents go, the omens are not good for this trip. *What does he want from me?*

But I am just being sentimental. It doesn't matter, not anymore. It is better this way. I am getting a taste for it – literally – for all my protestation of how morally repugnant I find the killing. The urges are too powerful to control: the need to drink human blood straight from the artery. Oxygenated blood is best – nice and fizzy. I still find this hard to admit, even to myself. The painful truth of the matter is that I like it. If I stay, I will succumb to the instinct and I will kill again and again. I feel it in my blood. Maybe this man can show me how to control the blood lust. Or maybe I am just clutching at straws?

"You can see in the dark?" I ask.

He doesn't look at me, just stares straight ahead.

"You're wondering why I have the headlights on?" he replies.

"Well, yes."

"To be invisible, so we don't get stopped."

When Mr Hrot says he will meet Gunnar back at the Château, I think to myself that he must mean the Old Manor house. So, when he takes the ring road out of town, it's crystal clear to me that he means somewhere else. I don't expect a straight answer from him, but I ask anyway:

"Where are we going?"

"You'll see. In time."

The cat's eyes glow in the headlights. The BMW pulls smoothly around the bend at ninety miles an hour. I rest my cheek on the cold glass of the side window and gaze out at the thick layer of trees that borders the side of the road. Parts of the landscape leap out at me in alarming shapes and then recede into the blackness of the background. I close my eyes. But my gaze only tries to burn its way through my eyelids. There is no off switch for their intensity it or so it seems. I

open them and fall back into the comfort of the car seat, looking out of
the windscreen at the road hurtling towards me.

"You gave us quite the run-around," Mr Hrot remarks.

"I went back to the house," I reply.

"Yes, I thought as much."

"But you had gone."

"Naturellement."

"It was all boarded up."

"After your, um, change. We left you alone for five minutes. Then
bugger me if you hadn't disappeared," he smiles.

"I don't remember..."

"No, well, I suppose you wouldn't."

Gunnar and Lady Francesca had a bit of a panic. So we had to close
down our base of operations, just in case."

"In case of what?" I say. I turn to look at him.

"In case the authorities get involved. We have friends in high places.
But you will be amazed at the trouble that your low-level salt-of-the-
earth type can cause – before we stamp on them that is!" A frown
crosses his brow as if remembering...

Outside, the car speeds past the grey shapes of hedge rows and trees.
Lit up briefly under the beams of the headlight, they are transformed
into white streaks, as if under moonlight, as they whizz past the car
window. There is no moon, not tonight, and there are no street lamps,
only mile after mile of alabaster shapes framed in blackness. The world
outside has all the details of a black and white photo and is visible until
the white bleach of the headlights startles the landscape into stark
colours. We pass a lone farmhouse, with a single upstairs light on, then
nothing but empty roads and hedgerow.

"How did you find me?" I ask.

"Well, it is simple really. I never forget a scent. It was just a matter of following my nose," he says.

"You sniffed me out?"

"Ha, ha. You could say that! When we first met, I could smell the others on you. They were easier to find than you. We were going to make them tell us where you had gotten to. We have ways of doing that. But all good plans and all that…"

I nod.

"But when we found the first two, they were dead. Then we knew you were going to go after the third one eventually. So we decided to head you off – before you got into real trouble."

"I see..."

"Nice work by the way, for a novice without tuition. Nice clean kills. You're a natural."

I am not sure how to take this. I peer hard at the side of his face to see if he is joking. I cannot detect even the glimmer of a smile. Still, even if he means it, this is nothing to be proud of: killing I mean. But part of me glows at the compliment. It mixes with a wave of guilt that comes crashing down on me. Confused, I have no idea what to feel, nothing that will be for the best – to feel nothing. To forget, that would be nice. In this enclosed space, warm and with the gentle hum of the engine: I can believe it is possible. Only something in my brain won't let me:

"What happened to the bodies…I mean…" I say, my eyes cast down toward my lap.

"I know what you mean," Mr Hrot says curtly.

"Gunnar, he disposed of them, with the others," he adds.

"So what now?"

"Now I take you to be with your own kind."

"You mean with other vampires?" I say. I instantly regret opening my mouth, when I see, side-on, the expression on Mr Hrot's face. He turns towards me. His features pinch in an expression somewhere between contempt and anger.

"Never say that, never think it and never ever use that word!" He says in a slow deadly sounding tone of voice.

I draw back in my seat.

"Why?"

He seems to relax. His face clears and he says:

"Seriously, you will do well never to use the V word. You can end up in all sorts of trouble."

"What then? We drink blood, so we are just like..." I trail off. I am not sure how to complete the sentence without using the V word.

"Our kind take that word 'Vampire!' as an insult. Rightly so in my opinion. It is a word made up by the humans to describe what they do not have the faintest notion of. You have to understand that humans are to us what cattle are to them."

"Ok..." I say, unsure where this is going.

"Would a human let a cow or a sheep name them?"

"No, I suppose not," I reply.

"So instead of human – they would be called a moo or... You know, I am not sure what sound a sheep makes. How silly!"

"Baa?" I say, trying to be helpful.

"Oh yes that is it! Baa!" says Mr Hrot, sounding delighted.

"Either way, you don't let your meal tell you who you are!" he says. He turns towards me. I try to gauge whether he is still angry or not. His face isn't giving away any clues. I wonder how wise it is to push this line of conversation. Clearly, this strange man has a lot of power. The last thing I want to do is to anger him. I ask anyway.

"So what are you... I mean what are we?" I ask. He looks at me, then turns his gaze back to the road.

"Well John," he says. "That all depends on your point of view..."

He continues.

"You have killed, yes? You know what we feed on?"

"Blood," I say confidently.

"No, that is just the medium, the thing in-between. What we feed on is life itself; we eat human souls. That is the core of it. It is what makes us special, top of the food chain if you like. What else do you know that eats people's souls?"

"Demons?" I say, horrified that I might have been eating people's souls. Killing them is bad enough.

"Demon's or angels: it's all the same thing. A race of beings above all others have always lived alongside humans," he says.

"There have been different names throughout history for us but we call ourselves 'Wonder-kind'. Forget your Gods and Devils. The Wonder-kind are the true immortals, born to rule. The earth is ours and humans only exist at all as our food."

"Oh, right" is the only thing I can think to say.

# Chapter 2

# Henry Hrot

*"I was christened Henry George Hrot."*

When I was human I owned a number of factories in the Midlands. Back when Queen Victoria was on the throne."

I nod, giving Mr Hrot the briefest glance to show I am listening. Meanwhile, my insides are churning sour milk. My future is forever and nothing about it is appealing in the slightest. More importantly, where are we going and who are these 'Wonder-kind' when they are at home? I am curious to meet them but judging by the three I have already met: I do not hold out much hope of it being a pleasant experience. And to think I used to consider school a living hell.

"Back then, we all thought that the best thing in the world was to be an 'Englishman'. Then one day someone showed me that there is something even better," he says. "I was born again at the same time that dear old Queen Vicky died. I thought I had lived before, believed I was important, but I was shown that I knew nothing about the way the world worked. I discovered what it meant to really live: what it was to really matter in this world."

I nod. He is getting really animated now. His eyes sparkle as he glances towards me and then back at the road. *Oh brother.*

"Can you even imagine that? Britain ruled and dominated most of the globe? I thought this was power. I was wrong, so wrong. I was shown that it all meant nothing. They taught me what real power is, what real influence is," he says.

"It was humbling, and liberating," he adds.

"It was as if I were reborn, baptised, this time in blood," he says.

I just sit in silence. I have every reason to hate this man. But, that is not it – not it at all. There is something about him that makes my insides physically recoil. I don't like him and he is supposed to be my mentor or sire or something like that. We are bound together. I don't see how I can stand it another minute. Eternity is going to feel very long.

"My wife did not share my enthusiasm for my new life," he recollects.

I like the woman already.

"She went off screaming something about it being about the 'work of the devil' or some such nonsense. It was a long time ago. That is the trouble with living for so long. You forget things, you know? There's so much stuff to remember that you have to forget some things to make room for more stuff. That's what it is like," he tells me.

"How old are you?" I ask

"Don't know... About a hundred or one hundred and one. I am a youngster compared to many," he replies.

"Anyway, that stupid wife of mine killed herself. Can you believe that? Killed herself and my son. Ran up to the top of the house and jumped out of the window. He would be about seventy now if he was still alive," he continues.

I find it very easy to believe. I understand why, of course I do, but I say nothing. *What good will it do?*

"Clearly the woman was mad. Can you imagine being married to someone so deranged for eternity? But my son... Well, these things happen," He speaks about his wife in a totally matter-of-fact way, with no emotion. He seems to consider that the reality of the situation so straightforward and clear that I must surely agree with him. Given the choice, I want to go the same way as his wife. He never asks for an opinion, so I don't give it. I am silent. Henry does not seem to mind. He just keeps talking.

We drive all night. Dawn breaks, replacing the monochrome with colour. The first rays of the sun go over the hills, then creeps down the valley.

Henry steers the car at breakneck speed. We run into a mist creeping along the ground towards us. White strands hug the land on either side of the valley, floating over the road in wisps.

*Fog?*

We drive down the hill, I look up through my window into the murky depths of the woodland towards the top of the hill. It is populated mainly by huge old oaks. Their enormous trunks support the huge branches bushed with green leaves. They look unwieldy due to the sheer size of the branches. The white vapour circles around the huge trunks and claws upwards towards the lower branches. I see someone walking out of the woods: human but too bulky, with the shape unclear within the mist. The figure holds a long metal poll lengthwise, protruding at the waist. Out of one end, a white steam comes spurting and spluttering out, eddying and swirling, joining seamlessly with the greater white ghostly bulk. The head of the figure seems deformed and he or she has a hump on their back. The body is oddly shaped. I squint, lifting a hand above my eyebrows to shield my eyes from the sun.

*It is just someone wearing a protective suit.* The deformed head is some sort of gas mask and the hump is a tank the size and shape of an oxygen one that a frogman might wear.

"There's someone up there," I point.

Henry causally glances out of the passenger window then looks away.

"Creepers," he utters, as if that explains everything.

"What?"

"The mist. See it?"

"Yes," I say, "It's hard to miss. It is everywhere."

"Well it isn't."

"It's not?"

"No, it's gas."

"Why would…?"

"It is a psychoactive agent. Anyone who wanders into this valley will get a hallucination the like of which will be more powerful than drinking several bottles of laudanum."

"Laudanum?"

"Oh, it's a drink, made up of alcohol and opium. It is a thing that my generation were pretty keen on actually. But take my word for it. Drink out of the neck of someone who's had a couple of glasses of that. You will be happy for days after," he laughs.

For a moment he is silent, lost in thought. Then suddenly, he seems to remember what he has been talking about.

"So, it is to keep humans out. Anyone who stubbles upon our little community will hallucinate so badly – that is if it doesn't send them over the edge into madness... Well, I believe that heart attacks and brain embolisms are also known side effects.”

“That is horrible,” I splutter.

“That's life: brutish and short. For humans anyway. I read that in a book somewhere. Damned if I can remember the name,” he says, rubbing his chin with one hand and lazily pulling the steering wheel around with other as he takes another corner.

“The point being, if they start jabbering about a colony of people with long razor-sharp teeth, it will be so intermingled with pink elephants and fairy folk. No one will believe a word they say. They will be locked in a padded cell before you can say ‘care in the community,” he adds.

“It is also to keep the humans – not that they have nonce to try anything like that,” he states.

“To keep humans in as well?” I ask, alarmed. Henry has been the first person I have been in close proximity with in a long time, who I do want to sink my fangs into – well, not to feed my hunger anyway. I do not really want to be around humans again – too much of a temptation. I haven't thought of feeding for the whole journey. Even Paul's slow and distant heart-beat has ceased to bother me, as he continues to sleep in the boot of the car. Purring in tune with the smooth sound of the engine, as the vehicle glides the road. I should be constantly thinking about his bloodstream. Usually, the thirst is like an electric wire sparking in the centre of my brain. For once it isn't.

“Oh, yes. The cattle. We don't want them to wander off do we?”

“Cattle?”

“What do you think we live on out here? Fresh air and cow pats?” He laughs.

I have a sudden thought:

"What about us? The gas, I mean," I say. Automatically, I stop breathing.

"Don't worry about it. We are immune," Henry says in his matter of fact way.

I think I can hear the sea: waves breaking against rock. Henry takes another corner on the winding road we are following. I am wondering if he even has a driving license. Did they even have cars in the late Victorian era? I don't know. All I can think of is Charles Dickens and Workhouses. And to think I used to be good at history! Then I see it: straight up ahead and on top of the hill. My thoughts draw to an abrupt halt.

The blue of the sea is glistening, rushing in towards the shore on my left, where the valley gives way to flat lands, bordered by sand dunes and beyond that the azure rolling expanse yawning out into the bay. The waves are crashing against rocks. One side of the hill is facing outwards, where the hill ends in a sheer drop: a dark grey rock face heading straight down to the sea. The nearest side forms a gradual grassy slope that ends in a plateau that abuts the long drop to the sea. This is where the dark tall castle sits. The very sight of it makes something in my stomach drop.

# Chapter 3

# Château Blanc

*It is a formidable sight.*

The base of the hill is surrounded by a high stone wall. Its ramparts score across the top like square teeth. Numerous towers stand sentinel at regular intervals along its long length. The biggest of them, guarding the entrance, is the gatehouse. It is composed of two stone towers joined on either side of a large wooden gate with a bridge over it. The road we are on has but one destination: the gatehouse.

Beyond the wall, leading from the gatehouse, a dirt road twists around the hill towards the strange looking building on the top: the Château I assume. It looks like it is part manor house, part castle and part something else entirely. There are towers, turrets and spires all over the place. There are too many, overcrowding the top of the structure and all wrapped inside an inner stone wall.

Towards the back of the castle, a bridge yawns out over the sea to a single tower. It stands alone among the waves that crash around it, leaping up against the grey rock like giant tongues around an ice lolly. Both the bridge and the tower look as if they are carved out of the stone of the cliff face itself. The remoteness and the sheerness of the tower appeals to me. I find it fascinating.

Between the outer defensive wall and the inner one that rings the main building there is an assortment of buildings that seem as diverse in style as they are in age. There are clusters of stone-walled hatched housing. Scattered in small hamlets and further up there is a larger group of thatched dwellings, with more modern farm buildings further up: sheds and long low buildings. People are walking beside the winding road. And on it, spewing white clouds of dust and stone chippings, two military style vehicles are moving up the hill on the road: a jeep and a lorry.

"Well we are here," Henry announces as we drove towards the main gates. He turns to me and smiles. The warmth in his smile surprises me. He appears how a wanderer who has finally returned home might look.

We approach the gatehouse. Two impressively tall wooden doors set in a stone arch stood in front of us. They look impenetrable, unless you happen to have an army and a full-size battering ram on you. Up close, I get a real sense of the size of the gatehouse. Made of large long stone blocks. It looks the epitome of strong and fortified.

The gatehouse reminds me of one of the British Heritage castles I visited with my parents when I was younger. These were smaller and for the most part in ruins. The black figures on top of the wall, behind the ramparts, tells me this is a castle that is very much still in use. They are aiming, not bows and arrows at us, but automatic assault rifles.

It is embarrassing to admit, but I only recognise the guns because of an Action-man figure I used to have when I was younger. He had a rifle just like it, only without the telescopic sights that these have. I think my brother has the figure now: any toys or clothes that have survived my rough handling always get passed on to my younger brother, much to my irritation.

Mounted on the bridge between the towers of the guardhouse, there is a heavy machine gun. Its thick barrel points down at us. I am no expert on military hardware; I don't even know what sort it is, but I can easy imagine the damage it could rain down on the car if it fired upon it. It would be destroyed in seconds. There is another modern addition to gatehouse: the video cameras on either side of the gate. They rotate on their fixed mounting to follow us as we approach. Henry sighs and shakes his head. He does not slow the car down until the last possible moment.

"Humans!" he exclaims. He bangs his fist down on the car horn in rapid succession: *Beep! Beep! Beep!*

The doors slowly open. Henry drives the car inside, screeching to a halt before the still-closed door at the other side of the stone passage. I crane my neck to look through the glass of the window and, for a moment in the ceiling above, I can see the murder holes, out of which four or five black nozzles emerge. A flame flickers inside the nozzle of each one.

*Flame throwers?*

I don't think I can die, but flame throwers... I am not sure about them. Even if it doesn't kill me, which seems to me likely – given my pathetic suicide attempt – I am not keen on being burnt to a crisp. That is the thing about this new life: I cannot die, but I can feel pain.

I shiver and squirm in the leather seat, expecting fire to come pouring down at any second, for the car's petrol tank to explode, for the fire to claim me and burn the little flesh I have off my thin skinny body.

But it never does.

Henry flashes me a dangerous look. I keep my mouth shut. I do not want to fan the fires of his anger.

"Bloody humans!" he repeats.

He winds down his window, sticks his head out and bellows:

"Get those doors open! Get them open right now. Or I will have your head on the end of a spike before the end of the day!"

Someone must have heard him, as the inner doors pull slowly open. Henry puts the car in first gear and roars out of the enclosed space. He stamps on the brakes. The car screams to a halt and stone chipping from the road surface flies in all directions.

A very scared looking man in a black uniform rushes over towards the car. He removes his black peak cap as he nears us. Some kind of officer I assume judging by the cap he wears, though there is no insignia on the uniform to denote any kind of rank.

Henry opens the car door and gets out. The man – the officer – looks to be a good foot taller than Henry. Still it is the officer who looks cowed, lowering his neck and head, to appear smaller than Henry.

"I am most dreadfully sorry sir!" the man pants. He must have run out to meet Henry.

"We didn't know... We weren't expecting..."

"Shut up!" Henry shouts at the man. Then he hits him. It does not seem more than a tap. But I know better, I know the strength we have. Henry's fist meets with the man's face. Then there is a mass of blood. The man's hands shoot up to his phiz, to stem the flow from his nose, and he falls to his knees. Henry reaches into his pocket and takes out a hanky. He gives it to the man, who holds it to his bleeding nose. One side of his face has already started to swell and turn a blue–black colour.

"If you ever, ever, keep me waiting again, I will personally rip open your neck and then do the same for all of your men. Am I clear?" Henry's voice seemingly calm but cold and hard.

"...Yes sir, ...Very clear sir, ...Won't happen again," the man exclaims.

"Better not."

Henry turns and gets back into the car. Then we are speeding up the road towards the castle on the top of the hill, stone chips spluttering out from under all four wheels as we speed on and up.

"Stupid bovine cattle!" Henry seethes. He continues:

"I have told the King, time and again, about using humans as security detail. The thing you have to remember about humans is that there not much use for anything greater than a good meal. Baa! Ha-ha!" Henry says veering from anger to contempt in one heartbeat.

Henry's hands are clamped tight on the steering wheel and his gaze is fixed upon the road ahead: a rough stony dirt surface with deep water filled furrows where heavy vehicles have frequented the road. I think to myself that this is not the time to point out that we were all human once or to say that it took less than minute to get through the gate. I cannot think for the life of me what Henry's problem is, but I decide to not to tempt risk his anger. So I remain silent.

Three military style trucks pass us, going the opposite direction. They are totally black, even the tinted windows. There are four humans walking in the opposite direction up the hill. They look like a couple of extras from 'Jude the Obscure'. Their eyes are cast down and their expressions are hidden from me. We pass by two hamlets, and on the right, I see more cottage-type housing: timber framed, with thatched roofs. It looks like a small village and could almost be described as biscuit tin quaint – twee, except for the mud everywhere and all the grime on people's faces.

"See what I mean," Henry says, screwing up his face, "They live like pigs. Disgusting!"

We pass by a low-roofed open fronted building that is being used as a garage for a range of military style vehicles: two black coloured half-tracks, a jeep and an armoured car. The car speeds on.

I look keenly out of the car window, from left to right, my eyes drinking it all in, as if there will be a comprehension test on what I have seen.

Another three troop lorries drive past us. In the rear window, I see them whoosh through a large and long puddle at the side of the road, splashing water over the ragtag group of humans, sending them running and tumbling down the hill.

"Ha, ha," Henry scoffs. "They could do with a bath."

I start to the sound of gunshots. Two of the black clad solders are taking pot-shots at the retreating humans out of the back of the lorry, laughing as the bumpy road ruins their aim. Another empties into the air as they bump down the hill. The sound of the shots sticks in my ear and the shrill nasty laughter grates.

They had better not scratch my car with their tom foolery!" Henry hisses as the car speeds up the hill rounding a corner. The two vehicles are now no more than a cloud of spluttering dust heading towards the gatehouse.

"They might hit someone," I say.

"Better not, else it comes out of their wages," Henry says.

"What!?" It seemed a callous thing to say, even for him.

"That is a joke. They don't get any wages."

"They might kill someone though," I say, even though it occurs to me that perhaps death is better than living here.

"If they do," Henry suggests, "the chap responsible will be taking the place of the dead man, as one of the herd. Send him back where he came from!"

I am shaking, both my hands and inside my chest, even though I know I am not human and that in another situation I would kill them and drink their blood, which is definitely worse than just shooting at them. And yet it shocks me. It is like something off the TV news, happening in some far away dictatorship, not here in the heart of England. I shake my head. I am being naive. Here, in their castle behind their impenetrable wall of fog, they can do pretty much as they want.

I am well and truly out of my depth. I dread to think what lies in wait inside those castle walls up ahead.


We reach the inner wall. I see the towers and spires poking over the top of the wall. We near two black ornamental gates, open wide in welcome. The car speeds into the inner courtyard. There are seven different cars parked up in front of the building: all highly priced and high-performance models: two black Porches and two Ferraris (one red, one bright yellow). There is at least one Lotus and a couple of other cars I do not recognise – they look equally sleek and powerful. However, all these brand-new cars are coated with brown mud splashes, which has somewhat spoiled the showroom impact of these powerful metal beasts.

The Castle itself doesn't look like it has been built, but more like it has grown up out of the rock itself and evolved over successive generations. It is, generally speaking, gothic in style with tall archways and high roofs. The central block of the building looks as if it is the original building, with the rest added on throughout the ages, now reaching the point where the building no longer knows what it is supposed to be anymore. It is a porcupine building with all its sharp edges, spires and towers.

Henry gets out and slams the door shut. I follow. I try to ignore the litter of kittens that are playing havoc inside of my gut. Behind those wooden doors... those giant-sized doors... lies what?

I start to feel it, flowing from the house, stronger than anything I have ever felt before: a miasma of pure and overwhelming malevolence. My tongue is so dry it sticks to the roof of my mouth. *I can make a run for it, but where can I go?* No, I am done for. This is where fate has brought me: possibly for good or, more likely, bad. I have to see this through. *No choice then?*

Has there ever been another way, other than the one that has brought me here to this place? Has there ever a chance to escape my fate? I cannot think of one right here and now. Henry mounts the stone steps leading upwards to the wooden doors. I follow, like a little lamb to the slaughter-house.

I hear something – feel it in my teeth – though I'm not sure what. Movement lots of it and the beating of small hearts, thousands of them. There is something familiar about the scratching and scraping sounds. Whatever it is, they are behind those doors. I swallow.

I glance at the two creatures, carved out of stone, on either side of the steps. One is a lion, but with a bird's feet and claws. Its body curves upwards to its roaring head. Its eyes seem to lock with mine and its aggression appears to be directed at me as I pass. On the other side is some sort of huge bird with four legs. The wingspan arches up and its beak looks as if it is shrieking at something, ready to attack a foe. I pass both of them, giving each several circumspect looks as I do so, half expecting them to spring to life and devour me.

At the top of the steps, Henry turns the huge ring door handles. I hurry up to join him. I expect him to ring the bell and for the servants to come rushing out to greet us, but apparently not. He pulls the door open and I peer into the gloom.

Inside, the hallway appears to be crawling. I feel every single hair on my body stand on end, with gooseflesh sprouting on every inch of my body. The floor, walls and even the ceiling is moving – swarming – and crawling. Something falls, with a shriek, onto the hard stone at my feet: a rat, a dirty black rat! It flips over, takes a look at us, then rushes back to join the throng, to mix with its brethren. I step back, nearly falling back down the steps. Henry catches me with one hand and pushes me back onto the top step.

"Ha, ha. Don't worry it gets everyone, the first time," Henry laughs. "It is part of the Château's security. Nothing for us to worry about though. You're safe as long as you follow close behind."

He steps towards the heaving mass of rodents. I feel sick at the sight, shivers zooming up to the top of my spine. I don't want to go anywhere near those nasty black things.

The rats part as Henry steps into the sea of their numbers. They scuttle away either side of him as he approaches. I follow, keeping close behind him. I flick a glance over my shoulder to see the mountainous avalanche of small furry bodies fall behind me, cutting off the outside world. The door is somewhere behind the seething mass of small furry animals with their razor-sharp teeth.

# Chapter 4

# King Theodore

*The inside of the Château is labyrinthine and vast.*

The corridors are high ceilinged and connect up a series of high vaulted rooms, with a collection of large framed paintings on the walls, each painting darker and gloomier than the last. Around the rooms themselves is equally gloomy furniture.

To my relief, there aren't furry rodents running around everywhere, though I can hear them run The running and racing behind the walls giving the impression they are following us around the building. Occasionally, a solitary rat will shoot out of a square hole, below the freeze, in the corner of room, then nip across the floor and shoot up the wall, disappearing into another dark hole.

We travel along a bewildering route, down corridors, through stately and disconsolate rooms. Then we enter a larger room, towards the back of the building. A huge stain glass window covers the whole of the rear wall. Daylight shines through the coloured glass. At first glance, unthinking, I think it depicts some sort of religious scene: the sort I have seen countless times in churches or cathedrals. My parents aren't religious: they never went to church or sent me to Sunday school. But they used to drag me and brother around historic monuments at the weekend and in the holidays: better than being dragged along to DIY stores. Now, that is child abuse, plain and simple! Anyway, I have seen more than my fair share of stained-glass windows, but never one quite like this one.

When I look a second time, I cannot quite believe the scene I am seeing; it is anything but religious, unless you include Holy Wars under that definition – then you would have a point.

The central figure is standing on top of a pile of bodies. It is a big pile. He is wearing a crown on his head. His head surrounded by a halo white glass that catches the sunlight as it shines through the window. In fact, there are dead bodies all over the place. Some are without heads, with trails of red leading into a red river, while others are merely impaled on the ends of spears. They have used a lot of red glass in the picture.

The crowned figure has a sword in one hand, which he is holding to the sky. In the other hand there is a severed head and behind him there is an army of knights wearing bulky suits of armour. It is this army that is doing most of the slaying in the scene. Like the main figure, the ones without helmets all have teeth – fangs pointing down out of their mouths. They seem to flow down and out on either side of the king's cape, pouring backwards towards the river of blood. It all gives me the creeps, just looking at it, but at the same time, I have to admire the detail, the craftsmanship and sheer size of it.

In the next room, there are more stained-glass windows, smaller this time, each depicting a different scene, usually with the crowd figure at the centre standing victorious. In each one, red glass is always in much demand. Red blood running in rivers. It picks something inside of me. I lick my dry lips, thinking of all that blood…

"That is our history;" Henry remarked. "The official version anyway."

"Who is the man in the crown?" I ask.

"King Theodore. Yes, that is who you are here to meet."

"I have to?"

"Yes, you have to... Tradition dictates. Also, as you may glean from the strain glass windows, he is not the sort of person you want to up-set…"

"Definitely not..." I agree. "But what do I say to him?"

"Nothing. Leave the talking to me," he snaps.

"Ok," I say, pleased and relieved.

"Oh, and when I first introduce you, get down on one knee. He likes that sort of thing. He is very old fashioned like that. Oh… and bow when you leave. Don't forget!"

"Ah, here we are!" he says.

Two enormous gold coloured ornamental doors stand before us. Two vampires – Wonder-kind – are positioned either side of the big doors. I can tell the difference: we smell strange, our heart beats are slower and our hearts themselves sound like someone squeezing wet clothes in a mangle. Both of the guards are bald and wearing black leather over-coats that reach their ankles. If I think Gunnar is big, then these guys are giant. They have a mysterious looking gun holstered at their sides, hidden beneath their overcoats until they pull them to one side, as we approach, revealing the guns. I have never seen weapons like them be-fore.

They relax on seeing Henry, but give me the once over with their little piggy eyes. They drop the flaps of their coats and move to open the door for us. Evidently, we are expected. I swallow hard. Walking two paces behind Henry, we pass through the doorway.

It looks like a scene straight out of a medieval painting. We are in a long highly ordered room with luxurious red carpet dissected the room down the middle like the cut from a scalpel incision. My shoes sink into its thick softness as I walk. It leads towards a throne on a raised step at the other end of the room, separating the ranks of Wonder-kind on either side: those dressed in yellow robes on the left of me and those in light green robes on my right. At the end of the room sits a small thin man with a gold crown on his head. The crown is a plain design, just a gold ring with a number of raised points around its circumference. It doesn't look impressive and the man on throne does not look anything like the giant man I saw depicted in the stained-glass windows.

To the thin man's left and right are two smaller thrones. A tall, thin woman sits on his right; on the other side is a man with shoulder length blonde hair and dark eyebrows.

The king is dressed in a white robe. The blonde man is dressed in an embroidered blue tunic and matching breeches. The woman wears a long and embroidered dress with fragile looking tassels around the shoulders.

To side of the three thrones are various other seated figures, men mostly, dressed in robes of dark red with white collars. On their heads, they wear small skullcaps, dark red in colour. At the back, standing, is a small and slender woman I can barely make out. Behind the others, she is like shadow, as if she barely exists. At the same time, once you notice her eyes they draw the woman out of scenery, refusing to let her disappear again. Then she looks directly at me. Wave after wave of sorrow flows out of those black orbs, undulating towards me to explode on the insides of my skull – a feeling that is too intense, too sad to bear. I look away.

There are paintings of supernatural beings all around the room. Behind the throne area and taking up the whole of the wall, is a painting of heaven. God, a big white bearded man, sits on his throne, with thunderbolts in one hand and a staff of light in the other. He looks down from the clouds into the room itself. Angels stand around his throne with swords and spears in their hands, with others flying in the air – descending downwards.

King Theodore's throne is perfectly framed so that it sits directly beneath the figure of god and his swarm of angels, giving the impression that he is sending his host down to protect and aid the King as the white bearded god smiles a stern smile, watching over the throne and its occupant. This is the last thing I expect to be on the walls in the hall of the vampire King. Then I remember what Henry said:

*I must not use the V word!*

As we enter, the room falls silent under the glow of hundreds of candles mounted on the wheel shaped chandeliers above. These cast shadows and light throughout the hall in equal measure. I have the eyes of everyone in the room falling upon and burning into me all at once. The frost of shyness freezes over my ability to think. My cheeks burn as if they are a bright red. I lower my eyes to look at the ground, keeping them down as I follow Henry towards King Theodore's throne. Every step of the way I feel them – hundreds of eyes staring. For the first time since being transformed, the muscles at the backs of my legs start to tremble.

I look at the side of Henry's face. He appears to be in a state of pure happiness. His face is positively lit up. He is smiling broadly and his eyes are bright, as he strides forward with a confident pace. *He is enjoying this!* He is completely at home with this pomp and ceremony. Me, on the other hand... I am just glad I do not have to say anything. I hate to think of what might come out of my mouth.

When we reach the steps, Henry motions for me to kneel down on one knee. I do. Then he too goes down on one knee, smiling up at the king:

"My King, my lord!" he says.

"Henry!" the king says. "We have missed you. Court is so dull without you! Approach! Approach!"

The king nods enthusiastically. Henry moves forward, still half bowed. He approaches the throne and falls back onto one knee. He reaches forward to kiss the King's extended hand. The hand has a ring with a huge ruby embedded in a gold clasp. It is the tip of this jewel that Henrys lips briefly touches. I wonder if the jewel is real. Of course – it has to be. If Henry is telling the truth, they are wealthy beyond all imaginings. Even if he isn't, he is Wonder-kind and can take anything he wants. No human can stand in his way, not if they want to keep their eight pints or so of red juice.

It is too much for my young mind to take in. The world swims, the low hanging chandlers seem to sway and the whole room blurs in and out. *This cannot be happening* I tell myself for the millionth time. But it is and I am standing right at the centre of it all. Really, I just want it all to just go away. I am jolted from my thoughts by the King's voice:

"So this is the new...um, the new member of my community then?" He says, looking down at Henry.

"He is," Henry says.

"Lady Francesca and Gunnar are not very pleased, I hear," King Theodore says. He arches his fingers in front of his face, tapping his two index fingers together.

"When are they ever?" Henry replies, shrugging his shoulders.

"It is a serious business, taking one of them as our own," the King says.

"I know what I am doing. I take full responsibility."

"I will hold you to it."

"Your actions have always paid off in the past; but one day your luck will run out."

"It is nothing to do with luck, Sire. It's about rising to the occasion, spotting opportunities as they present themselves and then, of course, making the right choice. This is the right decision, mark my words."

"I will. I rather gather he gave you a run for your money," the King remarks.

"True. He has killed twice already...at least." Henry replies.

"Ah a real killer, eh. Are you m'boy?"

I look up. I am thrown by the question and wonder whether I should answer. I glance towards Henry for guidance. He smiles and nods.

"Yes Sire," I say.

"And respectful too. I do like that!" exclaims the King. Then he turns back to Henry.

"He has arrived at a most opportune time. The festival starts shortly. We have an execution as well. I do enjoy those. We don't get them often enough. You have to make the best of them when they come," the King sighs.

"We have... er... a Capital Offence don't we Chancellor? Please tell me we do!" the king pleads like an excited child.

A large man with a big and bushy beard and a gold robe hustles up the steps, his huge frame hampering his movements. He bows and utters:

"Yes Sire. One Oliver Read-Dunn, to be put to death," the Chancellors' sonorous voice rumbles, the sound thundering from his huge chest, through the air, filling the entire hall with its sound.

"What is his crime?" Henry asked

"Attacked his master," the Chancellor replied.

"Is that even possible?" asks the King.

"Technically no, but intent is proven. Which is good enough," the Chancellor replies.

"Jolly good!" says the king. His face is childlike. Then it hardens into stone. His expression and tone becomes stern and deadly serious as he says to me:

"Obedience is something we take very seriously, and disobedience has to be punished."

I cast my eyes down from the severity of the King's gaze. My knees feel as if they will buckle and break. Then the King's mood changes completely and he scrutinises me with a childlike smile plastered across his face and says:

"How old is this rag-a-muffin anyway? He looks about ten!"

"Fifteen years old sire. I believe," Henry responds.

*I am sixteen!* I think. But I say nothing.

That is it. Then I am forgotten about.

"Henry?"

"Yes sire?"

"Stay. We have much to discuss."

"Of course," Henry smiles.

# Chapter 5

# Wearisome Night

*I can breathe once more.*

I am escorted out of the room by a gaunt vampire, whose neck is so long and thin that you can see his Adam's apple run up and down like a yo-yo whenever he speaks.

He leads me through several rooms and down more corridors than I can count, until we come across a wide, wooden staircase. The wood is dark and polished to a point of perfection; I can see my face in an elaborate curved shape that decorates the end of the banister.

A vampire who could be in his late teens is coming down the stairs as we approach. He eyeballs me once. His gaze is full of disdain.

"I say you there! Karl! Would you mind coming here one second? Would you mind – I know it is an awfully tedious task, but I simply must get back. Don't want to miss anything, you know," the gaunt vampire asks.

"Huh?" Karl responds. "What?"

"Find this young man a room. There's a good chap!"

"Ok."

"We haven't all day!" Karl barks by way of a greeting and then turns back to the stairs.

We climb the stairs. We go up about twelve flights, then through corridors lined with dark reddish wood panels and heavy wooden doors (though Karl pushes through them as if they are made of balsa wood).

I want to ask Karl how he came to be here, what happens at the festivities, who Oliver Read-Dunn is and what had he done. But Karl is marching at breakneck speed, always keeping four or five steps in front of me. *Not in a talkative mood then?* So we travel along in uncomfortable silence. Until, at last, he shoves one of the doors and grunts:

"This is it."

Then without another word, he turns on his heal and leaves me. However, I am all too pleased to be rid of his hostile presence. Clearly, the task of showing me to this room, which is now my room, is one he considered unworthy of his attentions.

"Why can't I ever meet anyone nice?" I mutter and I enter the space.

I spread out on the bed sinking into the mattress. It seems a long time since I have been on a proper mattress. I would say 'sleep', but I don't do that anymore.

I lift my head and scan the room.

There is cupboard, trunk and chair. They are all made of the same dark wood. They are simple in their design and very solid looking. I lie back on the bed. *Why have I a bed at all?* It is not as if I sleep. I find it hard to believe that I will never sleep or dream again. Surely It cannot go on forever like this. Could it?

The obvious comfort of the mattress starts to prickle my back. I don't deserve even that small level of comfort. It all feels wrong, completely and utterly wrong in every sense, everything about it, this new life of mine.

I remember them all, each person I have killed, vividly and up close, so close I can still feel their breath on my face as I lunge for their necks. The blood, oh, I remember that alright, sucking it into my mouth: bubbling and sparkling. The excitement and pleasure surging through my body and the deep need for more and more: to drown in it, to be one with it. I lick my lips at the thought. At the same time, I wince, all intense colour and high emotion. I put my hands over my eyes and screw my eyes tight shut, as if I can block out the moving pictures of their deaths: moving pictures with surround sound, screaming. Memory is a bastard.

Is this something that has always been there? Deep down, is this the real me? All you have to do is press the right buttons and your inner psychopath comes out to play. Or is it all just the fault of the monster they put inside me? I would not want... crave... the blood if I had not become this...Wonder-kind: a vampire by any other name. I have no answer for these questions. In sense it does not matter; it is all too late. I am a part of this world now and there is no way back: no way out. Maybe I deserve to be here. After all I can't die, but I can't live with myself either. *Perhaps being here with others like me is a way of controlling it?*

It is more likely that what is happening to me is an apt punishment for my crimes. I am among people who are worse than me. Are they worse than me? Or just the same as me? I do not know that either. God, I wish I could sleep. No rest for the wicked: the sleep-of-the-just and all that.

What worries me most is what they will expect me to do. Now I am a part of this place. *Wait a minute* – I have missed something; they say they are going to execute Oliver. Can we die? *So there is a way to end an immortal life. There is hope after all.*

Maybe it will only be a matter of time before it is my turn. I really don't know how I feel about that. Do I deserve it? Yes. Could I live with myself like this? No. Do I want to die? No, I really don't. Even after all this: the desire to live burns strongly within my twisted and black heart.

After a few hours – I am not sure how many – my mind quietens and the loneliness overwhelms me. In this building with hundreds, maybe thousands, of others like me, I am still alone, trapped in this small room. There is a lock on the door. But Karl did not lock it when he left. Even if he had, I could smash it open easily enough. And there is the window as well. I can feel a waft of air; it is open. So I can get out. I could drop down to the courtyard, and then I will be away: jump the wall and I will be gone.

I am too afraid. I curl into a ball on the bed and listen. I can hear people moving around – or rather vampires. I can hear the rats scurrying under the floors and in the walls. And somewhere, a distance away, I can hear screams and the sounds of feeding: the noisy slurping of someone sucking the blood out of its organic packaging. It sounds like a child sucking juice from one of those squeezy drink cartons. My stomach rumbles. I clench my fists and close my body into a tighter ball. A low moan escapes through my lips. And I wish that the world would come to an end, suddenly and without warning. But it doesn't.

# Chapter 6

# Blood Slaves

*The vampires are feeding openly on the humans.*

They are feeding on anyone they can get their blood-stained hands upon. They are, without exception, in serving roles of one sort or another. A good many of them are serving what appears to be red wine from large jugs. But my nose tells me it is human blood within those containers. This plentiful and readily available source of our favourite nectar, apparently, isn't enough for most of the Wonder-kind present.

"Having it served to you in silver goblet is convenient and civilised. But you can't hear the screams, you can't feel the fear, you can't taste it in the blood. Believe me... There is nothing like it, fresh from the vein, so to speak," a vampire with a long blonde beard and a balding head says to his companion, as I pass.

Most of the time they – the humans – make sure that the jug and goblets on the silver tray are stowed somewhere safe first: on a nearby table, stall or bench. After all, you never waste good blood, do you? After this is done, the vampires close in on their victim. They don't kill them – well, mostly they don't. The act itself is similar to what I had done to

Danny and James, but more skilled, brutal and a lot more heartless. They have perfected humiliation and cruelty into art form.

The stalls resemble your average church fate. They are colourful and full of things you can buy. The things on sale are of a higher quality than anything I have seen before. Everything is handmade: from custom built furniture to colourful embroidered tunics.

A young human who could be my age walks towards me. She wears a long black dress with white frilly cuffs and a collar (the same garb as all the female servers are wearing). She has long blonde hair, which is woven into long thick strands that trail all the way down her back. She is carrying a tray on her left side, which swings with her hips as she walks. There are three empty goblets on a circular wooden tray surrounding the larger wooden jug.

I smile. I have no hunger for any of this: the sickening violence, the cruelty. Even the sound of her quickening heart does nothing for me… except… except – *Shut up!*

The smile is supposed to be one that says *It's ok you want walk by me. I won't hurt you.* This is a message that is lost in translation it seems, because she freezes, her eyes widening into a 'rabbit in headlights' type of expression. I should have known better that a smile only means on thing here: *I am about to devour you.*

Two older vampires, a man with a short ponytail and a woman with long thick chestnut coloured hair and eyebrows that look as if they are glued to her fringe, silently appear behind her. The human woman's heart is hammering ten to the dozen. Her heartbeat goes faster still when the two vampires close in.

*Oh no. I didn't mean...*

I have to remember I am not the person I used to be. I am a monster just like them. Who am I to judge? But seeing it, seeing who you really are in others. Now that is chilling.

With big wide eyes, the woman glances up at the two vampires, to one then the other. She brings the tray around to her front and her shaking hand moves towards the jug.

"C... can I pour you a drink? I beg, sir, madam?" She asks, her voice small and trembling. She keeps glancing back and forth between the two vampires, hoping for an affirmative response, never once looking either of them in the eye, keeping her head slightly lowered – cowed – deliberately avoiding their gaze.

"Stagnant blood ugh! I think not!" the tall male vampire scoffs, as he runs his hand over the surface of his black hair. "What do you think dearest?"

"Oh, definitely not! I hear you humans top it up with pig's blood!" the female vampire replies.

"Quite! We prefer something fresher. Straight out of the vein, so to speak," the man says. He is staring directly at the human woman's neck, watching it as if it is the most interesting thing to him in the whole world. I know all too well what is holding his interest.

"But we would never..." the woman begins. Then her face falls and she gazes at the ground. Evidently realising that it is pointless speaking, that she is being toyed with. She sniffs twice and a single tear falls from her left eye. It plummets - exploding on the mud by her feet. Her arms are trembling, as pulls the black scarf she wears around her neck down. She tips her head to one side, exposing the left side of her neck. Her throat is white, slender and already covered in small red puncture marks.

"My... my blood is yours to taste," she says.

Her face flicks between submission and fear. I will never forget that look. The two vampires smile at each other, a savage glint to their eyes, with open mouths and their fangs out. Saliva spills over their bottom lips and their eye light up: ablaze with desire.

"Oh, we are going to do more than taste, wretch. We are going to feast!" the female vampire sneers. She runs her long pink tongue over her upper lip.

The body of the serving woman is now shaking in big and visible movements, leading the goblets and jug on the tray to also shake violently. She puts the tray down by her feet with substantial grace, considering how little control she seems to have left over her limbs.

Then the vampires are upon her. They pin her shaking arms behind her back, holding one arm each. She grimaces in pain, but says nothing. The woman vampire's foot shoots out. The jug flies over the grass, before landing, rolling over and then pouring out its content onto the grass: staining it red.

"Nooooo!" the serving woman moans.

"Shut up!" the woman vampire snaps. She slaps the server across the face. The woman makes a low wailing noise. It stops abruptly as the man grips her by the throat, as she struggles to get breath in and out of her lungs. The man laughs.

They both sink their fangs into the terrified woman's neck with untamed ferociously. They start to suck, making obscene slurping noises as the woman whimpers. Tears pour down her face in a flood. Then they simply drop her to the ground and she flops into a heap.

Still alive, the server moves slightly and I catch her heart beating, slower now. The male vampire kicks her shoulder. He laughs and I hear him say:

"Get away with you with your watery blood!"

The woman scrabbles to her feet. She holds her shoulder, wincing as she does, with half of her face swollen and starting to turn into a bruise. She turns and runs into the crowd, sprinting like a gazelle that has escaped the clutches of a band of lions, running out of desperation or disbelief at having survived the ordeal. The tray, goblet and jug lie forgotten.

# Chapter 7

# Blood Thirst

*My reaction takes me by surprise.*

I see those two vampires feed savagely on that woman, tears flooding her wide eyes and streaming down her cheeks, and the soft slight whimpers of pain and the humiliation. And the look on her face, like that of a wounded animal: the tears somehow touch something inside me, something that should be dead. My eyes prick and my stomach feels sick at the sight of this violence. I know that I felt for the girl, and yet I did nothing. I just kept watching. I feel repulsed, but I cannot deny I am also greedy for the blood they had been drinking so freely.

I want to block the memory out of my mind, but it is everywhere. It is almost as if there is a competition to come up with the most brutal way to prey on a human. As the afternoon wears on these thoughts become more savage.

Each human responds differently. It is a situation in which they can only lose; the only question is how badly. Most are terrified like the woman I have witnessed. Others act as if they enjoy it. They remove their scarves and bare their necks with a gleam in their eyes, as if offering sacrament to a god. And others just accept the violent assaults with dull bovine eyes.

It is hateful to watch.

I rush through the crowd. Another server, a man, appears in my path. He is all dressed up like an extra from Poldark. He looks at me with hopeful eyes, smiling and revealing two missing teeth. I have no idea whether he is hoping to be bitten, hoping not to be bitten or something else entirely. I just take the cup and nod my thanks, trying to avoid the disappointed look that begins to creep across his face. I carry on walking, putting the cup to my lips and drinking deeply from the goblet.

Like an alcoholic taking a drink, once the magical liquid has touched my tongue, the only thing I care about is drinking the red liquid. It isn't stale. It is fresh and delicious. I drain the cup. Then I look around for more. I find it. This time, the server looks terrified as I stomp up to her and take a goblet and drink it down in one go.

"More," I say

She pours me another goblet full. She is wincing as the cup, filled to the brim, spills over the edge. There is a look of pure terror there. I don't care. I have no intentions of punishing her over spilled blood.

This is how ridiculous this place is. They are all on a twisted power trip, picking on those weaker than themselves. They are all just like Danny, only the stakes here are higher: a matter of life and death.

I drink from the goblet of blood. I only drink half of the contents this time. And I look at the woman. She is standing there, literally shaking in her shoes. No one has ever been scared of me before. I find it irritating. I am even more irritated when she starts to nervously pull at her scarf. A low whining noise comes from her lips. I want to strike out at her, to hit or better to sink my fangs into her stupid neck, everything about this human chews on my nerves. The blood I have drunk is surging through my system now. All my senses light up. The woman takes a step backward, her lower jaw quivering.

"I beg..." she says.

Just like Danny, just like me.

"For god sake! I am not going bite you!" I say, then turn and stalk away. I am angry: at myself, at her, at the world – who knows. I finish the blood in the goblet and then throw it to the ground.

# Chapter 8

# Bloody Entertainment

*I have only ever seen this sort of thing in films.*

At the centre of the festivities there is an event that resembles one of those medieval epics: Excalibur, that sort of thing. It is behind a wooden waist-high fence, its perimeter annular in shape, enclosing an arena of mud and kicked up earth, where twenty-odd horses and riders are fighting it out. Outside, around the fence, there is a large crowd of onlooker, cheering and booing at the proceedings. The crowd seems to have its favourites and can make sense of the action, but from where I stand, it looks a free-for-all. If there are rules to the proceedings, they are beyond me.

Opposite me, there is a raised platform with a white tent-like canopy. It is open at the front, where the king and his retinue watch the fighting. The young female and male vampires flank him. Behind them are vampires in red robes. The arrangement is almost exactly the same as it was in the grand hall. At the back of the king's throne, a little to the side, there is the small blonde-haired vampire with the sorrowful eyes.

Something about her seems out of place. She just stands there, unmoved by whatever is happening in her field of vision. She just gazes ahead as if she is not really there: as if she cannot see at all. Then abruptly, something crosses her face. She frowns and then looks directly at me. Our eyes meet briefly. There is an intensity to her black pupils that is hard to endure. My eyes snap away and back to the arena.

The riders only wear light armour: a breast plate, shoulder, knee and elbow pads and a helmet. The helmet completely covers their faces with a tinted face visor. They ride at each other on huge horses, wielding a whole range of weapons. They hacked each other with speed and ferocity, sparing no punches.

In the middle of it all, I recognise Karl. He is riding without a helmet. He swings a large mace around his head. It has large spikes sticking out the sides and top. He hits out with the weapon, shouting and screaming, smashing it down upon shield of the first rider, the helmet of the second and into the flesh of his third opponent.

He hits a rider who is charging in the opposite direction. Under the blow, the rider is thrown, falling under the hooves of his own horse. He cries out, but it is impossible to hear the sound amongst the mass of cheering from the overexcited crowd.

This is not the chivalric world of King Arthur and his knights. This is brutal and savage. I see some of the fighters run through with swords or pikes, others hit the ground and their chests and heads are beaten in. The less said about the wounds inflicted by the battle axes the better – stomach churning and messy is all I am saying.

No, there is no gallant Sir Lancelot knocking his opponent off his horse here. This is just slaughter for its own sake. The crowd cheer at each beheading or disembowelling, becoming more worked up and frenzied at each piece of butchery.

Blood thirst flows through the crowd like electricity, lighting up each and every one of the blood suckers. meanwhile, the blonde-haired woman at the back looks on impassively, her face blank of all emotion.

All the while, there is no chivalry, honour or sense of fairness. There is no death here either. It is violent, brutal and sickening, in the sense that Tom and Jerry would be if it was made real, visceral and bloody.

I see the knight with blue tunic having his head cut clean off his body, falling to the crimson ground. He rolls, then is trampled upon by three different horses, as their riders are busily embroiled in combat. The body rolls over a few more times, before finally coming to rest at the side of the fence.

It is as if all the blood, flesh and bone has been magnetised. I blink. I suppose this is a natural response when you see the laws of physics (and biology) violated right in front of your eyes. I have seen it before: seen my own body repair itself from the embarrassing episode with the stake. But out here in the open and on mass, it seems more graphic, im-possible and unreal.

I watch separated body parts slither back together. I see caved in rib cages flatten out. I observe blood running up hill and back into a wound before sealing itself. All of it occurs as if it is the most normal thing in the world. It could be all the blood I have been drinking, but I think it more likely that it is the un-realness of it. I am seeing it but my brain just doesn't believe it.

Before my very eyes, as I watch, the knight in blue's head has squelched and slivered back into position – re-attaching and welding in its rightful place. He struggles to his feet, dazed, directionless, but in one piece. He turns, only to be hit over the head by Karl and his spiked mace. And then there he is: the only intact person left on in the arena, with his arms raised doing a lap of honour on foot – like James Cann at the end of the film Rollerball. Meanwhile, the still recovering bodies are dragged from the field.

"For the King!" shouts the knight and crowd goes wild with its cheering. King Theodore claps his hands enthusiastically.

I turn my head. My muscles tighten and release as if it is me receiving a blow myself. I have enough of it. I turn and walk away.

I drift away from the festivities and the noise of their enjoyment. The blood has gotten to me. *I've drunk too much!* My head is buzzing and there are strange flashes of light sparking before my eyes. The ground seems insubstantial and shifts with each step I take. Suddenly, I stop. It feels as if someone has just punched me in the stomach. I double over and vomit into the long grass.

"Uh Uruurh!" I moan as I come up for breath, only to double up to vomit once more and then a third time - just for luck. I collapse with the effort, next to the dark pool of liquid.

The taste in my mouth is bitter. It doesn't taste the way it did when I was drinking. I stick out my tongue in disgust. I rise my head and look down at the black sticky pool. The smell of it makes my stomach heave again. I clamber to my feet. I look around. There is no one about. I dig into the ground with my heel and sprinkle the excavated dirt on top of the black puddle.

Walking through the trees, I find a well-trodden footpath and follow it. It meanders down the hill, taking me towards the human village. I don't want to go there. I veer off to the left, where the path splits in two, taking me away from the village.

A green canopy of branches and leaves interlace above my head. The thick sentinel trunks stand firm on either side of the path. I keep walking until I find myself in a grove: a dead end. I look around. I am surrounded by huge old trees: Yews and Oaks for the most part. There is one Yew at the end of the path, a giant. Its cable-textured trunk makes it look as if it is a number of trees that are bound and twisted together. Yew trees can live for up to four thousand years, and this one looks really old. It could have been here for two thousand years, maybe more.

This tree must have been here, as a young sapling, when Roman soldiers walked on this soil. I reach out and touch the trunk's rough surface. I look upward, into its branches.

"Hmmm… Possible, definitely possible."

I start to climb, deftly, in seconds. I rest on a branch near the top. I wonder if any of the vampires here were around when time this tree was a sapling?

*Maybe...*

I watch the sun go down between the canopies of green above me. The red intensity is made soft by the green and yellow colours coming from the trees. A gentle wind blows warm and soothing air on my face, and circulates around my body. Night falls upon the hill and the colours fades to monochrome. The green glow that surrounded the woods has now turned to white, as if the contrast and the brightness has just been turned up too high. Sitting here on one of the higher branches, I can see the outer boundary wall, with its human guards walking it, automatic weapons slung around their waists as they saunter down the stone gangways.

I have to go back soon. They will come looking for me. I can already hear my name whispered in the distance. My name being used by strangers – people who I don't know – is, well…strange.

# Chapter 9

# Enduring Execution

*This is something I cannot miss.*

I have mixed feelings. Of course I do. I don't want to see some barbaric execution... of course not. Why would I want to see that? But I know they will find me eventually. And I don't want them in this grove. I like it here. I don't want them to come stomping in here and ruin its peace and separateness from the rest of the madness.

So I wander back towards the throng. The crowd parts to welcome me into their midst as I approach. I am 'helped' to the front by hundreds of anonymous hands in the crowd, pushing me forward, with force if I so much as slow my inexorable journey to the front. I stand once more at the fence at the edge of the arena. A very energetic woman who looks to be in her eighties yells by my ear. Her voice is a high-pitched shriek that is louder and higher than any other in the crowd. It makes me think of the noise you get when a TV station closes down and you have only the test card for company. Being so close to my right ear it is many decibels higher than I would like; it is a painful experience for my ear to endure.

"We know exactly how to treat criminals here!" she screams at me. "Not like where you come from!"

I glance at the woman who is yelling at me. I put a discrete hand to my ear; to give the appearance that I am cupping my ear to enable me to hear her better. But in truth, I am protecting my delicate hearing from what comes out her mouth. I am not only shielding myself from the volume but also the projectile saliva that flies towards the side of my head, as she spits out her words.

*Not like where you came from?* I repeat her words inside my head. It is a strange thing to say. Does she know who I am? That I am new to this place? Has she seen me earlier in the grand hall?

I do not think of the human world as mine anymore. It seems little more than a vague memory, or even a dream that I have woken from, if only to wake to a worse nightmare.

I hear the slow beating of thousands of vampire hearts, beating as one single mass, their smell dry and musty, myself repeated over. I am in a crowd with those like me: my own kind. I have never felt so alone.

The bodies behind me are pushing at my back, pushing me into the wooden fence. I don't like it; I don't like being hemmed in like this. I don't even want to be here. I am stuck with it – unless I go down on my hands and knees and crawl under everyone's legs, I will be here for the duration.

They drag him out: a gaunt pale figure, whose limbs seem longer and thinner than they should. His skin is peppered with cuts and bruises. He walks with a limp. But his asymmetric gait lessens as he walks. By the time he reaches the centre of the arena, his wounds look on the mend.

Like the newspaper photo from the trial of Brenda Spencer, about four years ago, his ankles and wrists are manacled, all linked together with a heavy chain that runs down the front. The heavy manacles seem almost too heavy for him to walk in. His movements are painfully slow.

King Theodore is still on his throne and appears to have not moved since the afternoon. The canopy has been taken down. Also, everyone else is still in place like manikins in a shop window. King Theodore stands up, harrumphs and starts to speak:

"The blood that runs through us, our community... Our nation is strong!" he says.

The crowd cheers.

"Blood must be pure. If it is diluted, it is weakened. If it is weakened, then we are weak."

"There are those amongst us who seek to destroy us!"

There is more cheering.

"The outlaw, the oath breaker and the anarchist cannot be allowed to weaken the blood: the red thread that binds us. They must be cut out. They must be spat out!"

The crowd is really screaming now, screaming for blood.

"Let the punishment be carried out!" The king shouts.

The crowd cheers even louder.

The King raises his hands to the cheers then sits back on his throne. Next to the king, the prince – if that is what he is – sits looking at his nails. The woman on the other side carries on stroking a king Charles dog that sits on her lap. The dog looks up at her bored face.

At the centre of the arena, they have built what looks like a bonfire waiting to be lit. There are large logs at the bottom of the pile, along with smaller ones and chopped branches as the stack goes up and thins towards the top. There is a thick and long wooden pole staked through the centre of the pyre. This is surrounded by metal scaffolding with large wheels at the bottom of each leg. At the top, there are planks of wood going over the metal poles to make a platform, and a ladder tied to the back of the structure. It looks highly dubious as scaffold structures go. It doesn't appear to be that stable – I can see it shifting.

Oliver is forced to climb the ladder. His progress is slowed by the manacles around his wrists and ankles. I can't understand it. He is a vampire; even with the chains on he should be bounding up that ladder. I could have done it in half the time. He is hauled up the final part of the ladder by two vampires waiting at the top. The two vampires chain him to the pole at the centre. He doesn't resist. In fact, he is very helpful and co-operative: participating fully in his execution. When they are done and he is securely chained to the post, one of the vampires asks Oliver something. I cannot catch it. Oliver shakes his head and the vampire nods.

One of the vampires picks up a steel jerry can and starts to dowse Oliver with the clear liquid. The stink of petrol fills my nostrils. Then, the other vampire picks up a similar can and starts to slosh the liquid liberally over the wooden pile beneath. After the last drop, they throw the cans towards the ground and climb down the scaffold.

The scaffold is pulled away from the wood pile. Another vampire wearing a bright yellow mantle comes forward from behind the King's platform. He marches towards the bonfire, as if launching a javelin, and throws a flaming torch though the air. It ignites the petrol instantly. Within seconds, the thing is alight with flames that rage, hungry to reach the top. Oliver screams.

The crowd goes wild, shouting and cheering.

I turn my head away. But hands from behind me grip my head, forcing my face back to watch. There are fingers around my eyes pulling at the flesh, making sure I cannot close them. Other hands grip my arms and hold them backwards. I struggle. I don't want to see. I really don't. I don't know how many are holding me. I only know it is too many to resist.

Seeing a man burn, even if he is a vampire, is something you don't forget. The screaming is bad enough. At first, the fire swallows the body into a ball of flame. Then the screaming reaches a higher register altogether.

The fat beneath the skin catches alight, eye balls pop and the flesh turns black and flakes away in chunks. I feel my skin crawl and flush hot. My mind just goes numb, seeing but not seeing. The worst thing about it is the fact that he is a vampire. If he was human, it would at least end eventually. But for Oliver, his nerve endings are seared and blunted by the fire, only to regenerate. Flesh attempts to reform, only to be instantly burnt away.

The smell of burning flesh finds its way to the powerful receptors in my nose, causing me to gag. As Oliver burns, fireworks are launched into the sky, exploding into bright colourful flowers of light. The noise of the explosions mixes with Oliver's screams. I am choking down a scream of my own but, instead, a strange whining voice leaves my mouth. The hands that have held me prisoner now release me and I fall to the ground. The grass is wet. I run my fingers through it, then curl them into the mud. Oliver's burning figure is indelibly printed onto the end of my two retinas. My stomach heaves, as it tries to find something to bring up. Finding nothing, I just wretch over and over again. Laughter surrounds me. I become conscious of eyes burning into the back of my head.

"Burn in hell, you traitorous scum-sucker!" the old woman shrieks at the top of her voice. I look up. Her features are distorted to resemble a plastic bag filled with water that is all squashed up to one corner by a tight knot. She turns to me and, reaching down, grips the bottom of my jaw with one hand; her grip is firm and strong. She screeches:

"This is how we deal with traitors."

I wipe the flecks of salvia from my face and turn away. I place my head back on the ground. I can still see it. Another image to add to my personal phantasmagoria of horror: its edges made softer by others.

# Chapter 10

# Night Noises

*I feel my skin crawl and my face flush hot.*

They have let the vampire called Oliver Read-Dunn burn on into the night. His suffering has been never ending, as has been his screaming. Even if he was silent, I think I would still hear his cries: they are etched onto the surface of my short-term memory: set on repeat-play.

*Bloody, bloody hell.*

I am not going to sleep. I know that much. I just want to get away. I need to be by myself, far away from these cold sadistic monsters. My mind needs to take shelter from all I have seen and that it means. Is it a threat or a promise? If I don't do what they want me to do, then it will be me they incinerate.

After seeing Oliver, I have changed my mind about dying; there is no way I can endure that kind of pain. Not for one hour, let alone hour after hour of torturous agony. I am stronger than when I was human, but my senses are keener. If that is what it takes to end this wretched life, I won't be doing it. What will be left of Oliver in the morning? Just cinders? Is that it? The only way for us to die is to burn until the body can no longer repair itself? That has to be it. Shit…

With my mind full of the horrors I have witnessed this evening and my imagination in over-drive, I return, with my head hung low, to the main building. Wearily, I slouch up the stairs, my eyes fixed upon their wood. I don't want to look at or talk with anyone. I hate them. I hate myself. I hate everything. I have never felt this way before. I don't like it. Not one little bit.

I close the door on their world and fall heavily on the bed. I am more like a sulky teenager than a blood-sucking fiend. I rub my eyes looking upwards at the ceiling.

Time passes. I have no idea how much. I just lie there. I think of Oliver's face and his blackened and twisted flesh. I think of Danny, then James. My mind replays the images over and over. I clench my fists and get up off of the bed. I go over to the window and look out. I see an array of lights: there are the big searchlights from the gatehouse and the towers along the walls. Their beams are wide and flowing as they swoop and trail along the length of the walls.

Below, there are a few lights on the bottom floor of the castle itself: the execution pyre that is still burning. And, of course, my old friend the moon – hanging in its fullness – is glowing far above the earth. Beyond that, only the shapes of the hills, like mightily shoulders, are shrugging towards me. *We must be a long way from the nearest city*, I think. However, it could be that, just over those hills, there is a town a couple of miles away. I could run there.

*Will they stop me? Did they have orders to prevent me leaving?*

I could out-run the humans anyway. I could run from this place and its violence and its fucked-up people. And then what? Start killing once more? No, like it or not, I am one of them. I am one of these blood thirsty creatures. It is a depressing thought, and one that weighs heavily on my shoulders as I walk back to the bed and sit on the edge of it. Then I lift my legs onto it, curling into a ball with my arms around my knees. I hold them tight to my chest and close my eyes, hoping against all expectation that sleep will come and take me from this place, this life, if only for a few hours. But, of course, it doesn't. I lie awake waiting for the dawn of another day – wondering what new horrors tomorrow will bring.

# The Abomination

# Chapter 1

# Sarah Sooth

*All of a sudden, awareness's bright light flicks on inside my head.*

And I know I am being watched. Alarm bells are going off in my head. My eyes shoot open wide. Quick as a cat, my neck snaps around and my spine curls up off the bed, my eyes seeking the sources of the intrusion.

Framed in the window, I see a strange, wild figure, silhouetted in moonlight behind me, bright against the grey visibility of the room. The figure moves, dashing from the window, travelling fast and disappearing for a second, before reappearing at the end of my bed: perching on the footboard, balancing perfectly – like a bird of prey.

Moonlight softly touches the side of the form at the end of the bed, illuminating the figure in the half light. The deathly pale skin of the face and the white silk night gown and long moon-lit silver hair gives a ghost-like quality to the visitation.

"Er...hello?" I venture.

I draw a sharp breath and start to retreat by shuffling up towards the headboard. I do not get very far. She leaps and lands on my chest.

"Oooph!"

I find myself staring into two black unblinking eyes. There is something mournful about them. I feel a wave of sadness rise inside of me. I blink. I can feel her two small hands on my chest, a bony knee to either side, but the pressure is light; she seems weigh nothing at all. Her long thin hair hangs down in front of her shoulders in long clumps. Intelligent eyes burn into me as if drilling into my very soul. The high intensity is that of the sun's rays through a magnifying glass, with me as the ant about to combust.

I know full well who it is. Her eyes tell me that. But what does she want? Does she mean me harm? Is she dangerous? I am being stupid. Everyone here in the castle is dangerous. We are, if nothing else, all monsters here. The thing with monsters though, is you know where you stand with them; they will always go for you, sooner or later. It is their nature.

Several seconds pass, with neither of us speaking. We just stare at each other. I wait for her to attack or at least say something. The persistent gaze of her eyes makes me feel uncomfortable. I want to look away, to the side, but I do not dare. When she finally speaks it is with one of the softest voices I have ever heard:

"Don't be frightened... My name is Sarah."

"Oh. Hello Sarah?" I say, my heart beating fast.

"I am John."

"I know."

Then there is silence once more. What does she want with me? I try to think of a tactful way of asking. But I have nothing.

She tilts her head to one side as if listening.

"No, no…no. I am going to tell him. Yes, alright!" she says, sounding annoyed, as if she is talking to someone else. It is my turn to frown. There is no one else in the room. All I can hear is the wind blowing outside, a heart beating in the distance and then a muffled scream, coming from somewhere inside the Château. I conclude that she has to be talking to herself and, more worryingly, getting answers. Then her gaze falls back upon me, forcing my thoughts to halt mid-sentence. I wait and realise that I am holding my breath. Then, she begins to speak again:

"Seeing the future is like remembering the past, only back-to-front rememberings. That is how it is!" she says, tapping my chest with an index finger.

"They come to me…um sort of like ripples…Hmm, yes that's it… And sometimes splashes," she says. She smiles.

"Oh?" I say, wondering where this is going.

"Yes. And it is full of you. You're going to end it. All of it. Everything will end with you. And maybe start anew! Big splash!" she adds.

"Me? I am a nobody. Are you sure you have the right room?" I say, almost laughing at the idea.

"They say nobody can do these things, but I know – yes I do – that if you are nobody then you must be him… ha-ha!" she smiles, eyes wild and full of excitement.

"Oh...?" I say, a frown pulling down my forehead.

"It is a joke!" She says slapping her hands down on my ribcage, "Well... almost. My timing is off! It always is."

A strange look comes over her face. She looks for a second as if she will burst into tears.

"It is a good one. I am just slow off the mark," I say.

"You are kind." She responds.

"I try."

"The future is not one thing," she continues. "It is like a ball of string, not just one thread, but lots; all pulling in different directions, like wiggly worms," she says, wiggling her finger to demonstrate. "So many worms, so many possibilities, it is hard to keep it all straight in my head."

She looks down for a few seconds and then directly at me once more. I try not to flinch under her gaze.

"Oh yes... Where was I?" she says. "Lots to tell." She creases her forehead then scratches the side of her nose.

"Oh yes… Of course… You must leave this place the first chance you get! Go! Run! Go anywhere!"

"Why? I have only just got here," I reply carefully.

"Soon. They want you dead. Not yet. But they will try. You must not let them."

"Why? I haven't done anything wrong. Have I?"

"Does not matter. They will come for you. If they could see what I see, you would be dead already. But I not tell them that one! Big secret, that one. If I tell them, it will be bad. Bad for everyone. Not just you."

"But why turn me into..." I pause considering whether Sarah is one of those who hates being called a vampire. I decide not to chance it.

She is a strange young woman, I think, but there is something about her: a sort of naive honesty that makes me want to trust her. Besides she seems to want to save me, which has to count for something. No one has ever done that for me before. I am quite touched really. Sarah is quiet for a little while, then she says:

"Can I stay here with you?"

"Yes, I guess" I say, slightly taken aback.

Then without a further word, Sarah jumps off me and curls up at my side.

"Lift up!" I say. She raises her head. I then put the second pillow underneath her head and she rests upon it.

"The future is such a lonely place," she sighs.

I take hold of the bed-covers and pull them up over her, up to her shoulders.

She puts her thumb in her mouth and starts to suck on it.

I pat her shoulder. She smiles. I rest my head back down on my pillow. I am at a loss on how to comfort this strange person.

*The future?*

My memory flashes up an image of Oliver – a human torch. I can almost feel my skin burning as I think of it, each and every nerve ending being razed to ash, only to regenerate once more – an eternity of screaming agony.

They are going to kill me. Just like that computer game where every time something kills you, you just disappear: "brup", then reappear as if nothing has happened. Being a vampire, you get infinite lives until you hit something that kills you over and over:

"Brupbrupbrubbrubbrub..."

In the end there is no other way to stop this eternal death other than to pull out the power plug from the computer and then start all over. Only in real life you don't get to do that. In this poisoned life, you just get to die over and over – without an end.

"Brupbrupbrubbrubbrub..."

I wrap my arms around my legs and stare through the open window into the moonlight-drenched landscape, towards the fortified wall that surrounds the hill, then to the smaller surrounding hills beyond the wall. I can hear the sea crashing against the rocks. I can hear Sarah's heart beating loudly and slowly at my side. Her breathing is soft and long. It has a relaxing quality to it. *Asleep. Vampires can sleep. So why can't I?*

I look down at the sleeping figure, her forehead creased and her thumb still in her mouth. I listen the rhythm of her heart and the slow steady sound of her exhalations. The sound contrasts with the sound of waves crashing in the distance.

# Chapter 2

# Bloody Breakfast

*At about six o'clock, Sarah curls out of bed and stretches.*

She makes her way to the chest of drawers and pulls out paper, ink and a fountain pen. Then, conscious of being watched, she whirls around facing me. She frantically waves a hand in front of her face.

"You not supposed to be awake! she says.

"I don't sleep," I reply.

"But you must!" she protests, "Dreams are really important!"

"Where are you going?"

"I... I have duties," she says, her head bowing and her shoulders sinking.

"Something I said?"

"Oh no, you have been kind."

"Will I see you again?"

"Oh yes," she says brightly. "Soon. Promise."

With that, Sarah runs towards the window and disappears out of it. For a second I think we can turn into bats after all. But as I rise from the bed, I see her land on the lawn below and then sprint around the side of the building, out of sight.

*What do I do now?* They are going to kill me, fine, but what do I do in the mean time? Twiddle my thumbs? Why has Henry brought me here anyway? Why has he turned me into one of their kind if they are only going to kill me? It makes no sense. Sarah said they didn't know they wanted me dead yet. Do I believe that? What am I meant to do in the meantime? *What do these Wonder-kind want from me?*

The answer to one of these questions comes with a knock at the door. Without waiting for a reply, the giant figure of Gunnar appears in the doorway.

"Mr Hrot wants to see you now!" he rumbles.

"O…ok," I start.

"Come," he beckons with a huge hand.

He leads me back down the corridor and downstairs and I get a feeling of Deja-vu. I feel like a dog following its master. *Well at least he isn't carrying me this time!*

"Here, some of the red stuff," Henry says. He doesn't mean wine. He pushes a silver goblet towards me, as I enter a large room full of chairs and tables laid with eating paraphernalia. He is sitting alone in the empty room in a comfortable leather-backed chair at the table nearest the door. He pours himself a top-up from the same silver jug. I sit beside him at the table.

"Hair of the dog," he says, raising his goblet.

"Only three fatalities: two women and one man. Quite a low compared to festivals of previous years," he says. "Got to keep the livestock numbers up, you know. Pity though. In the old days, we knew how to party… I remember one year… But never mind that. Drink up!"

I down the drink in one go.

"They just get a little too carried away. You should know all about that!" He laughs and nudges me with an elbow. It is bony, despite the fact he is not a thin man. He pours me another drink.

"But they deserved it," I say, thinking of Danny and James, though the excuse sounds hollow even to me.

"What for? A few punches and a couple of bad words?" He says.

"Aw! Poor John. Didn't the nasty bullies hurt your sensitive feelings?" he mocks.

"For making my life a living hell for years, that is why. They got off lightly," I retort acidly. Anger flares up in my chest, undiluted but unfocused. I am not used to it – feeling this way. It is like being drunk on the red stuff.

"Well, anyway, they're only humans. Plenty more where they came from," Henry laughs, putting his own goblet to his lips and pouring an elegant sip into his mouth.

"Only human, yeah." I am starting to think of them in that way. How long will it be before I am as just like everyone else here? I have already started to refer to them as 'humans', as if we are not of the same species, which I suppose we aren't, not really. But it is unnerving to think in those terms.

It is becoming easy just to see them as inferior creatures, lacking worth outside of cheap labour and food. How long will it be before I start to call them 'cattle' rather than human? I feel these things, but I hate it: I hated what I am becoming. As I sit here drinking human blood. I drain my goblet.

"Anyway," Henry says. "It's time to start your training."

"What training?"

"You didn't think I brought you here to sit on your backside, did you? You have just signed up to the Unseeyn Hand. Welcome aboard my son."

# Chapter 3

# The Bonemann

*"The name is Bonemann."*

He looks as his name would suggest: like a tall skeleton covered in a thin film of skin. He looks like a corpse that has been left out in the sun for too long. His eyes bulge from the sockets of his bald skull shaped head. He is not a nice man. He is our instructor.

"And I own each and every one of you."

"This..." Bonemann says, holding up an unlikely looking gun, with an equally unlikely long barrel, "...is the D-gun, or as some call it the Dum-gun."

I recognise it instantly. It is the same gun that the vampires guarding the grand hall had on their belts and the same one that all of Château Blanc's security detail have about their person.

"Anyone know what its primary use is? Or, to put another way, what do we kill with it?" Bonemann says.

"Wonder-kind sir! Our kind sir!" Karl shouts, as if he is a soldier on parade. His barrel chest is all puffed out.

"That's right! I am glad someone in here is awake!" Bonemann sneers.

In a way, Bonemann is similar to my old maths teacher, Mr Brookes. But there is a real edge to Bonemann's voice and something in his eyes that tells you he is a whole universe worse than Mr Brookes. After all, the worst thing Mr Brookes will do is throw chalk at your head if he thinks you are not listening. Instead of chalk, Bonemann will simply put a bullet through your forehead. So I pay attention: rapt attention.

"The D-gun sends out a sub-atomic pulse that destabilises and knocks the neurons out of place at the molecular level. Or, in simpler terms: it causes total molecular collapse," Bonemann explains, with a particularly ghastly smile gashed across his face.

"Which means what, Karl?" Bonemann asks, as his head swings towards Karl.

"No resurrection, sir?" Karl says.

"Exactly," Bonemann replies, taking the gun by its handle.

"You turn it on here," Bonemann explains, pressing a button on the side of the gun.

"Congratulations! You have purchased the D-type mark six point five side arm, serial number 24454233..." the gun says in a dull metallic voice.

"We don't need to hear this," Bonemann says. He then toggles another button and the voice dies.

"You turn the safety off here." He points to button on the hilt and presses it.

"Warning! Danger!" the gun warns.

"The safety is now off. If you do not want to fire, please return gun to the safety setting. Gun is ready to fire! Gun is ready to fire!" The gun screeches.

"The sighting is automatic. You just point in the general direction. The face recognition software will do the rest. Obviously, it is not much use in a hostage situation, especially if the target is holding a gun or knife to the captive's neck, unless the hostage is expendable, of course." Bonemann smiles his ghastly smile and mimes pulling the trigger. A ripple of laugher spreads through the room.

"Then go ahead and shoot..." he says.

He raises the gun and fires it. It makes a buzzing sound. A jolt of light leaps from the end of the barrel of the D-Gun. The beam hits one of the three life-sized man shaped dummies at the other end of the combat room. The dummy explodes – blue and white sparks fountaining in the air. Then it is gone, almost completely, except for millions and millions tiny flecks of coloured dust floating gently down from the ceiling.

"This is not a toy. Never point it at another unless you intend to kill them. And you don't kill anyone without my say so! Got that?" Bonemann is shouting now.

"Yes sir!" everyone choruses

"But what about humans?" asks Darren, a tall thin, fair hair lad who is standing at the back.

"What about them?"

"Can we try out the gun on them?"

"No you bloody well can't!" Bonemann shouts. "And I will tell you for why! Its bloody waste! You can break a human by sneezing at them. You don't need a gun like this. Got that?"

"Yes sir," the class choruses.

"Anyway, you won't be using the D-gun until you have been through basic combat skills. The powers that be don't want any of you getting vaporised at this point in your training. Though, personally, looking at you, I have never seen such a sorry bunch of losers. I can't see the harm."

Bonemann walks with the gun towards a tall cabinet at the wall at the far end of the training room on the other side from the shooting range. The room itself is a long oblong shape with a window high up on the far wall. The glass cabinet is at the other end from the observation window. Bonemann types a number into a key pad by the side of the glass cabinet. It clicks open. I guess that it is probably not ordinary glass. He put the D-Gun inside. It sits on the top rung and there are five others below it and six on the other side: twelve in all, nearly enough for one each. He shuts the door with a click. Then I hear the sound of several locks sliding into position.

Bonemann turns his attention to the metal cabinet standing next to the glass one. He opens the door and takes out a small pistol: a Glock semi-automatic hand gun.

"D-Gun or not. Not all of you will survive this training. Looking at some of you ugly wretches, that is no bad thing!" he says, looking at us from left to right. Then with the gun in his hand, he looks up and, with lightning speed, aims the gun and fires.

"Aaagh!"

My chest explodes with pain. I look down at my hands, which automatically cup the wound. Blood is pouring through my fingers. My head feels light as my consciousness tries to run away from the pain: I feel like I am going to die.

# Chapter 4

# Heart Shot

*I stare down at my hands.*

The blood has already started to dry and crust on my fingers, staining them an ugly red. The wound has already sealed itself. I know the bullet will not kill me but, standing there with a hole in my chest, I have to wonder. It feels like I am going to die, even though I know I am not. I look at the Bonemann. There is a sparkle of enjoyment in his eyes. Though his face remains impassive, the gash of his mouth is a straight and level line, with the thin flesh of his lips pinched tight together.

The throbbing pain slowly starts to recede, as my insides draw back together. It is a strange feeling: like having mice inside of my chest all nibbling at the flesh. But the feeling fades and everything goes quickly back to normal, or rather nearly normal: a ghost of feeling remains as if my chest still has a gaping hole in it.

"Too slow!" Bonemann says.

"Sorry sir," I respond.

"If that was a human, the heart shot would have been enough to kill. The head shot is better." Bonemann turns away from me. Even faster this time, he spins the gun around and fires.

This time I move. I hurl myself out of the way of the projectile: a bullet aimed straight between my eyes. It seems to slow as it passes. It is slow enough to pluck out of the air: so slow that I wonder how I was caught out with the first shot.

"Hmmm, good!" Bonemann says, then instantly changes his aim towards a blonde-haired kid called Kevin who is standing on my left.

"Aaaagh!" Kevin screams. His head is thrown backwards, as the bullet hits him. He is falling to the floor. He lies sprawled on his back with a red oozing circle in the centre of his forehead. The back of his head has blown outwards and his hair is clotted with blood. On the floor are pieces of bone and a whitish liquid. He looks as dead as a doornail.

"Ah!" says Bonemann. "Those of you who have not seen a full resurrection before, here is your chance! Gather around!"

We gather around Kevin's body. The wound seems to melt and the bone turns fluid. All the red and white matter seems to river, to flow towards the blown-out back of the skull, as if sucked back inside. The bone starts to move under Kevin's head. The hole in his forehead puckers. The surrounding skin is red and alive. As the hole gurgles, it reminds me of a plug-hole. I see the bullet plop out of the hole and fall from Kevin's forehead onto the ground with a clink. It rolls along the floor, leaving a thin red trail, to settle beside one of Lucy's boots. She frowns, then kicks the bullet away with the side of her boot.

Almost as soon as body has spat the bullet out from itself, the wound seals over. Kevin's whole body judders several times, before he shudders and then jerks up into a sitting position. He blinks his eyes and looks wildly around the room. His eyes are full of tears.

"Whaaa... Happp...?"

"Give it a few moments..."

"What happened?"

To Kevin's further confusion, everyone in the class starts to applaud him. Well almost everyone. I remain impassive and Karl just looks on indifferently. He's seen it all before.

"Full resurrection causes disorientation for up to ten minutes," Bonemann says in a matter-of-fact way.

"Enough time to be captured..." Bonemann continues.

"By humans?" Karl sounds appalled.

"More likely a rival kingdom. But they have the D-gun the same as us. So, chances are, you will already be dead – no resurrection."

To make his point, Bonemann walks over to the remains of the dummy he has zapped. He picks up a handful of the white dust and blows it into the air.

"Speed and agility are everything. You have to get in with a kill shot first or you are dust," he says.

"But won't we be fighting humans as well?" asks Lucy, a tall girl with long blonde hair, bound in a ponytail, and perfect white skin. Her mouth seems to be set, always in an impassive straight line. She barely breaks the line of her lips to get her words out.

"Humans, ah! For the most part we have them on a short leash," Bonemann says.

"Don't they get hacked off with that? Don't they ever want to... I don't know.... fight for freedom or rebel?" Another asks.

"What, them? The cattle? Nah. Not in a million years." Bonemann says. "No, if we're ever going into battle again, it will be against one of the twelve kingdoms or one of the breakaway outlaw groups."

"But I thought the rule of the twelve has banned such conflicts?" interjects another girl. She is tall and has black hair. I don't know her name. She reads a lot. That is all I know about her.

"True... Good point," Bonemann responds. "For now, anyway. But times change, and we have to be ready for that change. We all live for a very long time, remember. The only thing does not change is that there is always some bastard ready to glom what's yours."

I get the feeling, listening to Bonemann, that he would welcome a change in the status quo and that he would embrace it with all his black little heart – as if he is aching for the bloodshed. You can hear it in the way his voice rises, and the way his mouth turns up into a gruesome excuse for a smile, which divides the two halves of his head like two halves of an Easter egg.

# Chapter 5

# Underground Complex

*There is more underground than above.*

The combat room, or training room as it is also known, is located a couple of levels below the ground floor of the main part of the castle. As above, so below, the world down here is a rabbit warren of corridors and rooms. They call it the Complex. It bores down deep through the volcanic rock creating twelve levels: all linked by five different elevators.

To complicate matters more, when it comes to getting around the underground labyrinth, different elevators descend to different depths. Two of them descend the top five levels, the other two descend deeply, terminating at level ten. The fifth, marked with a red strip over the door, goes the deepest. That one, you need a special key to make the lift work. And, those who I have spoken to have either said they have never been down that lift or seem unwilling to say what is down there. They only say that it is the deepest and ask "Why would you want to go down there anyway?"

It is clear from all the diagrams of the underground complex that the red shaft goes deepest. But it is unlabelled, unlike the rest of the diagram that helpfully lists the rooms on each level according to colour and function. Each level is marked with a colour that corresponds with little plastic squares that are set upon the walls.

Despite the helpful colour-coded maps on each level, I get lost on more than one occasion. It is easily done. After all, this is a huge place and everywhere looks the same. The endless white corridors are all similar.

I am looking for the training room. I come out on the wrong level. I smell humans. *Strange? I thought humans weren't allowed down here.*

I can hear them, lots of them, and their beating heart – like the hearts of frightened rabbits. I am drawn along the corridor towards the sound. I come to a glass door. Two big security guards stand on either side. Their arms are folded, leaning against the wall. One of them shakes his head at me. I look through the window. The room is full of people. They are yammering on phones or waving pieces of paper in the air. They all appear in an extreme state of excitement. I can feel my mouth wetting up already.

"Don't even think about it," the guard who had shaken his head says. He draws back his overcoat to reveal a holstered D-gun. He rests his hand on the hilt in warning.

"What is this? What is in there?" I ask.

"None of your business sunshine," the guard replies.

I have to shake my head in wonder, with all the vampires wandering around these corridors, it is something of a dangerous, if not lethal, sport. *Suppose that must be what the guards are here for: to keep them in the room and to keep any passing vampire who might be peckish out.*

The only computer they have at my school is a BBC computer. It is a big long yellow keyboard plugged into a monitor. The computers behind the screen are all something called Apple Macs: clunky boxes with big bulky screens on top. There must be about thirty people in the room. They are all wearing long sleeve shirts with colourful trouser braces and wearing stressed and panicked faces. The smell of sweat and stress hormones is overwhelming, not to mention enticing: all those stressed little humans running around. It is hard to resist, until that is, the guard starts to lift the D-gun from its holster. I put both hands out in front of me in supplication.

"Alright," I say, "I am going."

"And don't come back!" The guard says, while the other laughs.

"Don't be like that!" The other guard says.

"Put it away," he adds.

The first guard returns the gun to its holster, frowning.

"He is just curious. Aren't you, boy?" the guard continues

"I…I suppose. What's in there?" I ask.

"You know what's in there."

"But why?"

"Ha! If I told you that, I'd have to kill you!" the guard laughs. The other guard smiles for the first time.

"You shouldn't be talking to him. We have a job to do," the guard who had threatened me with the gun says.

"Ah, he's only young," the other guard says, turning to face his co-worker.

"How do you know? Looks aren't everything. He could be hundreds of years old."

"Nah, he's Henry's boy. I saw him arrive."

"Isn't that right?" he indicates, looking at me.

"Yes," I say. I suppose I am. He has changed me over, so did that make him a sort of father figure? I don't know. I don't like the sound of it. It does, it seems, carry some weight with the less friendly of the two guards.

"Henry's boy. Oh, sorry mate, didn't know," he apologises.

"It's ok," I say out of automatic politeness.

"Don't take any notice of him. He is a miserable old sod. I am Jack by the way and this is my esteemed colleague. He's called Joe."

"How old are you then, kid? Twelve?"

"John," I reply, "I am sixteen."

"Aw!"

Aw? I thought. Not that. Anything but that! *I am not cute!* I think indignantly.

"Come on, I will show you around, if you promise not to eat anyone," Jack laughs.

"Ok," I agree.

Jack types in a number series into a keypad on the wall and the door slides open. I follow him through the door, into the room of temptation.

He introduces me to a human called Lucian, who offers me his hand, a limp thing, which I shake. Lucian is the first human who does nothing for me. I do not want to drink from him. He leaves me cold in every way. His skin is cold and clammy – pale grey in colour, and his eyes are two stagnant pools, watery but lifeless. His mouth is a humourless line that twitches from time to time. And his voice is as grey and monotone as his appearance. Nothing he says sticks: all of it, words, sentences and meanings, just disappear somewhere between his mouth and my ears.

But Lucian doesn't know fear; he is the only person in the room who does not eye me with fear. Evidently, he thinks he is too important for anything bad to happen to him.

"Boring guy!" Jack says after Lucien is out of earshot, "All that stuff – stocks and shares, bores the pants off of me. But it is important to the bigwigs upstairs."

"Anyway, this is more interesting," he adds.

I follow jack through another door. It leads into a room full of sombre-looking men and woman working at desks. The walls are covered in square TV monitors, hundreds of them, all the same size. The humans operate small controls built into their desks, which switch the TV channels on the screens in front of them. There are about twenty people in all. Some of them are speaking on the telephone in several different languages.

"Here we monitor the TV stations all of over the world," Jack says.

"Oh?" I say.

"Two reasons: to see how well we are doing, and to identify problems as and when they arise," he says.

"What do you do if you if problem comes up?" I say.

"We use the people we have in place," Jack replies. "If not, we send a team in to eliminate the problem."

"The Unseeyn Hand?"

"Ah yes, dead on. You are Hrot's boy, alright!" Jack exclaims, leading me towards a large doorway.

"And this is where what Mr Hrot calls 'the great game' is played out," Jack tells me, rubbing his big chin.

This is a larger room than the previous two. It resembles the call centre on the America Express TV Advert. Ranks of humans are all sat at desks, wearing bulky looking headsets. They sit in front of computer terminals, which are big and bulky. All the desks face towards the wall at the front, where there is a map of the world. It takes up nearly all of the wall. There are a number of brightly coloured lights clustered around all the major cities. The bigger the city, the more lights it has. They are all different colours.

"Red is for a high-level government agent, green is for military, blue is for police and so on," Jack tells me.

Lucian hurries in behind us. He goes up to one of the desks. A wide-faced woman behind it looks up at him.

"What is it?" he snaps, not bothering to disguise his annoyance.

"743. There's a problem. He has not been seen for two weeks."

"Who's the handler?"

"Hoffman, H. R."

"Give him a call. Get him to sort it out."

"Ok."

The woman presses a button on the desk and starts to talk rapidly on the phone. Lucian hurries back out of the door. He seems to be in charge here, or at least of the humans. I cannot see a vampire taking orders from him.

"Excuse me sir... A thousand apologies for disturbing you," she says into the microphone of her headset. Nervous isn't the word. Her voice is quaking.

"Yes sir."

"Sorry Sir."

"We have a problem. Yes, sir, 743 sir..."

Looking at it all, the coloured dots on the map, I begin to get a sense of what Henry had told me about the Wonder-kind running everything.

"The people? What have they to do with it? Democracy, government, it's all an illusion, a simple conjuring trick, to hide how the world works. People believe it because they want to. The alternative is too terrible for those too weak-willed sheep to contemplate," he had told me.

I hadn't believed him, not really, but there it is directly in front of me. The ground beneath my feet feels like it is no longer there, as I realise that everything I have ever believed about the world really is a lie.

"They're all human?" I ask.

"Mostly."

"The handlers and kill operatives are always the Unseeyn – Wonder-kind People we can trust."

"Now I see what Henry means. We do have fingers in every pie."

"Well he should know, he's the King's spy master," Jack says, as if I already know this.

"It's all in these rooms. We influence everything from the market to culture to politics worldwide. Not just here of course," he tells me.

"All of the other twelve kingdoms have rooms just like this. They operate to their own agenda of course, but broadly we are all on the same page. We are the ghost in the machine, everywhere and nowhere: The Unseeyn Hand that moves the world. That is how power really works," he explains.

"Oh well, that is the end of the tour" Jack says. "Mention me to Henry if you get a chance."

"Jack Smith. Tell him I was helpful," he says. This huge vampire who literally looks down at me, sounds almost pleading. I peer up at the mountain of a man and nod.

"Ok, I will," I say.

# Chapter 7

# The Watchtower

*I am drained and thinking dark thoughts.*

On returning to my room after another skull-wrenchingly awful day in the training room. I have no idea how I am going to hack it: day after day with the Bonemann. The fairest description of the man includes the word psychopath. I lean heavily on the door. Once inside of the room, I am surprised to see a folded piece of paper lying on the bed. I walk over, pick it up and read:

*8.00pm?*

There is a drawing of the watchtower, the connecting bridge and some very choppy-looking waves under the bridge. There is an arrow over the tower. Underneath that, it is signed with a large thick and highly patterned: S. The writer of the note has drawn the S to look like some sort of serpent, with a mouth and fangs at the top end of the letter and a pair of wings on the back. What does that make it? A dragon? Or a winged serpent? Either way, it has been drawn very skilfully with a steady hand.

*Sarah?* Has to be. I cannot think of anyone else.

The watchtower: I saw it the day I first arrived with Henry. I thought at the time that it would make an interesting place to visit. But it has completely slipped my mind. Not surprising really, all things considered.

I climb the narrow twist of steps from the fourth floor to the top floor of the castle. I take another set of circular steps and the passage is even narrower. I stoop all the way up the grey stone steps and it comes out on the roof on the main part of the Château. I walk over the roof towards its battlements. I stand on the edge of the fortification, looking down towards my destination – the watchtower.

The castle is built not only on top, but also out of the rock of what had once been an active volcano: thousands of years ago, perhaps, maybe millions. The bridge is made up what had been part of the coastline, carved out of the rock. It stretches out, over the sea, to the solitary watchtower. The tower itself is built out of a lump of rock that protrudes out of the rough sea. It is a circular structure, partly carved out of the rock and partly built of huge stone blocks.

I drop to the roof below, crossing it quickly and then dropping down another level. At the end of the roof is a gateway, guarded only by wrought iron gate. I open it and start across the bridge.

The gangway is a tight fit. It seems too thin a pathway to walk across. The stone walls only come up to waist height. The wind is racing over the bridge, making an eerie high-pitched whistling noise that contrasts with the more sonorous sound of the crashing of the waves below. It blows at my hair, pulls at my clothes and stings my skin numb with its ice-cold touch. I take a deep breath and then resume walking across the narrow bridge towards the tower.

*I am unafraid*, I tell myself.

The large stone blocks that make up the tower are worn smooth by the constant assault of the rain and wind that whips around the structure. Halfway across, I look down over the side of the bridge. Big mistake. The roaring waves leap up and come rushing up to meet me. The water looks deep and unwelcoming as its waves smash against the rocks. I sway uncertainly and a gust of wind catches me off-guard. I think I will certainly fall, but grab the side of the bridge to steady myself. I inhale: a breath that the wind tries to rip from my lungs. I close my lips tight.

I quickly cross the remaining half of the bridge, very glad to reach the archway on the other side.

"Pathetic," I say to myself. There is very little that could kill me, but I am still afraid of everything.

There is no door; both the entrance and the windows in the tower are open to the elements. The circular walls at least afford some protection from the wind, though it still finds its way inside the tower to make an eerie howling sound that echoes throughout it. I climb the stone steps that circle around the interior of the watchtower, up to the viewing platform at the top.

The platform is a square area of stone floor with a roof a stone pillar at each of its four corners. There is a waist-high wall that runs around the outside, connecting with the pillars. Above the wall and between the pillars unobstructed by any physical barrier, the blue stormy surface of the sea is rushing into my senses and the wind is blasting through the small space. It flattens my face as it pummels into me like a powerful hand.

I look around with watering eyes; the eyeballs themselves are blown dry by the wind. *No sign of Sarah? Where is she?* I look at my digital watch:

20:11.

I am late. This is the right place. I am sure of it. Maybe she has come and gone? Perhaps she waited for ten minutes and decided I would not be coming.

*Maybe something has happened to her?*

It is more than possible, in this place, with all its horrors. Just as the sharp blade of emotion finds my gut and begins to twist, I hear a voice:

"Up here!" it calls.

"Where is here?" I shout, looking around.

"The roof!" Sarah's upside-down face replies.

As I look at her head, it retreats back up on to the roof and the cool water of relief pours over me. My chest deflates back to its normal position. I hook my arm around the nearest pillar and with my other I pull my body out of the observation room. I look up. Sarah's small face is looking down at me. Her hair blows in long streaks. She looks calm – unbothered as the wind tears at her.

"Come on!" she shouts,

"I am not sure..." I begin.

"Come on!"

"Ok" I say, and hoist my body onto the stone roof. It has a slight angle to it. Its surface is rough and uneven. There are patches of moss growing in lines along the grooves and cracks in its surface. Hesitantly, I crawl over towards Sarah. She is sitting in the middle of the roof, cross legged.

"Look," she says pointing towards the horizon, "It is beautiful, is it not?"

I plonk myself down next to her and look.

The sea is a wild deep blue tumultuous expanse, a continuous bulging blanket of huge waves that power inwards toward the land. It reaches out towards the horizon and joins seamlessly into an equally intense blue, where the sky meets the water. It is impossible to tell where the sky ends and the sea begins: they fit together perfectly. The wind howls around the tower and the sea roars. I can taste the salt in my mouth, smell it too. I breathe in the fresh sea air. Everything is sharp and in focus, crystal clear and bracing.

I cast an eye towards the head-land, where a noisy bunch of seagulls are diving and rising above the white chalk cliffs that curve around the edge of the land towards the other side of the bay. They are massive, sheer and bright white in what remains of the day's sun: stretching around the headland and beyond, wrapping the coastline white.

It is easy to forget that there is another world outside the castle, with all its horror, where life is so tense and unremitting and everything seems a matter of life and death (or, rather, pain or the avoidance of it). I have just become caught up in the world within these walls. I have forgotten, almost, that there is anything else outside of the castle walls.

"Yes," I breathe. "It is."

"I thought you would," she says. "That's why I asked you."

"Pleased you did."

There is a lot I want to ask. But in this moment, not one of those things matter a damn. I am happy to just sit with Sarah and let the experience of this raw energy and beauty just wash over me, forsaking all else.

My English teacher, Miss Pander, used to try to get us interested in poetry. It left me cold. But, sitting here, I start to think that there might be something to it, the Romanic poets anyway. But at the same time that I start to glimpse what they are on about, I realise how inadequate they are. Their words seem distant and dry compared to this raw and keen experience that threatens to drag my conscious mind out through my senses, ripping it apart in its very act, to scatter its fragmented parts all over this place of fearful beauty and scatter it to the winds.

I don't know how long we have been sitting here, conscious of each other, but at the same time lost in the landscape. We don't say anything for the longest time. Then suddenly Sarah speaks. Her voice is so soft that I don't know how it makes its way through the roar of the waves to my ears.

"You really don't mind being here with me, do you?" she says.

"No of course not. Why should I?"

"You know what they think of me. I am an abomination. That's what they call me," she says.

Sarah's eyes are downcast. I know what she means. I have heard the needlessly cruel whispers that abound around the Château about her. Even before hearing these things, I have had the impression and picked it unconsciously that Sarah is not a person who it is ok to hang around with. She is touched with social exclusion – a scapegoat that can never be let back into the fold of the good vampiric sheep. The very act of sitting and talking to her: the stigma could rub off on me. I couldn't give a fuck about that. The sheep can go screw themselves. Being a monster changes you, for the worst mostly, but not always.

When Henry sees me talking to Sarah on the ground floor by the stairs and approaches. Sarah lowers her head and hurries off.

"I'd stay away from that abomination," he says.

"Sarah?"

"If you know what is good for you, you'll have nothing to do with… that poor wretched creature."

*If I knew what was good for me I wouldn't be here.* But why all the hate for this vampire? In my book, their distain only serves as a recommendation in my eyes. After all the horror I have seen, there is nothing left, no matter how base or depraved, that would surprise me. But, still, I wonder what has she done that was so terrible? Is she a mass murderer? Very possibly but in this place, we are all mass murderers. No, it has to be something else. Has she killed a bus-load of children? That thought bothers me. Do people get to a certain age and it is then ok to kill them? After all, Danny and James were only sixteen when I ended their lives. But no, I just can't see it. Not Sarah.

"I have heard. I see nothing to justify that name." It is outrageous and makes me angry each time I hear it.

"Talk about hypocrisy. We have all done terrible things and we carry on doing them. What makes you so terrible compared to the rest of us?" I ask.

"I did something, a long time ago," Sarah replies. Her eyes look up briefly, flashing darkly.

"I did something bad..." she continues. "...to get the gift. You know?"

"The gift has to be saved. To keep it in the blood. The gift of prophesy," she goes on.

"What did you do?"

"Drank from another of our kind. The gift lives in the blood. It has to be drunk before she dies or else all is lost. All gone..." Her voice is shaking now. She looks very small all of a sudden.

"And that is bad, is it?" I ask.

"Oh, yes, for our kind it is."

"Well makes no difference to me."

"Good. But you must never tell."

"Oh."

"You must never say, even that I told you. Never; you understand!"

"Ok."

"Good," she says. Then we fall into silence once more. I look at Sarah's face a couple of times. If she knows that I am looking she does not let on. She just carries on looking out at the sea. Then I break in:

"What is the rule of the twelve?"

"That is easy," she says, as she brushes a strand of hair from her eyes. Outside, I notice that she does not look as pale. She has a red flush to her cheeks.

"The world is divided into twelve kingdoms or sectors, more or less. Each is run by a King, Queen or Emperor; whatever they prefer to call themselves."

"And they rule our kind?"

"And the humans, of course."

"And they don't know?"

"No."

"How can they not know?"

Sarah shrugs: "Perhaps they choose not to?"

"What about us then... our kind, the Wonder-kind, or whatever!" I ask.

"Well, I think Theo rules about half of us in this sector. It could be more now. I... I don't know. But not everyone. That I am sure of."

There is more silence. Then, for no particular reason I ask:

"How old are you?"

"How old do you think?" She turns her head, smiling:

"Don't know: sixteen, seventeen, about the same as me."

"Kind, but no. I am old enough to be your great-great-great granny!" she says.

"You have been here all that time?"

"Oh, most of it. It is a long time to spend in a place you hate."

"So why are you here, if you hate it so much? Why not leave?" I ask.

"Because if I do, they will tell everyone what I did. Then they will kill me. Here, I am tolerated because I am useful to the king. But it is only his word that stops them turning on me. I have nowhere to go, except here." She says, as her eyes grow wet. Her body starts to convulse and tears rush down her cheeks. She makes no attempt to cover her face or turn away. She just lets them flood down her face.

I don't really know what to do. It lasts all of a second and a half. Of course, I understand. A deluge of emotions floods my brain, vaster and stormier than the sea out here. It is as if I am the watchtower being slashed by savage waves of steel. I have no foundations or schema to deal with any of it. I will snap off at the base and fall into the unbearable intensity of everything in me that is denied and my depthless compassion for this woman who has endured so much that I can only begin to imagine what it is like for her.

I put an arm around Sarah's small folded-in shoulders. The touch itself is surplus to requirements, I know; our minds have already encountered each other and neither of us has run away in terror. We are what we are and nothing more. But it completes the intimacy of the moment. Sarah places her cheek to my shoulder in response. Her body starts to shudder and my tee-shirt gets wet from her tears.

"I don't care what you have done. I will never lift a finger against you," I promise. This seems a strange thing to say. But it seems to work. Her body stills and she looks up. Her face is tear-marked but smiling, and her eyes are alight with enthusiasm once more.

She leaps to her feet and laughs, pulling me up, saying: "Let's jump in!"

"But I can't swim!" I protest. Too late. She pulls me to the edge, to the point of no return.

Pulling me over the edge... falling.

"Does not matter!" she says, as we both plummet towards the hostile-looking waves.

"We cannot die... We cannot die... We cannot be killed..." I repeat in my mind all the way down.

Sure, just like a computer game:

"Brupbrupbrubbrubbrub..."

And imagine myself hitting the water and dying over and over: forever.

There is no more time for thinking because we then hit the water: hard. It feels like smashing through a wall of ice. Then, helplessly, I fall like a stone toward the bottom.

# Chapter 8

# The Cave

*It is easy not to breathe.*

My body seems to know what it has to do. I want to – but don't. I want to breath in the seawater. Even though it will not kill me, it will not be pleasant. I would cough and splutter on the water, the same as any human. I don't know this for certain. It is not an experiment I am keen to try out.

I stand up. The strands of the seaweed curl around my ankles, flowing with the current. I am always forgetting I am a lot stronger now. I stand within the current, able to resist its pull easily. I look up towards the surface and the light from above seems to bend and shimmer blue within the water, giving no indication of its stormy surface.

*Well this is different!*

I see Sarah swim down towards me, her cheeks puffed out and her body pushing itself through the water using an S shaped movement that begins at her head and ends at her toes. She looks like a little mermaid or some kind of fairy tale water spirit. She comes close, putting a hand on my shoulder, and points in the direction she wants me to go in. I follow her: me walking along the sea bed and her swimming around my head like a little fish.

We come upon a ruin. By the size of it, it could be a whole village or a town, lying down here beneath the waves. Much of it has crumbled down and lies on the sea floor covered in a blanket of seaweed. What is left is the basic structure – a 'krypton factor' matrix: the skeletons of the buildings. They stand in long rows of decaying wooden beams that join the remainders of stone pillars and walls, stretching overhead as I pass underneath. They are covered in barnacles, seaweed and other underwater plants, concealing the stone surface with colourful life: feather-like tentacles and greenery, gently waving to the movement of the water.

We follow what was probably once a road, down into a gully in the seabed. Overhead, the Sea life encrusted arches make it look as if it is some kind of underwater garden. If Neptune or a bunch of mermaids (or mermen) popped into view, I would not be too surprised. After all, I am a vampire. Who knows what else is out there?

*Nothing good... probably.*

Suddenly, Sarah darts out in front of me and swims down towards the seabed. I speed up to follow, interested to see what she has found. She is prising something up from the sea floor. It is small, round and rough at the edges. Its surface is all covered in a green crusty layer. She rubs at the object. It reveals a dull gold colour. It is a gold coin. She hands it to me, enfolding it in my hand and curling my fingers around the coin with her own.

For me? I mime, pointing at my chest.

Sarah's head gives a vigorous nod, smiling at me. I smile back and, nodding my thanks, I put the coin in my back trouser pocket.

We follow the gully. It leads back towards the edge of the cliff. Sarah points upwards at the cliff face. I climb up. Sarah swims upwards. I break the surface of the water.

The sun is going down. The cliff looks foreboding in near monochrome. I look around for Sarah. She appears from behind a large rock within a cave inside of the cliff face.

"In here!" she says, waving.

The sea crashes over the rocks at the entrance to the cave and the roar of the water echoes as it gushes up through the channel between them, running up the centre, towards the back of the cave. Soaking wet, I haul myself out of the water and stand on a large flat slab of rock. The narrow channel through the stone runs up its centre and divides the cave into two halves. A larger wave hits the rocks at the mouth of the cave and spectacularly explodes white foam and sea water into the air, spraying us with the salty water.

"We are under the castle," Sarah says. "You can get through up there." She points to a narrow passageway towards the back of the cave.

"Yeah?"

"Yes, if you need to get away quickly, then this is the way to come. Or one of them anyway," she adds. A small smile breaks across her face.

"You're still trying to get rid of me then?" I say, using a jokey tone of voice. I mean nothing by it or, at least, that is the intention. I do not expect Sarah's reaction. Her eyes widen to huge globes and then she bursts into tears. Big teardrops stream down her cheeks, pushing through the beads of seawater on her still-wet face. My stomach falls through the hard rock floor. I didn't mean to make her cry. I feel like a piece of crap.

Sarah makes no attempt to hide her tears. As if she doesn't see them as weakness, only part of the body – to express certain feeling – no different from a smile or grimace in that respect. They are an outlet of sadness and nothing more. Sarah is always honest in expressing the full range of emotions that we all have, though I am certain she has a few more than anyone else does.

"No, I don't want you to go! I just don't want you to die!" she shouts.

I come forward.

"I am sorry!" I say. "I was only joking – bad joke!"

"You are warm. Not like the others. I will miss you."

"Maybe I will stay. They might not want me dead. I mean what is it to them?"

"They will, as soon as things line up. Big trouble then."

"What things?" I ask

"Don't know exactly. Could be stars, or could be something down to you," she says, then bites her lip. "Who knows with this sort of thing?"

I am at loss for anything to say.

"This way," she says a little too abruptly and then leads me to the back of the cave. We duck in to get through the narrow rock passageway. It is easy to slip though the space, as she is small and I have very little meat on my bones. I have to duck all the way down the tube of rock. The passageway goes on for a quite a length, sloping gently upwards until it comes out in the corner of what looks like a store-room. We emerge behind a pile of cardboard boxes. Sarah pushes them aside, ahead of me. We clamber out. I stand up and stretch – grateful to be out of the confined space of the tunnel.

Sarah pushes the boxes back towards the hole. I steady the pile of boxes as she pushes beneath me, until they are back in place. We dust ourselves down. Which is pointless as our clothes are still wet. I squelch with every step I take, and now the dust that has settled on the boxes has now found a new home, sticking to our damp faces and clothes. Sarah reaches for the door handle. It is unlocked. I follow her into the corridor.

# Chapter 9

# Level Twelve

*There is good news, bad news, and even worse news, Sarah tells me.*

The bad news is that she does not possess a key to the central lift. The good news is we don't need to take the lift: we can find our own way up. The worst news is that she has something else to show me. Admittedly that does sound like the worst thing in the world at the time, though not until I get close enough to smell it. When I do, its reek is as foul as can be, and looks a damn sight worse.

"Maybe this is a mistake," Sarah says. "We should go back the way we came."

"Too late. I can smell it! What is it?" I ask.

*Does suffering have a fragrance?* If it does, then that is what I sniff out long before we enter the dark cavernous room. Or do I mean cadaverous room? That would fit too. It is a stomach-wrenching stink, totally rank, like rotten meat left out in the sun. It is the stench of a lot of bodies that have not been washed for a long, long time. But it is more than that: within the scent of stale sweat and charred rotting meat, is the overwhelming, unbearable and choking malodour of despair.

"Why?" I ask Sarah in total bewilderment. Why has she brought me here?

"You need to see it. You need to know what is behind this place. So you have no illusions. It will help you make the right choice. I think," she says.

The heavy wooden door with an iron grill at head height is unguarded and unlocked. I pull it open with more force than is strictly necessary, old habits die hard, or not at all. I am trembling as I enter. It is as if the odour has infiltrated every pore of my body and is now somehow infecting my soul, making it sour and corrupting what is left of it; after all, it has been heavily pruned, hacked and mangled over the recent months.

Black shapes line every wall. Heavy chains bind them, holding them in place, or would do if they bothered to strain against them. I step over bodies on the floor, chained to rings of steel that have been driven into the stone. They are all curled up and unmoving. The aroma is now unbearable.

"Oliver?" Sarah says, and I turn to look.

I have only seen him once. At his execution. Yet here he is, alive, certainly not well. They haven't killed him. His head is bowed down and his face is covered within a metal mask with no eyes or mouth-hole. A low muffled moan comes from behind the mask.

"Why isn't his body healing?" I ask. My head feels light and I see colour spots in front of my eyes.

"Blood," Sarah says. "They don't allow them any human blood."

"They need it to heal?"

"A thimble-full a day will do. But cut off the supply and the body goes into degeneration."

"Then what?"

"A living death, like all these people you see here. The body just does not repair. It goes on living, but slowly falls apart."

"That horrible!" I say, swallowing down a lump in my throat.

"Isn't it."

"There are worse things than death, worse things in life," Sarah says.

"Oliver can you hear me?" She asks the figure, turning back to his slumped form.

"He can't talk with this mask on," I comment.

I kneel down to remove the iron mask. I undo the leather straps at the back. What is underneath is the stuff of nightmares. Oliver's face is blistered to charcoal. One side is completely black, the flesh seared away, and has not grown back. The other side is a fiery red fleshy colour, with a surface that appears to be melted, hanging heavily as it pulls downwards in bags of flesh that sit towards and then overlapping the jaw, hanging like melted candle wax. His lips seem almost completely melted together. It is difficult to look at it without instantly looking away. My stomach churns restlessly as I swallow rising bile.

I look down towards Oliver's throat – it is all but burnt out. I can see the shape of his windpipe melted into the flesh in and around his neck. I can hear the long and laboured rasping breath that is pulled in and out of his damaged lungs. It would not take a doctor to tell me that he will not be telling us anything anytime soon.

"We need blood," Sarah says.

"You can have some of mine," I suggest. I lift up my wrist. My fangs pop out. I am about to sink them into my wrist in the manner I have seen when vampires open up their veins when they have just turned a human into one of them. Well, on TV anyway.

"No! Don't!" Sarah says, her eyes wide in panic.

I look at her and then at Oliver. He cannot speak but his yellow-white eyes have widened as well, as far as it is possible, puss oozing out from the bottom of each eye.

"You don't know what you're doing. That will cause all end of grief," Sarah says in a quiet voice, as if regretting the harsh abruptness of her previous outburst. She presses upon my wrist pushing it back down to my side.

"Ok," I agree.

"It's a nice thought but no. It will not end well for you. They will throw you in here. I could not stand that. No, we need human blood," she insists.

"We will be back Oliver," Sarah promises, now standing.

Oliver just looks up at her, his expression unreadable. It is not altogether surprising as there is no way to read his facial gestures, only the occasional twitching of his charbroiled facial muscles that could mean this or that but most likely nothing. I put the mask back on, so nobody will know we have been here. I tighten the straps, careful not to make them too tight; only too conscious of his breathing and low moans.

I freeze. I hear voices approaching and getting louder. Sarah motions with her hand and I follow her into the shadows on the far side of the room. I hold my breath, looking towards the door.

I can see two faces at the iron grill. I pull further back into the darkness. There is too much of a stink in the room. Else, they might sniff our scent.

"I don't want him speaking to anyone."

I recognise his voice immediately; it is Henry Hrot's. He sounds agitated.

"How can he? He is too badly cremated. And we took his tongue out, remember?"

The other man is Bonemann.

"Even so, I don't want to take any chances," Henry retorts.

"We could just kill him?"

"Yes. Good. Not protocol, I know. The next demonstration – get rid of him."

One of them opens the door. They walk into the dank room.

My blood is frozen. I don't dare move. I look to one side. Sarah stands as still as a statue with one of her fingers to her lips.

"Which one is he?" Henry asks.

"That one I think," says Bonemann. He points. His back is to me. I cannot see where exactly he is pointing but his arm is raised. I assume that he is pointing at Oliver.

"You only think?" Henry says, his voice ice cold.

"I am sure," Bonemann tells him.

"Better be."

"Tut, tut. The trouble you have caused us! You're a very bad, bad boy," Henry scolds and gives a small kick to the man's leg.

The man behind the mask moans, a long sound that consists of only vowels. Then Henry turns on his heels. Bonemann follows him out of the door, closing it behind him. I hear their footsteps receding and their voices fade as they get further away. Sarah and I emerge from behind the pillar.

"We should go," she says. "If they catch us in here, they will do the same thing to us."

I am more than happy to leave. I cannot stop my arms from shaking. Sarah notices and puts a hand to both of my elbows, pressing on a nerve there. The shakes start to recede.

"It is a misjudgement on my part. I shouldn't have brought you here. I forget how young you are," Sarah laments.

"I am fine. I had to see it. I am not glad. But I had to see it."

I shake my head. I thought I had seen everything to the extent that nothing can surprise me anymore. My own arrogance. No matter how far you fall, there is always somewhere deeper to plummet to. How many more horrors are there left to see in this castle? I feel only despair at what the answer to that might be.

# Chapter 10

# Treat(y)ment

*Our Pact.*

"You still think staying is an option? They…will want to do this to you and I couldn't bear it," Sarah urges.

I swallow hard.

"I can't say I will be too keen on it," I reply.

"It's no joke."

"No, no joke."

"This is why you have to go – get away," Sarah tells me.

"I can't leave you here," I protest.

"No choice."

"Then come with me," I offer. "We can disappear."

She jumps up and hugs me.

"I did not think you would ask," she beams, the smile reaches her eyes and her face gushes bright red.

"Careful!" I steady her.

"But timing has to be just right, or else it's disaster, for you and me both," she warns.

"We'd better get back."

# Chapter 11

# The library

*I find the library after my first two weeks at the castle.*

I think it has to be the place to get to the bottom of things, at least to answer some of my questions – for instance: who are the Wonder-kind? Where did they come from? What are we? Stuff like that. I know it is big ask, but the answers I have gotten from in the castle have been illusive, incomplete and irritating, and that is being charitable. Even with Sarah, she is pretty vague and mystical in her account of the Wonder-kind:

"It all depends on what you believe. Different people believe different things. Some think we are descended from Angels and are the last squadron left on the earth to guide the humans, whereas others think that we are original Gods, like Zeus or Thor. It all depends on what you are trying believe about yourself," she says.

"That is what Henry said," I reply. "But what about turning humans into Wonder-kind? That is a vampire thing, right? Not Angels. Not Gods."

"Well you are just trading myths. One myth for the other. The human version versus the Wonder-kind version of the myth. None of it's real. It's just made up to justify stuff."

"Justify stuff?"

"Yes. It just a lie, a convenient one."

Well I do not get very far once I have gotten past the highly unpleasant librarian, only to find I cannot read a word of what is written in most of the books. They are written in a language, or languages, I don't understand.

I can speak and read in one language, English, and my grasp of that is rather shaky. When it comes to other languages, I don't have a clue. The fact that I am so obviously out of my depth is something that the officious librarian seems to enjoy immensely. Sarah says she will help, so I ask if she will come to the library and act as an interpreter. She agrees readily enough, but I detect a moment of hesitation: a reluctance. I don't know... Maybe I'm just imagining it.

The library itself is an enormous echoing room, filled – I mean packed – with books neatly presented on wooden bookcases. The shelves stand back to back in lines and around the edge of the room.

There are no paperbacks here, of course, and most of the books are the size of a large briefcase, some closer to suitcase size. Many are bound in the hides of animals. And I strongly suspect one or two of them could have been made with human skin. I try not to think about that.

Human book bindings notwithstanding, this is a library collection that will lead any Librarian or Archivist lucky enough to access to swear they have died and gone to library heaven.

We enter the library via its two large glass main doors. Inside, there is the hum of the dehumidifiers blasting out cold air. The air seems to cling to my skin, stinging it. My body gives a shiver in response.

"I don't like this place!" Sarah whispers. Even as a whisper it sounds loud in this place. The only other noise apart from the dehumidifiers is the sound of the librarian stacking books. I cannot see him. He is somewhere on the upper levels hidden within the rows of bookshelves.

We sit at the centre of the library. There is a circle of rather study looking tables directly under the skylight. We are sat at one of these.

The high ceiling above us is made up of stone arches that run from the edge of the hall towards the mid-line. At the centre (the part we are sitting under) six arches curve around the circle of the skylight. The skylight itself is a circular inverted dome of tinted glass.

"You don't like books?" I ask, surprised. I don't know why, but I have sort of assumed that Sarah is a book lover. I don't know why. She just looks like someone who would be happiest reading a good book.

"I like books, plenty," she says.

"What then?" I rub my eyes with both hands.

"The librarian is always mean to me!" she says, frowning.

"I think he is mean to everyone," I say.

"Even the King?"

"Probably not. But you never..."

The librarian reappears with a trolley full of books. He wheels them over to his desk, parks the trolley and walks around the desk and sits. He reminds me of a parrot, sitting there with his shoulders bunched together and his head jutting forward. He is writing something in a ledger. He is writing with a quill, just like a character out of a Dickens novel. He turns his disproportionately large head to scowl at us. I shrink back into the chair. He returns to his writing.

"Just ignore him," I say. "I need your help."

"Oh good!" Sarah brightens. "I would like to help."

Sarah pulls a book from the trolley. We have loaded it with books we have collected from the shelves earlier on. The book is bigger than her upper body, but she holds it in her hands without effort. She places it on the table in front of us.

"It's in Latin," she says.

"It all looks Greek to me" I reply.

"No, Latin. These other two are in Greek and this one is Anglo Saxon – Old English. Which is sort of like German or old German," she tells me.

"Good job you're here. I don't understand any of those."

"I know some, but she knows more," she says, pointing to her head.

I crease my brow.

"What?"

"Let's just hope she is in a helpful mood!" Sarah adds. She looks at me as if she has just said the most normal and mundane sentence in the entire world.

I am about to open the first book when the librarian's head whips around.

"Gloves, gloves!" he snaps.

I withdraw my hands.

"Happy to," I say. I sigh and reach for the white cloth gloves. I slide them on. Sarah raises her hands, wriggling her fingers to show that she already has her gloves on.

The librarian points to a sign that hangs over the desk:

GLOVES TO BE WORN AT ALL TIMES.

"If you don't know, you should not be handling such valuable documents!" he snips.

I glare back at him.

"Oh, very well!" he says and returns to whatever he is writing.

"If you so much as leave a finger mark. I will report you!" he says without looking up.

Luckily for me, the book has plenty of illustrations in it. So at least I have something to look at.

"It's called Wunderkind: Book of Kings" Sarah says as she carefully turns the pages.

"Ah here we are," she notes. "The family tree of the King."

I study the page. It looks less of a tree and more like a river of blood flowing down the pages. At various points, the red flow branches off slightly and there is a name on the page and a small illustration. There are twelve offshoots each with a name attached, with other names and branches shooting off of each of those.

"Here. This is Theo," Sarah indicates.

"Who are the others further down?"

"That's his son Frederickson and his daughter Greta."

I recall the bored looking man and woman either side of Theodore's throne. They are his children.

"And these?" I ask. I point across the other red lines that shoot off the main branch and then run parallel with Theodore's red line.

"That's the other eleven of the twelve. King Theo being the twelfth."

"And this stump thing at the top?"

"Ah that is the thirteenth. I am not sure if he ever existed or not. But at the conferences and feasts, they always have an extra seat at the centre of the royal table. It is always bigger than the others."

"Why's that?" I ask, frowning.

"It's a power thing. All of the twelve would all like to take the seat but none them have enough power to do so. Also, they are a little afraid that he might come back some day."

"That is his name. The myth says that he got tired of power and left to tread the earth for the rest of eternity, or some such thing. There is another myth that says he will return when we most need him," she says.

"Like King Arthur"

"A lot nastier, but yes. But then he could just be a myth, a story; we have lots of them. For practically anything you can think of, there is a myth lurking somewhere or other.".

I think that, for a family tree, there are not a lot of members. There are very few children and very few grandparents. However, according to Sarah, the tree goes back to the beginning of recorded history.

"What are the yellow lines for?" I ask. I trace the line from the top of the page and down King Theodore's line.

"That's God shining down his sacred divine will upon the chosen rulers of the earth."

"They think... King Theo thinks he is God's chosen one?"

"Pretty much. All the kings here think that. Even the human ones"

"Not very modest! And that entitles him to do what exactly?"

"Pretty much whatever he wants to."

"If the lie is big enough, you can justify pretty much anything... any act, however abhorrent, even the total subjugation of the human race."

# Chapter 12

# Killer Lessons

*Our training sessions are bloody affairs.*

The Bonemann says that death is only temporary, for those who just want a bit of lie down: "So get your ass off the floor and fight back!".

Everyone recovers from even the most terrible injuries, but they still leave their mark. After the flesh and bone has stitched itself back together and the blood has run backwards into the vessel of skin, there are still marks; there are still overlapping patches of dark red stains on the floor and walls. Worse still, you remember it each time you die or lose a limb. You remember coming back from the dead or looking with horror at your missing limb. The psychological and physical are pain are all real and screaming inside of your head. Desensitising training Bonemann calls it. It is where all this blood and guts horror show becomes normal, just another day in the training room.

Judy has taken a bullet to the head. She has been slammed against the wall and slowly slides down to the ground, leaving a trail of red liquid. The skid marks are still there, faded but still visible. And she is just one of many, serving as a visceral reminder of our deaths: dead and back.

Some of the stains are mine of course. I remember each one in second by second detail.

There is no fear of death, only fear of dying and pain. The worst place to take a bullet is through the jaw, with bone and teeth splintering, but the most painful is the hips, not a kill-shot but painful as hell, because there are so many nerves in that region.

To look at it is cartoon like – to see limbs and other body parts hacked off, only to see that limb crawl across the floor, to grow back again. It looks ridiculous: stomach churning but ridiculous. It is a gut-wrenching experience but at the same time there is no real consequence to any of this. Nobody has died. There are no real physical consequences any-way, psychologically those are different. When it is you, the experience is less than pleasant. Holding your skull together while it sucks in its vital bits, all because Karl has rammed an axe into your cranium, is an overrated pastime. And each time is as traumatic as the last. You always remember it, dying I mean: the sudden turning out of the light and then being suddenly thrown back into the world, conscious, your body in bits and pieces. It is as if death itself does not want me because I am so tainted and damned.

Bonemann smiles broadly as he lays down a selection of medieval weapons on a table in front of us. He has picked them out himself: two for each of us. I think he is genuinely interested in which ones each of us will choose.

"Take your pick!" he tells us.

He is clearly enjoying himself. This is his favourite lesson. I wonder whether this is because he is from the dark ages himself, or has lived through them, or whether he just wishes that he did. Everyone I speak to seems to have reached a significant age. It is possible I suppose. Or maybe Bonemann just likes seeing us hack each other to pieces.

"Sir!" announces Karl, holding his detached arm in place while the flesh and muscles knit back together.

"What is it Karl?" Bonemann retorts.

"What about if we decapitate one of our lot? Well, an enemy but a Wonder-kind…"

"Yes."

"Then we take the head and put it in a metal box. What would happen then, sir?"

"Good question."

We all stop fighting to look at the Bonemann. A cold shiver runs down my back. I have a nasty suspicion that he might want to try it out in front of the class. I am a firm favourite in that, and no other, respect.

"Well, it has been done in experimental conditions. It was in the Sixties, of course. Always the sixties."

"And?" Karl prompts.

"Mostly the head grows a new body, after a time."

"Really? What about box?" Karl asks.

"Can you rip steel with your bare hands?"

"Of course!" Karl smiles and flexes his shoulders and biceps.

"Well then!" Bonemann exclaims.

"Oh! I see!" Karl says.

"Carry on!" Bonemann orders. I raise my short sword and launch myself back into the fray.

With all this blood, you'd think that I'd go mad with hunger for the red stuff. You'd think I would be overpowered with thirst and I'd be crawling over the floor, scooping and lapping the stuff up. But I don't feel a bit of it. The smell of it – it is a perfumed smell – burns unpleasantly in the nostrils. Sarah has told me that the reason we find it unpleasant is that it is genetically engrained within us, because it is the final taboo – cannibalism. Wonder-kind may not drink from another. That is rule number one. There is a belief that the blood of another of our kind is poison to us. But that Sarah says she knows is not true. It is, however, one of the biggest and most sacrilegious of crimes for all Wonder-kind in all twelve kingdoms, the punishment for which is a long painful death that would make Oliver's non-fatal-execution look like a Sunday picnic.

*"There is no greater crime," she says.*

# Chapter 13

# Killing Time

*Bonemann is before anything else a showman.*

And as most showmen like to do, he loves to show off. This is evident when Lucy asks:

"But how do we know that these D-guns will actually work. Kill one of us?"

"One of us? I do hope you are not planning to murder someone here Miss Bryant?"

"I mean one of them. Wonder-kind but one of our... I mean one of the King's enemies!" she corrects.

"Well there's plenty of them. But it is a good question," he says.

Lucy gives a half smile in response.

"Well you could take my word for it?" Bonemann says, his hands on top of his razor-sharp hips.

"Ha, ha! Of course not!" he adds, laughing his dirty laugh.

"I have been waiting for someone to form that question!" adds Bonemann, his horrible Easter egg smile splitting his face in two.

"Guards!" he shouts.

It is all a set-up of course. The guards are waiting just outside the training room door with their prisoner. They come in, two of them, with a chained prisoner between them. For a second, remembering Henry's words, I think it is Oliver.

I can't see the face under the metal mask, but the body is all wrong. He is too tall for a start and his chest is much bigger, more barrel like. But he is a Wonder-kind, one of us, from that horror room on level twelve. I can smell it.

"Take the mask off," Bonemann commands. The two guards do as they are bid. The students hiss and many of them shrink backwards, appalled at the man's disfigured face. Then Bonemann looks at me:

"Give the man a drink. He looks thirsty," he says, looking at me.

"Now!" he shouts at me, gesturing to a silver jug on a nearby table. The table, jug, tray or single goblet is not usually here in the middle of the training room. They have been brought in as props for this particular lesson. Everything has been planned out in advance. This is how the Bonemann likes to play it. The table and jug have appeared this very morning. I noticed it when I first walked in the door earlier on, but thought nothing of it at the time.

How did Bonemann know that Lucy would ask that particular question? Experience maybe – more likely he didn't know if she would or not. But if the question had not have come up, then he would have gone along with his lesson plan anyway. Who knows what goes on behind those beady little eyes.

I pour some of the red stuff – human blood – into a goblet, not quite to the top, but near enough. Then I carry it the seemingly long distance, from the table to where the prisoner stands.

The prisoner – I don't know his name – has a nasty twisted grin on his charcoaled face. He looks at me with his one eye, his right. The one on the left is just a burnt-out socket. I hold the goblet towards him. I think that I might have to hold it to his lips and help him drink but he suddenly reaches out and snatches the goblet from my hands and downs it in one.

Bonemann places the D-gun on the other side of the table from earlier; he had it in his hands when we entered the room this morning. He stands by the table not looking at anything in particular. He is whistling the theme to *Callan* to himself. I remember the tune and the TV series. At the start there is light bulb swinging from side to side in front of this dingy brick wall, while the sinister theme tune plays, then the light bulb smashes. I think.

Bonemann's gaze falls upon the D-gun after a second or two. He starts to play with the gun on the table, twirling it around, with his finger in the trigger guard.

"You two, guards, go!" he orders, as he carries on playing with the gun.

The two guards look at each other, with uncertain glances.

"Now!" Bonemann shouts without looking up.

The nearest guard just shrugs and nods to his companion. Then, they turn and make for the door, slamming it on the way out.

"Behold, one of the fallen, one of the outcasts, about to be reborn," Bonemann says with a sneer across his unpleasant features.

The prisoner's skin seems to almost glow... after what? Only seconds of drinking the blood. His skin changes before our eyes and the charred black parts start to flake as the skin underneath, red raw, begins to scab, as new flesh grows. Most amazing of all is the prisoner's missing eye.

From the dark cavern of his eye socket a white round squishy globe starts to push forward into the light.

"Bonemann!" a voice rasps. It is a guttural sound, as if the prisoner has been in the habit of swallowing razor blades. He snaps the thick chains around his wrists and ankles as if they are paper decorations.

Bonemann roars, shoving me to one side. Taken by surprise, I fall back onto Lucy who is standing behind me and instantly pushes me away.

"Get off of me you little creep," she hisses.

The prisoner runs at Bonemann and, in that split second, Bonemann has already got the D-gun in his hand. He has already fired it at the prisoner. Whoever the prisoner had been, he is now no more than a circling collection of pink and white dust that drifts slowly to the floor.

"That my dear Lucy is how you know what a D-gun can do. And why you should trust your trainer when he tells you something is so," Bonemann says with his smug Easter egg smile splitting his face.

A hushed silence hangs in the air, along with the remains of the unknown prisoner. The dust particles are still drifting through the empty space at the centre of the room. It seems to take an age for the dust to settle onto the floor. No one will go near it. It is as if they are afraid that they too will dissolve if they come too close to the colourful dust.

After the demonstration, no one in that room feels as immortal as they once did.

# Chapter 14

# Henry's Army

*Sarah reads from a hardback book.*

It is in English, or an English of sorts. We are in the upper levels of the library. There is an eerie atmosphere up here, among all these dark coloured shelves populated with hundreds of sombre-coloured hardback books. They are red, black, green or blue: always a dark shade of the colour. There are no dust-covers or pictures or marking, apart from the title printed on the side. This one is called 'Wunderkind Society: Rules and Responsibilities.' It is comparably modern book, only about two hundred years old, so Sarah tells me.

"Listen," she says.

"The human should be the best of one's social grouping and an exemplar of good breeding and physical excellence. Such is the honour bestowed upon the protégé. To become one of the immortals, one of the all-powerful – to be Wunderkind."

"Good grief," I say. "I have no idea why they chose me!"

"You mean why Henry chose you?" Sarah says.

"Any ideas?"

"Only Henry knows the answer to that."

"And he is not going tell?"

"Oh yes, I am sure he will give you an answer. But it is not likely to be even remotely the truth. He is a great manipulator. He cannot be trusted."

"It may just be fate. I told you they don't know what I know about you," she adds.

"Even if I did believe that part; what makes you think they don't know?" I ask.

"You would be dead," states Sarah. There is no drum roll. No dramatic build up. She just says it in a simple matter of fact way.

"Though I suppose he is distracted..." she considers, looking down at the book once more.

"By what?"

"How many people are there in that murder-class you go to?"

"Murder-class?"

"The training where you go every day to train to kill. What else do you think you are doing there?"

"Oh, yes. There are twenty of us now. There were only twelve when we started."

"So there are more arriving every day?"

"Yeah, suppose so," I say, scratching at my head. I hadn't really thought about the new arrivals. They haven't had much to do with me. On the first day, they try to be friendly, until they realised the way the pecking order works within the classroom. Then they don't speak to me again. I am fed up of it. So I barely speak to anyone anymore.

"The point..." says Sarah, "...is that there have never been so many initiates. Two every ten years used to be considered a lot."

"Why so many now?" I ask.

"Simple: he is building an army. And you are part of it."

"I thought that was the Unseeyn Hand?"

"It is. But that is mostly to keep humans under control," she says, putting a finger to her chin, "No this is something different, new even."

"What then?"

"Everything is going to change, and he wants to be ready, I think."

"Regime change, on a large scale: big splash!" she says, a frown across her forehead.

"Could be very bad for everyone."

# Chapter 15

# Sleep Talk

*It is three in the morning.*

I have my eyes closed. I hear and feel Sarah move from the bed. I open my eyes to see her at the end of it. Her eyes flash upon me.

"Why are you the same?" she says, shaking her head. "What are you waiting for?"

"What?" I ask, confused.

"Do you want them to kill you? Do you want what that fool Olly got?"

Sarah turns and leaves the room. I lie there trying to make sense of what she has just said. What did it mean? About five minutes later, she comes back, her face wet with water. Without saying a word, she curls up into a ball and pops her thumb in her mouth and mumbles something. Then her breathing, though slight, returns to its regular rhythm.

I ask Sarah about what she had said the next morning and she tells me she doesn't remember waking up, let alone saying anything to me.

"I had such a good night's sleep" she says. "I didn't know anything until it was time to get up!"

She seems so convinced of her words and sounds so earnest that I begin to wonder if I have dreamt the whole thing. Except I think I see a
twinge of anxiety in her eyes, if only for a slight moment – a second –
but it is there. As quickly as it has come, it has gone again. So I just
shrug and shove the whole business to the back of my mind. Or I try to.
But something – I am not quite sure what – makes me uneasy, troubled
even.

# Chapter 16

# Lady Francesca

*"Look who it ain't!"*

For a split second, I think it is Danny's voice – just for a second.

"Karl," I say, turning towards him.

He stands at bottom of the staircase. It is a close thing but, if anything, it is worse than being haunted by the ghost of the kid I killed. And, if that isn't bad enough, Lady Francesca is standing by his side. She runs a long finger through Karl's short head of hair. Something about the act makes my skin crawl.

"Lady Francesca," I nod.

"I really can't believe Henry did it. I mean why?" She says, raising her hands to make the point.

"What is so special about you?" she says.

"Nothing," Karl smirks.

"The old man is losing his touch," he adds.

A flash of anger dawns in Lady Francesca's eyes. She cuffs Karl around the head. My jaw drops slightly. I almost laugh out loud. I stop myself just in time.

"Never talk about your betters in that way Karl. I don't know how many times I have to tell you," she says through pursed lips.

"Yes… Sorry. Wasn't thinking," Karl says meekly – or as meek as he is capable of being. He doesn't do that attitude well. Bragging, on the other hand, is a different matter.

Sarah silently appears at my elbow. I haven't heard her. She just materialises. She reminds me of the shop keeping in Mr Ben – *And as if by magic, the shop keeper appears!*

"John! I have..." she says, her voice upbeat and breezy. Then she stops mid-sentence.

"Oh!"

"Lady Francesca hisses, really hisses, like an angry cat or something.

"Get that despicable abomination away from me!" she screeches.

*This now? What is wrong with these people?*

Sarah has gone all tight-lipped and wide eyed.

"Why are you even still alive? You disgusting creature! Why do they keep you here?" Lady Francesca shrieks. She is looking at Sarah. The outburst could have equally been levelled at me. But she seems to have forgotten I am here for the moment, so great is her rage.

"You know why," Sarah says, her eyes cast down.

"Great Gods! Come on Karl. Let's not be seen with the likes of those two. It is would not be fitting," she hisses, grabbing Karl's arm and storming off.

It looks almost comical, Karl being hauled off, like a small child being dragged off by his angry mum.

"Honestly…" I say, turning to face Sarah. Her big black eyes are leaking huge tears.

"Hey!" I tell her. "They are just being horrible. It is all they are capable of. Don't let them get to you." I keep my voice soft and rub her shoulder with my hand.

"I know..." she sniffs. "...But it does."

We go up onto the roof. Finding the highest part, one of the oldest sections of the building, and climb up the tallest tower. We sit on the ramparts, our legs dangling over the edge. Out of the corner of my eye, I catch sight of Karl and Lady Francesca in the castle grounds below. I nod to Sarah.

"Down there."

"Why couldn't they have gone somewhere else?" I add, miffed.

"What are they doing?" Sarah asks.

I shrug.

I can hear Lady Francesca speaking:

"...Brought you a present, for us both really. Something we can both play with. I saw it on the way up. It is just so cute. I simply could not resist..."

I realise I hate the sound of her voice, but my hearing goes straight to it, as if I want to hear things that will only make me angry.

They are walking into the car park towards a yellow Audi.

"Open the boot," She purrs.

"What is it?" Karl asks.

"A surprise! Now stop being an old grumble guts and open the boot, will you!"

Despite myself, I am now interested in what is in the boot. I can hear it, faint in the distance. But I know full well what is in there. So must Karl. He is right next to it; he has to hear it. He has to be humouring her or is this part of a game they play? Who knows with those two.

"Yes Ma'am," he agrees in a serious voice.

The boot opens. Karl lifts the boy out of the trunk and raises him into the air.

"Well, well, what do we have here?"

The boy's face looks as if it is about to explode into tears. His eyes are huge and his lower jaw is quivering beneath a gag. He is bound, hand and foot. His body trembles and shakes: quaking with fear.

Karl takes the gag from the boy's mouth. When he does, the boy doesn't make a sound, too terrified I suppose. Then Karl snaps the boy's binding with an index finger. The ropes break apart as if they are strands of cobweb.

"We are going to play a little game…" Karl says.

"Hide and seek!" Lady Francesca completes.

They escort the boy out of the car park, towards the grounds at the back of the Château. Both have a hand on the boy's shoulder. They reach the green area of grass at the back. It is a big open space of green lawn, about the size of four football pitches. This is where the festival has been held. The fences and scaffolding have been taken down, but there is still a huge scorch mark in a circle where they have burnt Oliver. The ground surrounding the circle of seared grass is still churned up from all the fighting on that day. Karl taps the boy on the back and he goes flying face first onto the grass.

"I'll count to fifty. Then ready or not. we will come and find you," Karl says. He has his back to me but I can tell from his voice that he is enjoying this immensely.

"One, two, three…"

At first the boy does not move. He is too terrified and stays where he is, on the ground where Karl has pushed him.

"Ten, eleven, twelve…"

But then he staggers to his feet, and begins to run towards the trees, as if he is wounded. The gentle breeze carries the smell of his fear towards my appreciative nose. He runs in a shambling and panicked manner, his muscles refusing to cooperate. At the same time, adrenaline is flooding his system, pushing him on, despite everything.

Lady Francesca laughs. Her laugh is shrill, loud and unpleasant to my ears.

"Run little boy. Run!" she calls out. He isn't that young: school age, maybe fifteen at a guess.

"...forty-eight, forty-nine, fifty." Karl completes the count.

This is the first honest thing I have ever seen him do. I expect him to head out after the boy before the end of the count. He hasn't even sped up the count towards the end. But then it isn't much of a contest.

The boy has managed to make it to the trees on the other side of the lawn. He disappears into the undergrowth. Lady Francesca has already abandoned her high heels and ran with Karl after the boy. They are both fast.

Then they disappear from view. But we hear crying, and then the louder and shriller sounds of screaming. They must have been playing with him for a good half an hour before I saw both of them leave, coming out from under the trees. Both are grinning and talking about the 'game' they have been playing. I can smell human blood, hanging around them like an exquisite perfume. They walk up to the Château, entering through the French windows.

A short time later, I see one of the blood slaves leave from the kitchen, go into the woods and return holding a bundle. His face is ash-grey; his body limp and totally without life. I turn away.

"They're monsters," Sarah says.

"Yes," I agree, but my cheeks are flushing hot. The same could easily be said about me. After all, although I feel disgust at the cruelty, my mouth is awash with fresh saliva, so much that it threatens to run over my bottom lip and down my chin. I swallow.

# Power Play

# Chapter 1

# Psychotic Breaks

*"Kill everyone. Then burn it to the ground,"* Bonemann had said.

It was a simple mission:

*"Why else would we trust you toe-rags to carry it out?"* Bonemann had said.

What he hadn't said was why. Why are we doing this? It is not our business to know. It is our business to do, to do exactly what we are told, apparently.

Still it is a simple mission:

*What possibly could go wrong? I think,* one eyebrow raised.

Falling into the darkness... No, not darkness, not for me, and not for the owner of the thunderingly loud heartbeat either. Below on the ground, he has a torch that flashes its beam in my direction, finding me then losing me once more as I fall. He has some sort of machine gun. A spray of bullets whizz past. But he can't hold the gun and torch at the same time, and he can't steady his aim.

I am as nothing. I'm just a body, with fangs, side arm and boot knife: a body that knows only one thing – killing. After all that is what it is designed to do.

*Just give up thought and feeling and let it do its job*, or so I tell myself. After all, there is pleasure in acceptance: in submission.

I aim my body towards the light, towards the sound of his loud heartbeat; I am a heat seeking missile, heading for a big fat and easy target: falling too fast.

Without thinking, I twist the muscles in my gut, curling into a ball. Bullets are whizzing past me.

So much for surprise.

It is almost as if they knew we were coming. It doesn't matter though.

I unfurl and propel myself toward the man who is firing at me, falling on top of him. He collapses beneath me. My fangs are out already, my mouth dripping saliva.

"Just let go..." I tell myself.

He is a big man with a big heart. I heard his big heart all the way from the roof; down on the ground it's really loud. I have used the sound to guide me towards him. He is about twice my size, with a big meaty neck. My teeth go through his thick orange-peel-like skin easily enough. My hand is over his mouth, though it is too late for surprise, and my knee is in his back. He struggles but it is too late for that as well; too late for him. I rip through his flesh, towards the hot blood inside. At last, it floods into my mouth and I suck it down. Then little earthquakes go off inside my brain.

I hear gunshots, screams and lots of sexual swear words flying about. Inside, the sounds travel; everything sounds nearer. I drop to one knee, listening. I unclip my side arm from its holster, and take my boot knife out. I spring to my feet and sprint down the main aisle, towards the fire-fight: I can smell fresh blood.

I have to be quick. I turn into one of the side-aisle, as a hail of bullets travel down the main aisle. On either side of me is high metal shelving full of large cardboard boxes. I yelp. A bullet must have caught me just before I dart down the aisle. My shoulder smarts and blood colours the shoulder of my coat. I feel my body push at the bullet, until it falls from my shoulder. It pings to the ground and rolls along the concrete. The wound sucks together, stitching itself up. It stings like the devil, but that won't last long. It never does.

A man, tall with long hair, appears at the end of the aisle. He has some sort of semi-automatic machine gun slung low around his waist. It takes milliseconds to move his finger to pull the trigger, to move it the few centimetres needed to release a hail of bullets in my direction, and he is peppering my body with metal slugs. I have already shot him in the head. He falls silently and I move forward. Then the blood, from the dead man with the loud heart, really kicks in. My head explodes with feelings of ecstasy, and the promise of violence.

"I got one!" Someone shouts.

A human has just turned the corner. He aims a hand gun at my head. I smile insincerely back at him. My boot knife is stuck in his throat before the nerve impulse can make it to his trigger finger. I look into the man's staring eyes as he gurgles. I see nothing of interest. I let him drop to the floor.

I reach down, retrieving the knife. The blade is red, dripping. I lick the flat of the blade. It tastes sweet. Then I slink back into the main aisle, raising the Glock, and start firing at people's heads.

I plunge the knife into the heart of a grey-bearded man. It goes in quick and easy Due to a mixture of the sharpness of the knife itself and the force I can bring to bear on a specific point. With my other hand I aim at the head of a man running towards me. I pull the trigger and he falls down, then another, and another. To me, I am taking my time, to get the aim right. I have twenty rounds in the magazine and two more magazines in my pocket. I do not intend to waste one single bullet. But to the human eye, this will all be happening at lightening quick speed: too fast for it to keep up with. We are the Unseeyn after all.

There is something sickeningly pointless about all of this. It is like shooting fish in a barrel. Who are they anyway? Guards? Gangsters? Who runs around with machine guns in a warehouse? What are they doing here? I don't know. I don't even know why we are doing this.

*"Minds that are immeasurably more intelligent and knowledgeable than you lot have made the decision. All you have to do is try not to mess up," Bonemann had said.*

The lights go dead before we drop in. That is Lucy's job – kill the power. Kill anyone who gets in the way. Now the warehouse is illuminated with torchlight and gun-fire. Above me, I see Lucy running down the gantry, firing a semi-automatic machine gun. I can tell she has fed as well. She has lost her usual caution and is charging down the gantry, gun blazing. Blood has that effect.

*"If you've got to, then do it. But stay focused and stay disciplined! Use the blood high. After all, many battles have been won on the blood high. But don't let it control you. Don't lose control," Bonemann had said.*

Well that has well and truly gone out of the window. Along with everything else – the gunfire, the screaming – I can hear the incendiaries going off in the distance.

"Karl!" I sigh.

*It is too soon.*

When they go off, the incendiaries explode liquid fire everywhere like Napalm, only a lot worse and a lot faster. Incendiary grenades are nasty things. I hate them. First, the metal capsule explodes, firing thousands of small more fragile capsules into the air. On contact with any surface, they break and the liquid inside expands a hundred-fold, coating everything it comes in contact with: igniting, coving everything with 'liquid fire' that will consume everything it touches. It will not extinguish until it has burnt all it comes in contact with to ash, and then some. It is really nasty stuff.

Blinding bright light flares up, towards the ceiling, and then rushes down the aisle towards me, a wall of flame. I think about breaking into a run. But as I glance behind me at the direction I have come, another identical wall of flame comes roaring toward me.

*Before, in the back of the aeroplane, when we had been flying for just over an hour, I had not a clue where in the country we were, or if we were in the same country. It could have been anywhere. "You're going on a field trip," Bonemann had said. Bonemann had caught a punch aimed at the middle of my back. I turned to see Bonemann with Karl's fist in his hand; Karl looked surprised... No, he looked shocked, though not as shocked as me, I would wager – not at the fact that Karl had tried to hit me, but that Bonemann had stopped him. Wonders will never cease!*

*"No!" Bonemann said.*

*"But Sir...?" Karl began.*

*"Not here, not now."*

*"Here we are on a mission for the King. Here we put our differences aside. Here we are just one team. We don't mess about on the King's errand!" Bonemann said.*

*"Yes sir," Karl replied.*

*"John?" Bonemann asked, using my first name which had been unheard of up to that point: it had always been my surname or some insult or other.*

*"Yes sir."*

*"Right?"*

*"Yes sir."*

*Karl shot me a glance. I looked away, ignoring him. The plane circled, tilting to the left. The noise of the engines roared in my ears. It was a cargo plane, striped out of everything. The back doors opened and we poured out. We ran down the length of the gangway and leapt out of the door at the rear of plane, falling towards the earth below. I fell head first. My eyes opened and the wind dried all the moisture out from them. I blinked, then again, trying to keep them moist.*

*We landed in a farmer's field. We ran to the edge and leapt over the barbwire fence. We ran down the quiet country road towards our target. We would arrive within minutes.*

*We were all there, the whole class. We all had our tasks and our allotted entry points. Mine was the midsection of the roof. It was as good as any place I thought at the time. Now I am not so sure.*

There are about twelve or so bodies nearby, bleeding out, the blood meeting in the centre of the aisle in a pool. The concrete has a slight gradient on both sides so it pours towards the centre. I look into its dark scarlet surface. I see my unsmiling reflection looking back. The person in the reflection looks totally insane. I kneel and my knee goes down into a pool of blood, by the side of two bodies, their souls long since departed for the next world. I stir the liquid with the tip of my finger. Then I raise it to my mouth, tasting the fingertip with my tongue. I put the freshly sucked finger back into the pool.

"No way out then?" I say to no one in particular. I clip the side arm back into its holster.

I feel the intense searing heat rushing towards me. Soon I will be just like Oliver. The image of him on the pyre fills my mind: his flesh blacking and falling off as the fire consumed him. No way out for either of us.

"But no... That isn't right..."

He could have broken his chains. He could have run. Why didn't he? He stayed, a lamb to slaughter, or barbecued at any rate.

They would have got him anyway... Shot him down with a D-gun... Maybe we will never know. What I do know is that he chose to submit to the punishment, collude with it, accept it and acknowledge his guilt, (and for something he did not do). I don't have to do that.

"Sod acceptance, sod submission," I say smiling. They want madness – I have plenty of that to give, an abundance.

I stand up, the flames towering over me. In seconds they will consume me, not kill me, but take me to a living hell. That is ok. I don't need seconds. I leap into the air, catching hold of the bottom of one of the girders that help support the sloping corrugated roof. I climb up the metal towards it. On my left, the wall of flame is almost upon me. I punch through the corrugated roof, while holding to the girder with my other hand, rust crumbing from the metal. I fling myself towards the hole I have made and clamber through. My legs and feet as if they are on fire. I slide down the roof and land on the soft ground. Wet grass meets my fingertips as I crouch. I spring to my feet and run around the building towards the car park. I sprint out of the gates, down the road. The road is over-hung with branches from the trees that line the road. I peg it towards the black figures running away, up ahead. A few miles later, I run into a field, the noise of the waiting aircraft rattling from its dark shape. There are no lights on. The others hurry up the gang plank and into the plane. I put a spurt on. As the gang plank starts to lift and the plane starts to move, I leap into the back.

"Where the hell have you been?" Bonemann hisses.

"Oh, you know me. I'll be late for my own funeral," I say. It is the blood talking. I shoot Karl a look. He just shrugs.

Out of the back the plane, I see a billowing cloud of fire shoot up into the air. The blast consumes the warehouse, totally spreading out to eat the neighing building and greedily devouring everything in its path, only to explode out once more with the ring of destruction pushing ever-outwards in conquest.

# Chapter 2

# Like Me

*I get back to my room.*

Sarah is already there, lying on the bed, her head and back propped up with pillows. She looks up from the book she is reading. She puts the book down and regards me.

"You have been killing," she says. It isn't a question.

"Yeah, another of Bonemann's field trips," I reply.

"But you killed!"

"Yeah, I killed. It's in my nature. You know that."

"It's not," she says.

I am drained and at my wits end. I am not looking for a discussion on the ins and outs of Bonemann's missions. It's not as I if I have a choice. I can't stay in bed and say I am ill to get a sick note from my mum.

"You chose to," Sarah tells me. Anger, or the remaining effects of the large amount of blood I have drunk, flares up.

"You're Wonder-kind too. It's not as if you haven't killed. You know what the hunger is like," I snap.

"I have never killed anyone. Not ever," She says.

My jaw drops.

"Not ever? How is that even possible?" I ask, astonished.

"It just isn't in me," she says.

"That is what I thought about myself. But look at me," I retort.

How is it possible? I can't imagine it. I had taken it as a no-brainer that, because Sarah is a vampire like me, she will have killed, even if it is just by accident. It seems so normal, so inevitable. It is like she has just told me that the world is not round, as I have been taught at school, but in fact flat and made of blue cheese. I have a hard time believing it and I only do so, because I have not known Sarah to lie. If there is something she did want to tell me, she wouldn't, but she has never lied to me.

I need it too much, enjoy it too much – the red stuff that is. I just can't stop drinking, even if it means death for the person I am drinking from. I just cannot be trusted. Do I enjoy the power of life and death over another human being? I am not honest enough to be able to answer that one. I don't think I do, but clearly there was an element of sadism when I fed on Danny. Oh, poor old Danny. I can say that now, now he is dead and gone. If he was still alive and still making my life a misery – what then? I don't know. I am lost. Sarah makes me feel ashamed at my lack of control and the things I have done. I have blamed the monster in me for the killing, but it is *my* fangs that have sunk into their necks and *my* hands that held them down as I did it. It is *my* hands that are wholly soaked in the blood of others.

As if reading my thoughts, Sarah says:

"I am not judging you. I am just worried. Every time you kill, it chips away at you. So much so that soon you will be more like them and less like me. Then you won't want me around anymore. And I will be alone again..."

"Ha! That will never happen!" I insist.

"Don't make fun of me," she says.

"I am not. I just can't imagine that ever happening. That is why I laughed. I mean it."

Her eyes brighten.

"Really?"

"Really."

"Good."

I start to pull at my hair. The ends disintegrate as I pull out clumps of singed hair.

"What happened?" Sarah asks. Her head turns to one side as she watches my frenzied hair tugging.

"Oh, Karl set off the incendiary too early. I got stuck in the middle and had to get out thought the roof. It was close," I say. Looking down at the broken hair I hold pinched between my fingers and thumb, I rub it. It breaks down into smaller pieces that fall through my fingers to the floor.

"You smell of burnt hair," Sarah observes.

"Thanks," I say.

I rub at my eyebrows. They are singed too, crumbling as I rub them, raining motes of singed hair to the floor.

"Hair cells are already dead. So it won't grow back any faster than the speed at which our hair would normally grows," Sarah says helpfully.

"Hair doesn't revivify?"

"Not when it has been fried."

"How long?"

"Same speed as before."

"Great. I am going to be frizz-ball for months!" I say.

"We could cut it all off. Not the eye brows... the head hair, I mean."

"Do it," I say.

"It could have been worse," Sarah adds and produces a shaving kit she finds in the trunk at the end of the bed. It is complete with foam, a brush and a nice sharp cut-throat razor. She takes them out of the wooden box and lays them on the bed.

"Yeah, I suppose it could at that," I say, thinking about Oliver and his face as it went up in flame, as he burned alive.

"Take a seat" offers Sarah, indicating the one chair in the room. Then opening the razor, she looks at the blade quizzically, as if captured by her own reflection.

# Chapter 3

# The Gifts

*I am as ungifted as a student can be.*

Sarah's predictions about the future make no sense to me. They worry me. I keep getting the feeling she has the wrong person. I am no great vampire warrior, just a plain ordinary one. Karl, maybe. He is strong and decisive. Or Lucy: her brain is like a strategy computer, forever calculating the next move of her opponent so she can block, counter and then move in for the kill. Elliot has speed on his side and David's low cunning has won him many fights. But me: all I have is a startling lack of ability.

We are all meant, after anything between a week and six months, to manifest gifts. Here, a particular ability you had before will magnify and emerge in frightening brilliance. If you are good at it as a human, then you absolutely shine as a Wonder-kind. Or it could be a new ability, one that you have had all along, but has been hidden and latent. Where is my gift? Nowhere that is where.

What I lack most of all is the killer instinct: the desire to go straight for the throat and rip it out. I have killed, sure, but they were only human. I am in a whole different league here. The extra strength and keen perception can only take you so far. I mean what am I even doing here? I do not belong. Danny had more right to be here than I do. Why didn't Henry choose him? He would have fitted right in. After all, the majority of the Wonder-kind are predators. It did not take long for them to hon in on the fact that I am the weakest link in this particular chain. It was only a matter of time really...

"You 're up next," Bonemann says to me.

He turns, "Karl, Lucy you're up against Tiber here."

"Two against one?" I say. I am surprised.

*Sarah's bad influence.* She just says what she thinks, with no hesitation what so ever – she just comes right out with what is on her mind.

"You're the weakest in hand weapon combat, and just about everything else, so it is time for you to step up, Tiber," Bonemann says. I can think of another reason. But what is the use. I grab a short sword and a bowie knife from the table. I stick the knife in my ankle holster and hold the sword in both my hands.

Karl already has his favourite combination: a large two-headed axe and wooden club with a metal spike at the thick end. Lucy has a long sleek sword that looks a lot like one of those fencing ones, except that the whole of the length of the blade is as razor sharp as the tip.

"We're going to slaughter you, you little creep!" Karl says.

"OK now! Let's get to it!" Bonemann says, as he claps his long hands twice.

Lucy and Karl start to circle me. Every nerve in my body tingles with apprehension. A raw and very unpleasant sensation shoots up through my gut to my stomach, where it intensifies and sits like a thick poisonous miasma. I cannot die, not with these weapons, but I can be hurt –

badly. It is no longer about living or dying but winning or losing: it is all about avoiding the shame of losing. You would have thought I would be used to it by now.

Lucy holds herself back. Her blade points towards me as she circles. Her cold eyes lock onto me, unblinking. She is waiting for Karl to lumber in first. She does not have to wait too long. I duck as Karl's axe glides over my head. I drop to one knee. I grab the Bowie knife from its holster. I throw it. It finds a home in Karl's shoulder. I feel the mildest pang of pleasure at this.

The club falls from Karl's grip and clamours across the floor. For a split second, his body is open wide to an attack. But I am too slow. He growls as he rips the knife from his shoulder, still holding the axe. He throws the knife over his shoulder. It falls somewhere behind him towards the other end of the room. The wound has already sealed. The shirt itself is torn and bloody. He looks at it for a second, then back at me, staring directly into my face.

"Got any more tricks, or are you fresh out?" he smiles. He passes the handle of the two-headed axe from hand to hand a couple of times. Then, he grips it in both hands.

"He...argh!" he yells and charges straight at me.

I freeze for a moment, then decoy: moving to the right before darting to the left. Karl steams past me. But Lucy has correctly guessed my plan and darts forward with her sword. It hits home – passing through my ribs, slicing through my chest, but missing my loudly beating heart. However, it does feel as if it has skimmed the surface of the beating organ.

I pull backwards hard, falling off of the sword, stumbling. There is a spurt of blood as my body jolts off the sword. I fall backwards. I put a hand to my chest to cover the small wound.

"Well played, Lucy! Good lunge. You need to focus more. Find the heart and push through!" Bonemann calls, clapping, his eyes bright and his body animated.

Although I know the wound has to have healed by now, I circle my index finger around where the hole has been. The skin is smooth and unbroken. It still burns like hell. I feel the wetness of the remaining smear of blood. I put my bloody finger in my mouth and suck off the blood. The taste is sharp and explosive; it tingles and pops upon my tongue like moon dust.

There is no time for this. No time to think of the pain. I grip the sword in both hands and raise it to eye-level, Then, I charge towards Karl. He smiles an evil grin and then raises his axe to block my blow. The sword bounces off the silver surface of the axe head. Just as Lucy runs me through from behind, I feel the blade tear through the muscle of my back. But there is no time to register the pain. Because Karl brings down the edge of the axe on my left shoulder. My clavicle splinters in two as the axe tears its way through my flesh. The pain is out of this world. I fall to the floor. Blood pumps out, streaming down my body and pooling on the floor. I land awkwardly because of the sword still in my back.

Lucy pulls out the sword and I roll on my back. Karl laughs. He puts his size eleven boot to my chest and heaves at the axe handle until the blade comes free from my shoulder with a sickening sound. Then, the blood really starts to spurt out. After that, it starts going backwards, flowing like water uphill. It still seems impossible after all this time. It is like I have been conditioned for sixteen years to expect things to happen one way. Now it all works backwards. I watch in fascination at all the dark red fluid running. The pain seems far away now. It is like watching the TV. I am lost, looking at the dark wine-red fluid as it froths. I am here but at the same time I am far away: safe.

 I see the faces of Lucy, Karl and Bonemann. They all wear disappointment. Should that be worrying? I cannot decide. What are they expecting? What do they know that I do not? It is at this point that I realise it's not disappointment but hate in their eyes. And their eyes are all focused upon me.

# Chapter 4

# Punishment Duty

*My body is on the mend.*

I start to get the use of my shoulder back and can feel my legs once more. I kneel and then push myself to my feet. I hate it. My face burns with shame at being beaten so easily.

"That was pitiful," Bonemann says.

I nod.

"Stay behind. The rest of you, get lost until tomorrow," he says.

*Oh great*, I think.

"As for you, punishment duty!" Bonemann says.

The others walk towards the door. Their voices are raised in conversion, but their footsteps are silent. Karl, Lucy and a few others look back at me as they leave the room. Each has a smile for me that is closer to a sneer.

"Don't forget what is happening at the end of the month. So, I want you all sharp tomorrow. We have a lot to get through," Bonemann calls after them.

I know what he is talking about: the big feast and the meeting of the twelve. As well as the blood feast, there will be combat trials where four of the best 'protégé' fighters from each kingdom will fight. I do not expect to be among them. Not a chance in hell of that. Which I am glad about.

I scrub the floor and walls of the training room with a scrubbing brush and metal bucket. The mixture of soap, vinegar and hot water is not particularly good at removing blood from the stone walls and floor.

There is that small amount of blood that is not sucked right back into the body. If you are killed enough times, do you run out of blood? There are probably less than a couple of thimbles-full soaked into the walls, but the splatter makes it look worse: more abundant. A small amount goes a long way and it is murder to try and scrub it clean, especially when the scrubbing brush is little more than a piece of wood with the bristles ground down so far that using the word 'brush' to describe it at all is an act of pure optimism.

"So this is what a loser looks like: on his knees scrubbing the floor. A voice shatters the silence. "A regular Cinderella, aren't we?"

"Danny?" I do a double-take. Just for a split second, I think it is Danny's voice. I haven't thought about him for weeks. Then there is a female voice:

"Come on, Karl. Don't waste your time. He's not worth the effort!"

I am not best-pleased to see who is in the doorway.

"Come in and have a look, Luce," Karl smirks.

Lucy peers around the doorway. Karl walks forward a couple of steps.

"Great. I have seen him. Now let's go. If the Bonemann catches us here. We will be joining him," Lucy snaps.

"Oh, I don't think so. I have special dispensation," says Karl.

Special dispensation? What the hell does he mean? I do not like the sound of it. I do not like it one single bit.

"Haven't you heard? It is open season on this loser," sneers Karl. His voice is low like gravel being ground under foot. "He's got no friends to protect him now. Mr Hrot has withdrawn his protection. He has realised that he made a mistake."

"No friends? Are you sure? I have seen him with you know who... She's close to the king," Lucy says. Her forehead creases.

"The abomination? Ha, ha. They just use her for what she is good at. No one can stand her after what she did. She makes everyone sick to be around her!" he sneers.

"Karl" I say quietly.

"Eh?"

"Get lost!". I throw the bucket of water at his head.

He smoothly ducks. The pail flies towards the wall, water trailing behind. It crashes, its body pancaking against the wall and then falling to the floor with a clattering sound.

"Ha, ha...your days are numbered!" Karl calls out, as he turns on his heels and walks towards the door.

"Something else for you to clean up. That was really clever," Lucy purrs.

Then she follows Karl out. I just stand there. My fists clenched. My muscles are tight: too tight. They feel as if they might rip apart and tear away from the bones they are attached to. My face burns hot. I think about going after Karl, but I just crossed the room and retrieved the buckled bucket instead. I sigh. I sit cross-legged on the floor, then pull the bucket back into a rough bucket shape. It looks pretty pathetic. I try standing it on the floor. It falls drunkenly to its side and rolls around in a half circle. My eyelids flash open wide. I pick up the bucket and hurl it with all my strength at the wall, enjoying the sound of its destruction as it hits.

# Chapter 5

# Blood Feast



The Feast of Blood: the convention of the Twelve takes place over three days. Most of it is political, involving the meetings of heads of state. It has nothing to do with us and is only for the highest ranking of the Wonder-kind. For the rest, it is three days of celebration. There is the feast on the final evening. Before that, in the afternoons, there are the festivities and combat trials. Karl won all of his match-ups, making him more insufferable than normal. This is something I would not have thought possible; but there you are. If gloating was a competition, he would have won that too.

I nearly miss the main feast. That wouldn't have been a bad thing. Things have gone from bad to worse for me. Bonemann has scheduled me for another of his punishment details, but has had a change of heart at the last minute. Personally, I doubt that he even has one to change. It is certainly out of character for him. Then I find out it is nothing to do with him. The feast is something that everyone has to attend without exception: out of obligation. So it looks like Bonemann has been overruled. By who, I don't know. They haven't done me any favours; it will only give him another reason to make my life hell.

It doesn't matter to me one way or the other. I am the lowest of the low around here. I feel disconnected from the whole thing. I begin to wish to have been put on punishment detail instead.

The most ridiculous set of clothes I have ever seen materialises upon my bed. Bonemann tells me they will be there, and that I have to wear the damn things to the feast.

So I put them on. Both the trousers and the tunic are made from smooth black silk, with a pattern of yellow flames that circles the garment around the shoulders, elbows and hips, where the material flares out in round pleats. I look ridiculous. I look like some sort of peacock. I feel very visible and self-conscious as I go down the corridors towards the big hall at the other end of the castle where the feast is being held. But as I walk and see that everyone else is wearing similar – or even more ridiculous – clothing, I begin to feel less conspicuous. Even so, I am unable to shake off that uneasy feeling that everyone is looking at me and laughing behind my back. I half-expect to go into the hall to find myself the only one dressed bizarrely.

The Feasting hall is a long room with high ceiling and stone arches supported by ancient looking stone pillars. Stained glass windows are set into the walls down the length of the room, depicting vivid and violent battle scenes. Two of the windows have been covered for the period of the feast. Now, long dark green curtains hang in front of two of the windows on a copper rail that runs high up around the room. At the far end of the hall, there is a long table. It is raised about thirty centimetres or so off of the ground on a stone podium. King Theodore is sitting at the centre and his son and daughter are sat to the left. Sarah is sat on the right. The rest of the people at the table I don't recognise – the other eleven of the twelve, I can guess. They are all dressed in a more elaborate and puffed up clothing that is even more over the top than that worn by the rest of us. And that is saying something.

The other tables are longer and run down the length of the room. Each seat about twelve people. They are lined up one after another, in two lines on either side of the room. The centre is clear for the various serving staff, who hurry back and forth between tables. The tables are mostly full already. I walk down the centre aisle, looking for somewhere to sit.

"Over here!" a voice calls out. I don't recognise the voice at first. It is one I know all too well but because it is not punctuated with an insult, it sounds almost friendly. Because of this, it seems strange and unfamiliar.

"Over here," Karl repeats, his hand slapping on the back of a chair next to him. Lucy is sat on the other side drinking from a silver goblet. The others are familiar faces from the training room.

"Come on! Sit down!" Karl says.

Alarm bells are ringing loudly and violently inside my head. I think he must be drunk on either the blood or from his success in the trails, or both. But I sit next to him, instantly feeling uncomfortable.

"Have some of the red stuff!" he exclaims. "Fresh!"

"Here we go!" he says cheerfully.

Karl pours blood into my goblet until it is full to the top. The thick dark red liquid brims and a thin tickle of red flows quickly down the side. I smell it and my mouth floods in anticipation at the thought of its smooth velvety texture.

"Thanks," I say awkwardly.

I raise the goblet to my mouth. It fizzes on my tongue at the first taste. It is good, very good in fact. I drain the cup. I put the cup back on the table.

"More?" Karl says. He pours more into my goblet without waiting for my reply.

"Drink up!" He says, and slaps me on my back. It is something you might do to an old friend – an enthusiastic slap. So, of course, I am suspicious. I sniff at the blood. It smells like... well, blood: the strong smell of iron. But there is something else – something I cannot place.

"Yeah drink up," Lucy echoes, interrupting my thoughts. I turn to Karl.

"You're in a good mood," I comment.

"Too right I am, not only did I win every contest, but the King has made me his Team Champion!" he says, punctuating the sentence with another slap across my back. I wince. I swallow the blood, but come close to spitting it out over the table.

"Yes. Congratulations," Lucy says, her voice low and cold.

I look at her sour expression, surprised.

"Don't mind her. She is just jealous!" Karl says. He puts a big meaty hand on my shoulder to pull me back around to face him.

"I am not! It just isn't fair. That's all," Lucy retorts.

"What is not fair?" I ask. I have not had any involvement in the combat trials. I wonder what I have missed.

"Girls... Ok!" Karl says. Lucy reaches over and punches Karl on the arm. It is quite a powerful whack. Karl pretends to be hurt, then laughs: a deep throaty laugh, which sounds like a toad croaking.

"Women!" she corrects.

"Women?" I say, none the wiser.

"Women," she says glaring at Karl "aren't' allowed to compete in the trials."

"No?"

"No!"

"Why not?"

"Something to do with some ancient chivalric code: it goes back hundreds of years. Where a woman's place was at home doing embroidery and waiting for her husband to come home from the wars. As it should be," Karl says, as Lucy reaches for a long sharp meat knife.

*He really believes in that bullshit?* I shake my head.

Lucy slices the air in front of Karl's face. If she meant it, she would have had his nose off. No, this is just the way they play. Karl catches her wrist. With mock sincerity, he puts the hand to his lips and kisses it once.

"M' lady" he says.

Lucy pulls her hand away in one brisk moment. She holds it to her chest as if protecting it.

"What?" Karl says "I said I would make you my lieutenant, didn't I? What more do you want?" He throws up his arms, his eyes shooting up towards the ceiling.

"No pleasing some people."

My body relaxes a little. My mind on the other hand is racing. *What is this all about?* I wonder. It feels wrong, as if I have fallen into a parallel universe: a universe where cats bark and howl in alley ways and dogs meow and climb up trees. Here I am looking at the next generation of the Unseeyn Hand. They are all at this table and the next. I have to shudder.

There is food on the table: human food, meat dishes mainly. Elliot is eating the leg off of some large animal: a pig or a boar, maybe. He takes a bite and pulls the meat away in his mouth and then, with a sharp knife, he hacks the meat away from the bone – sucking it into his mouth. He smiles across to me with greasy blood-red lips. I don't know if we can still eat solid food. I suppose there is no reason why not, as we still have the same anatomic equipment we had when we were human. It has been modified, sure – in ways I still don't understand – for a diet of blood. I can still eat the meat on the table, except for the fact that solid food no longer appeals to me. Looking at the greasy carcass on the table, I reckon I will be able to hold it down but just seeing Elliot eat makes my stomach a bit queasy.

Awkward and restless, I glance around, looking at the others at the table, one by one: all of my classmates, all strangers to me. No sign of recognition passes between us. I turn back to Karl. He is talking about one of his fights. Everyone is looking at him in rapt attention. Even Bonemann looks towards him with half a smile on his face. Karl is at his happiest when he is the centre of attention. For me, neither he nor his story is of any interest to me. He has for some unknown reason started to act in a civil way towards me, but that does not change anything, not really. I start to look for somewhere to put my gaze other than looking at those at the table I am on.

On the next table one, one of the human blood slaves is having his head forced to the solid wood of the table, as two of them take turns drinking from his neck, the blood frothing into their eager mouths. *Revolting!* I look away. I become aware of the taste of blood in my mouth, marking me as a hypocrite. I glance over towards the King's raised table. I see Sarah. She is sitting next to Henry Hrot. He is leaning over, between her and the King. He has a silver goblet in his hand, which he holds on the table as if he is saying something to Sarah. She smiles and nods. Then she laughs. I realise she is looking directly at me as she laughs. It is a real Bonemann laugh: cruel and abrasive. Her face is full of contempt. My entire face burns under her gaze as I understand that I have her full attention, that is that she is laughing at me. I have been betrayed by the one friend I thought I had. I feel sick. God, I have been so stupid. Why do I do this? Why did I put my trust in another?

*They will always let you down.*

The room flickers, quivering as everything rushes in towards me. I see all the faces around the table laughing. But why? Simple, we are Wonder-kind and we crave two things: blood and cruelty. We need the blood to survive, but the cruelty... Well, that is just for fun. *How could I be so stupid to trust anyone here? They are all the same. Blood suckers. They lie, cheat and scheme as easily as breathing. I fume inside my head.*

"Have some more," a smiling Karl says, as he tops up my goblet with blood. I put the goblet to my lips and drink deep. My mind flips from feeling really stupid for being taken in, to devastating loss. I have never trusted anyone as I did Sarah. Too late…

I look back at the young man who the two on the next table have been feeding on. He lies on the table unmoving. His face is a white-grey colour and empty. I cannot hear a heartbeat. The man of the pair of blood suckers laughs and pushes the victim's head off the table. It falls into a heap on the floor. He raises his hands and clicks his fingers. Two terrified looking human slave-servers come over.

"Get rid of it!" he says and then turns back to the table and resumes talking in a loud and jovial way.

"And bring another!"

"Anyway! Then I say..."

This callous act is just one of so many I have seen. But it seems to say everything about this living nightmare... No, this is worse than a nightmare, because you can wake from a nightmare.

# Chapter 6

# Tainted Blood

*I have had enough.*

I just want the ground to open up beneath me. Most of all, I just want to die: if they are going to kill me, I just hope that it will be quick and that they will just get on with it.

I get up and start to walk to the door.

"Where are you going?" Karl's grinning face asks.

I say nothing. I just have to get out of the hall. I have to get away.

I walk with stiff, jerky, but determined moments, as if every muscle in my body is glued together, towards the wooden doors. I push through and storm down the corridor. I try to think if I have said anything compromising to Sarah, anything that they can get me with. Probably, but I cannot think of anything. However, that does not mean I haven't. I just can't think of it. Maybe the odd word or sentence when my guard was down... Perhaps that is why Henry has withdrawn his protection. Maybe...

"Are you going?" a gentle voice asks.

*The treacherous girl herself, who got me to lower my defences.*

My mind is white hot with rage. I want to punch my fist through a wall or someone's face. I have to leave this place. I have to run... and never stop. But I don't stop. Yet I cannot bear to turn around and look at her. I have no idea what I will do if I do.

"Yes..." I say, my voice hoarse and my throat a mass of tight muscles that barely let air in and out. A blur passes by me and then she is standing in front of me. Her black round eyes are locked directly onto mine. I look away, off to the side, unable to stand their intensity.

"You're angry..." she says.

"With me...?" she adds.

I try to nod. But I can barely move my neck. I bite my lip.

"You never told me you were so close to Henry!" I spit

"Of course. What did you think I did? I am the court Seer. The King's Seer... Henry is the King…"

"...Spy master," I complete.

"Yes."

"What did you think I did?" A concerned look flashes over her face. But I don't care.

"And you're his spy." I say the words slowly.

"...You...told him everything. All the time you are reporting all I did and said back to him," I say. I do not want to. I want this to be over. I want to get out of here.

But Sarah's face, in the very second of hearing my words and processing them, changes. It transforms from its small and pale shape to one that is animated with an explosion of emotion:

"Never!" she says. The word is spoken softly but has a real force to it, the force of capitalisation and an exclamation mark.

"I would never betray you. Not ever," she says.

"You are my one friend; the only piece of warmth in this cold and cruel world. I would never do anything to destroy that, to hurt you," she continues.

This stops me in my tracks. Suddenly, I feel stupid. The words themselves could have been feigned, but not the emotion behind them. I look down at my feet. I cannot think what to say. After a pause, I speak:

"...Sorry" I say, my voice weak.

"Do you think you would still be here, alive if I had told them what I know about you?"

That again.

"No."

"I just find it hard to trust. I thought –"

"NEVER" she repeats.

"Sorry I was really stupid to think..." I start.

"Yes, you were," she says simply.

"Will you come over later tonight?" I say, looking downward. I am expecting the answer no. So I add "I understand if you don't want to."

"Try and stop me," says Sarah, with a smile.

"I am sorry... I just get a bit paranoid, you know?"

"Henry has a reason for why he recruits who he does."

"How is that?"

Sarah seems to ignore this question. "What's that smell?" she asks, her nose wings moving as she makes a sniffing sound.

She puts a finger to my upper lip. I think that she is signalling to me to be silent, but no. She runs a finger over the surface and then takes it to her nose as she sniffs it.

"Psycho-active," she says.

"What?"

"The blood you have been drinking. It is spiked."

"I thought Karl and Lucy were being bit too friendly," I sigh. "They were very keen on my drinking it. I wondered why."

"Hmmm. Hoping you would act out, maybe..." Sarah suggests. "You noticed the guards all have D-guns. Maybe that was the plan? Who knows? You need to be more careful."

"What is it meant to do?" I ask.

"It distorts reality. Makes you see things. Makes emotions run riot, so that everything seems out of proportion. It would explain a lot," Sarah replies.

"It would," I say. We both look at each other. I look into the big black centres of her eyes, uninhibited.

# Chapter 7

# (Un)Just Sleep

*The drug is starting to wear off.*

The simmering distortion of reality has settled down and my emotions have been dampened. Things return to normal. This has been a strange experience. It is manageable as long as I can remember not to believe anything I see, hear or think. It is as if Rene Descartes' demon is taunting me. But it is harder than you would think. The slightest thing will set me off. I see things that are not there.

"Remember, remember, remember..." I say to myself.

"Are you feeling better?" Sarah asks.

"A bit."

"You know you can sleep" Sarah says to me, as I stare up at the ceiling. I sigh heavily.

She turns over to look at my face. Her face is at an angle.

"How?" I ask.

"Well you just close your eyes, think of something nice and wait! It's easy."

"That doesn't work for me anymore. Not since... I changed. I feel too wired and too awake all of the time."

"I must have a valve broken in my head somewhere," I say.

"Nonsense!" declares Sarah and her arm shoots out for her to pinch the bridge of my nose with a finger and thumb.

"Sleep," she says.

"No..." I protest, but I do. I sleep the sleep of a thousand years, even if it is condensed into ten actual hours. After this, I never have trouble sleeping again. I have trouble with dreams, dark and disturbing dreams, but never with sleeping.

# Chapter 8

# Future Tense

*My Clarks shoes squelch in the mud.*

I look down. The dark red-brown liquid rises up over the tops of my shoes. The sides flood with the cold wetness. Every blade of grass in this meadow is coloured red.

I feel the intense heat on my back. I turn to look. Beyond the outside walls and the towers, everything is in flames. The hills are no longer visible and are hidden behind walls of flame. In the distance, mushroom clouds billow up into the sky. The world is burning. It warms me. It feels nice on my face. I close my eyes, feeling its warmth. I sigh because I know I cannot stay here. I have to finish my pilgrimage. I have to go up the hill; I am coming home.

I ascend the hill of bone. You can tell the human bones from the Wonder-kind ones. The Wonder-kind are not dead, not really, they still move and twitch, endlessly trying to reconstruct, but unable. I climb up over them towards the great hall.

"All-hail-the-conquering-hero!" Henry calls out, as, I enter the great hall.

The red carpet oozes and squelches the red stuff as I walk up towards the single throne. It is made of entirely of bone. Henry's head bobs up and down on top of his spine. His spine and everything else, below the jaw line, is stripped of its flesh. His head is woven together with two others to form the back of the chair. The ribs of the three ribcages have been broken open and the bone woven together with golden thread. The heads are the only parts still covered in flesh and hair: barely. Henry is smiling a big smile of pure happiness – no, that isn't it - it is pride. He is looking at me with pride. I can see it in his eyes. The other head, the one next to Henry, is the king's: King Theodore. He looks at me, his eyes glaring at me with hate, his lipless mouth sewn together with thick rows of zig-zag stitches. Whatever it is, he is burning to say it to me. He can't. Have I done this to him? The third head is Bonemann's:

"Proud of you. Never thought you had it in you," Bonemann says smiling.

"I told you! He is born to rule!" Henry says excitedly.

"My Lord," a small voice behind me says. I recognise it.

Sarah is knelt at the foot of the steps to the throne. Her head is lowered. I can't see her face. Her knees are on the sodden red carpet, which is staining the long white silk dress she is wearing.

"Sarah? What are you doing down there? You don't have to kneel to me?"

"No?" the dead voice says. It is heart-breaking to hear.

I walk over to Sarah and reach down to her arms and start to pull her up. I gaze down at her as she looks up.

I can't breathe. Everything hurts. It is as if someone has swung at my stomach with a sledgehammer. I can't bear it. I can't bear to be alive for another second. As the small white face looks up from under her blonde matted hair, I see where those big bright eyes should be, where now only two black and empty sockets lie. She speaks, but it isn't her voice that comes out of her mouth:

"She sees the future much better now, since you took her eyes," the voice chuckles.

And then everything spins around and upside down.

"NO!" I scream.

The scream vibrates, joined with both the dreaming and my waking state. I jerk bolt upright, looking around wildly. My night clothes are drenched in sweat. I look around the room.

"Sarah?" I whimper.

Sarah slides through the window and drops to the floor without a sound. Her black eyes are big and her face is creased, full of concern.

"What is it?" she asks. "I heard you from the roof!"

"Nothing. Just a dream," I say. I am more relieved than I could ever put into words.

I am looking at Sarah's eyes, bright and alive. Not like the hollow sockets in the dream. I feel an immense sense of relief. I get off the bed and hug her: a real bear hug, unbreakable and tight. If she were human, it would crush her. But as she isn't, she hugs me back with equal ferocity.

"You should always listen to your dreams. You never know what they are going to tell you," she says.

"They can be prophetic," she chirps.

*I hope not. God, I hope not.*

The message of the dream is plain enough. I am going to kill everyone. Worse, I am going hurt Sarah. I hate and loathe the second part.

The world... Well, I have always felt that to be over rated. But we all need somewhere to put our feet, don't we?

I hug Sarah tighter.

"Urk!" she says.

"I will never hurt you. Not you. You know that, right?"

"Yes, I know!" she insists, eyes wide and trusting.

I silently and dearly wish that it will always be true.

# Regime Change

# Chapter 1

# Future Signs

*The night is brighter than daylight.*

The moon, full and colossal, looks down upon us, shining brilliant and bright: like a new sun. Its rays play upon the furrowing sea, as a silver sheen.

We sit on the roof of the watchtower, watching the waves push endlessly towards the shore, Sarah with her legs crossed and me with my legs stuck out in front of me. My elbows support me as I lean back. The wind blows around the structure like a giant tin whistle.

I look out at the sea, watching the waves roll towards the shore and my eyes follow up tracing the outline of cliffs, tall, magnificent and indifferent.

Darkness has gone for me, forever, I will never look out upon a dark and foreboding sea again; all that has gone for me. There is no more concealment, no more fear at what lies out there invisible to my eyes. I can see perfectly. I will never again be able to shut out the horror that passes in front of my eyes.

We have spoken about everything, said everything that can be said. Now we sit in silence, out of words, with both fatigue and repose joint at the hip.

Everything is the way that it is in its full horrific reality.

My eyesight improves every day; things are getting sharper, more vivid and clear. With that, my night vision has improved and I have started to see the night in colour as well, so much so I can barely distinguish between night and day now, except for the presence of the moon and the sun. I know the difference between those two.

I lie back on to the roof. Sarah does the same. Hand in hand, we just stretch out there looking up at the sky and the stars. There are so many of them now. Spread across the night sky in clusters of bright white light, they seem brighter than usual.

Suddenly, a light shoots in an arc across the blue-black sky, and then plummets towards the horizon.

"It's a falling star," Sarah says.

"It's an omen, a harbinger!" she adds excitedly, leaping to her feet. Turning to face me, her eyes are ablaze with the sparkle of excitement.

"An omen of what?" I ask.

"It's the beginning of the end," Sarah replies.

Then her face softens. She is looking directly at me, into my eyes, as if trying to see what lies in that dark void beyond my black pupils.

"I am afraid you are going to have to suffer – a lot. I am sorry," she says.

I just look up at her, uncomprehending. The shooting star arches across the sky over her left shoulder: falling. And something in my stomach follows it down.

# Chapter 2

# Fangs Out

*"Fangs out," Lucy screams over the radio static as we fall into hell.*

Hell is very green. I fall upon a giant fleshy leaf from some sort of tropical plant. I have no idea what it is. It's not as if they teach you anything you actually need to know in geography. Still, after all this time, I still feel cheated. I wish I knew these things.

I bounce off the leafy plant, grateful for the soft landing. At least I don't have to waste valuable time on resurrection. The heat is intense and pushing against my body: an invisible hand of heat at baking temperature. I am pouring with sweat already. I try to pull the thick hot air into my lungs. It is like breathing wet concrete. The jungle is alive with the pounding of a particular beat: human hearts. I don't need Lucy's orders; my fangs, long snake-like things, are already extended, screwing up my upper lip into a fleshy pinch of skin. Salvia pours in buckets out of my snarling mouth. I can feel my blood coursing through my veins: it boils within my flesh. But it's not my blood that holds my attention. It is blood of others.

They come out of holes in the ground, down from the trees and through the densely packed forest; eyes burning with the light of fanaticism and the promise of some higher purpose. But they are just kill-dogs sent out by their master to eliminate trespassers. Only, we don't care about death. We are Wonder-kind – we *are* death.

They have been waiting for us. That much is clear even to me. It doesn't matter though. Nothing does. Maybe one thing. I lick my lips.

This is not me.

I sink into the red.

The side arms in my hands are going off like sparklers. Each shot slows. Seemingly, it is minutes between each bullet: time enough to aim and find the target. I never miss, ripping through cranium-bone, taking brain tissue out of the back of the skull. But still they swarm at me. I bring my elbow around, nearly taking the acolyte's head off. Bonemann says every part of our body is a deadly weapon. You just need to know how to use it. Besides, they are only human.

It's an eerie sensation: the sounds of death in the real close up, so close you can feel the spirit leave the body. At the same time, death screams all around. But most chilling of all are the crackles of the headset mixed with the sounds of gunfire and dying. It gives all this death a sort of three-dimensionality. There is a sense of absolute totality to it.

I feel the crack of breaking bone. Or is it *the sickening crack*? I can't tell anymore. I am played out and burnt out. Only blood matters – the drinking of the soul of another. I find a neck to sink my fang into, his body hot as the jungle itself, and the red stuff flows into my mouth upon my grateful and excited taste buds.

I guess that Sarah is right. I am moving away from her, closer to these psychopaths. She is losing me. I am losing her. I am not sure which is the most heart-breaking. It is wrong: not what I want. But when did what I want have anything to do with anything? After all, Sarah has shown me the future. She has shown me the thing that I will become. No, I am not the same as these other Wonder-kind cunts. I am a million times worse. This way is better: away from Sarah. I should stay away. Stay here maybe. Before I take her eyes and her soul.

She had said some other things that night. After seeing the shooting star from the watchtower. They were mostly to do with different coloured balls of wool, all tangled up and batted around: played with by a bunch of cosmic cats or something like that. I love Sarah to bits but when she goes off the deep end... Well, I can't make head nor tail of what she is on about.

And, in the morning, they come for me. Through sleepy eyes, I see Sarah disappear through the window, then the knock on the door. There is no waiting for an answer. Karl barges in. Karl, the new team leader, is with Lucy and has one other in tow.

"We 're at war," he says. "Combat room in five minutes."

And then he is ramming a handgun under my jaw, telling me, "Don't mess up, or I will kill you."

"Not with that you won't," I say, forcing his finger down on the trigger.

The bullet takes out half my jaw and a couple teeth, leaving a hole at the back of my throat. I feel the crunch and pull of bone as it is already re-ossifying back into one piece, and the flesh crawling across my jaw to melt back together. It hurts a lot, but it is worth it to see the look on

Karl's mug. Karl rages at me, shouting and waving his fists at my face. I just laugh at the stupid bastard. The Bonemann sighs:

"Maybe there is hope for young Tiber after all."

I think I am losing my mind. I can feel it all unravelling. But it is the god-awful numbness that frightens me the most: feeling nothing and caring less. Fugue. Every time I close my eyes I see Sarah's face: two empty lifeless sockets – black. She is looking up at me – sightless but still seeing – through me. I know full well that it is me who did this to her. The pain of our knowing is too much. I say over and over: *Just a dream*. It doesn't help. It feels too real – too much like something I am going to do. I will cut out my own heart first, rather than do that to her. So my mind takes flight and runs from the image – from everything. I am still running out here in the heat and the green. Maybe I will never stop.

We are somewhere in South America. Even I manage to figure that one out. I have never seen airplanes like the ones that brought us here. It seems to me that there is a whole armada of them: all prepped and ready to go. I have never fallen so far, as one of hundreds of us, raining out the sky. Why am I here? The Wonder-kind don't like this sort of direct open conflict. But this is an exception or so I am told. What the exception is or why we are here is on a need to know basis and I don't – apparently.

No, they prefer to keep their activities covert here – hence the name: The Unseeyn Hand. But this is as far out in the open as you can get. Things are changing rapidly aright, but for those who don't do well with change, it doesn't seem right.

*So why all of this?*

The Unseeyn Hand's shock troops are all around: dark ghosts that move in a blur, disappearing almost before you see them. They are spreading out up ahead of us. I can see Bonemann just after them and, behind him, the other prodigies are peppered throughout the woods: killing and feeding. The only way you can see the shock troops properly is if you slow down what you are seeing in your head. Then you can make out their silently flowing bodies with their heavy armaments: some sort of heavy-duty D-gun in the form of a chunky and ugly looking rifle. The whispers in the group say we are only a mile away from the target. The other Wonder-kind nations are advancing from all sides.

*I don't care about any of this.*

*"Don't go getting the idea that I give a shit," Bonemann says. "It is simply the case I will have to train another bunch of toe-rags."*

So, I am a child soldier. Is that it? Well I am seventeen now. Is that too old? I have never known what I wanted to be when I grew up, but I am pretty sure this was not it. I lick at the crud on my lips. When that doesn't work, I scrape it off with a thumbnail.

Something not human falls from the tree. It is upon me before I can react. I am pushed to the ground. He is Wonder-kind: one of King Lanzón's El Niño's storm warriors.

*"Some of the best solders you will ever come across," Bonemann says.*

*"So stay out the way. You are there for support only," he adds.*

The El Niño punches me hard across the face and the two handguns go flying into the greenery. I have nothing except the two knives in either boot to defend myself, if only I could reach them. No D-gun for me, or any other Prodigies, not until we graduate. And this is looking like something that is never going to happen.

*"You will be going into battle naked," Bonemann informs me. "Play-time is over. So far, you have only gone up against humans, who unless they are lucky in the extreme, can't hurt anything other than your feelings. That's over. There are wonder-kind out there with the means of your destruction. They have D-guns, while you have only regular weapons."*

*"The grown-ups will be doing most of the killing. So, stay close and make yourself useful."*

*"What about if we come face to face with an in a combat situation?" Karl asks.*

*"Shoot for the face, then run. You can't beat an armed El Nino. But most likely you will already be dead. Dust on the wind," Bonemann says.*

He is on top of me, pushing down and crushing me, his fangs out and his knife, a long thing that is shaped like a dagger, coming towards my face. Then he explodes into pink dust, sliding from me as the rest of his body crumbles. I look up to see Bonemann with his D-gun, recently fired, at the end of his extended arm. He turns and walks towards the fighting up ahead, disappearing into the weird and wonderful vegetation.

The D-canons fire, hissing with electrical charge before their beams shoot through the dense forest, exploding the dark figures out of trees, making them instantly disintegrate, no more than particles of dust, before they hit the forest floor, to be blown on the furnace-like breeze.

There are whole sectors of rainforest stripped bare by the D-Canon blast. We march through the empty spaces, with coloured dust at our feet, like small dunes of sand. The sun burns down on my head as if wanting to burn me to a cinder. The idea is not unwelcome.

Entering the jungle once more, I run into a wall of bullets. They tear my body to shreds. Bone and flesh rend apart. It comes so quickly that I don't feel a thing. I twist downwards, still conscious, as I crash to the ground. Now I feel it: the sparks of electrical jolts as my brain tries to reboot itself. I can taste my own blood. The bullets have to be 50 calibers – when you have been shot as often as I have you know about these things. I have had plenty of practice in the murder games back at Chateau Blanc.

# Chapter 3

# Newly risen

*I resurrect in the shit and the dirt of the jungle floor.*

A dead man reborn out of the filth and muck. I hear the blood rushing in my ear and feel that my wreck of a body is screaming, as bone snaps back together and flesh reconstitutes itself. My spine snakes up into shape and my eyes open. I am alive. It is always a surprise no matter how many times I die. Then I remember the first rule of resurrection – move!

Half formed, with my insides still hanging out along the jungle floor, I crawl at full speed. I am full of holes and bleeding out everywhere, sliming a trail of blood over the jungle floor. My insides are trying to escape, hanging down and dragging on the filthy ground. I speed towards the heavy machine gun emplacement. It is made out of the tree logs and smeared over with mud. The gun spits out led like a swarm of angry mosquitoes. I know what I need, with my body peppered with fifty calibre wounds, and I know how to get it. I am nothing but a crawling slab of bloody meat. But I am a carcass with intention. I know what I want. The pounding of human hearts up ahead, louder to me than the rattle of the gun, calls me on.

They shriek and scream as I break into their log emplacement. One of them shakes so much that his vocal cords barely make a sound as the other two make a run for it. Suits me fine. My fangs pop through his neck and the red stuff floods in what is left of my mouth. I must look monstrous. For once in my life, the outside resembles the inside.

My body burns as if it is covered in molten lead. Inside, my brain nerve synapses are going off, firing to the sky. As the blood hits the spot, my skin crawls back over my ripped apart body: whole again. My chest pops bullets like rain falling to the damp ground. Then I am screaming, out of my mind. I run after the two fleeing prey, leaping through the trees. I descend upon my prey – no ego, no conscious thought – only fangs and cold hard steel. I go to work.

Nothing makes any sense to me anymore. So what is there left to do – except embrace the insanity? You have got to be crazy living a life like this – a real straitjacket and padded cell candidate. When I lose control, it's like a sparkler going off in the centre of the nervous tissue of my brain.

I want to kill everyone. I want to rip this world apart and burn it to the ground.

With all this violence and death all around, I am a far cry from the person I am with Sarah. But this madness becomes me. It seeps through the skin, the eyes and the ears. Am I even the same person? Or am I two separate ones in the same shell? I'm damned if I know.

I haven't lost my temper in a long while, not even with the people I've killed, and before that, never. When I was ten, my brother threw an action man at me and it hit me on the head. Enraged, I jumped on him, action man figure in hand, forcing him to the floor. Holding the action man up high, I was ready to bring the figure down upon my brother. Before I did, I could feel my rage, knowing that if I started, I would keep hitting him until…No I just would not stop. That scared the hell out of me. After that, I was too scared of my anger to even lose control for a second. But now the safety is most definitely switched off and my hair trigger is going in all directions. There are no moral restraints here, only the endless choleric feeling, and yellow bile pouring from every pore. The ocean of ire within me is flooding up into my brain. I scream out for more blood.

*"War is real, maybe the only truly authentic thing you will ever engage with. It is pure and simple, like touching the divine, something greater than yourself,"* The Bonemann had said.

I really am a loathsome creature: truly ghastly.

All around, it is like trees are crying out with ear-piecing screams. The many voices merge into one heart-stopping terrible noise. Those huge trunks, shooting straight skyways into the greenness of their thick canopy of leaves, seem to have found a voice for the misfortune that we have visited upon them. Only the screams are all human. The Wonder-kind are taking their time with the killing.

The anger and everything dies in my throat. As huge and infinite the feeling of rage feels, I am disconnected from it. The endless tide of enjoyment that promises satisfaction expires within my chest. It is the most god-awful feeling. Suddenly, I am alone and very small in this giant's landscape, with its mammoth tress and triffid-like plants. I just want to curl up into a ball and weep.

And then death walks out of the trees. Two bodies are dangling upside down from a tree to the left of him. He is tall, brown skinned and young looking – really young. His arms are outstretched straight, holding the D-gun – aiming straight at me. I tilt my head to one side, considering this development.

I smile warmly at death and saunter over to meet him. After all, we are always missing each other. I am starting to think he is avoiding me. Yet here he is with his fangs out. The El Niño has me in his sights. All sorts of wild thoughts rush through my head as I break into a run to meet him: to embrace death head on.

His fangs shrink back into his mouth. His arm is shaking in big physical movements. He lets go of the gun and drops his burden into the grass by his feet. The D-gun lands with a gentle thud. Then the El Niño turns and runs into the trees. And I see death doing a runner, scuttling away from me with all the might he can muster. I can only conclude he really doesn't like me. And so much for these fearless warriors, the El Niño's. More lies. Death is just a scared kid. Five minutes ago, I would have torn him apart, Wonder-kind or not.

I walk over to where Death had been standing, kneel and pick up the D-gun. Just touching it sends shivers racing in relay up and down my spine. I have never held a D-gun in my hands before. If a prodigy is caught with so much as a finger touching one of these things, they face instant termination. With the ability to deliver death to the immortal, these D-guns are the power behind the formidable wonder-kind. And yet the gun looks unimpressive and plain. With its long lack barrel and its stubby little handle, it doesn't amount to much.

"I'll take that, if you don't mind," a voice from behind me says.

"Huh?" I respond, reaching the handle.

But a hand has already gripped the barrel and is prising it away from me.

"Before you hurt yourself," the Bonemann says, with one of his ghoulish smiles strewn across his face.

"Oh, I just found it," I say, feeling like I am ten again and back at middle school, caught red-handed. Though he is in his rights to just shoot me on the spot. Bonemann considers it, or perhaps something else. I can see the pupils of his eyes flick from side to side. But instead he just says:

"On your way, boy. There's still killing to be done."

# Chapter 4

# Mind Meandering

*I have been walking for hours.*

The rags that used to be clothes are drenched in sweat and blood and hanging limply, made darker with shades of brown: my blood and that of others. It stains my mouth and the insides of my nostrils. Dried on my skin, under my nails, and crumbing off in flakes from my hands, each still holding a blade – the steel dulled to the colour of dried blood. My bullet-hole racked trousers chafe again on the inside of my leg with each step. I have to walk full circle, back to the clearing where I left Bonemann hours ago. I recognise the two humans strung up in the trees, hanging upside down tied with rope by their ankles. And, of course, their throats have been ripped out. I walk into the clearing. I have no idea where either the El Niño or the Unseeyn Hand troops are. My radio headset bit the big one when I was peppered with bullets. I hear explosions and guns going off somewhere behind the trees.

*It is simply mind over matter, the Bonemann had said back in Chateau Blanc in the combat room. I don't mind: you don't matter. The class laughed even though the joke was at their expense, even though the*

*Bonemann wasn't smiling and did not look like he regarded what he had said as a joke.*

"The enemy will have D-guns but you won't. I would prefer it if none of you see action until after you graduate."

"You are not ready. But fate dictates events and not me. There are things that even I can't control," he continues,

There is laughter.

"So who is the enemy?" Karl asks.

"Anyone we tell you," Bonemann replies.

We are all just being used. Pawns in a bigger game, bigger than any of us will ever understand. It is certainly beyond my sick and tired little brain. And it is all for some twist: a so-called greater purpose.

I have had my fill.

It is a mind-body problem. My body has changed beyond all recognition. It enjoys the killing and blood, especially the blood. It lights me up bright. But I am not my body. I am my mind wrapped up in its flesh. Most things we tell ourselves about who we are really are just fictions on top of the stories our parents and teachers told us and anyone else who happened to be in the vicinity at the time. The only thing we can say truthfully is that we are organic machines that try to make sense of all that experience thrown at us. We are meaning machines in a meaningless universe – talk about sadomasochism.

There is no exit from my fucked-up life. I can't bring back yesterday. If I could, would I? Danny would have killed me eventually. If not by his hand, he'd have made my life so nasty and miserable. Well I was just not that strong – not back then. After a while, the abuse just eats you away from the inside out, like a cancer, until there is nothing left: nothing remains and there is no strength left. Now I am the killer. My moral fortitude has been reset to zero – the last vestiges of humanity are disappearing in the steam and humidity of this place. And I don't care. I remain as an empty shell – brought alive only by the thrill of the kill.

It is the heat. The sun burns down on my stubbly scalp. The blood seems to boil within my veins as the sun pours down on top of me. I wipe the sheen of sweat from my scalp. I have never known anything like this heat. Not even in the summer of '76'. It feels like my brain is being boiled.

Everything around me slows to a stop. Blood is roaring and there is a high-pitched whine in my ear, then silence: everything stops, everything is still and everything goes quiet. Even the sound of gunfire and screaming subsides – like someone has turned the volume down on life. It is as if time has gone backwards; at the same time, there is a sharp sensation in the middle of my forehead. It is like my head is splitting into two halves under the impact of an ice pick.

Everything is distant and flies away from me, seemingly far away, as if on the edge of something new. It is the sensation of standing on a steep gorge looking down, waiting for the terminal wind to take me and blow me over in the valley of razor-sharp blades filling every part of my conscious mind. I'm just waiting for it to happen.

The glow that surrounds the trees looks like green flames that flicker and swirl upwards, flaring towards the blue cloudless sky. The sun is fierce and a near-perfect red sphere that expands, as a circle of fiery red gloriole surrounds its main mass: spreading outwards. Something flies out of its centre, akin to an egg giving birth to a bird shape spectre, with huge wings ablaze, made out of fire. It comes hurtling towards me and hits me with full force, dragging me out of myself.

I have the impression of dropping backwards, though my body seems to stay where it is. And I have lost contact with anything palpable. *Am I dying?* That's what it feels like. *How do I know that? I have never died before.* Has someone killed me after all this? I have wanted it for so long and now it is finally here? No, that's not right. I have only wanted to live – but not as a monster – just to be me. Whatever that means. No, my body looks fine, standing in the clearing – it's just that I am not in it anymore. I shoot skywards.

I am above the trees, with a conflagration of green light covering the rainforest, leaping up from the trees. A wide and flowing expanse of green-black water separates the forest, serpentine and formidable. Further down the river, I see the oil and chemical refineries burning. I have no idea who set light to them. I only recognise the way that fire leaps from building to building: someone has set off incendiary explosives. The fires will burn and burn. There is thick black smoke pouring into the sky and a dirty yellow haze that pollutes the mix of clear blue and green on the horizon. I have no idea how they are going to put out the fire once the fighting is over. The wonder-kind are proving to be nearly as destructive as their human flock.

I am touched by the sheer power of this green landscape and its rawness, though it is not through any mask of fake sentimentality. That was been ripped from me long ago: gone forever. This is different. From the rainforest's roof, with its billions of green leaves, the pale green aura pulses upwards, reaching and bathing me in its rich glow as it passes through me. Despite the fact I have no lungs up here. I breathe in the glow. It feels like life: being alive. There is a warm honey-like sensation in the middle of my body as it is wracked with waves of delight.

And I know what I want. What I need is far from me, but at least I know what is. That is a first for me.

Light blurs as I speed up. Then, the leap is quantum and I am back in Chateau Blanc in the corner of one of the high vaulted roofs, looking down at Sarah. She is standing with Henry and the King. Her head is down as she speaks the words and sentences, as if they are of little or no interest to her because they are not hers. I hear nothing. Everything is silent apart from a roaring sound – like a very strong wind blowing directly into my ears. Only my ears are about 2000 miles away.

Suddenly, Sarah's head snaps upwards, looking directly at me. Her head tilts to one side at first and then her smile broadens, the warmth of which cannot fail to penetrate even my dark heart. *She can see me.* I smile back. A beam of pure radiance shoots out from her stomach and hits me: green and flaring just like the trees in the rainforest and a giant hand of heat pushes through my chest – warming my ice-cold soul.

It is possible. There is a way out of all of this. I just have to get back to Sarah. I made a promise after all. And you should always keep your promises. I want to stay but I know I can't. I have to go back and collect my body. I snap backwards, back to the rainforest.

Is it real? Did it really happen? I don't know. But I do know what I have to do. I have to get back to Sarah. I will listen more carefully to her prophesies, except perhaps the thing about the cosmic cats.

My body isn't where I left it. It has wandered off. I have to wonder what else it has gotten up to while I have been away. It has somehow found the others. They are converging on large stone building: a pyramid with sharp edges and an infinite number of steps leading upward. It looks like a tomb.

# Chapter 5

# Empire's Heart

*The Heart of all Empires are truly rotten.*

This one is no exception. I wander out of the trees to find the others, massed outside of what looks like a stone temple. I see the square status in the front before the thousands of stone steps. I see its square face, its melodious smile revealing two huge fanged teeth protruding down either side of a top row of square stone teeth. And I understand want is going on here. In front of the statue is a long stone trough. Millions of flying insects puncture the surface of dark red going on the black substance inside: half fluid, and half coagulated and jelly-like. It smells rank: stale and rotten human blood is my guess. Its scent turns my stomach. It's enough to make the most bloodthirsty Wonder-kind turn vegetarian. The Wonder-kind swarm en masse up the steps, towards the entrance. I do too, but for a different reason: this is my path back to Sarah.

I wish I couldn't see in the dark, to see those things around the edges of the temple crawling and writhing, those tortured and severed body parts that should be dead. They move and carry on.

There must be a hundred or so D weapons trained upon the lone figure of King Lanzón, but it is Bonemann who steps forward. Following the central gangway toward the stone platform.

"Bonemann! I knew it would be you," the tall man at the centre of the cavernous hall exclaims. I take him to be King Lanzón. He had been present at the Feast of Blood, but I was drugged at the time. I remember very little of the central table of dignitaries in the great hall.

"It's over," the Bonemann says, as he saunters up the stone footway toward the dais where the King stands.

"I knew it would be," the King nods approval. "I had a dream and it was you," he confides.

*Not more dreams! Whatever happened to dreaming you are naked in front of the whole school or that your teeth are all falling out like a waterfall... Dreams where you wake, realising with relief – 'thank god that was just a dream'. Why aren't dreams just dreams anymore?*

The ghoulish-looking Bonemann towers over the king. As if on cue, the king kneels before him, lowing his head. Bonemann points his D-gun downwards at the crouching figure.

"You would kill a God, Bonemann?" the king asks.

"There are no Gods anymore," Bonemann says and pulls the trigger.

The King's body explodes into a million tiny pink pixels that are carried with the draft, lifting upwards towards the apex of the inside of the pyramid as if we are witnessing an apotheosis.

# Chapter 6

# Final Analysis

*My body is shitting bullets and jungle detritus.*

It is slowly working its way out through my flesh. This has been going on for days now. I am well and truly sick of it.

On the left side of my jaw, where the bone meets the skull, a lump of lead is protruding out of the skin like an angry infected pimple. The bone has given the bullet up, which now sits in the flesh, working its way slowly out. I can't help myself. I jiggle the thing from side to side to try and coax it out of the soft tissue. It starts to bleed and I stop my tampering. The thing irritates me, but it is nothing really; I have a number of things pushing out of my back, my left hip, arms and legs. I even have something trying to work its way out of the back of my head.

Pttp…

Something falls out of my body and rolls onto the floor.

"For Pete's sake," I groan.

More planes are starting to arrive. Now that the fight is over, the danger is minimal. Henry and the officials of the remaining eleven kingdoms disembark. They are already arguing with each other. This tells me the negotiations will be long and tiresome. I am just glad to be on the next flight out: back to Chateau Blanc.

"Ah Bonemann!" Henry says.

The massive figure of Gunnar is standing behind him. Lady Francesca crosses the tarmac towards them and Karl moves forward to greet her.

"Any problems?" Henry asks.

"None," the Bonemann replies. "It was a pushover."

"As I said."

"It looks like our friend King Lanzón was so paranoid that he executed most of the talent."

"Yes, yes. My Intelligence said that is so" Henry replies. "He killed nine out of ten of his most experienced generals."

"Worse than that, he excommunicated or kill anyone he thought to be a threat, which is pretty much everyone, except the protégées he tried to compensate by recruiting on mass. But, as you know, numbers are no match for an experienced warrior," Bonemann muses.

"Better for us though," he adds.

"True, true. It is good job we arrived to save the situation," Henry agrees.

"Henry, Bonemann, good to see you both," a tall man says, walking runway towards us on the runway. He speaks with a slight Spanish intonation.

Bonemann grabs me by the arm and pulls me away.

"Don't say anything. Just move!" Bonemann urges.

"What?"

He pulls me towards the airplane, pushing me up the gangway towards the others already on board.

"That's the American," he hisses.

I have heard of him. He is one of the eleven, the only one who doesn't call himself King or anything else for that matter, just 'the American'. If I had expected him to dress as a cowboy, I would be disappointed; he is a snappy dresser, with a thin black overcoat and black shirt and trousers – well pressed and immaculate. He looks like a businessman – like a CEO or something. Nobody knows anything about him, only that he had masterminded the last successful regime change. Turning Middle America into mass grave for its natives and worse for its vampires. They existed before the word Wonder-kind had even been thought of, and every last of them exterminated at the order of this vampire called 'the American'. All reference to their existence has been removed from books and records. I only know this because the wonder-kind live such a long time and some them were around when it happened.

"So?" I ask.

"And that guy is bad news," Bonemann tells me. "Don't ever cross him. It will be the last thing you do."

"I never knew you cared," I reply.

"I don't," he retorts, "but I am responsible for bringing the full team back to the castle in one piece. That includes you, worm!" He says, pushing me away.

Regime change: so that is what this all about. King Lanzón's kingdom was vulnerable, as it has weakened itself to the point of collapse. In other words an easy kill, and what Wonder-kind can resist that?

The twelve are now eleven and King Lanzón's kingdom is divided up between the others. Four thousand years of tradition goes flying out of the window. To say that no one is disturbed by that fact would be a lie. I saw Bonemann's normally rock-steady hand shake when he pulled the trigger. It was only slight but I saw it. And, I feel it in the air now, as we're flying back, despite all the jokes and cheers of celebration: the disconcerted flicker glances, pupils that can't sit still, restless feet and fighting hands. The wonder-kind don't like change. Even us youngsters have internalised that fact. Change means uncertainty – and that signifies danger. We have opened up a whole hornet's nest. The fact that one of the kingdoms has been successfully deposed means that every strategist, official, King or Queen are busy figuring out which of the remaining kingdoms is weakest and ready to be taken down. Regime change is a spiral that never ends once it has started. Me, I don't care. They can all kill each other. The only part of the universe I care about is back in Chateau Blanc. Once I have found her, we will leave these mad creatures to their own devices – after I have promised Sarah. And promises have to be kept. Otherwise you have nothing and are less than zero, on a terminal velocity towards living a life worse than the living dead.

# Sarah Sooth

# Chapter 1

# Rat Runs

*I hear her voice coming out from one of the rat holes.*

I am egotistical enough to expect Sarah to be waiting for me on the runway with a welcome home banner flying. But at the same time, I have been hoping to see her soon after returning. It has been two weeks now. I have not seen hide nor hair of her. She has disappeared before, for days or sometimes weeks and on returning, her only explanation has been that she has duties. *So where is she? Is she avoiding me? Doesn't she want to see me anymore?* Her smile seems to counter that particular argument, but only if it is real and not just a hallucination brought on by heat stroke or some tropical delirium. I have never asked for anything from her and I'm not about to start now. It is not as if we are married or anything. We have, from the start, gravitated towards each other and stayed in each other's obit. But still I miss her – more than I would be prepared to ever admit.

Walking back from the combat room, feeling tired and depressed, the emptiness of my Spartan room is the only thing waiting for me. My ears prick up and I hear Sarah's voice, distant, but it is definitely her.

356

Above me is one of the rat runs, one the numerous exits for the rats to pour in and out of in the pursuit of intruders. They are the white blood cells of the house.

Sarah's voice is being carried out from the hole in the wall. It is quite a large hole as holes go and must be one of the main junctions for our furry friends. I have seen plenty of others of a much smaller size, just large enough for the fattest rat to squeeze through. It is about a foot square. My pulled in shoulders fit easily through the square hole. I begin to crawl towards the source of Sarah's voice and, to my ears, it feels like water on the tip of a parched tongue. I just hope I will not meet any of them coming the other way. They won't do me any harm. I am considered part of the house... unless I do something like attack the King. But I don't like them. They are horrible little dark hairy things with sharp teeth and scratchy claws.

I am in the tunnel-end of a room that is 14 foot by 8. It is swarming with rats, brown and black, and the floor is thick with their number, with a large mound of them in the middle of the floor attacking something beneath them, as they screech and carry on. A hatch opens in the end of the room and something drops in. It is long (about 5ft, 10.) and bound in a hessian shroud. It falls into the middle of the rat pile. They swarm all over the package, gnawing through the hessian and getting stuck into whatever is inside.

*I wonder what they feed the horrible little creatures with?* This is a random thought, but suddenly it is one I wish I have not had. It is so obvious what they feed on: leftovers of course. When the human body has been totally drained of blood, the greyish meat remains; it isn't an empty husk and what better to feed to the animals that form the security system than meat from the very creatures they are meant to attack? It is a disgusting thought. My stomach does a cartwheel and bile tries to find its way up into my mouth.

On the other side of the room, directly opposite and high on the wall, there is a further entrance to the rat run, to take them to the other side of the house. There are another two square holes on the two adjacent walls. This must be their lair. I crawl out of the hole and launch myself at the one opposite. I grip on the stone and pull myself into the hole. I quickly reverse as a single rat comes running down the tunnel. It jumps over my head to land into the mass below. I lose my grip but, out of pure fright of landing in with those furry monsters, I quickly grab the stone ledge, my shoes scuffing up and down on the stone as I pull myself back into the tunnel. I resume my journey towards the source of that voice coming down the tunnel, much louder now. I have to be close.

"I hope this is not another of your vague prophecies that turns out to be completely wrong," Lady Francesca says. "...Like the last time, remember!"

I see them from out of the rat hole: the tall Lady Francesca towers over Sarah. Her face is one of rage. Sarah's eyes glance downwards at the floor.

"Sometimes I wonder if Cassandra is even in there," Francesca says, peering down at Sarah, who looks up as if bewildered. Lady Francesca cups Sarah's chin and looks directly into those large black pupils of hers.

"We need the prophetess. We don't need you. If we didn't need her, we would have gotten ridden of you a long time ago," Francesca says.

"You know what I see when I look into your eyes? Absolutely nothing – just a vicious bitch," Sarah asserts, looking directly into Francesca's glowering eyes.

In truth, though more than deserved, this sounds nothing like Sarah.

Lady Francesca's hand flies towards Sarah in a savage blow, but Sarah catches her arm before it makes contact with her face:

"Don't hit me. I don't like it," Sarah says.

"Why you... I could..."

"Do nothing of the sort," Henrys arm strikes out, taking Lady Francesca's from Sarah's grip. Her eyes blaze with anger.

"You saw that. It's...her!" Lady Francesca protests.

"Enough," Henry snaps, "We have work to do... You know a kingdom to run."

He picks up a piece of chalk and starts to draw a series of overlapping circles on the drawing board.

"Now, where are we?" he says cupping his chin.

Sarah's gaze turns towards me, it is cold and mocking, totally different from the one I have seen in my mind-trip, not to mention totally alien to the woman I have come to know. I yelp silently and turn and flee, feeling that cold gaze burn into the back of my head all the way back through the rat run.

# Chapter 2

# Healing Properties

*"Want to go for a walk?" Sarah says.*

"Sure," I reply.

She sounds and looks like... well, Sarah. I relax. It *is* her. Who else is it going to be? Am losing my grip on reality? Since getting back from South America, I have gotten worse. I just am not sure which parts I am imagining and which are real. *But can I trust her?* Why not? Because she looked at me in an odd way? I am being paranoid. Maybe they are still putting stuff in my blood?

But I am just overwhelmed and so pleased to see Sarah once more that all these worries just melt away into nothing. And pretty soon it is like we have never been apart.

Outside, walking in the grounds of the castle, Sarah has been talking. But now we fall into silence, just walking and happy to be in each other's company. This is a real treat after the corrosive and harmful company of others; it feels better than I can ever imagine: to be with someone who means me no harm and who is the very opposite, despite my paranoia, and who has only good will towards me. It makes all the difference.

Traversing the chateau grounds, we head into the woods and the green
swallows us up. Surrounded by the trees, under the canopy of glowing
green branches, you can forget where you are. Here, cut off from the
sight of the chateau, it is like being somewhere else entirely. We walk
down the stone path, coming out on the other side of the woods. I can
see the human village, up ahead. A woman is running towards us. I can
hear her pounding human heart beat, beating faster than her footfalls.

The back of my neck stiffens and my gut tightens. I point to the
woman. Sarah nods her head slightly. We stop as the woman runs directly towards us, then skids to a stop. She looks at me. An expression
of doubt and fear crosses her features. Then, in a heartbeat, she turns to
Sarah and starts to babble sentences with no spaces or gaps for air –
just a continued grating sound.

I can't understand what the woman is saying. It sounds foreign,
vaguely German, but I can understand the occasional word. Sarah nods
and responds in the woman's own language and then follows her towards the village.

"Come," Sarah says to me.

"No, can't," I respond.

"Why?"

"Can't be trusted," I say.

"Not around humans," I add.

"It will be fine," Sarah tells me.

"Hmm, I am not so sure."

"I won't let you do anything you will regret," Sarah encourages.

Reluctantly, I follow her. The woman leads us over the square patch of grass, down a narrow muddy alleyway, towards a small thatched house at the end. The door is already open. They stride into the windowless hallway. Uncertain, I amble after them.

We are led up some rickety wooden stairs and into the bedroom. A simple bed sits in the centre of the room. It is made of wood, with a single grey dirty blanket crumbled in the middle. There is a small wooden cot in the far corner of the room, with a shroud of mildew upon the wall behind it. By the cot sits a single wooden chair. A small window is set in the thick grubby walls, letting in next to no light into the room.

The woman prattles on, making frenzied gestures with her hands and pointing towards the baby in the cot. Sarah nods calmly, listening. The baby is small, with very little meat around its bones; it looks underfed. It can't be more than a year old – if that. Sarah uncovers the small child from the dirty rag that serves as a blanket and lifts her to her chest.

"There, there..." she says.

The crying child quietens, looking into Sarah's eyes, as if mesmerised by her huge black pupils. Sarah settles on the nearby wooden chair. I would not have trusted the chair with the weight of a hamster, but Sarah perches happily on the rickety old thing. It does not surprise me: whatever she does, she does with a poise and grace that any ballet dancer at the top of her game would envy.

The child's clothes are as grimy as her blanket; they do not seem to be much more than rags. Her face is covered in streaks of dirt, her nose caked in snot and there's a scar on her forehead. It will be too much to bear if I see teeth marks on the babies' neck, so I do not look there. Underneath all the grey-black daubs of dirt, the baby's skin looks inflamed, bright red. The rash covers the child's exposed flesh: face, feet and hands; my guess is that it covers most of the child's body. The child begins to cough violently and Sarah holds her little body, rubbing a hand up and down her back.

"There, there...it's ok, it's ok," Sarah coos, breaking into the strange guttural dialect that these humans speak. She carries on speaking to the mother. I have no idea what she says, but it sounds comforting.

Sarah lays the baby's back on her knees. Then, she leans forward and spits on the child's face.

"What?" My mouth drops open. *What has gotten into her?*

The saliva lands on the child's forehead and Sarah starts to rub it on the skin in circular movements, all over the baby's face. Then she spits again, into her hand this time – the tips of her fingers – and lets it run off into the child's mouth.

"Wah! Wah!"

The child is less than impressed with this treatment. I can't say I blame her.

The mother, who has been sat on the bare floorboards in the corner, wringing her hands and taking to herself, suddenly looks up, her eyes wide and her shoulders trembling.

"Any of our fluids are medicinal," Sarah tells me. "Our spit is just the most convenient to use. It will clear up just about anything. It's good stuff."

"Oh!" I say, now understanding.

The mother makes a dive. I think she is going for Sarah. I react instantly, my fangs snapping out into place. I hiss at her. The poor woman retreats, yelping like a scolded puppy, back into the corner of the room.

"It's ok," Sarah says. I assume she is directing this at me, as she is speaking modern English. But the look on both the child and the mother's faces seem to have eased. The tension has dissolved, although that does not stop the mother from looking at me with fear from behind her hands: hands that she holds to her face, wringing the loose flesh there.

"They learn from a very early age to fear us. They have some very bloody fairy tales about us. Unfortunately, they're not that far-fetched either," Sarah says.

"But you're helping," I point out.

"It is still difficult to trust after a lifetime cruel treatment," Sarah replies.

The baby has stopped crying. The red rash that covers most of the child's body has paled, and is now disappearing before my eyes. The baby just sits on Sarah's lap, looking at her and laughing. The mother and the child, their heartbeats, could not be more different. The mother has big loud beats, going fast –incredibly fast – and irregular. The baby's, on the other hand, lets out smaller beats: steady and relaxed. I can only wonder at Sarah's self-control. She seems unmoved by the presence of two tasty snacks being so near. Whereas I am finding it hard to concentrate, without thinking of what the two hearts are beating around their owner's bodies. I will have to go soon. I know I will not be able to take much more. As long as Sarah is here they are safe. But the strain is considerable.

Sarah stands up and walks over to the mother. She presents the baby to her. The mother snatches the baby out of her hands. She clings to the baby, who seems alarmed at the rough treatment. The mother begins to rock back and forth, mumbling incoherently as she does. The alarmed baby is crying in fits as it is rocked.

There is nothing left to do, so we leave the little thatched cottage. The air smells fresh and so good after the humid atmosphere of the cottage. But I am gripped by a sensation of complete and utter guilt, so much so that I find it hard to breathe or put on foot after another. Sarah has the same hunger as me, she has to: we are both Wonder-kind – we are vampires. Yet she has chosen to do something positive with her life, healing the sick. Whereas it is all I can do to stop killing. I think of my dream with the throne of bone and Sarah... No, I can't let that happen... I could not bear it. But spilling blood, lots of it, is a part of me and I can't change that. I look down at my hands as if they are already soaked in the red stuff.

# Chapter 3

# Down Below

*"You're lucky," Bonemann says.*

I doubt that I am, in the extreme: Lucky and on punishment duty. There is nothing in those two things that go together. I doubt this is going to be very lucky for me in any way at all.

"Not many people get to go down here," Bonemann says.

"Where are we going?" I ask, although I might already know.

Bonemann turns the key and the control panel lights up. He punches in a number with his long bony finger. The lift doors close smoothly. The lift rumbles downwards.

Lucky, no. I know where he is taking me.

The lift rumbles to a halt, the doors open and we walk out into the corridor. The lift is flanked on either side by two muscle-bound security guards. They look identical to the ones who are guarding the lift on the floor where we got in. No, that is wrong; they are bald headed large chaps, but not quite the same. It has to be the uniform: the type. Put a man in uniform and he becomes like all the others in his colour of cloth.

"Can I have the key?" I ask.

"No, you bloody well can't. You think I going let you run around down here?" Bonemann retorts.

"How can I get back up?" I ask.

I know how to get back up another way: the one Sarah has shown me. However, I am not telling him that because it will mean letting on that I have been down here before. And that isn't a good idea.

"Ask the security guards to send you up," Bonemann tells me.

He shows me to a store room. It is not far from the one in the hole in the ground from the cave. He decks me out with a bucket, mop, scrubbing brush and cleaning solution in a grey bottle.

"Need anything else?" He asks, rubbing his thin pointed chin.

"Don't know. You haven't told me what I supposed to be do yet," I grumble.

"No, that should be enough..." he says, as if he has not heard me. "Come on."

He leads me to a leaky tap at the end of the corridor. The stone walls on both sides just end in a blank wall: bare except for one metal tap that leaks water down on the ground, where it run towards a small metal drain.

"No hot water down here," says Bonemann.

*That is just great! Cold water is practically useless when it comes to cleaning up the sort of mess I have to clean up.*

I put the bucket under the tap and turn it. Water splutters out, most of it going in the bucket and some of it splashing up my trouser legs. I fill the bucket three quarters and turn off the tap.

"Come on," Bonemann says, turning on his heel.

I know exactly where we are going now. Sure enough, he leads me to the heavy door and I know what we will find behind it: the dungeon full of the walking dead. The Wonder-kind who have been starved of blood and left to rot in their own decaying bodies.

"What is this place?" I say, trying to act all 'butter wouldn't melt' and innocent.

"This where we keep the excommunicated," Bonemann replies.

"Excommunicated?"

"Scum who are no longer fit to share in the blood-life of our community," Bonemann simply states.

He turns to face me, a ghastly smile upon his face, and says:

"It's somewhere I can fully see you ending up some day... if we don't see some improvements."

"Oh?" I enquire.

"But today you're just cleaning the place out. So do a good job of it, else I may consider leaving you down in there with the rest of these poor sods," he says.

"Yes sir," I reply.

"Don't talk to any of them. It's forbidden. Not that they can talk. Most of them have their tongues hacked out," Bonemann adds with a laugh: his dirty sounding laugh. It sounds a lot like an electronic lawnmower with hiccups.

"So get going," he says, pushing open the door.

"If this place is not spotless by the time I come to inspect it, I will personally clean the floor with your entrails," he threatens. I suspect that he would like to do that if he could: I further expect that he would enjoy the experience.

I set to work with the mop and bucket. I hear Bonemann turn and exit the room. He leaves the door open. It isn't as if anyone here is going anywhere, me included.

"I'll never be finished here. It will take me all night!" I sniff.

Through the miasma of less than savoury smells, sweat riddled with every negative emotion you can think of, I catch a whiff of something very familiar, a smell less terrible that the others, sweet in fact.

"You might as well come out now. I know you're here," I say.

And very welcome.

"Sarah!"

"I thought you would be here. I thought you could do with some company to cheer you up!" she responds.

"You thought right." I have to smile, as she slides out from behind a stone pillar.

"Blood," Sarah holds up a small glass tube, with a dark red liquid inside.

"Will it be enough?" I ask.

"Plenty. Any more, after a period of depravation, and his body will just overload," Sarah answers.

"I think I might have seen that," I say, thinking back to the burnt man with one eye. At the time I thought he was just consumed by hatred for Bonemann, which, as far as I'm concerned, would be more than understandable. But, thinking about it now, there is perhaps something else to his rage. Maybe fifty-fifty: half rage, half overdose. That would make sense. But, really, who knows...

I remove Oliver's mask and flakes of burnt skin peel off as I lifted it away. His condition seems to be getting worse. I think of Bonemann's words: his promise to put me down here. It has to be worse than hell for these people. I can barely bring myself to think about it. I put the mask down on the ground, face-up.

"Here," Sarah says. She loosens the chains on the wall, unhooking some of the length, so that although the cuffs are still attached to Oliver's wrists, the chain lengthens so that he can lower his arms to his side. He rests his hands on the ground. He gives a grunt.

Sarah lightly takes his chin in her hand, drawing his wasted jaw bone downwards. She pulls the rubber cork out of the end of the tube with her teeth. Then, she puts the end of the glass tube to Oliver's lips, slowly pouring the liquid into his mouth. There is a sound of liquid trickling down, followed by pumping, squelching and gurgling noises. For a couple of minutes, nothing much happens. Then Oliver's skin seems to almost glow. A film of skin falls from his face: black and sticky. Half of his face appears as if it is falling away, leaving an angry red bubbling surface underneath, which expands and grows before my eyes.

After about half an hour – maybe more, maybe less – I can see Oliver is anything but healed. His skin is still an angry red and covered in lumps. But he at least has the shape of a face and can talk – after a fashion. He forms the sounds slowly at first, then more quickly, until he is speaking so fast that he is tripping over his own words.

"Slower. Slow down," Sarah instructs.

"A... Anymore? Blood? I bet I know where it's from! He-he!"

"No. But it is too dangerous anyway."

"Dangerousss? Look at me!" he says.

"It must please you... that I was excommunicated – ssso sssomeone is worse off, worse than you, eh abomination...?" he taunts.

"Not in the least..." Sarah tells him.

"And less of the Abomination. Her name is Sarah," I say.

Oliver spits. His spit is tainted red and lies on the floor at his feet.

"S...so you're the new one?" he says, looking up at me.

"You won't last. I can tell," he adds.

"Why? Why did they do it to you?" Sarah cuts in.

"Ah. That is the question isssn't it?" Oliver responds.

"And?"

"It wasn't what they sssaid."

"I know that..."

"What doesss your little birdy say?"

"Nothing. So tell me."

"I found out something. I couldn't live it. Sssilly really. I alwaysss wasss too sentimental..."

*I should feel sorry for him but I don't.*

"It was my favourite blood slave – Jules was his name. We are er, um... close," Oliver says, looking down at place on the ground where he has spat. He puts his finger into the salvia and starts to draw a circle, then a smaller one inside the first.

"He wasss not from here, not from the village – was being the operative word. He was into things I liked," he says. He starts to draw lines in the dust.

"I fed off him. My favourite, as I said. We used to talk as well – for hours. Then he just vanished. Like I say, we got on. Sso I tracked him, by sssmelting him out. And when I saw what they had done to him. I..." he trails off and a tiny spec of water appears at the tear ducts of one of his eyes: not enough to be called a tear, but it is there.

"I went to my master - Markus. He said I was being sentimental. There are plenty of other cows I can have to play with."

"Cows?" I ask.

"Humans. We call them that sometimes, male or female. It doesn't matter."

"I said I didn't care," Oliver continues.

"I said I thought it was horrible..." he says. "I flew at him. I was just so angry. I didn't think it through. Of course I couldn't touch him. Something in the blood. I thought the worst that could happen was that they would kill me. They should have killed me. I wish they had," Oliver laments.

"So what did they do to Jules?" Sarah asks.

Oliver points down to the ground, to the shapes he has been making in the dust.

"You have to see it to understand, properly..." he says, as he points to the marks in the dust. I see what he has been drawing in the dust. It is a crude map. I can make out the shape of the castle, the human village and, beyond that, the word 'FARM'. He has drawn a number of squarish shapes and buildings, and between them he has marked an X.

"X marks the spot!" he exclaims. Then, he wipes the whole thing away with his foot.

"Don't tell them I told you and don't let them catch on. Or you will end up in here, the same as me," Oliver warns.

"If I were you, I would just forget everything I just told you. Go back upstairs and forget it. But if you can't, take a look at the farm. Then you will understand. And then we will talk," he says.

"But I bet you don't, bet you're too chicken!" he adds, looking directly at me.

# Chapter 4

# Casual Violence

*"Oi!" Karl shouts as I walk down the corridor.*

"Come back here. I am talking to you!" he booms.

I have had a gut full. More than that, my guts are overflowing. If life was a cartoon, then right now steam would be shooting out of my ears.

"Where you going anyway!" calls Karl.

"None of your business!" I call back.

To say I have not forgiven him for spiking my drink couldn't be more wrong. That would mean there was some trust there to begin with. He has done exactly as I have expected. If only I had been quicker off the mark. Well, hindsight is wonderful science with an accuracy rate of 99.9%.

Since becoming the Team Champion, Karl has become worse than unbearable. He has been giving me a lecture on all my faults and failures, which is no small list. But I have had enough. So I walk out on him, leaving the training room and storming down the corridor. Someone with more sense and less ego would have just let me go. Not Karl.

I speed up to put some distance between us. But it seems that Karl is also picking up the pace. He overtakes and turns towards me. He raises his hand as a stop sign.

"Off to see your..." Karl starts.

*There are just some people you can't talk to. You can't reason with them. What is the point of all this? What purpose does all this serve?*

"I get it," he says, "I do. 'Cause everyone hates your guts. She is the only one who will talk to you. That is why you hang around with the abomination. You poor sad moron. You know why she's call that? Eh? The abomination. Shall I tell you?"

"Oh, just get lost, Karl" I say. I could have used stronger words to get my point across. But what would be the point? It is not as if he is going to do what I say: "Oh yeah. I never thought. I will leave you alone and go my own way. Sorry to have bothered you!"

*Yeah right! ha!*

"I am not surprised you hang around with **her**! You're both a disgrace, an embarrassment to our kind. You could get married. You are made for each other," Karl continues.

"Shut up" I say.

"No, wait. Don't do that. You might have children. We don't want any more of you diseased wretches gumming our world!" The sooner you are wiped from the face of the planet the better!" asserts Karl.

"And who is going to do that?" I ask.

"What?"

"Wipe me from the face of the planet."

Karl's grin changes to a sneer. He starts to open his mouth, to impart more abuse, I expect. But I cut in first:

"Just do it or get out of my face!"

I find it hard to believe that the words are coming out of my mouth, but before I can reconsider, they are out there. In big neon lights. Karl stops as if I have slapped him across the face. His eyes are uncomprehending, as if someone has rewritten the script – a twist instead of a scripted predictable ending. Taking advantage of this, I say:

"I am sick of your face, sick of your words, sick of you!"

Karl's face twists. His arms shoot up. His hands find my neck, as he shoves me back against the wall.

"Ok, so you want it. I'm just the person to give to you!" he snarls through clenched teeth, his spittle finding my face.

It is at times like this that, in a fair world, someone steps in and saves you from a beating. The world is anything but fair, but sometimes...

"Leave him alone!" a voice growls from down the corridor.

We both turn to see Sarah stalk down it, towards us. Then suddenly she is there, inches away. Her eyes are two black pools of intense concentration, locked onto Karl. She moves soundlessly, with the pose of a panther hunting prey.

"Looks like your aberration of g..." Karl starts. He releases my neck as he turns to face the new target.

But he never finishes the sentence because he finds himself smashing against the opposite wall. The white stone cracks and detritus falls with the force of impact. He falls to the ground. Sarah has swung him around into the wall. I have not even seen her move. And neither it seems has Karl.

"You little bitch!" Karl roars, as he springs to his feet, with his left fist raised and his right fist at the ready. Small pieces of white stone and dust fall from his shoulders and clothes as raises himself upright.

It looks an absurd fight, as they face each other off: big Karl towers over little Sarah. His fist rockets towards her small round face. I take a sharp breath:

"No!"

It is a powerful punch. Only Sarah's face is not there anymore. She ducks down under his arm and drives a punch into his stomach at the same time. He doubles. She brings her fist up under his chin. His head flies backwards, then forwards. Sarah grabs his hair and pulls it to her knee, as she brings it up hard to meet his face. There is a sickening crack as the knee and the face connect.

Then Sarah stands back. Karl slumps backwards against the opposite wall. She walks over to him and pokes a small finger into his barrel chest:

"You don't know everything!" she says. "With age comes power. You would do well to remember that!"

Karl slumps forwards in a nod. His nose is bleeding buckets. He is either acknowledging the point or more likely dropping out from the conscious world.

"You're not as mild mannered as you appear," I observe, nervously.

"I am. She's not. I have to admit that she is sometimes in the right," Sarah adds.

I wonder what this means. Sarah has said something similar before: spoken about herself in both the third and first person: as if she is taking about two different people.

"Come on," she says, turning on her heel.

"Where are we going?" I ask, following her, looking back at Karl and glancing at him over my shoulder. He is still slumped against the wall, his face a bloody mess.

"We need to talk. There is something I need to tell you," Sarah states.

"Sound ominous. What is it?" I ask.

"I need to tell you what I did and why I am the way that I am," Sarah says.

"And you won't like it" she adds.

# Chapter 5

# Sarah's Confession

*"It should never have happened."*

But it did, Sarah explains. We are outside in the castle grounds. The breeze is cool and fresh. We walk under a thick canopy of green leaves. The trees that surround us are all ancient and expansive – blocking out the sun from view. We follow a path that leads down beyond the human village. The yew trees and oaks that surround us are all of a thick girth and extraordinary twisted and gnarled in shape.

"The original, the first court seer, is over two thousand years old. Older than even the King. Older than most. Can you imagine that? Living for that long?" Sarah says.

"Not really," I respond truthfully, as I am only slowly inching towards my seventeenth birthday. I have no idea at all. When is that anyway? The time that the Roman army are stomping about Britain? That sounds about right.

"Ha, ha, of course. No. I keep forgetting you are a youngster!" Sarah laughs.

"Don't call me that!" I say in mock protest.

"Aw!" she taunts.

"Or say that!" I push down hard with my hands in my pockets.

Sarah smiles, then her face falls once more. Her expression is deadly serious.

"She was dying," Sarah tells me.

"How come?"

"This is back when the twelve were continuously at war with each other. Not all at once, but they would often fall out over the slightest thing. One of the other kingdoms – they still don't know which – poisoned her," Sarah says.

"Really? Why?"

"They all want power to be the king of the other kings. They hate it if one of the others has something they do not. They don't like the fact that King Theo had someone who can look into the future. It made them uneasy and very jealous," she explains.

Sarah pauses, peering up at one of the larger trees. The grooves of its thick bark zig-zag up its length. She places a gentle hand on the glowing surface. Her hand glows purple and its fiery tongues leap out towards the trunk of the tree and merge with the slight radiation of green coming from it. She takes a deep breath before continuing.

"I thought at the time, why didn't she see her own death coming? Now that I am older, I realise she did. That is the one reason that she sought me out and transformed me many, many years earlier. I already have the gift, you see. Though no one was as powerful a seer as her. What I didn't know at the time was why: why me? Well, she had the whole thing planned. I was quite a sensitive person, sensitive to the point of being able to see into the future."

Sarah stops and looks down at the ground. She ruffles the dirt with her shoe then sighs and carries on talking and walking.

"...But now I think... She knew how it would tear me apart inside, bring me close to brink of madness. Oh, I am certain she knew all along and is still having a good laugh over that one." There isn't so much bitterness in Sarah's voice and expression: only a sort of lonely sadness that dims and brightens in her face as she speaks.

I say nothing. I just listen, fearing where this is going and knowing there is no happy ending to this confession. I am dreading the punchline, which is hurtling towards my pensive ears. Sarah carries on talking:

"Henry must have been in on the joke too. Later, he is not as old, but it would have amused him no end. You asked why he chose you. Well, he likes nothing more than to turn the kindest, most sensitive person in the world into a killer. He gets a real kick out of it. If you turn a killer into a vampire, then they are the same, only stronger, but if you take, say, a pacifist and turn them, then after their first kill, everything they are is destroyed, morally, psychologically, spiritually – they're easier to manipulate and more vicious, because they have nothing left to lose."

"What about if he can't? What about if they refuse to go that way?" I ask.

"He gets rid of them of course," Sarah replies.

I wince.

"Unless they are useful. Like me." she adds and continues:

"Anyway, the two of them... He likes his games and, well, she does too. She likes to use people, to use them right up. It's all a game to them. A bloody brutal and pointless game. Like it or not, you're part of the game. Me too."

"What game? I don't understand... Part of what?" I enquire – confused.

"The reason that everyone is on your case in the training room is because of Henry."

"I know. He revoked his protection. I heard Karl..."

"No! You probably never had it in the first place. That is how he works." There is anger in Sarah's voice now.

"But Bonemann..." I counter.

"Especially Bonemann. The Bonemann is Henry's little pet. Does whatever he is told."

"Well that makes a kind of sense, I suppose," I agree. "Anyway, we're getting off track. The old woman was dying..." I say, stopping next to a great oak tree, its boughs so heavy that they slope downwards towards the ground and run along it, like a giant green python. Sarah explains:

"The poison works on the molecular level. It is similar to the D-gun tech, but using chemical reactions rather than light frequencies. So she was physically falling apart..." she says, looking down at the ground. She runs her shoe along the earth, back and forth, making a line in the dirt.

"Ok."

"But her vision, her gift, was too valuable, too important to King Theo to lose. Sure, there were other seers but she was the brightest and most gifted. Some say she was one of the original oracles at Delphi," she says

"Do you believe that?"

"No. She used to say it as if it was true. But she was always... She *is* a bit of a bragger. I think she wove so many stories about herself that she forgot which ones were true and which ones she'd made up."

"*Is?*" I muse. "She didn't die?"

"Well, yes and no. Anyway, I am coming to that. Hold your horses a second or two." Sarah's face falls and her shoulders sag.

"Anyway, she survived, but her body was not resurrecting. It was weak. Then Henry came to me. He said there was something I have to do, for the kingdom, for the community, something only I can do. It is dangerous, and could kill me. I said, stupidly as it turned out, that I didn't care and would do what I could... I don't know. I should have guessed. I was so naive and stupid back then.

"When I found out what it was he wanted. I was horrified. I said no. I said I changed my mind. They... *He* said it was too late. He said I would have to do it. They made me..." Sarah breaks off and closes her eyes. It is as if the act is too horrible to think of, to relive. But I know what it is. She had already told me at the watchtower. "I had to drink from another..." she says. Tears form in the corners of her eyes.

"...They made you drink her blood." I finish for her. I put my hand gently on her shoulder. I think she might pull away. But she doesn't.

"Yes... They said I had to drink. Lots, too much – all of it. This was so a strong impression of her psyche would be transferred across. Oh, they enjoyed that. I was known at the time as 'Sarah the sipper'. Because I only took enough blood to keep the hunger at bay: a thimble full, half a pint at most, maybe, but no more. Not enough to kill anyone. They hated that."

I smile a gentle smile at her tear-stained face. It seemed so like her. Me, I never had that kind of control. I hold her gently as her tears come in a flood, marking the front of my black shirt with long wet lines.

"Sorry..."

"Don't be. It's ok," I say.

# Chapter 6

# Soul Juice

*"Whether you live or die, you will be remembered forever", Henry had said," Sarah recalls.*

"Remembered?" I ask.

"Oh yes, and he was right. He just did not say how I will be remembered. I would be remembered alright: as an abomination, as a violator of our most sacred law, as something untouchable and disgusting."

"He's a right royal bastard in other words," I say.

I mean it. I have gone through the rounds with the man emotionally, from hate to toleration, to dependence, to fear. But now I hate him for hurting Sarah. And that is far more venomous than for anything I have had done to me.

"Let's climb up," Sarah exclaims suddenly.

We both peer up at the ancient looking Yew tree with its knotty skin and twisted cables that run up into the branches towards the top.

"It is better to do something when you're talking about things you don't want to. It gives your hands something to do," Sarah explains.

I follow her up the gnarled trunk.

"Obviously I survived. Only I contracted rather more than just the seer's prophetic gift," Sarah tells me, as she speeds nimbly up the old Yew tree. She stops, turning her head to face me, looking down.

"More than?" I ask.

"The seer herself, the late great Cassandra lives and breathes... Well, she doesn't breathe exactly, but she is here inside of me. Inside here." Sarah points to the middle of her forehead.

"She's what?" I ask, disbelieving. It makes sense. But I don't believe it.

"She found a way to cheat death." Live and kicking, up here." Sarah is still tapping her forehead as she says this.

"But that is not possible," I counter.

"Not possible? Are we possible? The Wonder-kind? I bet this time last year you would have laughed at the idea!".

"No, well yes, but..." I trail off.

"I don't pretend to understand it. But it is what is. I have to accept that. I feel her moving around all the time. I can hear her voice. She hates me. She is always an icy cold person. I just thought it is the way she was, but it takes sharing a head with someone to really know a person. I never knew how much she loathed me…" Sarah swings down one handed on a branch towards me, as she speaks.

"She hates you?" I couldn't think of one reason why anyone would. Is it even possible to hate Sarah? I tried it once. Even though it was drug induced, it didn't take. Sarah answers:

"Always has, always will, I expect. As you know we live a long time. I don't know whether I am her prison warder or if she is mine. Sometime it feels more like the latter. But it is how it is."

"But..." I start. However, Sarah puts a finger to my lips to silence me and explains further:

"It's something to do with who we are. The way we feed - we drink blood: yes? That is what distinguishes us from human beings, right?"

"Yeah, don't remind me," I say wearily.

"Well, what I think happens is that our digestive system strips out something from the blood – the essence. That spark of life. Not exactly the soul, but close to it. How could it be? The soul is a nonphysical thing. Maybe blood touches it, or they are connected: you know, blood and life. Whether the soul is something eternal and mystical or just the source of life, the energy that makes people tick makes them move." She says, "That's why we call it soul juice. Because it's full of life. We drink life itself."

"But nothing like that happened with Danny!" I protest, horrified at the thought of him stomping around in my brain, causing chaos.

"It is different for humans. I don't know how. But it is. Maybe their souls are not directly caught up with blood. Maybe their subtle and physical bodies are more one, in humans. I don't know. But for us it is different. I think it's behind the first sacred law of our kind. I used to think it is just another cannibalism taboo. But now I think the reason is that the personality is literally transferred over when we feed on another Wonder-kind," Sarah pauses, then continues:

"...So I looked it up in the library, and there used to be a lot of that sort of thing in the dim and distant past. There is one tale of a King Eli who fought and beat King Frederic and drank his blood, in battle. He thought he had won only to find that he was haunted by his enemy. In the end, or so the story goes, King Frederic eventually took over Eli's body completely. The other version is that King Eli went completely insane, driven mad by his passenger, so that he only thought he was King Frederic. In such cases, it is impossible to tell." Sarah is now hanging one-handed.

"And if you drink the lot, you get the lot. Hence, I have a two-thousand-year old pain in the ass living in my brain," she says, heaving herself on to a thick tree branch.

"And she is far from happy about the situation" she adds, now lying on a thick section of the branch, putting her head down on its surface.

"She's not?" I ask.

"I think she wanted me to die. I could see it in her eyes as her body died. But I spoilt it for her: her great plan for me to die and leave her in my place," Sarah tells me, calm as you like.

"Good grief!" I exclaim, as I take in the full magnitude of what has been done to Sarah.

I blow out air from my cheeks.

"Two thousand years. That's a long time. She must have done a lot of living. Seen everything. Done everything. Why does she even want to go on living?" I challenge.

"Well there is always something new to do," Sarah sighs. She climbs up higher. We are near the top now.

"Can you see anything?" I ask.

I don't know why I asked. We can see almost everything this high up the tallest tree in the grove. The chateau sits on the top and the watchtower stretches out to the sea and down the hill – the human village, the road, the trees and the outer walls; beyond that, are the hills and the white of smog of the psycho-active gas that surrounds the hill side and woods.

Sarah answers my question:

"I think so. Down the other side of the hill. There are three long sheds, just as Oliver said."

Sarah jumps, landing without a sound. She straightens and looks back up at me.

"Coming?"

"One sec..."

I drop to the ground.

We are in the heart of the village. I haven't been paying attention: just thinking how nice it would be to ring Henry's neck. Even though I know I can't. He has seen to that. We walk over the square of green. It is bordered on each side by a collection of timber cottages with thatched roofs. I hear human hearts beating all around me.

I can hear Sarah's heart if I want. I just have to focus in on it. But it is different when it comes to something you can eat. Well, my body takes a rather keener interest in that respect: the absolute desire to gorge myself on soul juice. The sound of a human heart beating is the sweetest sound to my ears. It's a bit like a big juicy steak grilled just the way you like it; succulent and tasty – but a hundred times better than that. I have not drunk since this morning. I am not sure I can be trusted to be around this place. I am not sure I can control myself. I am just about to tell Sarah we should go. I see one of the villagers walking towards us. It is a woman in a black dress and white bonnet: a working dress streaked with dirt. She nods to Sarah before lowering her head.

We walk through the houses. Another human – a man this time – passes us. He nods to Sarah. He gives me a look that is part fear and part suspicion. I think he fears I might feed on his family while he is out. I don't think he would be surprised to come home and find his family brutally murdered, not in this place, where the average human, or any human come to that, has all the rights of livestock: badly treated livestock at that.

"They're not afraid of you," I comment.

"Why would they be? Besides, it is because of my gift. They respect that sort of thing. Second sight. They sort of revere it. Though it can be embarrassing," Sarah reflects.

"You have to remember that they have always been separate from the outside world all their lives. They would be shocked at the world you come from. I think I would be too. I have been here for such a long time. In my day, we travelled on horse and cart, or we just walked."

"You have lots of modern stuff here: computers, cars, weapons..." I suggest

"Not the same. I keep up to date with books. But it's not that same as living in it, walking amongst it, feeling it and seeing it. You just take all that for granted, don't you?" Sarah challenges.

"I suppose not everything about modern human history is so great,"

"I know. I read."

"But you never been out. Outside of these walls?"

"Not since I was brought here. No, never... Well, nearly never. I have been out a couple times on trips with the King."

"But you never get to see much. I liked Switzerland. With the cuckoo clocks and the houses with the funny roofs."

"You have seen more than me then. I have never left the country."

"No? We should go. We can live in the mountains in houses with a red roof. I think I would like that!"

"With a cuckoo clock as well?"

"Oh yes!"

"When?"

"Soon!"

"How soon?"

"When you are ready."

"What does that mean?"

"You will see," she says, turning away from me.

# Chapter 7

# Small Gestures

*Leaving the village.*

We head for the group of farm buildings we saw from the Yew tree. We follow a dirt-track downhill. There are deep tyre track marks in the mud, from frequent use from heavy vehicles such as tractors or heavy military vehicles, I guess. We approach the three farm sheds. They are long and single story, and made out of some sort of corrugated plastic.

"It started with the looks," Sarah tells me. "Everyone would just look at me, then turn away. That is horrible enough. Then I heard what they were saying. They would stop when I came near. But I heard. With our hearing, how could I not! I think they must have known that! Whenever I passed two or more people – groups were the worst – they would say things like how shocking it was that I was allowed to live after what I had done. They would say how, in the old days, this would never have happened." Sarah looks up at me, as she walks beside me. Her eyes are big and full of tears.

"But if it was Theo's and Henrys idea, why didn't they put a stop to all this...back stabbing?" I venture.

"They wouldn't talk to me about it. Or anything else. Outside of my job as seer, that is. They wanted to know all about the future: for their plans and stuff. The King never speaks to me though. He always gets Henry to speak to me, for the sake of appearances. The King cannot be seen to be talking to me. I just stand in the background."

I wince as I think of how I imagined that Sarah was in cahoots with them. I must have been hallucinating, which in fact I was. I could not have been more mistaken.

"People really are little shits. Wonder-kind are same, only worse," I assert.

"People spoke to me only when they had to... when they wanted something. When they wanted what I can do," Sarah reflects.

"But..."

"No. I could see it in their eyes. The hate, the distrust – the loathing. They could not wait to get away from me. Then, they became braver, talking out loud in front of me. It was as if they were deliberately trying to hurt or humiliate me. That was when they started calling me 'the abomination' and other equally colourful names that I choose to forget."

"But if you are helping them, I don't get it... Why?" I ask. I am horrified at the way Sarah has been treated from the start. But with each new revelation, I grow even more appalled. She doesn't deserve it. Of all of us here, she just doesn't!

"Didn't matter," Sarah says, her voice sounding desolate. "I was tolerated just as long they could use me. I am sorry. I have to be honest."

"No, I am sorry... No one should have to go through what you did." I attempt to assure Sarah. It sounds inadequate and it is.

"It ok. You're here now, unless this has changed your mind about me?"

Sarah stops abruptly and looks at my face. Her big black pupils dart around it, looking for telling signs. My face flames. Sarah takes a step backwards. I think she is desperately afraid of what I might say.

"It has hasn't it?"

"Never!" I say. It is a word of fire and steel. I meet her intense gaze; looking into those dark pupils, gazing into the person that lies behind them. I continue:

"Get this into your head once and for all. I wouldn't – I won't – ever abandon you. So, you see, you are stuck with me."

"You mean it?"

"Absolutely."

"Forever?"

"And all time."

Sarah smiles broadly – a smile that beams the brightness of a super-nova.

# Farming Paradigms

# Chapter 1

# The Farm

*"Think this is it? The place Oliver told us about?" I ask.*

"I think so," Sarah says.

We approach one of the sheds. It is about the length of a football pitch. We go up to the front of the building, where there is an opening large enough to drive a fighter jet through. The roof is arched – made of corrugated steel. The building looks quite new, as the shine of the metal has not yet faded to dull silver.

"Serfs?" I suggest, finding the word that Sarah had been searching for.

"They are owned by Theo?" I venture.

"That's right. Though slaves, more like, worse – cattle really."

"How come some of them speak English?"

"They all do, just different varieties. They are a bilingual community. Those who come into contact with the Château learn the Kings English, but the others not so much."

"Ah, is that it?" I ask.

Sometimes it seems to me as if everything that I am has been smashed to pieces and that the person I used to be has been utterly destroyed.

Sometimes I feel I am pure vampire. Other times, I feel as if I have not changed at all. Sarah has helped to bring that back, of course – if not bring back, then strengthen it and bring it into the open... for better or worse.

I don't know what to feel anymore. I'm constantly torn between two polar opposites: who I used to be and the demands of this utterly insane life.

I still don't think anyone has the right to own anyone else. I am un-comfortable about being served in a cafe, let alone in the feasting hall. Nor is it easy to square this belief with my behaviour. I still drink blood. I may not be doing it straight from the organic vessel like some do, but out of glasses poured from jugs which come from... well let's just say I am not fooled. And I cannot square it in my mind. The best that I can do is not think about it. The only thing for that is drinking more blood. It takes the edge off of things. As well as nourishment, it sedates and stimulates. It is my drug as well as my food. It is my soul juice: reinvigorating and life enhancing. I suppose my position at this point is a lot like people who eat the meat of animals. They happily gobble up a nice juicy beef steak, but do their best not to think about where it comes from. I think that is me or something similar anyway.

"If Oliver is to be believed, then there are worst things to come," Sarah admits, biting her upper lip.

Sarah tells me that when she drinks, it is not very much. She has a rec-iprocal arrangement with a number of the humans in the village. She gives them healing and prophecy in exchange for what she needs. 'Sarah the sipper' she is called, because she does not see the need for violently taking the blood and takes such small sips of the red stuff.

"The violence, the way the Wonder-kind feed is totally unnecessary," she explains. "It is all for show, all bravado, as if to say 'Look at me, look at what I can do to this person. I can take what I want, and there is not a thing they can do to stop me.' That sort of thing sickens me."

I am not sure what to expect when I enter the building – maybe cows lined up in rows in milking stations. Alternatively, it could be full of farm equipment or storage for the many military vehicles I have seen about the place. But why would Oliver want us to see anything like that? What does any of that have to do with the future? Just inside the entrance we are confronted with a raised concrete platform that runs the length of the entrance. It is about shoulder height, with steps going up to the top: a grey-silver steel rail by the side of the steps. Sarah mounts the steps. I follow.

At the top, there is concrete pathway, three feet wide, with ridges marked into the concrete, mud and straw ground into the grooves between. It runs down between what appear to be square concrete pits on either side of the pathway. The pathway spans the entire length of the shed. I follow Sarah as she strides down it and glance down into the pits on either side. I am sure I can see things, lots of them, moving down there.

The pits are deep, maybe twenty feet in depth, stretching down below floor level, with smooth concrete walls. There are hundreds of these cells in lines, one after another, marked out with a matrix of rectilinear walkways.

There is definitely something moving at the bottom of the pits. I find it hard to make out. It reminds me of the rats in the corridor when I first came to the Chateau: lots of creatures crawling over each other, only these are much bigger. We progress down a good many concrete cells before I get the nerve to look again. I regret it instantly.

I see humans that look like pigs at first glance, covered in mud, too many of them in such a small space. They are hemmed in by the walls and squashed together to a point they can barely move without crawling over each other. The noise they make sounds like pigs too: high pitched squealing cries. I do a double take.

"Human? There are humans down there!" I exclaim.

Sarah turns to face me.

"Yes. I don't think this is going to be worst thing we will see today either."

"Worse?" I wonder senselessly. Isn't this enough? What are they doing here? There is of course only one answer: food. They are our food. The glass of wine I drank so eagerly from this morning suddenly seems to weigh heavily in my stomach – threatening, with no promise to come back up.

# Chapter 2

# Cattle Market

*I peer down into the bottom of the pit to see what once must have once been human beings, now reduced to their most primitive and base state.*

They are grunting rather than speaking: fighting over dirty scraps of food in a long metal trough. They are so covered in mud and strands of straw I can't tell the difference between them in terms of gender or skin colour. All but a few act with savage aggression, growling and nipping each other. The ones at the front, heads down in the trough, are greedily helping themselves to what smells to me like rotting meat. They snarl at each other and ram and shove away at anyone trying to get to the trough. There are a few who do not approach the trough and stay back: whimpering, forlorn and despairing. It is as if they have just given up all hope. These ones look painfully emaciated.

I can hear their hearts beating, but my hunger has completely left me. My mouth is dry. I feel empty inside, unable to process the full horror of what I am seeing. I am trying and failing to think of what lies behind all of this senseless cruelty.

I try to speak. But I am having trouble forming words, let alone sentences. I have nothing. This is so obviously wrong and beyond the pale.

I catch a glimpse of a blue light out of the corner of my eye. This is followed a second later by a crack, the sound of electricity and then a scream. Loud and shrill, this scream echoes throughout the building. I turn around, instantly alert.

Further up the walkway, two humans dressed in green overalls stand on the walkway, leaning over one of the pits. A blue light flares once more from down below, then there is another scream of pain. My overly sensitive nose catches the faint aroma of burning flesh. It is almost invisible under the overwhelming odours of the shed. It smells like the cattle market. It even looks like one. I used to go to the one in town with my grandparents when I was young. My lasting impression of the place was the pong and the animals all squashed together in little concrete cells. This is what this place is too. It makes perfect sense. The idea disgusts me.

The two men in the overalls each have an elongated metal rod. At first glance, it is not unlike the ones people use to unblock drains. Both of them have long unkempt hair: the nearest one has a greasy grey colour, while the younger man has thick and matted blond hair. Each rod is clearly designed for a different purpose. The blond-haired man has a rod with a metal loop at the end. Meanwhile, the grey-haired man has one that is ended in two short blunt points: some kind of kind of electric cattle prod, designed to admit an electric shock, I guess.

The two men look up when we approach. They both give, one after the other, a sort of nod of deference in our direction and then turn back to their work. They are dragging a human, streaked in sweat and mud, out of the pit. Caked in mud, the prisoners' long matted hair hangs in solid clumps on the sides of their head with very little on the other side. They are not making a very good job of it. There is a woman, for I think it is a woman, covered in all that grime and clothed in tattered rags. It is impossible to tell for certain. She bangs her hip and then her shoulder against the concrete wall, as she struggles against the attachment – whimpering and whining as she is pulled towards the top.

The men with the rods resemble a couple of anglers, one of whom puts down his own rod in order to help the other land a particularly big fish. The woman is pushed face down on the concrete pathway by one of them, while the other pulls her arms backwards to a position that cannot be anything but very painful. They then attach white plastic restraints, which are looped around both wrists, which they then tighten, pulling the woman upright.

"These animals are vicious, my lord, my lady. Don't get too close," one of the men warns.

"They will take a bit out of you if you are not careful," the other says.

The two of them speak about their captive as if they do not consider her – or any of the others within the pits – to belong to the same species as them. I find that quite astonishing. I suppose I shouldn't. That is after all what it is all about: us and them.

At this point, all fight – though it is evident there isn't much to begin with – seems to leave the woman. The younger man attaches a metal collar around her neck. The collar has four arms: front, back and two sides. Each arm has about a foot and half in length, each with a handle at the end. The blond man holds and pulls the woman by the handle on the front. The older man follows up at the rear, holding the handle in one hand and the rod in the other, the cattle prod, at the ready. Sarah and I follow a small distance behind. We look at each other, both reading what the other is feeling.

The woman walks with a sideways twist that rotates through her spine, throwing her left leg out of kilter. Her shoulders are hunched and her head is bowed over as low as the metal collar will allow. She is making a low, throaty whining noise, which after a while I realise it is a tune: 'Sweet-dreams,' I think, although the tune is barely recognisable, through the rasping gasps of air she emits. It is a song I know well. It was number two in the charts only recently even though this feels like a lifetime ago – back in my old life. But that is by the by. No, this means something else. She couldn't have been taken from the village: she is from the outside, which means they are taking humans from the world I came from. And I can only think of one thing a human would be used for in this place – food. This is a fate that could have been mine. I could have ended up here, if not for Henry's intervention.

Suddenly, the woman yelps and her heels jump about an inch off the concrete. The older man giggles; there is a hard, cruel twang to the sound. Then, he jabs her again with the cattle prod. A blue flash sparks against the skin of her back and she cries out once more. She hasn't done anything. She has only been walking, led by the man in front, not looking up, just singing gently to herself.

Anger flares inside of me. The cattle prod is no obstacle to me. I could rip open the necks of both of the men before they know what is happening. Sarah must see the expression on my face because she puts a restraining hand on my arm and whispers:

"No. Not here. Not now."

"It will get worse... I think... It will... but keep your head. There's nothing to be done. Yet," she urges.

I really do not see how it can be – worse I mean. But Sarah's long solemn and unsmiling face tells me all I need to know. Then, I am equally certain that, whatever it is, I really don't want to see it. But I have to, now that we have come this far. Otherwise, it will prey on my mind, like some silent terror in the cellar that I am not brave enough to face.

# Chapter 3

# Whatever Lies

*We follow the two men and their captive outside.*

They exit through the opposite end of the building to the one we have entered by. The captive stops suddenly. She tries to raise her arms, but they are still tied behind her. The man with the prod gives her another zap. She screams. There is no need for extra cruelty. They aren't even vampires; there is no excuse for tormenting one of your own.

"L.l.ll-light...too...b..b-bright!" The captive chokes out the word as if they are foreign body lodged in her throat.

The blond man in front pulls at the captive's collar and she follows, as meek as can be. They cross over the dirt track that cuts between the shed and a different building. The other building is white brick, two stories high, with a flat roof. In the entrance there is a heavy door, made of metal, and a black door with "keep out!" written in red just below eye level.

I glance at Sarah, who looks back at me. She nods as if to say *This is it. This is the secret they have been keeping.* Whatever it is, whatever lies behind this door is nothing less than the future: what the entire human race has in store for it.

We follow the captive and captors into the building, going down several flights of stairs. But at some point, we lose them in the underground maze. We go down more stairs and along blank white painted corridors. They all look exactly the same. Sarah doesn't seem perturbed that we are no longer following the woman and her two warders. I relax a little. But I cannot get that tune the woman had been singing out of my head.

We pass a large room, empty, but for shower heads that hang from ceiling. The walls are lined with white tiles. The floor is set at a slight angle so that water can gutter down to the drain at the centre of the room. It is like a big shower room, only with no changing facilities. It seems obvious who this room is for: the poor sods back in the cattle shed. Just looking in gives me an ominous feeling and my stomach ties itself into knots. I am dreading the secret that this building is going give up at the end of this journey. I really don't want to see it. I want to say to Sarah: "Look lets go. We know it's bad. We don't need to see it to know that!" But I don't. I just keep walking, my muscles coiling around themselves, tightening, as I chew on my lip.

"I have been dreaming about this place for months now. I can see it in every detail. In my dreams I just see the corridors and hear the screaming. Half of the time I am not sure whether the screaming is coming from beyond the doors or if it is me that is doing the screaming," Sarah tells me.

"So you don't know what we will find down here?" I ask.

"Oneiromancy is confusing. I don't know the last time I had... you know... just an ordinary dream. There is a difference. I can tell. I just get confused sometimes. Living in the future and the present does that. And the past – I go there too. Not so often though...” Sarah replies.

“But we are not expecting anything good down here,” I warn.

“No. It is very doubtful we will. I can’t stop crying after I have them... the dreams. The reality is only reliving the same dreams. I can’t tell if it is better or worse or the same. I have seen so many bad things.” Sarah’s voice despairing. We reach a door.

“Here it is! I can feel it. This is the place,” says Sarah, throwing open a heavy steel door with ‘Keep Out’ written on it in large red letters. Something Sarah obviously does not think applies to her. We walk into a large room. Inside, it is about the size of the insides of the sports hall back at the school. My footsteps echo as I walk over the floor. Sarah’s footsteps are as normal – silent. I look up at the gantry: at the machines and the monstrous organic shapes trapped within all this metal and technology. I am uncertain to what I am actually seeing.

# Chapter 4

# Parasitical Ma-
chines

*It is a bleeding machine.*

Made out of steel, it is five levels high. Each level is divided into separate cells, and within each cell is a human. I am using the term human
loosely to label these distorted bulbous and swollen shapes. Everyone
is hemmed in with restraining straps, electronic wiring and coloured
tubes. The medical paraphernalia would not look out of place in an in-
tensive care unit. Only here, they brutally penetrate the bodies, with the
main purpose of taking from, not giving to, these swollen bodies. The
blood is drained away into clear tubing, running downwards toward
towards large see-through vats on the other side of the room. The blood
enters the vats in spurts, where a plastic whisk-like protrusion rotates at
the centre, reminding me of those slush puppy machines you see in
newsagents, only much bigger in size.

Even the heartbeats of these poor wretches sound wrong, deformed,
laboured and struggling as if on the verge of total collapse. The excite-

ment I nearly always feel is nowhere to be seen, only pity, the most base and sickly of emotions. It fills my stomach and I taste its bile in my mouth.

Sarah walks over to a bank of terminals and white metal machines by the side of the metal structure.

"Look at this!" she says, sounding appalled.

I follow her over to the first monitor.

"They are 'leeched' almost continually," she says, pointing to a timer on the screen under the legend in bright green: Leaching Cycle. I look at the other information on the screen then at the other screens. Sarah follows and continues to observe:

"There is a control and monitoring system here for red blood cells and haemoglobin production. This one is to pump them full of hormones to stimulate cell growth."

"Good God!" I respond.

"And have a look at this," adds Sarah as she leads me over to another computer terminal. On the screen, there are rows and rows of wavy lines making their way over the screen. I press the downward button on the keyboard and scroll down the screen, where there are hundreds of these patterns, all numbered. It is not too much of leap to realise that the numbers match up with those on each of the cages. According to this, there are about ninety-five 'disposable blood units'. What I can see now is only the front row.

There are steps up to each level and a steel pathway along the front that disappears around the back out of sight. There must be more people racked back there I think. *Must be.*

"They are pumping them full of all sorts of drugs, but for what?" I say as I scroll through the green screen.

"Designer blood, to improve the favour of the blood, to intoxicate maybe, or anything they want. Maybe even poison. I have heard the King talk about such a thing." Sarah replies, a frown drawn across her forehead.

"But what about them?" I point in the general direction of the racks. "Are they conscious? Do they know what is happening to them?"

"I hope not. It looks like the process takes its toll. It must place an incredible strain on the body. It must be an existence of pure pain. Horrible is it not?"

"To say the least."

"This is what Oliver found out. What he wanted us to see," I suggest.

It is hard to look away. I don't want to look at all. My eyes are drawn to one particular prisoner on the third level. I spot him as soon as I enter the room. I can't for the life of me think why this aspect stands out.

I leap up, not bothering with the steel steps and look directly at the man. There is something familiar about him. I cannot put my finger on what. It is difficult to see how it can be so. The head is hanging down, distorted with bulging cheeks, sprouting out from behind the respirator and a food pipe that covers his nose and mouth. His belly protrudes outwards, pushing the rib cage up and out, to allow the massive expanse to escape and hang down, unsupported over stubby short legs. His neck lolls back and forth, as if unable to lift up his head, because the neck muscles have atrophied. His mouth emits a long low moan. It is a soft noise, filled with pain. It is hard to bear. The sound seems in some way familiar. I look once more onto the face of this creature. Then it comes to me. I know this... this person. I speak the words as they pop into my head:

"Paul?!"

He is barely recognisable under the mass of weight he has been forced to accumulate. Yet it is there, something that tells me this is Paul, or what is left of him at any rate.

Sarah leaps up to stand beside me.

"Do you know this one?" she asks.

"Yes."

"A friend?"

"No. He was once. He got a better offer... I should have killed him when I had the chance. It would have been better than...." I am unable to finish the sentence.

I reach out towards him.

"I am sorry..." I say.

With my other hand, I hold up the food tube and bunch of other wiring so I can thread my other hand through. I place a hand at the back of his neck, just below the unsupportable mass of his head. I feel his back-bone through his hot clammy skin, just touching its greasy wet surface gives me goose flesh. I feel the points at the back of Paul's vertebra, in amongst all the layers of flesh. When I have the long column in my hand, I grip it, driving my thumb into one of the vertebrae: fast and sharp.

Crack!

His neck snaps and his huge head falls forward onto his chest. I hear a beeping sound coming from one of the computers: beep, beep, beep... Then there is silence.

"Take me out of this place," is all I manage to rasp. There is a lump in my throat so big that it feels like a great big cooking apple.

"Please..." I add. Even in the most trying of times. I manage to be well mannered.

"Ok" Sarah says softly, taking me by the hand and leading me down the steps and back out of the room. Outside, in the fresh air, I take a giant intake of breath. My shoulders and hands are still quaking.

# Chapter 5

# Escalating Cabal

*"I am sorry" Oliver says.*

His face is pointing toward the ground. "I thought you should see it for yourself, I did not know your friend was there."

"He is not my friend, not for a long time. But no one deserves that. Anyway, you did the right thing." I try to smile, but fail. My mouth just stretches into an uncertain tight line. I don't know what to feel about Paul. Besides, I know fake sympathy when I hear it.

"So that is the future? For everyone?" I ask.

"Yes. I am afraid it is. Humans anyway."

"So that is what all the military build-up is about. They are going to take over?"

"What? Oh no. That's already done. They took over thousands of year ago."

This is what Henry said. More or less. I do not know whether to believe him or not.

"It is the change from one form of domination to another. Or a rather a return to a more feudal, direct form of rule, instead of the more delicate behind the scenes type of thing..." Oliver explains. He rests his heel down on the floor, then runs it across the ground, straightening his leg. He looks better, but his face still seems more like a Halloween mask. Sarah puts the rubber stopper back into the empty glass tube and pockets it.

"But there is no way you get the humans lined up to go into there!" I say. "As soon as they see it, they will go mad; there be war and revolution, and no one will willingly walk into one of those cages. Believe me, I used to be one."

"It is an all a matter of managing perceptions," Oliver says, "and that is what Henry does best."

"They're going to pull the plug on the world economy. They already control it. They're going to make everything crash and burn," he adds.

"The room I saw on one of the lower floors with all the computers?" It suddenly dawns upon me.

"That is where they will make it all happen, or rather where they will pull the trigger. They have people in governments, police and the army, worldwide, to do their bidding. Humans hoping for an upgrade."

"They want to be Wonder-kind?"

"That what they want. I doubt that is what they will get. If they are lucky, Theo being in good mood, they might get a quick painless death."

"If they're not?"

"Then they will just be another human boiler in a hutch." Oliver laughs.

"I still don't see how..." I retort.

"The Wonder-kind have been around for a long time. Can you imagine a multi-national company that has been around ever since the first cavemen started trading with neighbouring tribes? That is them and more. They have been around since the beginning."

"Even so," I protest.

"Even so, nothing. It's a piece of cake for these people. They already own everything. Well, between the twelve anyway." Oliver smiles – or tries. A crooked line curls across his face.

"God!"

I don't want to believe it. How can it be so? Clearly, they are a powerful organisation, but crashing the world economy and crippling it, irretrievably? That will take some doing. Is it even possible? I hope not, but I get a feeling in the depths of my gut that I am wrong: that they can do this and more besides. Oliver could be wrong of course, but I get the sense that there is little hope of that.

"They can do it," Sarah nods.

"Things will break down in a very short time span," Oliver continues. "They will go bad very quickly. So bad... Riots in the street, mass hunger, everything breaking down, law and order failing, so what do they do?"

"Don't know..."

"Bring in martial law. Because there is no choice, not really, and at first the they will be grateful – at last someone is taking control of the situation."

"But?"

"But this is only the beginning. Pretty soon afterwards they will introduce work centres, which become work camps, which will become what you saw today. Only on a mass scale."

We leave Oliver. Sarah promises to return, to help him get out of the castle. I agree, but I still don't trust him. He is enjoying his role as harbinger of doom a little too much. And I definitely don't like the guy. Anyway, he expresses his thanks but say that he doubts that he will be well enough to be move anytime soon. The blood is working but it is taking its time. Oliver's body has just been destroyed too many times. It will repair but it will take time. Time we don't have.

# Chapter 6

# ...Have Ears



*"Shhh! Not here, the walls..." Sarah starts.*

"I know. '...have ears'" I agree.

"Literally," she says. I look at her black eyes. They dart around my face.

We exit the Chateau, via the French windows and head towards the ancient wood grove. We hike up our favourite Yew tree, talking as we climb.

"It's all true," Sarah says.

"How do you know that?" I ask.

"I am the Kings seer, remember? The door is open now. I hear things, worse I see them. Or *she* does. I just get to watch... For me, it is like it has already happened... It's bad, really bad." Sarah turns to me, tears pouring from her eyes.

I climb up to sit on the branch beside Sarah. I put an arm around her, as the tears pour in seemingly endless rivers. I don't question or prod. I just wait for her to speak.

"It's ok," she says, before correcting herself: "No it's not, it really isn't."

"But why do it at all?" I ask. "If they have so much power, so much influence, then why not just carry on feeding on the human race as they have done for centuries. What is the point of changing?"

"Well, even with all that power and influence, the human race is a destructive force. They're still hell-bent on screwing things up. The wars in my time were bad enough – but with nuclear weapons? And when they are not doing that they are destroying the rain forests. If they blow the planet up and each other with it, what will be left for us? No food and just a burnt cinder of a planet to live on."

"Well that is true, as far as it goes, we... *They* are rather self-destructive..." I suggest.

"That's how these people think just thinks that this would make a better solution. Take out the unstable element in the equation... But they can't do this. They can't!"

I say nothing at this point. I don't see the things the way Sarah does. I don't feel the things she feels. In fact, I feel very little. I feel nothing for the human race. Wonder-kind and humans deserve each other in my book. They are just shades of the same thing. But Sarah does care, so I start to as well. The feeling fills the void inside. It is as if receiving the emotion via her synapses the impulses leap towards another, rather than around one brain: mind to mind.

"What are we going do?" Sarah asks.

"What *can* we do?" I reply.

"Well..." Sarah whispers her plan to me.

"It's doable," I agree and she smiles.

We descend the tree and start back towards the Chateau. We approach the walls of the castle; they seem taller than usual, more forbidding. Night is fast approaching, with darkness descending in a manner that seems to harbour a feeling of finality.

# Chapter 7

# Henry's Office

*"What about finger prints? Don't we need gloves or something?"*

"No. We don't have any."

"No gloves?"

"No fingerprints. We have no finger prints."

"What? Why not?"

"Our bodies are in constant flux, constantly repairing themselves. So no fingerprints."

I examine the tips of my fingers. Sarah is right. They are smooth. I look at my palms. There are next to no lines on them. Why didn't I notice before?

I look down over the edge of the ramparts, towards the ground.

"And you're sure he's not in there?" I ask, with a nervy tang to my voice.

"Relatively. I think he left about an hour ago," Sarah replies.

"You think?"

"Yes. I said I did."

"Where'd he go? Do you know?"

"No. He would not tell me. Even if I asked."

"Oh well, let's do this." I say, throwing my legs over the ramparts.

I drop down, landing upon the back of a gargoyle. I perch with feet and hands on the stone surface of the beast. I move closer to the wall. Sarah lands silently behind me. She crouches, bird-like, her feet curving to the shape of the gargoyle's back. She looks around, then fixes her gaze on the window she wants and leaps across. She catches the window ledge and in one continuous moment pulls herself up and slides through the tall narrow window, disappearing from view. I follow with considerably less grace.

I slide through the window into a throwback to the Victorian era. It looks like a room from one of those houses owned by the National Trust. There is nothing in the room to suggest we are living in the 1980s. The room is all dark wood and green padding. There is a drinks cabinet, brandy glasses and two decanters: one is filled to the top and the other half is filled with the red stuff. A wooden filing cabinet and a couple of tall book shelves take up all the space on one wall. The books are all dull coloured hardbacks. They look old and well-thumbed. The majority of the room is taken up by the huge old-fashioned desk. A leather-bound chair is parked next to it. On top of the desk, there is a writing set: an old-fashioned ink pen, ink well and ink bottles containing blue, black and red. There is also a square flat leaning pad, a writing pad and green blotting paper on the desk. To the left is a photo housed in an elaborately decorated photo frame. It is black and white, and faded. The photo is of a young boy who looks as if he has been cemented into his school uniform, appearing too rigid. He is smiling at the camera, but only just. However, his eyes look... lonely.

*Who is he? Henry's son?* No time for that now. The only other thing on the desk is a brief case on its side, with its leather flap open: an invitation for some nosy parker to have a look through. But it is far too obvious for a man as fastidious as Henry. It is as if he has left it here to be found and rifled through

"That looks suspicious," I say.

"Shh! The walls," Sarah whispers, holding her hands above her ears and wiggling her fingers.

I nod.

Sarah goes over to the filing cabinet and starts to go through it, one drawer at a time. I take the contents of the briefcase out and start to sort through the paper work, laying the documents side by side on the desk. I glance up. Sarah has finished searching through the filing cabinet. She turns to me with a hands-up shrug to say she hasn't found anything. I beckon her over.

There are plans, diagrams, maps and other documents. The plans are architectural blueprints of the building to house the 'cattle' and all the equipment. They resemble long slaughter houses, which is apt I suppose. According to the scale, the building will be vast, much bigger than the setup they have here, but little more than a shell: a roof and walls to contain the workings of the parasitical machines. Half the building is for storage, while the other half is for the machines. If I think there are too many in that room, in the white building, this building is on an industrial scale: built to contain thousands of cages, ten thousand to be exact. The diagrams are of the leaching machinery, the cages, feeding equipment and the other paraphernalia we have seen. All the parts are numbered and referenced to lists of parts and order numbers on sheets of crisp A4 paper. In the other papers there are lists of locations that reference the geographical maps on which the locations are marked in red ink. I turn to the final pile, where there is a selection of miscellaneous papers: signed agreements, site reports, medical reports and minutes of the meetings of the twelve. *Only eleven now.* I read the medical report first:

*"...Due to the strain put upon the animal., the average life span is considerably shortened. The average life span is thought to be no longer than one year, much less in some cases. It is therefore a necessity that a plentiful supply of cattle be kept on-hand..."*

I pass the report to Sarah. She nods. I pick up the minutes to the secretive meetings of the twelve. I rifle through the pages, scanning the sheets, looking for anything interesting. I see nothing until I get to the last page. I start to read:

*"32. We recognise the importance of maintaining the food supply and of the importance of reducing pollution and sustaining the environment.*

*In order to achieve the above, the committee approves:*

*1. use of force.*

*2. initiation of Project Planned Response.*

*Preparations to begin as soon as possible. Resources to be allocated from each Kingdom as specified in appendix iii of the agreement signed by all parties.*

*It is also agreed that Henry Hrot will be acting Project Manager for the duration. King Theo will act as Executive, but all major decisions are to be approved by the meeting of the full Project Board. This will meet every mouth to monitor progress of the project..."*

There it is in black and white. It all sounds so mundane, boring even. Just words on a page. It is hard to believe that it spells out something as terrible as the end of the human race as a semi-autonomous concern, transformed into caged cattle at the stroke of a pen. These words illustrate the end, and the beginning of the untold suffering of millions... no, billions. It is too big, way too big, to even comprehend.

*God...* I shake my head. It is all real. And there is even a completion date. I put the sheets of paper back on the desk. Sarah picks them up and looks through them, shaking her head.

I can hear movement in the corridor. I stuff the paperwork back into the briefcase and click it shut. We dart for the window and shoot out into the warm night air, scuttling back up the walls to the roof.

We have found what we are looking for, but I can't help but feel it is a little too easy: as if we are meant to find all those documents.

I decide I am just being paranoid and that I just don't like it when things are simple and go the way I want them to.

# Chapter 8

# Bad Bet

*I walk to the training room.*

I know today will be difficult, but we have to go about things as if they are perfectly normal and we are not planning to do something that will be considered treasonous. We agree that it is be best not to show our hand; they can't find out until we are long gone. Anything else is suicide.

"Tiber, may I have a word?" a voice behind me enquires. I whirl around. It is Henry Hrot standing in the doorway. His arms are folded and his eyes are hard and unreadable. There is a marked change in the man. Or not. I always thought that much of his initial friendliness was an act. I remember what Karl said about Henry revoking his protection of me. I still don't know what that meant exactly, other than what the word seemed to imply at the time. But now Henry's attitude and composure is markedly different. It seems almost as if a different person is standing in front of me now.

*He knows...*I think; *he knows we are in his office*. I don't see any cameras, they could be hidden, or maybe he has just smelt us in his room. Whatever, I am screwed.

"What is it, Henry?" I ask with a polite tone to my voice.

"It would be best if you addressed me as Mr. Hrot or Sir from now on," he retorts.

Well that is pretty telling I think. It is just like being back at school.

"Ok, Mr Hrot," I say.

"Hmm...good. Not beyond all hope then."

"Pardon?"

"Never mind, never mind! I got a lot of flak from Lady Francesca, Karl's donor, over what that girl did to him."

"It wasn't unprovoked," I venture.

"Not the point. The point is your actions, and the actions of that thing, came back to me. If you had of sorted it out between you then no one would have batted an eyelid. But as things stand..." He raises his hands and drops them down to his sides again.

That *thing*? He means Sarah. *Don't get angry. They are only looking for an excuse. To kill you. You only have to get through this day and then I – we – will be gone.*

"Hmm, yes. Well this whole thing means I have to let you... Well, I just can't protect you anymore. I know a bad bet when I see it." Henry rubs his forehead as if he has a headache.

"A bad bet?"

"We have a sort of rivalry. Me and the lady. And Karl has outstripped you in every respect. Even Lucy has proved more loyal and tenacious than you."

Now is probably not the time to say to Henry that Sarah kicked Karl's arse well and truly.

"You're something of a disappointment. I had expected more of you," Henry continues. "Frankly I am downright embarrassed."

He *does* know! How could he know? Keep your cool, Tiber, you can get away with this.

"I am sorry I let you down Mr Hrot," I say, relieved.

"Quite. I took a chance on you, by changing you to one of us and bringing you into the fold. So far, you have failed to live up to expectations. Today will be your last chance to prove you are made of sterner stuff: a last chance for you to shine."

"Or what happens?"

Henry puts his finger to his lips.

"You don't want to know," he says. "I have already said more than I should." He winks at me.

"Oh?"

"Just don't let me down." Henry's voice is stern.

Then, Mr Hrot turns on his heels. I hear his shoes click loudly as he walks away. I stand perplexed. *Was that a threat? I guess so, but what is it I am being threatened with? Will they kick me out?* That would be a dream come true though I have never heard of it happening. No, that is as likely as Karl and me becoming friends. It is more likely I will be excommunicated: burned alive then left to rot downstairs in the dungeon.

I really hate Henry: for what he has done to Sarah and for his character; he is not a nice man, not nice at all. Slimy, that is the word. He uses people and if they don't turn out as winners, he discards them and

leaves them to die. I don't feel frightened of him anymore, but I know I
have to tread very carefully now

The others arrive in dribs and drabs. Karl even nods to me as he enters. But I just nod back, hoping he will not start anything after yesterday's little incident.

I have the creeping feeling that something is up; something is really
wrong here. I am ignoring it. The only thing different is that we have
started the day practising with hand guns with targets pinned to the
walls rather than shooting each other. I just empty a clip of bullets into
the small red target.

There are no signs that anything is out of the ordinary in the training
room. "Just another day in hell," I mutter under my breath.

# Chapter 9

# Cleaning House

*Something is very wrong.*

When we return to level 12, later that day, it is deserted. The chains all hang empty and the bodies that have been spread out through the room have all gone. It is like walking into an invisible wall. It smacks you in the face, but you can't work out why or what has hit you. I look back at Sarah, who is still holding the little tube of blood she has brought for Oliver.

I take a couple of hesitant steps into the room and a feeling of dread shoots through my stomach. I instantly know what has happened. I feel it underneath my Clarks shoes.

"No..." I say out loud.

"I am afraid..." Sarah begins. She is just behind me.

"No! This is just too horrible!" she continues.

"It is."

I am looking down at my feet, at the floor – at what covers the floor in little piles. It is fleshy in hue, mixed with black and few other colours. There are piles and piles of the stuff – all coming together to make the

427

colour of the sand you used to get in glass ornaments from the seaside: a carpet of the broken-down bodies of Wonder-kind – immortals all reduced to dust.

"My God!" I utter. "They have killed them... all of them."

They must have executed each in turn: one after the other, or several at a time. Maybe they just opened the door and started shooting with their D-guns. We will never know.

"Is this our fault?" I ask, "because we went to the farm?" I am weighed down enough with the guilt for all the people I have killed and all the bad things I have done. I don't need this massacre on my conscience as well.

"...Because we spoke to Oliver?" I add.

"Yes, because we spoke to him" says Sarah. "But it's not our fault; We weren't the ones to pull the trigger."

"As good as," I retort, looking around the room.

"No. We didn't. Blame lays with those did this, not us. They did not have to do it. But they chose it."

"What now?" I say, weary. I don't want to argue about it. I don't want to think about it.

"Now we get the hell out before we are discovered. From now on, we tread like angels: very carefully. If they know it's us...then we are in a lot of trouble. We need to be ready." Sarah answers.

"Let's just go. The cave is close – let's just..." I suggest.

"Can't." Sarah says, a crease folding the features of her face. Her eyes look distant and far away, as if she is thinking about something unpleasant.

"She can't help you this time, this you have to do on your own." It is Sarah's mouth moving but the words do not fit. Something about them freezes my blood.

"Why not? If they have done this, then they will think nothing of killing us," I ask.

"Less than nothing…" the cadaverous Bonemann interjects, standing in the doorway, D-gun in hand and Karl behind him. It is then I realise what Sarah means. It falls upon me like a ton of bricks.

"It is already too late…" I say.

They know everything and they are already coming for us. We have been playing this as if it is a game against wonder-kind, who have been playing this for centuries and who have been several steps ahead of us all the time. And now it is time to pay for that nativity.

"It's over, sunshine, you're as good as dead," Bonemann sneers.

I turn in panic, about to shout: "Run, Sarah, run," but she is no longer here in the room. I think I hear her say "I am sorry," but she is not there to say anything. Only the Bonemann, Karl and two guards are here now. They close in on me. This is it. *This is the end* my mind says, stating the bleeding obvious.

# End Game

# Chapter 1

# Plasma Heart

*The sun is far too big and much too near.*

Seemly, through the heat haze, it almost touches the black tarmac of the road leading towards it. It takes up most of the horizon. It is a blood red and fierily orange colour. Solar flares arch in giant loops all across its huge plasma surface.

People run past me – in fear, in terror – their skin and hair alit: human candles trying to out-run death.

Fat chance.

Their screams are shrill and penetrating, playing discordantly on each and every one of my nerves. Each are on edge as I walk towards the burning globe.

*It is me it wants.*

Buildings burn, the tarmac running in black rivers that flow around my ankles as thick as treacle. I look into the sun's brilliance, the light blinding me, as tentacles of flame reach down to cradle me. *At least it will warm me; never again will I feel the coldness of this world and its people.*

It takes me up in its fiery arms to draw me beneath its convecting surface of fire. The flesh burns from my bones, then my bones turn to ash and I enter the surface of the burning orb and connect up with its centre. My heart, that black hated thing, somehow survives, becoming at one with the suns pulsating core. It beats louder and louder – the sound is deafening. With each beat, a million hydrogen nuclear reactions explode, expanding the incandescent surface bigger and bigger until it swallows the whole earth in fire and flame. I feel the screaming and agony of the billons of humans who have inhabited the earth, all burning inside of me. Their bodies are popping like bubble wrap. I can feel the suffering of every single living soul, as they burn and I feel the ecstasy it brings me. I am without sympathy or mercy – the sadism of my revenge know no bounds. Soon my black heart is the only living thing in the solar system. It continues to expand and reaches out into the void, beating its savage rhythm. After all, there must be life on other planets. I look forward to embracing them all in my blazing embrace, because I am so very hungry...

"Aagh!"

I start away. My arms are numb and I try to pull them towards me, but they are suspended about my head. Metal grates against stone as I move them.

"Oh," I say as memory returns.

Another crazy dream: wish fulfilment and not prophecy, as Sarah has said. I am just a sad nonentity who never did anything with his life. Even when I have superhuman powers of the wonder-kind, all I do is bring death. It makes sense to dream that you are the sun or some super warrior king rather that the nobody that I really am. The only prophetic element of the dream is being burnt alive – surely they mean to execute me in front of the Wonder-kind community – just like Oliver burned me at the stake? I only hope that they kill me after, not keep me around like they did him – as one of the living dead. I shiver. The wonder-kind are not really known for their kindness – I can expect no mercy.

I am not even seventeen years old, but I feel so old and tired, as if I am 4000 like king Lanzón. If only it could all be over. If only the pain, guilt and suffering could come to an end. Well, the cost of my life it is cheap at half the price.

I cannot imagine all those intense and terrible feelings just dying; they seem as if they will keep going on long after my body is dust. Knowing my luck, I will come back as a ghost... Why not? I am already a vampire – the veil of credibility has already been broken.

They will kill me, for sure, and there are guards: two of them outside the doors. I can hear them, but that does not mean I have to go the same way as Oliver did. Karl took great pleasure in locking the manacles that held up my wrists much too tight. It is strange how we take imprisonment and all its paraphernalia as read: that we accept that you have to obey the implicit instructions to stay – even if there is no real need. There is no real reason why I should remain chained up; I am not one of the living dead after all. I reach one hand over to the metal of the manacle and snap it in two. I do the same for the other and let my arms fall gratefully to my lap, the blood rushing to fill the two limbs up once more. I have pins and needles.

"He's awake. Radio the Bonemann." I hear the voice of one of the guards outside.

I wonder where Sarah is. Back in the bosom of the Wonder-kinds' little community or in a cell somewhere being tortured? Why did she do it? She promised she would never betray me. Has she told them where to find me? Or did she just run after hearing them coming? As someone who can see the future, she could have given me a heads up. I would have told her to run and save herself, but I turned to find she had just disappeared. I feel betrayed and hurt. The feeling burns most bitterly in my chest. Only, deep down, I know it isn't her. I have heard that voice before, when Sarah was sleepwalking and then again in my dreams. As crazy as it sounds, when Sarah ran out on me she wasn't at home. It is that other woman driving – the 4000-year-old Cassandra. I didn't twig at the time, yet at the same time I did – I know then as I know now. Sarah would never betray me. But I have let her down. I cannot help her. I should have been more for her, but then I let everyone down. I always do. Just ask anyone. All I can bring myself to say is:

"I am sorry, Sarah." The words seem to echo around the empty room.

# Chapter 2

# Sweet Dreams

*"See anything you like?" Henry probes.*

Entering through the door this time, I look around Mr Hrot's office. Bonemann is standing in the corner of the room, leant against the wall with his arms folded. Apart from that, everything else looks the same; even his brief case is still on his desk. Oh, yes, there is one more change: Henry Hrot is slouched in his leather chair behind the desk. He holds a glass of the red stuff aloft. He swirls the half-full brandy glass around before putting to his mouth and draining it. It piques my thirst. I lick my lips automatically.

"Sure you wouldn't like another poke around?"

I say nothing.

The guards push me to stand at the front of Mr Hrot's desk and then retreat, shutting the oak door on the way out.

"Treason is something we take very seriously around here," Henry says.

"You made that clear, when I first came here," I agree.

"Did I? Oh, the execution of the boy Oliver? Ha, ha. So I did, but that is not for you,"

"It isn't?"

To my surprise, Henry roars with laughter.

"No of course bloody not!" he says, recovering.

"You're not good enough for that," he tells me, smiling his supercilious smile, before continuing:

"That is only for the Wonder-kind. To be a part of the community, you need to have completed your combat training. That will never happen. So, you see, you simply don't deserve the pomp of a public execution."

"And then there is your co-conspirator," he muses, pouring himself another drink.

"...That Sarah woman."

"She has nothing to do with it," I say.

"You have me, let that be an end of it," I add.

"Oh, very noble I am sure, but we know everything. You needn't worry though. She may be an abomination but she is one of us. She won't have the freedom she used to have; we will keep her on a shorter leash than she is used to," Henry tells me.

"Besides she is useful. You, one the other hand, are not," he adds.

"Sweet dreams, eh?" I say, more to myself than Henry, remembering the words to that particular song.

"Pardon?"

"Nothing."

"Quite. But don't worry. Your death will be put to good use," he jeers before going on:

"What we don't tell you prodigies is that only half of you will survive. If you don't die in training, you can only graduate by taking the life of one of your fellows. And I think Karl has taken rather a shine to you," he says, considering the blood in his glass and then taking a sip.

"Who knows you might even win," he continues. "Stranger things have happened."

"What then? Then you kill me?"

"Good lord no! We are not savages. You will be exiled."

"That's it?"

"True, you may be killed on sight if you set foot on our lands, but I am sure you can live with that."

Henry licks the blood from his lips.

"Hmm, this is good," he says.

"Here," he gestures, pouring out another glass and pushing it across the desk towards me.

"The last meal of the condemned," he laughs.

I pick it up and sniff the red liquid. Nothing funny about it. I knock it back in one. I would probably do the same thing if I had smelt something odd about the blood. I need it.

"Ok, take him away." Henry nods to Bonemann.

"I'll be watching, so make sure you put on a good show," he laughs, before draining his glass.

"I don't care", I snap back.

I really don't. And there is strength in such a feeling. I am led out by the two guards. I walk with long strides, no longer cowed or with my chest and head bent forward, nor afraid to meet anyone's gaze. I walk tall towards my death, which is surely waiting in the wings to jump out at me and say "Boo". And it is hardly before time.

No more dreams, no more prophesies and no more make believe –
only the grim bite of reality: I am going to die soon and that feels as
unreal as it can get.

Bonemann calls the two guards, who come in and take me away,
down to the underground complex to the training room for one final
and terminal combat lesson: how to die.

# Chapter 3

# Combat Play

*I glance up at the at the observation room.*

It is set high up on the main wall, with a long rectangle of glass through which visitors might view the proceedings below. And, in other words, watch us hack each other to pieces. I have never given it a great deal of thought because it is usually empty and unlit. It is just there. Today, that is clearly not the case; today, the light is definitely on and it is packed. There are a number of people already inside and more are shuffling into the room. Henry is there, of course. He looks down at me, unsmiling; his lower jaw looks as if it is locked in place, superglued to the upper one.

The two guards on either side of me make me look a small piggy in the middle compared to these two giants. They certainly know how to pick them around here. They give me a small shove to my back and I stagger forwards a couple of steps. I look around at their smiling faces. One looks as he is going to say something, but instead just shakes his massive dome, then turns with his companion and heads towards the door. The Bonemann walks up to me. A Glock in his hand, he presses the side arm into my palm.

"Get some practice in," he says, as if this is just another day in the training room.

"Make sure you put on a good show," he tells me.

I turn to the target. I look down at the pistol I am holding. I wonder if the glass of the observation room is bulletproof? Probably. I empty the magazine into the target at the opposite end of the room. My aim is perfect. With my eyesight, that means nothing. I'm no better than anyone else in the room. I let the empty clip drop out and then take another one from the table and put the fresh one in the slot of the handle, then ram it in place. I raise the pistol once more and take aim.

I am not the only one who notices the VIPs in attendance. There is an excited chatter in the air. When I finish firing, I put the gun down and turn to see that Bonemann is standing in the centre of the room, his bony arms in the air.

"All right, all right, so we have guests. Get over it! It shouldn't make any difference to you lot. It's the same drill as usual – focus, concentration and doing what you are bloody well told," he shouts.

The room falls silent.

There is no announcement, no speeches and no summary of my many crimes. It starts the way it always does, but everyone knows today is different. Everyone is on the same page – we all know what has to happen here. We begin in pairs, using hand guns and short daggers on each other. Then, just for me, it becomes three to one, then four to one... then six. I do ok, for me anyway. I take two out completely, but the numbers are against me. Then Karl wades in. He has two bayonets.

I lose my gun with my arm when Karl joins the fray. He comes from behind, one bayonet cutting through my shoulder and his trunk like arm wrapping around my neck, as the ultra-sharp bayonet slices through the muscle. The game has changed, not that it was ever that. It is deadly serious. It becomes clear that the others are just there to grind me down, wear me out and make me waste energy. Karl could have taken me on his own, but this is a fixed fight, so the outcome is assured. It is a demonstration and well- exercised piece of theatre. The only one who is not in on the script is me, though I can tell that, before very long, I will be exiting stage left or wherever it is you go when you're dead.

# Chapter 4

# Undisputed Death

*All things run the course of their necessary lives.*

Everything comes to an end. "No matter how bad it is, it will come to an end, sooner or later" I used to say when I was human. The Wonderkind are, as far as I can tell, immortal, but how many of us will live forever? How many of us will just die killing each other for little more than a glint of approval in the eyes of those who run our lives? How many will end their lives after living so long that they are sick of living, tired of the same things repeating over and over? Or, if the humans have their way, how many will destroy everything worth living for? Either way, no one lives forever. Not really.

It is the day everything goes to hell and the day my life here is over. We have reached an impasse, Karl and me. Sarah had my back. I am sure of that, as sure as blood is blood. But Karl has everyone else. So he wins.

Like I say, nobody lives forever.

"How does that feel? Eh? Like it?" Karl asks me, as he twists the bayonet deep into my gut, forcing it upwards into the space between my rib cage, cutting through anything that gets in its way. My left arm is snaking its way across the floor, trying to make it to my shoulder, so it can reattach itself.

The pool of blood I am lying in has lost its warmth. It clings and squelches beneath me. It could be worse. It had been a craze in the training room for a while; two fighters will aim especially for the artery, just because of the spectacular geyser it produces, and they cheer if it hits the roof. It is messy of course, but no one gets killed. I am less keen, as it is usually me who has to mop up the mess.

The space where my arm had been only minutes ago has stopped bleeding now. All the tubes that link to my arm have sealed themselves off, waiting for the arms return, so they can reattach themselves and continue their normal business of supplying blood. This is another advantage of being Wonder-kind: we are keen on drinking the red stuff, but reluctant to give up our own.

Anyway, before my arm can manage to sneak its way back to its proper place, Karl sees it and kicks it away. I think it lands somewhere on the other side of the room. I cannot see, but I know that wherever it has landed, it will be once more resuming its slow journey towards me.

I can still feel my disconnected arm as it creeps along the floor. I have some control over it, though not much. I can clench and unclench my fist, for all the use that is. I have heard of, though never seen, Wonder-kind claiming to be able to fight with their remote limb, but I have always been sceptical. The Wonder-kind are always bragging about something. I can feel fingernails scratch across the floor and its cold surface under my fingertips and the lower side of my arm. I have no idea how that is even possible. It could be that I just imagined it all.

When I am wounded, the pain rushes in and my mind often goes off elsewhere, trying to get away from the pain: to try to out-run it. So, really, anything is possible when you are in that a state.

Karl puts his hand back onto the second bayonet that he skewered through my other shoulder, pinning me to the ground. At the same time, he works with the other one: the one inside my gut. He twists the bayonet so it hits on a nerve. The pain tells me to do something. It tells me he is killing me, even though I know he is not. *He can't, not yet anyway*, I tell myself. He can only inflict pain, that is all, but the panic in my chest just keeps rising. I can hear a roaring in my left ear. I can see Karl's face twisted with hate and, at the same time, a large smile leers, telling me just how much he is loving this: enjoying hurting me.

Another twist...

I cry out between clenched teeth. I regret the cry the instant it leaves my mouth. As Karl's grin widens, I bite down on my lip.

*Uh! Take it, take the pain, all of it. Don't give him the satisfaction...*

I wonder when he tears into me, how much is out of malice toward me and how much is duty. I even wonder how much is out of fear of losing face. We have not spoken about the time Sarah had knocked him down so easily the evening before. Let sleeping dogs lie I had thought...

"This is for what that bitch of yours did to me," he says, as he forces the bayonet in my gut closer to my spine; the tip scrapes over bone.

*So, he isn't not the type to forgive and forget: no surprise there.*

"Uh...not mine...she doesn't belong to me...and for what? kicking your ass?" I gasp, knowing full well this is probably not the right thing to say, given the circumstances. But what the hell I think. After your pain levels reach a certain pitch, that is it, they don't go any higher, and it is not as if all this is going to kill me. Or not like this anyway. That has to come later. This is the warm up to make me suffer before the end.

Karl pulls the bayonet out. There is a horrible slurping sound as the blade exits. I bite down to prevent myself from crying out once more.

*You've been through worse.* Telling myself this works for a while, until the pain gets too much once more. I need this to be over, right away. But it is all too clear, from what I see in Karl's eyes: the hunger – pure hatred even – and maybe that is too mild a description of what I see here. There is no escaping this trial by bayonet.

Karl holds the blade, still dripping with my blood, to my left cheek. He is still grinning. He presses down with the flat side of the long blade, wiping my blood down my cheek, smiling all the while: dragging it out. My insides lurch as the many severed surfaces, organs and flesh force themselves together. It is like having a rat in there chewing at my insides. At least I am healing, I think, but then I realise Karl properly plans to rip it all open again. But not yet. In the meantime, he is amusing himself by carving his initials into my cheek with the point of the bayonet.

"So much for chivalry..." I manage to grunt, holding back a scream.

From over Karl's shoulder I see Henry. He nods to the King, who is on the other side of the observation room. I don't know if it has been planned this way. Probably, but from where I lie I can see up to the observation room. I have a perfect view.

There is occasionally the odd visitor or two sitting up there to watch our training sessions. Henry has been there a couple of times, along with a few other people I do not know, or wouldn't recognise if I ever saw them again. But, now, there is a full house. Alongside the King and Henry, the big body of the chancellor is squeezed in on the right and there are a number of other people from the court. I don't know their names. They all appear to be waiting, on the edge of their seats, expecting something spectacular, and it isn't my fighting skills that they have all come to see – that at least is for certain.

I wonder if Sarah is up there. Then, I see her a little way behind the King, in the back row. I am not the only one looking over in her direction. Henry keeps gazing over at her, looking at her face, expecting something, but her face is impassive: a mask. That means nothing, I know. But at the same time... Even Karl flicks a glance to see what I am looking.

"Heh,"

He yanks my head up. I think he believes I will get a better view, but it isn't necessary. I can see everything from where I am.

"Looks like she's grown bored of you. Looks like she doesn't care about you anymore," he spits at me.

But he is wrong. He doesn't know Sarah. None of them do. This means he is bound to get it wrong and pick up the message she wanted them to see: indifference. Her small white face shows no emotion. But her bright wide eyes do. The soft black centres seem to reach to me, generating a warmth in my ripped open gut. They radiate outwards and upwards. She knows there is nothing she can do and that any expression that crosses her face will only give Karl pleasure and make him more vicious and lead him to enjoy his sadism even more. So she keeps her face blank, not even granting him so much as a frown.

Karl places the tip of the bayonet on my barely healed stomach and then, with a sharp thrust, pushes the sharp blade into my intestines. He laughs.

Then Henry steps forward, knocks on the glass and says in solemn voice:

"As we agreed Mr Bonemann."

The Bonemann gets up starts to walk towards us. Meanwhile, Karl the King's psychopath is really getting into his thing, thrusting the knife in and out like a steam piston.

"Enough!" Bonemann roars.

"But sir..." Karl pleads. There is real whine to his voice, like a child being told to go to bed when his favourite programme has only just started.

Bonemann grabs \Karl's wrist and pulls him off me. I groan in relief.

"Enough I say!"

The fact that Henry has put an end to my suffering makes me feel, a rush of warmth towards him, even though I know it is foolish and misplaced. I look towards Sarah, who ever so slightly shakes her head and mouths:

"Don't trust him."

So this is going to get worse, not better. I can't say I am surprised.

"Enough I say" Bonemann repeats, his tone lower and more menacing this time. Karl stops struggling and Bonemann releases his hands. They fall to his sides and he nods.

"Ok?" Bonemann says to Karl

"Ok." He confirms.

"Sorry Sir. Won't happen again, Sir."

"That's alright, boy. We all get carried away, but now you have to set an example. Stay focused, disciplined and, most important of all, follow orders. After all you are the Team Champion now. You have a tradition, a legacy to uphold!"

"Yes sir," Karl agrees, and I wonder if he is going to salute Bonemann.

I look back at Sarah. She is mouthing individual letters to me: "W...O...R...K...I...T...O...U...T."

*Work it out? Work what out?* I try to think, desperately, but I just do not know what she wants me to do.

"As part of your rank, your office, you will have to make choices, some of them meaning life or death. You will need make sacrifices. You need to cut out the dead wood, lest the rest of the tree become infected," Bonemann goes on.

*That doesn't sound good. I am not liking the way this speech is going, not one little bit.*

*What have I got to work out? They want kill me? I got that much myself.*

Bonemann pats Karl on the shoulder.

"It's time," he says, and walks over to the locked cabinet on the other side of the room. There is a sinking feeling in what must be my exposed stomach. Who knows, it could have been really my gut sinking down – literally. But I am not thinking of that. I am thinking about the cabinet and what is inside – death and, in particular, mine. I realise that I want to live after all.

I am thinking this just as Bonemann brings out the long sleek shape: the D-Gun.

"In your hands, duty," Bonemann says.

"The will of the King," he adds, walking back towards Karl.

"The will of the King," Karl repeats.

*Bloody hell!*

Karl takes the offered D-gun, not giving the task any thought at all. He just walks over to me and places the end of the barrel against my forehead. It feels cold. He flicks the safety off and the gun whirls to life. I feel it vibrate against my skull.

"I could say I am sorry it came to this...but, well, I am not!" Karl smiles at me, his lips twitching.

"Last words?" Karl smiles.

I say nothing. This is it the end. Death has caught up with me. I only wish I knew what Sarah had meant. I am obviously too stupid to live. This is it: termination.

"No? Good, because no one wants to hear them. Don't you want to beg?" Karl taunts.

This is it: The end of the line. Curtains.

I should have known. I should have known better. I really should have. I ought to have grabbed Sarah's hand and ran from this place, far away. We said we were going to; why did we wait? Now it is too late.

Did we really have some crazy notion of putting a stop to what we found down on the farm? Only, we were not sure how to go about it. How could we do anything, just the two of us against all this: the full might of the Wonder-kind? What could we do against all that? Nothing. We ought to have just run. I hope Sarah still will. I hope she will be ok. She survived so many years before she met me, didn't she? She is stronger than me, stronger than Karl even. It seems unfair that I will never see her again... In seconds, I will either not exist anymore or be trapped on the other side of the dark veil. I wonder if I will be able to see through it. Could I bear that? I don't think I could.

Anyway, there is nothing to be done, other than to die.

# Chapter 5

# Molecular Collapse

*One minute you're here, next minute...*

"Stop!" It is Bonemann's voice.

I open one eye. *What now?* I am not afraid. Not anymore. My mind clears, no longer a pea soup of worry and confused thought. That is all gone. Now it is icy cold – oh so very cold – and clear as crystal, in the face of death.

"Remember this is an execution. It's not personal. Stay detached and professional," Bonemann instructs.

*Oh for the love of...*

"I can't enjoy it?" Karl asks. He flicks the switch of the gun back and the whining noise of it stops.

"Sure you can. But at that distance the back blast from the gun will kill you at the same time it kills him," he elaborates.

"Oh, ok," Karl agrees. Then, lifting the gun, he steps backwards a couple of steps and aims once more. He tuts and flicks back the safety switch. The gun purrs into life once more.

*Oh, this is just so comical: a complete farce.* I think bitterly.

*What is it I am meant to work out? What is it that I am too stupid to get?*

I haven't a clue.

*Maybe I deserve this, to die.*

I feel a tingling at the centre of my brain. It expands into a fiery point of intense heat – burning through to my forehead, hot and searing, like a pin point laser beam. I frown – *what is happening?* Then it is in the middle of my forehead, an intense and angry point. My sight leaves my eyes, as consciousness ignites. Then, it explodes into the room. It is as if time is running backwards and something in my mind has clicked into place like an ancient and rusty machine just starting up after centuries of neglect: an old, old machine, older than me or the Wonderkind or anything else I can think of. Nothing will ever be the same for me ever again. I see it: bright, clear and sharp in focus. I see everything as it really is, in microscopic detail. *I am going insane.*

Everything is just patterns of energy, binding molecules forever circling around. Neutrons and protons racing: that is all that we all are. But it is the energy that is the important thing. It binds us to matter but, at the same time, it is separate – the real soul juice. It is not the blood running around our veins, pulsing through our arteries, but souls in motion that are changing, fluid and in flux. They are in time and outside of time with the molecules the soul juice attracts and controls...

It seems as if I can reach out into the very minds of everyone here and can hear what they are thinking.

Then a voice comes in, sharp and clear:

**Just get it over with. Just kill him.**

Except it is not my own.

Another:

***Boring. Just do it!***

***Pity I thought he might just...*** another voice says. Or is it a thought? I can't tell. The world falls out of orbit for me. *Am I going insane?* I have to wonder.

I know, of course, that I can't be seeing this. It is a sort of virtual space, but no less real – in fact it is more real than reality.

Then my mind snaps to one thought pattern in particular: one that is so familiar. I can cry tears.

***You've got it. Now use it!*** Sarah's thoughts urge.

My body is filled with power surging through me. It feels as if my blood is boiling and my nerves are on fire. All I need to do is...

"Wait!" I say.

I raise my hand and make it into a fist and then open it as if releasing a butterfly. This is, for my part pure, theatrics. I want them all to see what I am about to do. I want them to know it is me doing it. I want them to all know it is me who is responsible for what is going to happen next.

*It is all so simple.*

I reach out with my mind and punch into dark swirling energy mass that goes by the name of Karl, disturbing the delicate and intricate dance of the bodies' molecules, sending them spinning off in every direction, colliding, repelling and attracting, like an amorphous cloud trying to hold its centre, but gyrating out of control. Like a cancer, it flows through Karl's etheric and physical body, tearing it apart as it goes. The soul juice that holds everything in place binds it and keeps it in stasis. It tries desperately to hold on, to cling on to matter, but fails at every turn, as the chaos increases, oscillating towards total collapse.

The result is inevitable. There is no moral debate going on in my head. If it is this or death, Karl's death or mine, Then I choose his. For the first time in my life, I feel I exist and have a place on the earth, a connection. I can feel it vibrate through the heels of my feet and pulse behind my eyeballs. If you were to ask me if I would relive this moment, with ability to do something less drastic, would I do that less drastic thing instead? If you were to ask me, I could only say I don't know.

Sight returns to my eyes. My view shifts and the psychedelic vision ends abruptly, like taking my eye from a microscope to refocus on the classroom: the science bench with graffiti carved on its surface, gas taps for the Bunsen burners and students in white lab coats. I am back in the world, or rather back here to the training room.

I mainly see pink, white and black. I am sure there are other colours as well, but those are the ones that stand out: the ones I see explode into the air, then raining down like a storm of dust. It reminds me of one of those egg timers with the different coloured sands pouring through the hole, rushing to get to the bottom.

Silence.

It is a silence that stretches out: uncomprehending. Then, disbelief and horror take over. All eyes are on the circulating dust that drifts to form a film of colourful dust on the floor. Maybe they think staring hard enough – or wishing, bargaining or praying hard enough – means Karl will resurrect: that he will rise up from the floor, magically reforming from dust to flesh and blood. But we all know nothing like that ever happens. When you're dead you are dead, even if you are Wonder-kind.

I can still hear them in my head. Bonemann looks towards me and the cabinet of the D-guns. My eyes meet his, mine narrowing and waiting for him to make a move. I spring to my feet. The movement seems easy and my body feels light. I rip the bayonet out from my shoulder and throw down. It clatters over the stone floor. The sound is loud in comparison to the previous silence of the room.

In terms of the rest of me, my arm has at last crawled over the floor, leaving a red trail in its wake, now flopping against my shoe, like a small puppy hoping to be petted. I squat and grab the wayward limb, not for moment taking my eye off Bonemann. Holding the arm at the elbow, it feels strange, alive and part of me, as if the separation is only illusionary, a trick done by mirrors. I hold it in place in the shoulder area, where it has lived until recently. There is a squelching sound as both sides suck together, healing the breach. I flex it a couple of times and flick my wrist. It is almost back to normal. Full service has almost been restored.

More seconds pass by. Karl doesn't resurrect and never will, of course. Every Wonder-kind knows that. The destruction is absolute. There is no coming back from total molecular collapse.

I walk, with long strides towards Karl's remains. I put my foot into the coloured dust and kick handfuls of the stuff into the air.

I look into the eyes of everyone in the room, one by one. *What now?* I wonder. What am I trying to do? Antagonise them? What if they all rush me at once? What then? Can I take them all? I don't know.

I can hear their thoughts. They are scared, but that only makes them all the more dangerous. My mouth moves. Words come out. I cannot believe I am saying them. It doesn't even sound like my voice. It is a deep and nasty-sounding voice: harsh and biting, not like me at all. But the words come out of *my* mouth. I can't deny that. One after another, I speak them:

"So, who's next?"

# Chapter 6

# Murderous Thoughts

*I hear footfalls in the distance, getting closer: the sound of raised voices alongside angry little thoughts, flying around – indistinguishable.* But most of all, I see fear in the eyes of everyone. I see it in Bonemann, in my classmates and those up behind the glass window, except for one pair of eyes: Sarah's. She is smiling. There is only the smallest hint of a smile but it is certainly there: her huge black eyes glisten with warmth and relief.

Bonemann backs away, his arms raised to shoulder height. My classmates back away, until someone's nerve breaks. It is someone towards the back of the group in the room. I cannot see who it is. They just turn and run. Everyone else apparently thinks this a good idea, as they all run. They move at the same time, or maybe a little before or after. The ones behind the glass window run from their little room, helped along by a couple of big men in black. I see someone, the chancellor I think, grab Sarah's arm. She resists but is pulled along towards the exit. I move forward. Henry throws me back an unreadable look before he disappears with the rest of the fleeing crowd.

I feel a spike of anxiety in my stomach and concern for Sarah.

"Kill him! Kill him!" I hear the Kings shout.

I want to run after them to try to reach Sarah. But first things first. I have some pressing matters to deal with. There are two of them in observation room, one banging on the window with what is clearly a D-gun. Another one is framed in the doorway. I raise my hands. I can hear their thoughts, loud and feverishly murderous. So I insert a thought of my own. I don't know how I know I can do this. I just do. Something has woken up inside my brain and is starting to stretch out, to flex its muscles.

I imagine the room, empty, and push the image out towards the three bodyguards. I turn up the clarity of the vision until not one of them can see the room as anything other than the image I put in their heads.

"The room is empty...?" one of them says helpfully.

"He must have got out..." another replies, blinking.

"We have to get him. He can't have gone far," the third suggests. They run. The two in the observation room thunder down the stairs and the man at the door turns and pelts down the corridor, closely followed by the other two. The sound of their footfalls fades.

Then I am alone. The silence in the training room is oppressive. It seems more silent and desolate than anything I have known before. I look around the room, at the blood stains, remembering all that has happened here: all unnecessary and cruel. I take one last look. Then I make up my mind: I must find Sarah and then get the hell out of here. I turn on my heels and head for the doorway. Before I reach it, I pause.

Whatever I have become has been burnt into the central part of my forehead. It feels powerful, pulsing and throbbing in time with my heart beat. But will it be enough? It is intuitive, but I have no idea how to use it properly, to its full potential. No. I need something else as well. Something more concrete when it comes to fire-power. I need a D-gun.

I walk over to the glass cabinet. The one that Karl had been intending to use on me is nothing but dust on the floor, now mixed in with what is left of Karl. I reach out towards the cabinet and the glass surface starts to ripple, beginning to move away as if it is averse to my hand. The surface looks similar to ripples on water. The glass material melts, pouring down the surface of the cabinet like candle wax. I put my hand into the gap at the front of the cabinet.

I take out two of the long black weapons from the cupboard. I have a slight quiver in my heart at their touch – these coveted items. All the prodigies have dreamt of earning one of these, but I have received two by theft. I wedge one inside of my belt, where it hangs on my hip. Then I walk back to the centre of the room. I look down at the gun. It seems simple enough to operate, just an 'on' button and a safety switch – then I point and fire. I press it into the 'on' position and it starts to hum. A mechanical voice starts to say "Welc..." and I remember Bonemann's words:

"If you are out in the field on a covert mission – say, an assassination for example – or you are just in a place you shouldn't be and you need to take someone out, the last thing you want is for your D-gun to start yapping!"

There's a button underneath the barrel, next to the trigger guard. I flick it and the voice dies. I hold the gun in my hand, feeling its heaviness It is no weight at all, but looks ridiculously big in my hands. I point it at the cabinet with its door still dripping to the floor. I pull the trigger. There is a blinding flash. The cabinet and a large chunk of the wall behind it are now dust showering towards the ground. No doubt there are plenty more of them. Theo's guards all have them, but as far as I am concerned, the less of these things in circulation, the better.

I know everyone will be looking for me; I am a marked man: marked for death.

*Take no chances, just do what you have to and then get out.*

Good advice, but it is not as if I have done anything like this before. I feel a slight tremor in my gut. Then it dies. Just vanishes. There is something new inside me. It is a feeling of calmness and of burning anger: ice and fire.

I sneak along the corridor, with every nerve on red alert, listening for slightest noise or any incoming thought. I edge along the corridor and press against the surface of the wall.

*Where is she? Where have they taken her?*

# Chapter 7

# Heart Pangs

*So where is she?*

Where have they taken her? And what are they doing to her? A hundred horrible fates flash through my head, fast, one after the other and many at the same time. It isn't helpful.

Are they torturing her to find out how I do the things I did back there in the training room? I can't put it past them. They will do it just for fun – something else I will be to blame for. *What have I done?*

It seemed the right thing to do at the time, but now, was it really? I haven't any choice. I have to act or die. But what are the consequences of my actions? What price is Sarah paying on my behalf? She is tougher than she looks, I know that, and she is several centuries old, so she has learnt a thing or two in that time, but she is not invulnerable. She is easily hurt if you are skilled in the art, as most of the Wonderkind definitely are. The idea that someone is hurting her makes me feel nauseous and sick to my soul.

My breathing becomes short and fast. I run down the corridor, pausing at the end, listening and waiting for any sounds. I come to the lift. *No, I'll take the stairs.* I pass by the lift and mount the stone steps upward.

*This can't be happening, not after all we have been through. It can't end like this. It just can't.*

Then something deep inside moans.

# Chapter 8

# Reaching Out

*I try to reach out: to tune into Sarah's thoughts.*

So far, I have only been able to hear the thoughts of others when they come within range: if they are in the same room. But, then again, this is all pretty new to me – so what do I know? I have to at least try. I stop climbing the stone staircase. I try to reach out, to listen. It is not a lot different from using my regular ears., In fact, back in the training room, with so many people, I had a hard job telling what was coming out of people's mouths and what was pure thought – it all sounded the same.

Faintly, I hear something trapped in a lot of background sounds, buzzing like white-noise. Then there is a familiar tinge. My conscious-ness leaps on it, following it, as lightening down a lightning rod. It is trace to the source.

***I am here. Listen...*** It is her: Sarah.

"Sarah?"

I speak aloud and think it at the same time.

***Yes.***

"Where are you? Are you alone. What have they done to you?"

***Go without me. I will only slow you down. You can get out through the cave. Go. Please. They are looking everywhere for you. Please just run.***

At these words, my heart sinks deeper than I would have thought possible. I do not believe what I am hearing.

"What? No. Why?"

***They will use me against you...I see that now...That is the last thing I want.***

"No!"

I start to run up the stairs once more, taking the steps, two, three, and then four at a time. Speed is not a problem. I have had my body ripped apart in a fight that I thought I could not win, but now it has healed very nicely. My arm, the one that got hacked off, still feels a little stiff and a little strange, but all things considered...

***Please, don't, get out, they will kill you!***

Then she is gone. The silence is unbearable. I drive a fist into the wall of solid rock. It breaks open. Fragments of rock pour from the large hole.

I feel empty: my stomach, head and, especially, my heart. There is no point to anything without Sarah. Everything is a waste of effort. Then, a raw feeling flows into those empty places, like lava consuming all other considerations in their path.

Rage burns in my stomach now. *If they want me, then they can have me, but I will take as many of Theo's men down as I can.* After all, what has my life been leading to but this? I have killed so many – too many. What have those dreams been about if not this? I am akin to death walking these corridors. Right now, I am all about sharing it out.

Insane thoughts rush through my head, murderous and ugly: thoughts I have never thought possible, not me. I always hoped it would be down to the nature of the beast. I had hoped the hunger for blood, the thing they have turned me into, was responsible for all those deaths, but not me. Not really. But there is no hiding from it now.

Here I am exposed to the truth of it. I want to kill everyone and gorge myself on their blood. Taboo or not, I don't care. I don't care about anything but the rage that consumes me – totally.

# Chapter 9

# Eyes, Ears...

*"You're really not going to go without me, are you?"*

Sarah is sat on the bed, facing the doorway. It is a small cramped room. My room is hardly large, but it is positively huge compared to this cupboard of a room.

I brush a hand through the stubble on my head. I have a feeling that something of the leftovers of the two guards who are stationed outside Sarah's room have got into it. As I come through the doorway, it itches. The rest of the guards lie on the floor in heaps of dust particles. I think I trod some into the carpet when I walked in the room.

There are two cushions jammed into two holes in the wall, one on either side of the bed. The holes are about five inches square. One has a red cushion, with one corner sticking out. The other cushion is brown.

I walk over to the bed and pull Sarah up by her arms. She lets me lift her to her feet. I hold her by the shoulders.

"No, I am really not," I finally answer.

"But why?" she asks.

"Because you are the only one I have ever trusted in this god-forsaken world" My voice sounds tired, even to me.

"You know they will use me against you at every opportunity. I don't have a destiny, but you have. I can't stand in the way of that. It would not be fair."

"Screw destiny. You think I want to be some sort of super-vampire, someone worse than Theo? Ruling from a throne of vampire bones, perched on a hill of human corpses? You think that is what I want?" I raise my voice, and the words come out of my mouth thick and fast. They are the right words just for once.

"No... I don't," Sarah says quietly.

"Without that – trust and kindness – without you... It all means nothing. Don't you understand that?" I ask. My eyes are wide and pleading. Or at least I think they are.

"If you don't want to come... Well..." I venture. It sounds played out. "...I won't make you. It won't be any kind of picnic – I know that. Theo will chase us to the ends of the earth to kill me – you too if you come..." I trail off, realising in this moment that I don't really have anything to offer, other than uncertainty, a life running and constantly looking over our shoulders, fearful, fraught and stalked by every Wonder-kind on the planet. I have nothing to offer after this big show.

*I ought to leave. I am just making things worse for her. I have nothing to offer anyone. Not anymore.*

I turn away from Sarah, unable to face those big black eyes, open wide, gazing and solemn. I continue:

"If I were you, I would stay. You're safe here. Just don't tell me it is for my own good." My anger is beginning to return, tinged with I don't know what.

I start to pace up and down in front of Sarah, my hands behind my back, as I wait for the final pronouncement. I am waiting to be told I am no longer wanted in her life.

"I want to come to you but..."

"But what?"

"She told me I would ruin everything. I have to let you go."

"Did she tell you how it will all turn out?"

"No. She won't show me. She says it is unclear, undecided – murky, but that they will use me to get to you. After today, I thought..."

"Well then. It is up to you."

"You think I am being stupid, don't you?"

"No, of course not."

"So, you're not going downstairs to go out in a blaze of glory?"

"Probably not."

"But your thoughts... I heard them loud and clear." Sarah sounds unconvinced as she says this.

"I was angry. I am calmer now," I explain.

"I... I just don't want to be used to hurt you. I don't want to be a liability – a millstone around your neck."

I walked over to Sarah.

"Good god, Sarah... You're never that!" I say, with emotion filling my voice and the corner of my eyes pricked. I place my hands on her shoulders and squeeze gently.

"No?"

"Of course not. You're very dear to me. You're a necessity. not a liability." These aren't quite the right words. But they are true. I can see from Sarah's big eyes that she understands. I put my arms around her and squeeze. She hugs back.

"Can I still come with you then?" she says.

"Of course."

There is a sound.

"What is that?" Sarah asks, listening, I can hear it too, like a thousand-thousand tiny feet scrabbling on stone.

The red cushion falls from its position in the hole. It flops to the floor. I mean to ask Sarah what they are for: the cushions, but I am overtaken with the heat of the conversion. Half a second later, I know exactly why she has stuffed the cushions in those holes. The face of one of the biggest rats I have ever seen pokes its head out. It glares at us, looking first at me and then at Sarah. It launches itself out of the hole, screeching as it travels through the air.

"The King has found us!" Sarah shouts. "The rats are his eyes and ears!"

# Chapter 10

# ...And Teeth

*The rat shrieks.*

Bearing its razor-sharp teeth at us, it leaps. I step to one side, catching the horrible creature by the scruff of the neck, as it passes. I swing it around and throw it out through the open window.

"Eeeek!" the rat protests as it flies through the opening. It's not much of a reward for its valiant bravery against the Kings enemies, but I am not letting those sharp teeth anywhere near. As soon as I have got rid of the rat, the room starts to fill with a multitude of them, smaller ones, but with equally sharp teeth, falling and leaping from the square hole. The cushion from the other hole is forced out of its position, so that more can spill out on the other side of the bed. Outside, through the door, I can hear people running; I can hear their thoughts, all of them to do with killing me and anyone who gets in the way.

We kick rats left, right and centre, but they keep coming. They're not launching a frontal attack like their larger comrade, but falling on the floor, then charging en masse. The ground is covered in a carpet of brown and black fur.

"The window!" Sarah urges. "We have to get out."

No kidding.

She leaps onto the window sill. I follow. The opening of the window is small, even when opened to its maximum, but Sarah is also small. I am taller but painfully thin. So, I am able to sliver out head-first, snaking the rest of my body out of the window, where we cling to the stone work on either side of it. The rats swarm up through the window after us. Some fall, flailing down to the court yard below, while others are pushed forward by the bulk of bodies following at the rear, forcing them to fall over the edge. We don't hang around. We start to scale the wall towards the roof.

Pffff!

One of the gargoyles on my left explodes into dust. We speed up the wall, climbing like spiders, swinging over the crenellations, and land on the flat roof surface. I hear the sound of masonry exploding. I take a chance, kneeling and peering down over the rampart, just for a second: the grounds are full of black-clothed figures firing their D-guns at us. I pull out one of the D-guns I have wedged in my belt and fire off a couple of shots. Then I duck back down. With my back to the parapet, I turn to see Sarah beckon for me to follow her. She scrambles across the roof space. I don't know if I have hit anyone. I don't look back.

We run between the towers and chimney stacks. Sarah leaps over the hatchway that leads back down into the castle. Beyond the far walls, I can see the watchtower: our place of sanctuary, or at least it was. If we can get there, we might be able to get away. *Not much hope of that though.*

Sarah leaps onto the battlements and then jumps down, landing on the roof space below. I land next to her. There is a sort of spire at one corner of the roof, three towers on the other three. I stand up. Sarah stops dead, she is ahead of me, halfway over the roof. One of her feet still in the air. I frown. Then I see it: a movement over the inside of the mouth of the tower door on the far-left side; there is somebody there.

Between us and the tower, there is a raised structure: a long slightly curved glass dome. It's the skylight in the library.

Next to me are a chimney stacks with six chimneys built upon a brickwork base.

I pull the other D-gun out of my belt. Sarah half turns to look at me with an index finger to her mouth. I throw the second D-gun towards her and she catches it. She leaps in a backwards flip towards me. At the same time, a man dressed in black steps out of the tower door and his arm reaches out in front, with the long black familiar shape of a D-gun in his hand. He fires. I don't think or stop: I throw my body one way and Sarah goes the other. A flash of white light zooms between us. Behind us, the chimney stack explodes at its middle. Blinding light dissolves brickwork, before the top half avalanches onto the roof surface in an eruption of bricks and red dust.

I fire the D-gun, but the wonder-kind ducks back into the tower. The gun blasts a chunk the size of a man out of the side of the stone work. I can see inside: the spiralling stair case that winds up to the next and top level of the tower which is now visible. Sarah leaps over the skylight and runs to the right of the tower. The King's guard, who has been hidden behind the staircase, raises his head and his gun arm to fire another shot, only to find his arm broken, as Sarah darts forward to grab it and snaps it into two as if it is a twig. She then jumps onto the staircase and her foot shoots out. She catches the guards jaw with the bottom of her boot and his head snaps backwards, his body flying toward the wall behind him. I race over in time to see the guard crash into the wall, smashing the stonework behind him on impact. He drops, collapsing to the floor, chunks of stone falling on top of him as he sits like drunk in a shower of masonry.

I hear more noise – more footsteps and more voices – coming from below. I glance down the tower staircase and see the black clothed arms and body parts of more Wonder-kind. I fire the D-gun and see the one just below me dart backwards.

"More guards," I breathe.

Sarah nods.

"We can't take them all," she says.

"Let's get out of here."

We run from the tower in time to see more black-clothed figures in the archway of the tower opposite.

"Quick! "Sarah says, grabbing my hand and pulling me towards the skylight. I follow her lead, leaping onto the low dome, to land on the glass of the skylight. Glass breaks as soon as our boots land on its sur-face, disappearing under our weight, shattering in large shards that fall inwards and downwards. And, along with it, we plummet.

# Chapter 11

# Library Drop-in

*We fall.*

The broken glass falls alongside us, down through empty space. I think I may have left my stomach up on the roof top.

There is an almighty bang as we land on one of the sturdy tables on the ground floor. It breaks under the impact, all four legs flattening to the floor. The heavy wooden table now resembles an MFI flat pack. I straighten and look up in time to see one of the guards taking aim from the skylight above. I pull Sarah forwards and we run for the exit. The Chief librarian is standing between us and the door.

"Wh... What is going on? How dare you. Look what you have done! You vandals!" The librarian's words come thick and fast, like bullets.

Behind me, out of the corner of my eye, there is a flash of white light. This tells me that the table where we have been standing is now just dust. Sarah raises the gun level with the librarian's eyes, which widen considerably.

"Out of the way!" she commands between clenched teeth

The librarian looks torn, even now, between extolling his outrage upon us, and I can see plainly see fear in his eyes. It takes all of about a second for him to reach the correct decision: deciding it will be better for him if he is somewhere else. He turns and flees, heading towards the end of the library's north wing. He runs through the exit, not bothering to slow down as he crashes through the glass doors.

# Chapter 12

# Fugitives Flight

*I hear running footsteps.*

They are nearby, possibly outside the door. Sarah puts her index finger to her lips. I don't think this is necessary. It isn't as if I am going to shout out: "Here we are! Come and get us!"

I stand statue-like, not moving a muscle. The footsteps pass by, pounding down the corridor and then receding. I look around the small room. There are mostly boxes stacked on top of each other, three-high-.it is some sort of Storage room. I seem to be spending a lot of time in rooms like these of late: *not a healthy occupation.*

"It will only be a matter of time until they start searching room to room," Sarah tells me.

"Ok," I say.

"We can't stay here."

"Got that. Where to?"

"East Wing."

"What's there?"

"It's blocked off. Not in use."

"Ok. Sounds perfect."

I listen at the doorway for sounds of the search party. I hear nothing. I slowly open the door and slide into the corridor.

"All clear."

Sarah shadows behind me. I feel her rather than hear her moving.

"This way," she whispers.

Sarah sets off down the corridor. I follow, my stomach clenched into a tension ball. I hear voices, shouts and footsteps, but they are all way off. My exceptional hearing makes it feel as if they are much closer. I start in alarm, then relax once more. The journey seems to take longer that it ought to. My nerves are constantly on tenterhooks.

# Chapter 13

# East Wing

*We grind to a halt.*

The entrance to the East Wing is via an absurdly huge pair of wooden doors. They have to be twice my height, if not three times. We have a worm's-eye view of the intricately carved patterns of curves, circles and ellipses on the doors. There is not a straight line to be seen. The shapes run parallel, in transverse to each other, but never cross. It is a hell of a piece of craftsmanship. On each door, at eye level, there are two circular brass handles, each the size of a rubber swimming ring. I pull on the handle. The door doesn't even move.

"Fee fi fo thumb!" I exclaim.

"Oh, Jack and the Beanstalk. I like that story!" Sarah says.

"How do we get in?"

"Easy. Just not this way."

"Where?"

Sarah walks past the doors down the corridor. I follow. The corridor ends in a stone wall. I put my hand to my forehead, confused.

"Up there." Sarah points and I follow her finger to the corner, where the two walls and the ceiling meet. There is a large square hole with plenty of room for a person to squeeze through.

"The rat-runs are bigger in this wing, because it's older," Sarah says.

"There aren't any rats inside, are there?" I ask, remembering my encounter with them the last time I went into the rat run.

"No, I can't hear any. But if there are, then the game's pretty much up anyway." Sarah frowns.

"The King's eyes and ears," I say, repeating her earlier words.

"Yes, he has some sort of remote-view telepathy with the wee beasts." She nods. My skin crawls.

Sarah jumps up at the hole, catching the lower lip, and hoists herself into the opening.

"Come on!" I hear her say.

I see her feet disappear into the square opening. I leap up after her into the passageway. I can see her up ahead; with my elbows and knees, I shuffle along the cold stone, behind her.

We don't have far to crawl. The rat-run goes onward, for miles I expect, but there is a square hole in the wall every twenty metres or so. On the third exit point, we jump down into a dusty, unkempt room.

The room is in a state of decay: the paintwork on the walls is peeling and mottled with dark patches of mildew. There are white cotton sheets everywhere, draped over furniture and covering the floor. Cobwebs connect every surface, and thick layers of dust cover everything. It is easy to see that the East Wing has not been used for a very long time.

We move from room to room, each resembling the last. Dampness hangs in the air. I can feel it cling to my skin as we walk: cold and dank.

"Aren't you glad you decided to come with me?" I suggest. Sarah misses the sarcasm. In fact, I don't think she even knows what it is. I have never heard her use it or pick up on it. It is as if it blows straight through her, never touching the sides.

"Yes, I am!" she answers, her voice honest and genuine. I have to smile. How can I not. Out of admiration, not condensation. In a lot of ways, Sarah remains untouched by all the horrors that life has thrown at her. You have to admire that, you really do.

I wipe away the cobwebs around the door handle and then take hold the brass globe. I turn and it snaps off in my hand and crumbles as I let it fall to the floor.

"I don't know my own strength," I admit.

"I have always said so." Sarah smiles.

She gives the door a quick series of taps around the part where the lock is located. Then she taps again, quick and hard, with her palm to the centre of the square. The door gives way, not quietly; it screams its protest: the sound of swollen wood against swollen wood. Then we are through to another room, identical to the last, except for the shapes and location of the cotton sheets covering the odd forms of chests, tables, and chairs. There is even a grand piano in this room. That is new. Even under white covers, the shape is unmistakable.

After another three rooms, we come out in a corridor, full of dust, cobwebs and fallen stone work. I look uneasily at the ceiling which seems to be bulging downwards like a discoloured bruise. I suppose that if it hadn't already fallen in due to god knows how many years of neglect, then it is unlikely to fall in now. I hope so anyway, but I have my doubts.

"No lifts in this wing, I guess."

"No, lifts are a bad idea anyway."

"What about stairs? Are there stairs?"

"Yes. Up ahead. Just keep going."

The stairs, like everything else in this wing, have not been in use for some time and are in a similar state of disrepair. There are large chunks of masonry missing from some of the stairs. This is a minor issue compared with the chunks of stone, rubble and wood that litter the stairwell, which are more worrying altogether. Beggars can't be choosers I suppose. We are well and truly out on a limb on this one. I am not even sure what we are trying to do. The plan is to get to the cave or dive off the watchtower, to escape that way. The former is well and truly out of the window, and the latter – well, I am not even sure how to get to it from where we are.

"We have to go back into the main section of the underground part of the castle to get to the way down to the cave," Sarah says.

That makes sense, but with hundreds of Wonder-kind swarming all around the place, the task of getting there without being detected seems unlikely in the extreme. And there is also the thing I have been trying not to think of, which Sarah voices:

"But can we really walk away from all of this?"

"Bloody well right we can."

"But you saw your friend. You want them to do that to everyone?"

"Not my friend. Anyway, the human race has always been hell-bent on its own destruction."

"What about the people you knew before Henry changed you? The ones you told me about. Do they deserve that fate?"

Good grief, what am I thinking? No one deserves what they have done to the humans in the farm. I know I can never see them again. I still do not want anything bad to happen to them: my parents, my brother, Miss Sped and the many others I have never even met. Can I stand by and let them be used in that way – as battery chickens with no life and no hope? Can I stand by as they are reduced to cattle whose only purpose in life is to pump blood to supply King Theo and his breed with an everlasting source of food, until their bodies give out and die?

"Damn it, Sarah!" I say.

"You know I am right!"

"Yes, as ever, but what can we do?" I say slowly.

"You just turned the King's most promising warrior into dust, and you are asking me that?"

"That's different. It's all so new, I… I am not even sure I can do it again."

"That's what we can't do. So what can we do?"

Sarah is right. Of course she is. We can't just leave, not knowing the things, we know. How will we ever live with ourselves? I can have a damn good go, but Sarah... It will destroy her to know we do nothing.

"I just thought of something," Sarah says. "It might not make a difference in the long-run, but if we can get there, it will put a stop to their plans for a while."

Sarah tells me her plan, and I feel a smile spread out over my face:

"Maybe. Not perfect. But maybe," I say.

Getting there: that's the problem, isn't it? It could be worse. We easily navigated various obstacles and pitfalls. After all, we are Wonder-kind. If nothing else, we are agile and nimble on our feet.

# Chapter 14

# Going Underground

*"The training room is on this level," Sarah says.*

It does not seem possible. We have been going for about an hour in what seems to me to be an ever-increasing circle. My sense of direction was never particularly great, but, when we come back out into the underground complex of the castle, I now feel totally bewildered.

There is no one around. I wonder how long our luck will hold out.

"We need to go down four levels and then cross over to the other side of the complex," I say. Looking at the floor plan map on the wall, I may not have a good sense of direction but I know where I want to go.

*It is Sarah's plan. It difficult to believe that I am contemplating doing it, me of all people. No, we are doing this; not just me. Not this time.*

"What are we doing here again?" I ask.

"The Armoury."

"If you say so."

"I do. Let's go."

The corridors, at least, do not have ceilings in danger of collapse, but it is still disconcerting. We are not safe anywhere, not even in the East

Wing. But it seems unlikely that too many of the search party will venture down there before they have searched everywhere else first. The risk of discovery down here is almost certain. Funnily enough, it is the fact that they are all out looking for us that means that we have not been discovered yet. Usually these passageways will be buzzing with Wonder-kind going to or from the many rooms down here. I wonder how the search is going. On thinking about it, I feel even more uneasy than I had a second ago.

We pass the training room and I look briefly though the door, seeing the faded stains of blood on walls. I have had to scrub the walls after each day, but it never all comes off; there is always a stain left behind. How much of it is mine? With a quick shiver, I walk past the doorway. This is no time to wallow in the past. We have to get this done and then get out fast.

# Chapter 15

# Safe Door

*The door is made of five inches of solid steel.*

With a good kick, Sarah has it off of its very solid hinges. We go inside.

"Just had a thought... There isn't anything nuclear in here is there?" I ask.

"Good Lord, no. That is definitely not approved of!" Sarah replies.

"But regular weapons, grenades, Clayton mines, plastics... They're all ok, are they?"

"If Theo had his way, they would only use swords, axes and that sort of thing. But even he is forced to admit that, while it won't kill us, a human armed with an automatic machine gun can inconvenience us, and the human guards would not fare well at all without modern weaponry"

"I see," I say.

I have the Bonemann to thank for this. Without his training, I would be lost in here. While everyone knows a gun or hand grenade when they see one, I don't know much more. But thanks to him, I know how all of this works: the racks of machine guns, sniper rifles and small arms. I also know all the good stuff is down on the other side of the room behind the door of the walk-in safe. This is the bit I am not too sure of: a good kick is not going to do the job of bringing down that door. Only Bonemann knows the combination number. He kept it a secret from all of us, even Karl – when he was still alive that is.

We cross the room, passing by the weapons racks and metal ammunition boxes piled in stacks. The opening to the safe is a dull silver colour and about the size of a garage door. A square of metal takes up all of the wall, with the square door at the centre. I put my hands on the metal surface, which is cold to the touch, remembering how the locks work. There is a metal wheel at the centre of the door. You spin it after you type in the correct number in the keypad at the side of the door. There is also a card swipe; I don't have an access card either. Turning the wheel also turns the huge cylindrical bolts within the vault door, each around eight inches in diameter. These wind back into the safe door and the door opens. There is some sort of complex mechanism in the door itself. I can only begin to wonder at its complexity.

I try to remember what I did to Bonemann's glass cabinet back in the training room; my only hope here is that I can I do the same thing to something a damn sight bigger and more solid. I am not hopeful. I can't think for the life of me what I did or when it happened. It just unfolded before me. I think I know what to do, just by thinking about it. I am about to remove my hand when I feel the door getting warm.

The door is the same as anything. However strong the steel, it is just a bunch of molecules strung together until you stop them doing what they have been doing. All I have to do is reach out and gently nudge one of the neutrons, so it spins out of its orbit, disrupting the chain, accelerating its half-life and then ultimately all falling apart.

I remove my hand once the heat gets too much. There is a sound of metal buckling, as if under immense strain. Then, the safe door, with its four-foot width, starts to melt in front of our eyes, pooling on the ground and running towards us. I take a couple of steps back, not wanting to come into contact with the liquid. It isn't white or red hot or anything, just a mass of silver goo. It starts to solidify, resembling plastic that has gone too close to a fire. I put my hand up to signal to Sarah that we ought to wait for a bit. Then after about a few minutes we step over the solid metal pond and enter the vault.

"How do you..." she starts.

"...do that?" I venture.

"Yes."

"No idea. I just sort of think about it and then something takes over."

"Fantastic," she smiles.

"Fantastic?"

"I have never seen anything like it before."

"I think it must be my very late arriving gift."

The vault is an Aladdin's cave, if you consider devices of destruction as treasure. One thing is for sure, once the jinni popped out of these boxes, there will be no putting it back again.

"Is there everything we need?"

"Oh yes, and more besides," I reply.

I break into another box. This one is full of incendiaries: those nasty little bombs that explode liquid fire. I feel guilty just holding one in my hand. Can I seriously do this? They are really nasty and, alongside the plastic, Claymores, old fashioned dynamite and even more besides, they are going to do a lot of damage. I only hope we are not still here at the time they go off. *Boom* and everyone will fall down.

# Chapter 16

# Time Set

*"All done" I say.*

I walk out of the vault. I stop in my tracks. Sarah is juggling with incendiary grenades, six of them. They form a perfect arch as, one by one, she passes each of them to the other hand and throws it up in the air with the other five, which are airborne at any one time and in a room full of ammunition and explosives. She is juggling with incendiary grenades and liquid fire. My heart quickens.

"Please don't," I say.

"Why not? I won't drop them I promise." Sarah makes the arch higher, nearly touching the ceiling. I don't like the way she takes her eyes off of what she is doing every time she speaks.

"All the same you are making me nervous," I say.

"Ok!" she replies and then throws all six grenades into the air. I take a sharp intake of breath and my stomach clenches. But as each grenade comes towards waist height, Sarah catches it and places it back in the box. After this, she returns her hand for the next then the next, until they are all safely back in the box. I sigh.

"See if you can find a couple of bags or something," I say.

She comes back with a couple of large yellow-brown rucksacks.

"These do?"

"Perfect," I say. Sarah smiles a broad smile.

I start to load up both the rucksacks with grenades:

"Definitely not for juggling!" I add firmly. Sarah just shrugs.

I add a couple of hand guns, then do up the strap on the top of each of the rucksacks loosely, just in case we need the contents in a hurry.

"Will it work?"

"Hope so."

"Where now?"

"We've got to get out of here, out of the castle and away as far as we can go," I say. "Let's go, we have got forty-five minutes."

# Chapter 17

# Humans Go...

*I duck back around the corner.*

I look to Sarah. I put my fingers to my lips. I hold up two fingers with my other hand, indicating that there are two of them in the corridor ahead. Sarah nods. She strains her neck and peeks around the corner and then pulls quickly back behind the wall again. She shrugs. I put my index finger to her nose and tap it. She screws up her nose and smiles. I point to my chest.

"I'll do it," I mouth and Sarah nods enthusiastically.

I peek around the corner once more. I am relieved to see that the two guards are not Jack or Joe. I haven't seen Jack since he showed me around. I don't feel any fellowship, as such. It would just feel a bit embarrassing meeting those two again. Even more so if we're prodding and manipulating their minds. No, it is better with strangers. These two are perfect.

One of the large muscly men picks up a mobile phone, taking it from a clip on his belt. It is about the size of a brick. The other one looks at him, a puzzled look on his thick fleshy features.

"I didn't hear it ring."

"So? Get your ears washed out!"

"Hello...yeah...level seven. What? Now? Ok, we're on our way."

He clicks the 'off' button and returns the phone to his belt.

"We have to go."

"What? Why?"

"The king is under attack; they have got him cornered in the throne room. He needs back up fast!"

"What about these then?" the man says, banging a palm against the glass door.

"Forget 'em. It's just a bunch of dumb humans. It's the king who's in trouble. If anything happens to him, we will get it for sure. One-way trip to oblivion city!"

"I suppose."

"They will be ok for a bit. Anyone taking a bite from these pale-blooded parasites, will more than likely die of apoplectic shock, drinking their watery blood."

"Especially, that Lucian. Yuk!" the other guard agrees.

We slide further back into the darkness of the corridor, as shadows on the wall.

"Let's go then." The guard takes his D-gun out from its holster deep inside of his black overcoat and starts to thunder down the corridor toward the lift. His companion follows, drawing his gun and running after him. I hear the lift doors open and then close again. Only then do I look into the corridor.

"All clear," I say, stepping out of the shadows and into the corridor.

"The King is under attack?" Sarah asks, an eyebrow lifted.

"It's all I could think of at short notice," I shrug.

"What happens when they find out they have been tricked?"

"Doesn't matter much. They come back, we will be gone."

I stride over to the glass door. I put a fist though the protective glass and open it from the handle on the other side. They have been locked in to keep any passers-by out, to stop them from coming in for bite to eat, and killing the key personnel for their big project. I can empathise; my fangs have extended. At first, I don't even notice, but the smell of humans and the sound of so many hearts beating in such a small space alerts me. Well, that and the fact they are all so obviously betraying their own kind. They have to know what they are doing. They just have to. I don't have a lot of sympathy for those who will betray everyone else just so they can live. I can't think of anything more contemptible and that's coming from a blood-drinking murder.

It is difficult to resist such a temptation. Anyway, this is neither the time nor the place. I consciously retract my fangs into my gums.

"Everyone out!" I shout. The room falls silent. Those who are talking on telephones just hold them limp in their hands and those who are typing stop dead. All eyes are on us. And I bare my teeth at them. We don't have time for this. Personally, I could easily have left them.

"Anyone still in here in five minutes will be dinner!" Sarah says, baring her teeth as well.

They can't run fast enough. They swarm past us towards and out of the door, keeping a reasonable distance from us, I note. Their hearts are beating out a familiar beat. And I am so hungry.

"Focus...keep your mind on the job" I think, echoing Bonemann's words.

Once Sarah has finished herding any remaining humans out of the Remote viewing room, she walks towards me, smiling.

On the other side of room, beyond all the desks and filing cabinets, there is a glass wall with a sliding door in the centre. Behind the glass, I can see tall units, each about the size of a large wardrobe. Lights flash on their surfaces, wires hang down and tape runs around large reels. They look like giant tape recorders stood on their sides: not the ones with cassettes, but the older ones with the tape reels.

These are the computer mainframes, telephone exchange and everything they need to hack into everything and keep them connected to their operatives in the human world. They could have done it legitimately – after all, they have the money for it – but I cannot imagine a BT engineer turning up on the doorstep to install all of this stuff. I have never seen material like this before... Maybe in Sci-fi films or James Bond – something like that. But not in reality.

"That must be the computer system and the telephone exchange." I say, stating the obvious.

Sarah nods.

"We don't have much time," she adds.

"Don't need much!" I reply. I take out the D-gun and turn it on. It winds up to full power. I aim at the glass wall and fire. Sarah also raises her gun. We blast a hole in the glass wall. While white power fills the hole, we hear the sound of falling glass as the remains of the glass wall start to fall to the ground. We fire once more into the dusty gap, hitting the large lumps of metal beyond it, reducing the mainframe case and anything else in it to fine dust.

I look at my digital watch.

"Thirty minutes," I say.

"I wonder if they will make it out? Those humans," Sarah wonders.

"Doubtful. But at least they have a chance." I suggest.

I don't hold up much hope for their prospects. I don't really care either. They have betrayed their own species. *But isn't that what we are doing right now?* It isn't as if we have a choice or anything... Maybe they don't either...

"Let's go!" I say, cutting off my internal dialogue.

# Chapter 18

# Turning Tables

*We fly out of the room, hurtling down the corridor at top speed, which for Wonder-kind is just a blur for ordinary human eyes.*

"Do we risk the lift?" I ask.

"No. Better not. Take the stairs."

This is it. At last, we are leaving this wretched place. Sarah leads the way through the rabbit warren of stairs and corridors, going down all the time. I am glad that she seems to know where she is going, namely because I sort of do, but mostly do not.

"Twenty minutes" I say.

"That's ok. It's just down here."

Then we are back in the storeroom once more. I freeze. I have not been down here since the time I had come in from the sea with Sarah. When was that? I cannot remember. It seems a long time ago.

"Have you been down here? Since..." I ask.

"No. You?" Sarah says, frowning, looking at the same thing.

"No."

The boxes that covered the hole have been moved. The hole is open for all to see. Someone has been down here.

"Twenty-seven minutes"

"We have no choice. We have to chance it." I say.

"I agree."

I look down into the hole. I nearly say darkness, but that is just habit, as I can see equally well in light and dark now. There is nothing down there, or nothing that shouldn't be there. I jump into the gap. Sarah follows after a slight pause.

We clamber down over the wet rock. I think of all the activity that must be going on above us. I have to smile. I am surprised that we haven't come across more Wonder-kind in our descent through the underground complex. It seems almost as if they have been told to leave us alone.

Is there someone down here with us? Bad for them if they are. It can't just be that someone needed the supplies and has just taken the boxes without noticing the hole. Yeah right! How likely is that? Not very. I look at my watch: fifteen minutes to go. No choice then.

"Wait. What about the sheds, with the experiments?" Sarah's hand flies to her mouth.

"Nothing we can do." I say.

"I suppose not. But wouldn't it be better to die, than living like that."

"I would say so. But it is not our choice to make."

"But shouldn't we at least set them free?"

"In truth, I have no idea; they won't be able to walk and, even if they can, it won't be very far. Even if we are to get them out of here, they will need care for the rest of their lives. Which isn't very long. Months? A year at best. In any case it is too late. Fourteen minutes to go," I add.

I don't mention the human village. They ought to be out of the range of the blast, but who knows with these things? Everything is far from perfect. We did what we could and that was all that was possible. Life is full of mistakes and half-measures. I would have preferred better but what can I do? Nothing, that is what!

"You're right, I suppose" Sarah laments, sounding as unhappy as I feel about the situation.

"We can't do everything." I say, looking down at the rock.

The sound of water rushing and crashing against rock is getting louder. I know we are near now. The cave is just up ahead. Then, we can just get the hell out of here. That last thought feels good...

I can smell the saltwater and feel the fresh breeze of air coming up through the tunnel, brushing gently over my face, feeling too good against my skin.

We come out into the cave: freedom beckoning out beyond the rocks. A wave rushes into the cave as we walk down the small ramp of stone. The waves smash against the surface of rocks, worn smooth by this very repetitive action. The waves come rushing up the narrow gully at the centre of the cave, its roar echoing and stretching for the back of it.

Ten minutes: plenty of time. It will be nice to be far away when they find out who has done this to them. They are two of the most reprehensible people of their race: they would not like that – they would not like that a lot. If they have wanted me dead before, then that will go for triple after this...

My thoughts stop dead in their tracks. Two all too familiar figures appear at the side of the cave, from behind a large black rock that had at one time been part of the cave roof.

Why didn't we hear them – their thoughts at least? Both of them advance toward us, pointing the long black barrels of the equally familiar and unwelcome shape of D-guns.

"I knew you would come this way." Henry says. His voice is puffed up and gloating.

"What, you think I don't know about this place?" he adds, seeing our reactions.

"I suppose."

"And you didn't see this coming, I suppose?" He looks at Sarah.

While I can hear the thoughts of others and can even insert a thought, an idea or sensation in the head of another, Sarah is the only one I know who can talk back to me. I do not know whether this is due to our closeness, our thoughts being attuned or Sarah's other strange powers. Either way it is her thoughts I hear in my head now. I am beginning to be able to tell the difference between what is said and what is thought, though I still make mistakes.

*I am so sorry! I am so sorry I let you down!*

*Forget it, where is your D-Gun?*

*In the rucksack. Why?*

*First chance you have. Get it out and start blasting. Then run. Get out of here.*

*No.*

*No? What do you mean, no?*

*I am not leaving you.*

*This is not the time...*

But before I can continue, everyone else's thoughts flood into my consciousness:

Lucy: *He had better be right about this. That is all. He had just better be damn well right!*

Then Henry comes in but there are no words. Just a tune. It's something classical. Beethoven's fifth or ninth? I know next to nothing about classical music. What I do know is that he is hiding something.

"Tell you what..." I say. "You let us go – walk right out of here. And you walk away from this. No one will ever know."

"And why would I do a thing like that?" Henry asks.

"Because then I won't reach inside of your head and melt your brain like a piece of cheese under the flame of a welding torch," I say, leaning forward towards him, my eyes fixed on his.

Seven minutes... Crap! Crap! Crap!

"Ha, ha! As threats go, that's pretty good!" he laughs.

Lucy: *This isn't going to work; this isn't going to work!*

I look at Lucy for the briefest of seconds, as I hear her thoughts.

*Well whatever it is Mr Hrot has up his sleeve it's coming. It is coming now.*

I look back at Henry. His face seems relaxed. He looks confident, like a gambler who knows he has an ace of spades up his sleeve. All he needs to do is get it to the table without anyone else seeing...

"You know..." Henry muses, "...there is one thing you have not thought of."

"What's that?" I ask. I eye him with suspicion. I am worried now.

"It is me who took you from your mundane world and changed you: gave you life, real life, strength and power undreamed of..."

Is Henry trying to make me feel guilty? Is he trying to make me feel I owe him something? Is that all he has?

I yawn. "Your point?" I question, with an edge of sharpness in my voice.

"My point is I can make you do anything I wish, because I made you."

He takes a step towards me. I don't take my eyes off his face.

"Part of it, part of that process, is that something of me is in you. You belong to me. You can't lift a finger against me. Me on the other hand..." he threatens.

"No, you don't..." I start.

"I own you, body and soul..."

"I've heard enough."

I have already started to reach out with my mind towards his, to hurt him. I am looking forward to making his brain pop like an exploding cucumber.

Only I can't. Blood rushes to my cheeks as I realise he is right. I can get so far, and then it will stop, frozen in mid-air. But Sarah is behind me and she has whipped out the D-Gun. I hear the gun whirl into life as she flicks the safety button. Henry continues taunting:

"The same goes for you Miss Muffet. Put it down. You look ridiculous!"

*Sarah: Why aren't you doing anything?*

*Me: I can't. It doesn't work. Shoot him!*

*You can't make me.*

Sarah attempts the trigger...

*Can't either... Can't pull the trigger...*

*Shoot them both!*

"There really is nothing you can do. You can't harm me – either of you." Henry takes a step towards me.

"Stay back! You're my little pets, and what fine pets you both are!"

"No!" Sarah and I both say in unison. "It will never happen," I complete.

Henry moves in on me. One hand grips upon my neck and the other twists my arm. I am unable to move, as he pins my arm behind my back.

"You know the trouble with our kind?" he asks.

I can think of a few things and I am in no mood to play guessing games, so I say nothing. My forehead throbs as I strain to move from this invisible grip that holds me placid and useless.

"Torture," he says.

"We don't die: our bodies repair and come back to life – again and again."

"Your point being?" I gasp. I am finding it hard to breathe now.

I can feel Henry's chest behind me and that twisted little heart of his beating. It is a slow thud, quieter than a human heart, perhaps an inaudible sound to human ears. How I hate the sound.

"The thing is, we can suffer indefinitely with no hope of release. You can't imagine the things I am going to have done to your little friend over there." Henry nods in Sarah's direction.

"No! You can't!" I almost scream.

"Oh, I think you will find that I can. But don't worry. I will let you visit and hold hands for an hour every day. Just so you can see her suffer. See what they have done to her and know that it is all your fault: your stupid stubborn fault." He smiles.

"Ok, I will do it. I will do what you want!" I agree, not believing the words I am saying. But what choice do I have? None.

"I know you will, after a couple of months, maybe years. After all, what is time to us immortals?"

"I said you win. I will do what you want," I say.

"You will come on your hands and knees begging me to stop her pain, telling me you will do anything..." he continues, as if he hasn't heard me plead.

"Why do it at all? I said I will do what you want." My voice sounds desperate.

"You're not ready yet. You need to be broken. As does your little bitch!" Henry roars.

"No!" I cry out.

"Isn't that right, Cassandra?"

I finally manage to strain to turn my head around and see Sarah's face: to see her eyes, change from black to pale grey.

"I told you it is him. Ye of little faith Henry boy," a voice from Sarah's mouth says. Its sound has all the warmth of a downpour of broken glass.

# Chapter 19

# Intimate Betrayal

*"So how did you know?*

"She told me," Henry says, pointing at Sarah. I look disbelievingly at her crumpling face.

"No..."

I feel as if a jagged knife has just seared through my heart.

"No. I didn't. Don't believe him. I never would!" Sarah says, her eyes black once more and open wider than I have ever seen them.

"Why?" I ask weakly. My heart is broken, as if ripped apart by rabid dogs. If only. Then this would all stop.

I am thrown off balance. Then Sarah's face contorts, as if some new emotion is trying to break through.

"No..."

"But I would!" the voice comes from Sarah's mouth, sounding from her vocal cords, but at the same time it seems totally foreign to her form, as if she is possessed or taken over by some other malign entity, twisting the body for its own uses, destroying the personality that is there before it, claiming the body as its own.

"We planned it all from the very start! I saw you in my visions. I let Sarah see some of it, but kept the good ones just for me..." Cassandra laughs. "I had Henry pick you up, change you. It all went according to plan with the right nudging to show you your real self: your potential. After all, you're a bigger monster than all of us put together! Such a bright future. Full of blood! Full of death!"

"It is me who sees the future, not this dumb bitch. Honestly Henry, I don't think you could have chosen such a wet behind-the-ears idiot if you tired!" she says, wagging a finger at Henry. He just looks up to the roof and says:

"She was disposable: the best option at the time. Beggars can't be choosers." He smiles back.

"Hmm!"

"So Sarah didn't know?" I ask, grabbing hold of that small lifeboat of an idea, even though it is sinking rapidly.

Cassandra answers:

"What, that ninny? Not a chance and, before you ask, it will still be her that does all the suffering, when Henry here puts the Château Blanc's torturers to work on this soft and sensitive body. I won't feel a thing! Ha! Ha!"

Henry chips in:

"Have you met the King's torturer, by the way? Such a nice chap. He is so good at his job too. So hard to find these days: someone who simply loves his job."

"Planned it?" I challenge. "But you had Karl try to kill me!"

"What, that buffoon? He couldn't execute a sentence. No, he is just an incentive to spur you on a little bit. It worked a treat!" Henry says, smiling.

"What the hell? What the hell is happening?" Lucy speaks, looking not at me but at Henry and then to Sarah.

"What is she doing here?" Cassandra asks acidly, pointing to Lucy.

"She is ok. I haven't told her everything, but she knows which way the wind is blowing. She's likes to be on the winning team," Henry says, his arms folded.

"You always did have a weakness for pretty little idiots didn't you Henry!" Cassandra exclaims.

"Now, now! No need for that. Now we have him. Why don't you tell him the future? I am sure he would love to know his horoscope," Henry sneers in response.

"Would you like to know?" Cassandra turns to me, smiling a smile that seems to stretch Sarah's face in way that is alien to her features.

"Know what?" I enquire. I am not sure whether I do or not, but Cassandra tells me:

"Our King Theo wants more... power! Being king is not enough for him. Oh no!"

"Oh no. He wants it all. To kill the other Kings, to take their kingdoms and have the lot! King Lanzón is just the first," she continues.

Suddenly Cassandra's expression changes. In a flash, she points the D-gun straight towards Lucy's surprised face.

"Don't even think about it, girly girl. I will have you before you get within two feet."

"I'm not...," Lucy protests

"You little liar." Cassandra says, "Now drop it."

Lucy drops the D-gun to the floor.

"Kick it over here"

Lucy does as she is told. Without breaking eye contact with Lucy, Cassandra drops down to one knee and scoops up the gun. She stands, the barrels of both guns pointing towards Lucy. Henry just shakes his head.

"Tut, tut!"

I have heard Lucy's thoughts; she is thinking "Sod this for a lark" and deliberating about whether to make a break for it. I don't say anything. Lucy is no friend to me, but neither are these two.

"So..." says Henry. "We – or rather *you* – are going to help him deal with the other ten. Then, who knows, maybe even he will get careless. Too long in the job, you know."

"Isn't that treason?" I suggest.

"Well naughty old me. It's not as if you can tell him," Henry sneers.

"Even if you did, he would kill you out of hand. I am afraid you are helpless in this matter. You have no choice but to do exactly what I tell you to," says Henry, smiling, before explaining further:

"I am a power broker. The kings spy master. Without me, the King would just go on daydreaming of the old days in this dreary castle. I want more."

He kicks a small stone across the rock; it bounces and lands in the gully to be claimed by the swollen wave that is rushing up to the back of the cave. Then he says:

"I helped him get where he is today and it is time for him to move on."

"You're going to kill him?"

"No, you're going to kill him. Drink him dry."

"No…"

"Cheer up. You're going to be king."

"King?"

"With me as your lord and master pulling the strings, of course."

"Don't you want the job?" I ask, puzzled.

"God, no. Too dangerous. Kill a king and everyone wants you dead: relatives, favourites, mistresses, other Kings and King Theo himself. I expect he will want you dead too, being alive and kicking inside of you… And Cass here can't do it."

"Thanks to you, sweet Henry," Cassandra mocks. "But we get to rule through you, boy."

Henry almost yells, his voice an echo in the confined space of the cave:

"You have seen the plans! I left them on my desk for you to find. The future is going to be glorious, not only do you have a part in it, you will have a front row seat!"

My insides burn and twist at the thought, but he is right: he has me. There is nothing I can do. I don't like it though. I am seething with anger.

"I am sorry, Sarah," I whisper. I know I am beaten.

# Chapter 20

# Sky High

*"Got it all worked out then,"* I say.

I strain with my neck. I look down at my watch.

*Oh crap!!!*

The first explosion sounds far off. It is muffled and distant, but gets louder until it is a deafening reverberation: a boom that shakes the cave's walls, loosening rocks. It is portentous to the fact that the roof of the cave is just about to come crashing down upon of our heads...

# Chapter 21

# Cave In

*Blood runs down the side of my head.*

I can feel it. It is like a river running backwards. I look around through the cloud of circling detritus, at what is left of the cave. It hasn't collapsed completely. I think I might have to punch my way through half a mile of rock to the surface, where I will no doubt find an angry welcoming committee. But, no, the large – and I do mean large – slab of rock that had been the roof of the cave has fallen at an angle, wedging itself between the straining rocks above the ground. Big as it is and made of solid rock, I can see it is not going to be up there for very long.

I look around. Henry is staggering to his feet, with Lucy just behind him. They both look like ghosts, covered in the white mist of particles that still fill the air. Behind me, Sarah or Cassandra (or both) emerges from the rocks.

It comes to me in a bright flash of light so clear and sharp that, for the first time in my life, I know what to do. I know how I can turn all this around. Without another thought, I lunge...

# Chapter 22

# Sharp Exit

*It is probably not the best idea I have ever had.*

When the chance comes I take it. Henry is distracted and disorientated. It gives me more than enough time: enough to let my monstrous self out of its cage. This has nothing to do with being Wonder-kind. What surges up from my unconscious is my human side. The part of me that has been brought into being by Danny and his ilk is the part brought to maturity by Karl, Henry and the rest of the Wonder-kind. This is the part of me that remembers every slap, every punch, every put-down, every insult and every bullet. It rushes up through me, snarling, breathing out fire and billowing out black smoke. My monstrous long buried humanness rears up. I twist my body, straining my neck, and bring the razor-sharp ends of my bared fangs down into Henry's neck. My aim is perfect: I hear his artery pop as I sink quickly through its hard wall. I drink deeply. I cannot get the blood into my mouth fast enough. It sparkles upon my taste buds and tingles upon my lips. It is the best thing I have ever tasted – it is pure and unadulterated pleasure.

I hear Cassandra scream, as Sarah punches her way back into her own body.

"No, don't!" she shouts. Hearing her voice again is good, so good to hear. I release Henry's body. It falls heavily. His head cracks against the stone and then flops limply. It is too late. Lucy just stares wide-eyed at me. I am Frankenstein's monster realising what he is. The blood at the side of my lips runs down the side of my chin, to fall onto my black shirt, producing a dark, barely visible stain.

"Tastes like Champagne," I smile, through bloody teeth.

And I have a moment of perfect clarity: I now understand the dream where I wound Sarah. It is what happens when I become what others would have me be: if I do what I am told to do just like I have always done. It can only lead to the destruction of everything I have ever loved and is dear to me. I am not going to ever hurt Sarah because I am not going to do what I am told – not ever again.

They both look at me, mouths open. I really regret Sarah seeing me like this. Lucy, I do not really care about, but Sarah... But it is out there now. It is not as if I can take it back. Much as I might like to. It is done. Lucy looks at the two D-guns still vibrating nosily in Sarah's hands, then to the one that has fallen from Henry's hands. Then she looks into Lucy's eyes, before turning greedily to the gun on the ground. Sarah levels both the guns at Lucy's face. Lucy takes a step backwards her arms raised, palms showing.

"You shouldn't have..." Sarah says to me. And she is probably right. I can hardly stand. I am conscious that I have a massive smile spread all across my face. It is so big that it feels like my upturned lips are taking up all of my face and more besides. I want to break down in fits of laughter. But I have things to do. I pick up the fallen D-gun and point it at Lucy. Her shoulders start to shake. She looks from the gun to the ground and back to the gun again. I hear her thoughts:

*This is it...I am really going to die, I thought...I was promised I would live forever...More lies...*

"Just do it. I know you're going to kill me," Lucy says, her bottom lip quivering.

"Not if you do what I tell you, which I think you will. After all you are the strategist – always playing the long game – that's your gift. No?"

"What do you want me to do?" she asks.

"Simple. In a moment, you are going to leave. Go back up that tunnel, back to Theo and your kind. You're going to tell him what happened here. I wouldn't mention Henry and Cassandra's machinations if I were you, but it's your call..." I say.

"Ok" she says.

"You will probably have to dig your way up. But you can cope with that. Avoid the training room area."

Lucy: *Am I really going to get out of this alive? Where's the catch? It can't be this simple...*

"Yes, you might" I say, answering her thoughts. She draws in breath, looking alarmed and confused in equal measure, so I push on.

"Tell them how Henry died. Tell them what I did... I am leaving now, with Sarah. Tell them that if anyone follows us, I will do the same thing to them. I will be without mercy."

Lucy: *If the bastard doesn't shoot me in the back...I am almost out of here. Just don't say anything wrong...so close...*

"Understand?"

"I understand."

"Then what are you waiting for? Scat!"

She turns on her heels and runs towards what is left of the tunnel. She is just a blur; she does not turn to look back.

Which is just as well. her I couldn't stand for one second more. I drop forward upon my knees. It is surprisingly painful as my knee caps hit the rock.

"What is it? Are you alright?" Sarah says, a look of concern on her face, as she closes the gap between us.

"I feel so wired!" I tell her. I am shaking. I can't hold one single muscle still.

"It's like that. In an hour or two it will pass, hopefully..." she says.

I am still smiling inanely. I want to collapse on floor, roll over and laugh until my jaw falls off.

"Too long," I say smiling. My face feels like it will break, the constant nag of wanting to laugh pulling at my mouth.

"Can you get me out of here? I can hardly move. Sorry," I add.

"Yes of course," Sarah assures me. Out of it as I am, Sarah voice sounds mellifluous, like honey pouring into my ears.

She gathers up the three D-guns, then gently puts them inside of her rucksack. She throws the rucksack on her back, adjusting the straps; I hope that it is waterproof.

Then she takes my shoulders, gripping me under my armpits, and pulls me backwards towards the sea, into the cold water.

"Cold!"

"Are you complaining?"

"Of course not. As if."

"Good!"

She drags me deeper into the water, the waves rushing at us. They roar and sweep over my body: me like a baby, powerless and trusting. My body slides under the raging surface.

Sarah kicks off, starting to swim underwater through the strong currents that buffer me as she drags me along, with one hand on the scruff of my tee-shirt. As my eyes are open, I can see the remains of the sun overhead shimmering through the blue water, its liquid shape waxing and waning. I am aware of a bright yellow-orange glow on top of the cliff, leaping into the air. But I don't really attend to it. I just think it pretty. Even as fireballs explode into the sky, and red-hot debris splashes into the water, sizzling as it disappears under the waves, I just smile a stupid smile.

In my delusional state, things seem even more vivid and bright, but also strangely peaceful and safe. All I know is that I am being taken away from that dreadful place that has been home for so long. No, not home, never that...

Sarah swims harder, pulling me deeper still. I am dragged downwards. Then, after a while, I have the sensation that we are going upwards towards the surface, my limp body following. I could be imagining it but I suddenly think I am outside my body watching us – both of us. Passing through the gloom, I think she looks like a small mermaid rescuing a sailor from the water depths.

It seems apt.

# Afterwards

# Chapter 1

# Stone Beach

*Sarah drags me up on the beach.*

A little way beyond the headland, I feel the shingle under my legs. After a few minutes, I sit up. I rub the sides of the bridge of my nose. I am feeling better than I was. Just cold: my still wet clothes cling to my body as a second skin. I look around the deserted beach, at the pebbles and drift wood, then up at Sarah who is standing, looking down at me, smiling.

"Ready?" she asks.

"Ready."

She offers me her hand. I take it. She helps hoist me to my feet. I stand there, unsteady for a moment. Then we head up the beach toward the cliff. We climb up the white chalk and rock. At the top, we stand looking back at the hill where the Chateau had once stood. The outer battlement that surrounded the hill is still intact. I can see the small village where the humans lived, which to my relief is also untouched by the explosion. But the castle is gone: just a pile of rubble with a long curling plume of smoke at it centre, pointing to where the building should have been, and where a fierce fire now rages.

I know as I watch that they will soon be crawling up out of the ruins, like worms sliding out of the wet earth after a rain storm. And when they do, they will be coming for us. We have to get as far away from this place as possible.

"It won't stop them; it will only set them back. We can't do everything," I lament, shaking my head.

Sarah only nods and turns away. Walking down the cliff top path, I follow.

Neither Sarah nor me have much of an idea of where exactly we are: in England somewhere, somewhere north, but that is about it. So we just head away from the chateau: south I think, though I cannot swear to it.

We find a car and steal it. It is parked outside of a rather twee looking cottage, which lacks the baseness, dirt and the griminess of the ones back in the human village. I thought the sort of thing here only existed on dinner plates belonging to great aunties. Sarah hot-wires the car. I raise an eyebrow.

"What? Basic training," she explains.

"Well, we never did that!" In truth we never did much in our training sessions outside of ways to hack and slice each other apart. But that is all over now.

Sarah climbs into the driver's seat. She adjusts it so that her feet can reach the peddles. It is a BMW. I don't think it is the same model as Henry's one, though it is a similar shape. It is strange to be leaving in a similar car to the one I arrived in, but there you are.

After driving about twenty miles or so, I warn Sarah:

"We need to watch out for police."

"Because of Theo's influence?"

"No, besides the fact we are driving a stolen car, I look about thirteen. You don't look much older, and I'm betting that neither of us has a valid driving licence."

"Those things matter?" Sarah challenges, with a frown on her face.

"I think you need to be seventeen to drive a car," I suggest.

"But I am hundreds of years old!"

"Don't look it, and it's still a stolen car."

"Ok, we will stay away from major cities..." Sarah agrees, but then turns to me and says:

"Oh, damn it, why don't we just get out and run? You feel up to it?"

"Fine with me. We can probably run faster than this thing anyway."

She stops the car abruptly. We get out. We run. We run and it feels good, really good. We lope through trees and over open fields. Running is easy and we can cover a lot of distance. Two hours is the maximum time we can run without needing a rest. We speed through the night, resting under trees and watching the bright stars and moon above. We pause under an oak for a rest. If we find the right bit of coast, we will be able to take a ferry over the France and then make our way towards Switzerland.

"...where we can live in one of those houses with the funny roofs in the mountains," I say.

"Oh yes!" Sarah agrees with lots of enthusiasm, "and we can buy a cuckoo clock and hang it on the wall!"

"If you want."

"You don't like cuckoo clocks?" she says, her face fallen with disappointment.

"They are all right. I can't say I have given them a lot of thought. But have one if you want one. I insist."

"I will like that!" She brightens once more.

Later, in the early hours of the morning, I tell Sarah what Cassandra had said.

"I sort of know..." she admits. "It is like being in your body but not able to do anything. It is horrible."

"Is she going to come back? Where is she now?"

"Not if I can help it. I have her locked away in little box in my mind. I won't be listening to her ever again. That is how she got strong enough to take over in the first place... Anyway, you have the same problem now – with Henry I mean."

"I know. I thought as much."

"When I saw you, you scared me a little. A lot."

"Doesn't matter. You know I won't ever hurt you. You know that, right?"

"Sort of. Yes. I don't know why..."

"I am just not wired up that way. You're such a gentle soul, I could never..."

"I know. I just needed to hear you say it."

We curl up under the trees, which gently rustle in the wind, and somewhere in England we fall asleep.

# Chapter 2

# Two Outlaws

*It is a modest room: not the penthouse suite by any stretch of the imagination; we are after all trying to stay below the radar.* We are outlaws in the true sense of the word – outside and unprotected by law. We are trapped between two different worlds: Wonder-kind and human, belonging to neither one, each wanting to do us harm. We are alone, only having each other. We depend on each other absolutely.

"How are we going to pay for this?" Sarah asks as we descend in the lift, eleventh floor, tenth...

"We are not; we are going to make a run for it first thing in the morning," I answer.

"But that is dishonest!" Sarah protests.

"It is better than sleeping on the streets," I point out.

"I suppose so." She considers the option with a frown.

# Chapter 3

# Cityscape Surfing

*Sarah looks down at the traffic below, speeding past, with headlights and tail lights in white and red: a continuous stream through the night.* They look like toy cars from this high up. The wind blows at Sarah's hair, which is thicker now and wild: her face has always been bright and alert, but now it has softened. Even up here, I can tell from the side of her face. It seems to have relaxed into a creaseless surface that glows coral-pink. She no longer lowers her head in deference to the world; instead, it springs from her shoulders at the end of her flexible neck: sharp and smiling.

Sarah pads to the edge of the roof. Her bare feet are dancing as she skips towards the edge. She raises herself on to the tips of her toes. The wind pulls at her black drainpipe trousers, though there is not much for it to grab on to and flutter about. She bends her head forward so that her neck and then the rest of her spine follow her head downwards. She pushes off, falling head-first towards the hard pavement below. I follow, falling behind her. She crosses her arms in front of her chest with her thumb in her mouth, sucking as she falls. In many ways Sarah has changed a lot as have I but the thumb sucking business remains. But so what? The ground rushes up to meet us.

At the last moment, Sarah pulls up, turning in the air, so that she lands feet-first. Then she leaps up, jumping over the stream of traffic, to disappear into a dimly lit alleyway. We sprint to the end and start to climb once more. At the top we sit, looking up at the stars, the moon and the city lights.

# Chapter 4

# Feeding Time

*"It is so bright, so full of lights"* Sarah says.

"I have never seen so many," she adds.

"Yeah. It is at that," I agree.

"It is pretty in the city – pretty bright lights – but I prefer it green or blue... I like being by the sea the best..."

"Me too."

"Will we see the sea soon?"

"Yes, the south coast. It's very beautiful."

"I can't wait!"

"We used to go on holiday there, Cornwall mainly, all around that area."

"Is the sea very blue?"

"Very."

"I think I will like that."

"So blue you can get lost in it... Come on. I am Hungry. You promised we can eat soon." I change the subject, my mouth watering at the prospect of the red stuff.

"Yes, ok," Sarah agrees.

We climb down the building. Halfway down, Sarah alerts me:

"This one."

The steel framed window is half open. Without disturbing it, we slide through into the room. There is a couple lying in a double bed, with the covers pulled up to their shoulders. I hear their sleeping hearts beating slowly. My heart quickens and salvia floods into my mouth; I lick my dry lips.

***Now, gently, like this.*** Sarah pushes her fangs into the woman's neck. She sucks gently and the woman makes a slight noise. Her eyebrows draw together but she does not wake. After a few seconds, Sarah releases the woman's neck.

***Now you try.***

*Ok.*

I try to be as gentle as Sarah. I fail but, under her watchful eyes, I do not fall into a gulping frenzy, not that I don't want to. As soon as the blood hits the tip of my tongue, savage and greedy thoughts strike me; I just want it all – to drink this human dry... But Sarah puts a gentle hand on my arm – as if to say that's enough. I ease back.

We slip back out the way we came. As we climb back up the wall, I think to Sarah:

*This is going to take some practice to get used to.*

She thinks back:

***We've got plenty of time.***

We reach the top of the building.

"So they will just wake up with sore necks," I say.

"They will think they have been bitten by an insect. They may feel a bit faint, but as long as they have a cup of tea and bite to eat, they will be none the worse for our attentions..."

"Good. That is good," I say

With that, we turn, run and jump from building to building until we are easing ourselves through the open window of the small hotel room.

# Chapter 5

# Found By?



*6.15 a.m.*

I sit up bolt upright, every nerve ending awake and alarm bells in my head ringing loud. Sarah is already up. She is crouched on the floor as if she is going to pounce on something.

"You smell them. Don't you?" I whisper.

"Wonder-kind." She nods.

"Yeah, quite few of them."

"How?" I wonder aloud

"Doesn't matter. They're here."

"Get your stuff. We're out of here."

"Already done." Sarah tosses the second rucksack at me. I put it on my back.

We have thoughts of climbing out of the window. But that will be too obvious. They will be waiting for us: some of them on the roof and some down below. If we are going to fight then it is better to have solid ground under our feet and places we can hide, or corners to hide behind...

So we decide to walk out like two ordinary people. We take the lift to the ground floor. The pit of my stomach is out accelerating the lift: nothing to do with the lift going down, just the thought of more death, maybe our own. Why can't they just leave us alone? I clench my teeth. I reach for Sarah's hand and takes it and squeezes.

"It is ok; we can do this," she assures me.

"I hope so."

The lift door shudders open...

I am expecting to see a D-gun trained army, all in black, at the lift. I am pleasantly disappointed, which makes me even more suspicious and on edge. There are only three suspects: two rather overweight and tired looking business men making their way to the breakfast area and the bored receptionist, who looks up occasionally from reading her colourful magazine. None of them smell like Wonder-kind, but it is there: the smell of our own kind, in the air, distinct and strong.

My eyes scan the room. We move cautiously out of the lift. Then I see them. There are two of them, a man and woman, both tall, straight and lean. They have just entered the hotel. The receptionist looks up, interested in the new arrivals. The man looks back at her, then she seems to forget that they are there and goes back to reading her magazine.

He turns to us, and starts to walk across the lobby towards us. The man's eyes seem bright and alive, while the eyes of the woman who walks easily at his side her eyes are the opposite to his, looking distant and far away. However, I have the sensation that we are the focus of her attention.

"Ready?" I whisper.

"As I will ever be," Sarah says.

The man sticks his hands in the air in mock surrender. The woman looks at him sideways and smirks. The man speaks:

"I want to say 'We mean you no harm. You can trust us.' But in my experience, anyone who says that... Well, let's just say you should check your pockets before leaving..." A smile draws across his lips. As a smile it is not a bad one. It has a certain warmth to it.

"We are not from Château Blanc or any of the twelve kingdoms," says the woman. She opens her palms towards us.

"The woman's a truth seer!" Sarah asserts.

"Got that," I say.

I reach with my mind towards the man, but instantly hit a mental wall; it feels as if I have just head-butted solid brick. It feels old, really old. This guy has clocked up a lot of years and has learned more than a few tricks on the way. I have to be careful here.

"I can keep you out all day. But as I have nothing to hide. Knock yourself out," the man says. "It may speed matters up".

I delve into his mind. I am shocked to discover they have told the truth.

"They're telling the truth, they're not..." I say

"Where are you from?" Sarah asks.

"I am Howard and this is Cate. We are part of the non-aligned vampires... Wonder-kind if you like. I have always found the name a tad pretentious. We are all blood suckers here after all is said and done."

"I told you they will be wary!" Cate says.

"What do you want from us?" I ask.

"Want from you?" Howard seems to consider this.

"Nothing. We've come to offer you a home: a place where you will belong. A community if you like," Howard adds brightly.

"We hope you will accept. Give us a chance," Cate adds.

**I think they are telling the truth.**

*I think that too.*

To cut a long story short, we accept the offer made by the strange pair.

"Great, we have a car outside." Howard says.

"I am so glad." Cate beams, her eyes coming into sharp focus, smiling bright.

"This way," Howard leads us toward the exit.

"You're like me aren't you?" Sarah says to Cate, as we walk.

"I see the future...yes. It is going to be great having you two around – liven things up no end," Cate agrees.

And she is not wrong. I feel it in my soul.